TYRANT

Books by Conn Iggulden

TYRANT

PART II OF
THE NERO TRILOGY

CONN
IGGULDEN

PEGASUS BOOKS
NEW YORK LONDON

TYRANT

Pegasus Books, Ltd.
148 West 37th Street, 13th Floor
New York, NY 10018

Copyright © 2025 by Conn Iggulden

First Pegasus Books cloth edition May 2025

Snake illustration copyright © Artur Balytskyi/Alamy

ISBN: 978-1-63936-889-1

10 9 8 7 6 5 4 3 2 1

Printed in the United States of America
Distributed by Simon & Schuster

www.pegasusbooks.com

To Detective Constable Alan Bray

N

BRITANNIA

River Thames

River Medway • Gesoriacum

←*River Somme*

•Lutetia

GAUL

Lugdunum•

Po Valley

GERM

HISPANIA

Cyrnus

ITALY

Rome•

Ostia

Sicilia

0   500 miles

0   500 km

The Roman Empire, First Century AD

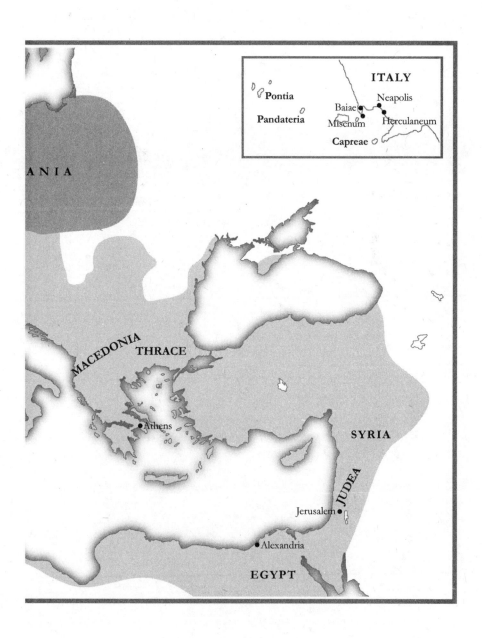

ITALY

Pontia

Pandateria

Baiae
Miscnum
Capreae

Neapolis

Herculaneum

ANIA

MACEDONIA
THRACE

Athens

SYRIA

JUDEA

Jerusalem

Alexandria

EGYPT

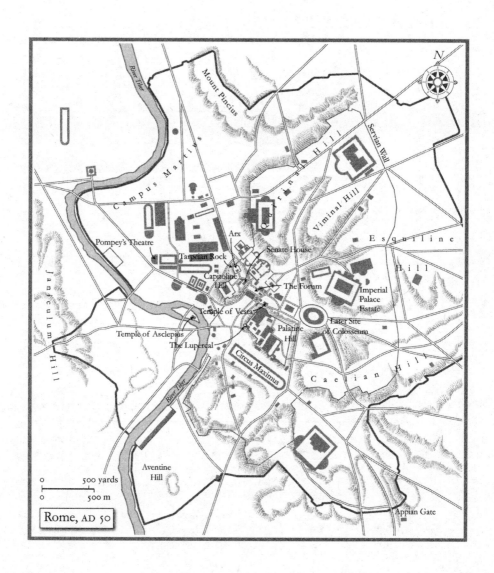

River Tiber

Mount Pincius

Campus Martius

Servian Wall

Quirinal Hill

Viminal Hill

Esquiline Hill

Pompey's Theatre

Arx

Tarpeian Rock

Senate House

Capitoline Hill

The Forum

Imperial Palace Estate

Janiculum Hill

Temple of Vesta

Temple of Asclepius

Palatine Hill

Later Site of Colosseum

The Lupercal

Circus Maximus

Caelian Hill

River Tiber

Aventine Hill

0   500 yards
0   500 m

Appian Gate

Rome, AD 50

Julio–Claudian Family Tree

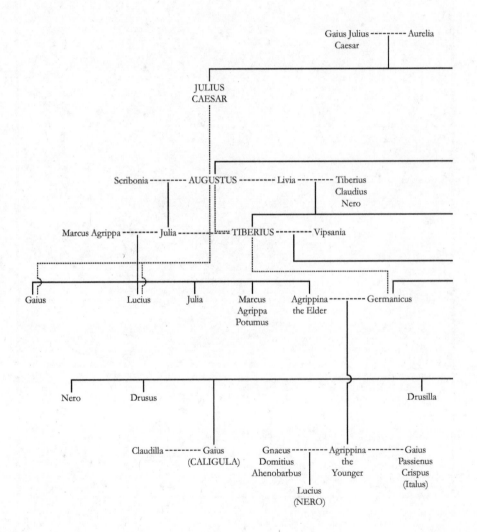

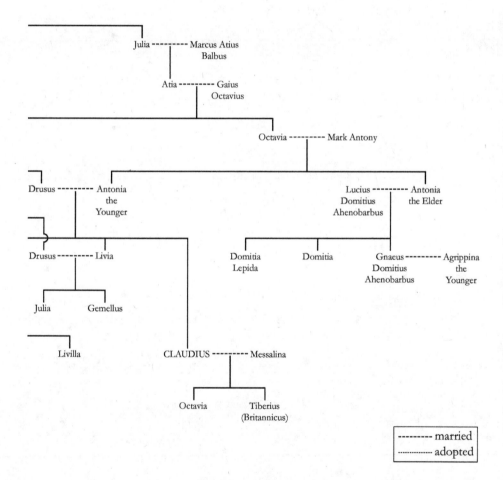

Julia --------- Marcus Atius
                 Balbus

Atia --------- Gaius
                Octavius

Octavia --------- Mark Antony

Drusus --------- Antonia   Lucius --------- Antonia
                 the   Domitius   the Elder
                 Younger   Ahenobarbus

Drusus --------- Livia   Domitia   Domitia   Gnaeus --------- Agrippina
                           Lepida   Domitius   the
                                                   Ahenobarbus   Younger

Julia   Gemellus

Livilla

CLAUDIUS --------- Messalina

Octavia   Tiberius
            (Britannicus)

┌─────────────────────┐
│ --------- married   │
│ ·········· adopted   │
└─────────────────────┘

Prologue

Bells sounded across Rome. Thousands were struck, over and over. Every temple acolyte wielded handbells or rapped a bar against a curve of bronze. Like thunder, the notes rolled out, over the seven hills of the city and past the great walls. The result was both patterned and tuneless, filling every street, echoing through temples and arches.

Workers stopped their hurrying to stand in awe at a sound they might never hear again. Their own lives went on, their hopes and tragedies, with the grind of work and the struggle to raise a family. For just a morning, all that was interrupted. The emperor would marry that day, before the sun rose to noon. He would put a gold ring on the finger of a woman many of them knew by name. Agrippina. Daughter to General Germanicus, whom they had loved. Sister to Caligula, whom they had feared. Of the bloodline of Augustus himself.

As Agrippina was in her thirties – with a son of her own – Emperor Claudius had found no blushing virgin to ease him into old age. Both saddles and gloves grow more comfortable with use, so the men said. Fires do not have to rage to warm a bed – and for some, the companionship of a woman can be something he does not even know he needs. Until she has told him so, many times.

On the crest of the Caelian hill, Junius Silanus faced the

praetorians who had come into his home. It was too late to think about how he might have prepared for such a threat. They had brought an iron ram to smash their way in. His door had seemed a fine and solid thing the day before. They had broken it with two blows, like bell notes themselves. Nor had his servants been ready for an armed assault, not in darkness. Before the sun showed, soldiers were crashing through his home, searching every room until they arrived at his bed.

In the pale dawn light, the praetor hid his fear as best he could. Junius was twenty years of age and carried a gladius he had snatched up. The house was large, a symbol of Silanus wealth. He had managed to pull on a robe and sandals, but his hair was wild as he faced them.

He blinked at the uniforms, recognising the regiment that guaranteed the safety of the emperor and his family. In turn, they ignored him, fanning out around the room, checking doors and windows, making sure he was truly alone.

The threat of a single sword did not seem to worry the men who had come into his house. Junius felt his heart hammering so hard he wondered if he would faint. Yet a worm of hope uncoiled, almost painfully. They were imperial soldiers, men of discipline and order. Junius Silanus was both senator and praetor, law officer and one of a gilded eight across the entire empire. His official title was second in rank only to the consuls – with Emperor Claudius above all.

The sword that trembled in his hand suddenly felt foolish. The young praetor tossed it onto the bed.

'I am Praetor Junius Silanus Torquatus,' he said, forcing his voice to calm authority.

Prologue

He could hear bells in the streets outside, the sound spreading across the city. That sense of joy clashed with acid in his mouth. He breathed slowly, sensing confidence in the men who faced him. His older brother would know what to do. Marcus was the head of the family, married with children and already the image of their father. He had protected Junius from tormentors more than once. If he could have been summoned by sheer force of need, he would have stood in the doorway at that moment.

'Gentlemen, there has clearly been a terrible error,' he said. 'I am praetor of the city, a senator – you may present your written orders to me. Perhaps you did not realise this is a private house.'

It was subtle, but two of the praetorians turned slightly as if to question another. That man wore no badge of rank. He was the oldest of them, around fifty, broad and compact-looking. His arms were criss-crossed with thin white scars and Junius saw two fingers were missing from his left hand. The legions were built on men like that, Junius knew. He could sense the violence in him, the battles he had seen. Junius had none of his own to set against that store. Men like that were not much given to sentiment, but neither were they blocks of stone. They could hear reason.

'If you command here, what is your name?' Junius began again. 'Who gave you the order to break into my home?'

His hands were trembling. He clenched them together behind his back. He needed time, to settle the heart that hammered his ribs and made him feel sick.

'Centurion Sextus Burrus, praetor,' the man replied. His hair was white and tightly cropped. It looked like rabbit's fur. The eyes that met those of Junius were so dark they appeared to have no ring around the pupils. It made his gaze uncomfortable.

Burrus grimaced, as if he suddenly tasted something unpleasant. Junius was not half his age and struggled to read the man's expressions. The centurion looked ill at ease, but he could not discern the reason. Junius stumbled over his words as he spoke again.

'You w-will have to describe . . . to explain this extraordinary action to Prefect Rufrius, centurion. Do you understand? Your commanding officer is a close friend of the Silanus family. He too is a praetor.' Junius felt his patience fray at the impassive expressions of the intruders. '*Do* you understand or not? There has clearly been an error. I am a praetor and a senator. I am of the *Silanus* family. If you hope to keep your rank, if you hope to keep your back unstriped, you will take these men and leave my home.'

'I'm afraid there is no error, praetor,' the centurion said softly.

Burrus looked away for a moment, running a hand over the bristles of his scalp. The sound was a rasp in that cramped space. Junius realised he could smell acrid sweat and was not sure it was his own.

'What do you mean, no error?' Junius said.

He heard his voice rising and clamped his mouth shut. He glanced at the sword on the bed. It remained there, tantalising. The threat of violence was still in the room. He could smell it on them, see it in the way they exchanged glances. He could not fight his way out, not with praetorians ready to lunge at him. Only the best were accepted into their ranks, he recalled, his mind fastening on anything but his fear. Soldiers of twenty-eight legions tried out when they needed recruits, with an elite chosen for duty they regarded as sacred. Of course, they also spent their fighting years in Rome, with all the other legions making sure no foreign army ever came close.

'I'm afraid . . . my orders are clear, praetor,' Burrus said. 'You stand accused of incest. I have already . . .'

He was interrupted by a bark of laughter from the young man who faced him.

'Incest? My mother is dead, centurion! Or am I meant to have defiled her ashes?'

The praetorian went on, his voice dull.

'Your sister is the subject of the accusation, praetor. I have spoken to her – and to her husband. He confirmed what I was told.'

The praetorian looked uncomfortable and Junius suddenly understood. The man was lying – and he *knew* he was lying. Burrus had enough honour to detest what he was doing. Perhaps there was a lever there, something to turn him away.

'I demand a hearing to defend myself from these falsehoods,' Junius said. 'My sister is a chaste and honourable woman. Her husband, though . . . Yes, I see. There is malice there, I am certain. He is a weak man. Well, I can convene a court under my authority as praetor. My sister will be called as a witness and the truth will come out. You have my word.'

'Your sister is being taken to exile, praetor,' Burrus said. 'I'm sorry, but this . . . Understand: there is no salvation here, no way out. My orders are from the emperor's household – to make a quiet ending, without fuss. There will be no trial, no public accusations. You are a young man, sir, without children. You have brothers to carry on your family name.'

Again, Junius saw the discomfort in him.

'You may take your own life with dignity, praetor. Or it can be . . . hard, bloody, more vicious than you would believe. Those are my orders. Believe me, I would choose the quiet path if I could. I do not want to beat you to death, dominus. You are young . . . and in good health. It would not be quick. Understand me, praetor. Whichever path you choose, you will not leave this room.'

The younger son of the Silanus family stared in astonishment at the man pronouncing his death. He opened and closed his mouth.

'I have never been incestuous with my sister . . .' he said faintly.

'The accusation is enough,' Burrus said. 'Now, if I lend you my knife, praetor, will you do something stupid with it? I don't want any of my men hurt. This is a distasteful business and they are just lads doing their jobs.'

'Lend me . . . ? You expect me to cut my own throat? To go meekly just because you break into my home and smash my door down and demand it?'

'Lower your voice,' the praetorian muttered.

He took a pace suddenly, so that he stood very close to the younger man. Junius' bed was touching his legs and he could not step back.

'This is an honour, praetor, due to your rank – and yes, the influence and wealth of your family. If you cut your wrists or your throat, if you do that by your own hand, your sister will live in peaceful exile and that will be the end of it. Your family will be told you took your own life in shame. Do you see? This comes from the imperial household. There is no backing away, no reprieve. Nor do I have the morning to waste debating with you. I can put a sharp knife in your hand. Your rank deserves that much.'

'This is madness,' Junius said under his breath. 'The accusation is . . . a lie.' He frowned suddenly in thought. 'And too serious to be some scribe's slip. The imperial household? I am betrothed to the emperor's only daughter! When Octavia is of age in a few years, she and I will marry! I *am* the imperial household, or will be! By the gods, man, will you stop and think for a moment? What if you have come to the wrong family, if the name you were given was meant to be another . . .'

He trailed off as Burrus unsheathed a vicious-looking dagger, wide at the base. It was a legionary blade, as good for hacking down a pine sapling as cutting a throat. It glinted in the dawn light and Junius leaned away from it. Understanding flashed into his mind and he stiffened.

'That's it, isn't it? The betrothal. By Mars, it is! That damned woman is behind all of this. The one who has the emperor tangled in her skirts, who marries today. The source of those *cursed bells*!' He shouted the last, driven to it by the constant clang and jingle that had only grown since he'd been wrenched from sleep.

Slowly, Junius sat on the bed. Burrus held the blade out.

'I am sorry, praetor, truly,' Burrus said.

He did look regretful, but there was no give in him, no change. For the first time, Junius understood, really understood. There would be no last-minute salvation. His brother would not hear until he was dead – and Marcus would do nothing, not if the emperor's wife stood behind it. Emperor Claudius was getting married that morning and if his new bride had marked Junius for death, that would be her wedding gift.

'Give me a little time, would you?' Junius said. 'To write letters to my family. If you do that, I will take the knife from you and cut my wrists.'

'I need to get back to the Palatine, praetor,' Burrus said.

He glanced aside to where a small table held the bits and pieces needed to send a letter. Sealing wax and vellum rested there, with a dark ink block and a little jug of Tiber water. A night lamp was still shuttered, the flame tiny over its reservoir of oil. The praetorian's mouth twisted as he considered it.

'Please,' Junius said. His voice cracked. He had accepted there was no escape, but the reality of what that meant was still dawning. There was fear in his eyes as he met those of the centurion.

'Very well,' Burrus said.

He'd thought this would be an ordinary duty when he'd been given it. A young praetor offered a chance to take his own life rather than bring shame on his family. Burrus shook his head as Junius bent over his desk. Ignoring the clay jug, the young man spat on the ink stone, working a scraper back and forth until he had a smear he could use.

The praetorian no longer believed the accusation, but that didn't change anything. Burrus had sworn an oath to protect the imperial family – and to obey their orders. Of course, Agrippina was not quite a member of that family, at least until Claudius made her his wife. That was a distinction that mattered about as much as the guilt or innocence of a young praetor. Burrus didn't know if Agrippina had someone else she favoured for the praetorship, or another suitor for the emperor's daughter. Nor was he still certain she would look favourably on his chances of promotion, as she had promised. In its own way, Burrus knew his life was as precarious as that of the young man mingling tears and ink on page after page. Agrippina understood power – both in the reality and the promise of it. If she could bring down a praetor with the right words and a few hard men, the life of Sextus Burrus would be of little consequence.

After an age, the centurion laid a hand on the young man's shoulder.

'Finish the letter, would you, son? That's long enough, I'd say.'

He watched as Junius signed his name with a swirl, folding the vellum. With the ease of long practice, the young man opened the little lamp. He lengthened the wick and passed a stick of wax through the flame. It dripped where he placed it on the letter, a circle of red and soot like a bloody coin. His own ring sealed it before it dried hard.

'Give me the knife,' he said.

The centurion nodded, passing the blade to him, hilt first. The others were all watching, ready to move. It might have been the dagger in his hand, or the presence of death that had come into that room. One of them licked dry lips in anticipation. This was better than some dull duty in the barracks or keeping crowds back from the emperor's carriage. The noise of bells had risen to a great crescendo outside, so that the entire city rang with it.

Burrus stood very still as the young man rose from his seat at the table, the knife in his hand.

'Don't try it,' the praetorian muttered.

Junius nodded, then stepped forward suddenly, with all the speed of a young man driven to desperation. Burrus began to duck, but froze as he felt the edge of his own knife pressing his throat. The lad had moved like a rattlesnake – and the truth was, Burrus hadn't seen battle for many years. He felt himself growing hot as his cheeks flushed. Before he could speak, Junius took the knife away and held it up, as if he surrendered.

'I just wanted you to know,' he said with a shrug. 'I *could* have taken you with me.'

Burrus blinked, caught in rising anger that had nowhere to go. It was such a young man's move! A pointless show. He touched his neck and saw a faint smear of red. He'd sharpened the thing himself for that edge. By the gods, he loved the young praetor then for his moment of madness.

Burrus nodded rather than speak, conceding the point. He knew the others would mock him when they were heading back to the barracks. A man at fifty can't match the speed of one of twenty! They would know that just as well as he did. He scowled. He would have to knock one of them down. He saw them exchange worried glances at the fierceness of his expression and nodded to himself, breathing like an old bull. Good. Let the bastards fear his wrath.

'I . . .' He caught himself. The young man's eyes were wide in fear and rage. Nothing Burrus could say would ease the moment. 'There's no more time, son.'

Junius laid the dagger against his left wrist and cut with huge force. The gash was appalling, blood gouting in an instant. He made a strangled sound as he tried to change grip to cut his other wrist. His left hand hung limp so that the knife slipped from its grasp. He staggered and Burrus took the blade as he sagged onto the bed. The centurion watched the young man's eyes grow dark. The praetor saw something coming. He tried to turn his face from it.

Burrus cursed when he saw it was taking too long. A healthy male could cling to the world and make dying a hard, hard thing. He couldn't have that, so he made the second cut himself. Redness sank into the bedclothes, spreading beneath and rising as points through the weave. The praetor sagged onto his side, breathing slowing to a halt.

Burrus waited a little longer.

'That's done, then,' he said, grim with anger.

He'd thought his men might make some joke at his expense, but they saw the way he glared and decided not to say a single word. They watched him burn the letter to ashes in the lamp's flame. He and his men left the estate then, the sound of bells still on the air.

As they marched back towards the Palatine, Burrus stamped as if he wanted to break in a new pair of sandals. He knew his men exchanged worried glances, but he didn't care. He'd obeyed the orders he'd been given, to the letter. There *were* times when a senator took up some vile perversion, slept with the wrong wife or just crossed the wrong man. There were no public trials then, Burrus knew, no accusations back and forth until the whole city knew everything. Those men were given a knife, or sometimes poison – told to choose suicide rather than disgrace. He *knew* that was the way Rome worked! Until that morning, he'd seen the sense of it. Some things were best handled quietly, without the plebeians of Rome learning all the sordid details. For the dignity of the emperor or the senate, such things could be justified. It wasn't a matter for law, but a deeper justice.

He still remembered the senator who murdered his slaves, apparently for his own enjoyment. When a much younger Burrus had been sent to his door, that old man had scorned him, claiming the right to do exactly as he pleased with those he owned. He had refused to cut his wrists, Burrus remembered. Death had come quickly even so, the old man strangled by a praetorian's hands. A younger Burrus had lost no sleep over him. He'd felt worldly-wise with his new understanding. To be a praetorian was more than just parades and helmet plumes. It meant unpleasant work on behalf of the empire's heart.

He clenched his jaw. If he'd known then it would mean a quarter century with no promotion, that his career would stall and become cold ashes, he might have gone sick that day. Year after year, he'd had to watch lesser men rising through the ranks – and Rufrius made prefect of his beloved legion. All because Burrus' hands had been the ones around that senator's throat.

He had tried to be a good man, but the unfairness had eaten at him. He'd followed his orders and put a savage old dog out of his misery. In return, Rome had forgotten him. There had been a time when senior men had marked Burrus as a star on the rise, a centurion with a quick mind and good sense. A man others followed. That had all vanished like morning frost, until she'd found him.

He looked up at the Palatine hill as he reached it. She was up there in the temple to Juno, marrying the stooped figure of her husband, Emperor C-C-Claudius. Burrus knew the Persians and the Jews talked of angels. She had seemed like one of those when she'd come to him and walked at his side. A chance to redeem himself, with the promise of an empress's favour. It was the sort of thing he'd daydreamed over the years, while he watched Prefect Rufrius strutting and growing too fat for his uniform. Redemption. Another chance.

Burrus blinked as his eyes stung. Every time he closed them, he could see the ridiculous bravado of the young man who'd chosen to press a knife against his throat, to reclaim a single moment of dignity in a move so pointless it made Burrus want to embrace him. He hardly remembered being so young! Leaving Junius Silanus behind with his wrists opened did not feel much like redemption.

PART ONE

AD 50

I

Agrippina stood at her husband's shoulder as he read. She knew Claudius could devour records and histories at great speed, running his eye down a page with one finger, then flicking it aside. He may have sounded like a fool when he stammered and struggled with words, but he was not one. Just as he looked like an emperor when he sat still. The moment he moved, the limp and shuffle made her wince, the great head that wagged with every step. She told him it was the weight of his thoughts that bowed him down and made his back ache. The truth was somewhat simpler. Claudius had been born badly, drawn into the world by some backwoods Gaulish midwife instead of a matron of Rome. His body had been twisted in the process.

'Are you still reading?' Agrippina prompted.

Nor was her new husband an innocent, though Caligula had treated him as one. Her brother had made Claudius the court fool, humiliating him in front of senators and slaves. Claudius had accepted every blow and jest without a sign of resentment. In Caligula's court, that had kept him alive while many others perished. Her entire family had been plucked by fate and men in power, one by one, until Agrippina was the last, beautiful as summer – and empress of Rome.

'N-nearly f-finished,' Claudius said.

She nodded in reply, her face perfectly still. She'd assumed she would stop hearing the stutter after a few months of marriage. The reality was different, like a squeaking gate in a storm. It grated on her and she had to struggle not to interrupt, to hurry him along to the end of the sentence. If her patience failed, he fell back into his old acceptance, the image of a meek man. Yet she knew how much those old wounds stung, how the poison still brimmed, ready to spill over. Claudius was more complex than her previous husbands. His power was absolute, and yet there were times when she could lead him, gentle as a lamb with her rope around its neck. It was a dance be-tween them, or a debate. She could use his awe at her beauty and a woman's caresses. He reacted to her hand like a colt to its first bridle, looking into her eyes in a sort of wonder until she was tempted to check her own reflection, to see what only he could see. She rubbed his head when he was weary, but it was more than the comfort of warmth or her hands. He wanted to please her and so gave her whatever she wanted, like adopting her son into the im-perial family. In return, she talked to him, enduring his stammer until she wanted to scream, helping him order plans and ideas until he was ready to make them in stone.

Her previous husbands had not wanted to talk, she thought wryly. Claudius would not be racing chariots or leading men to battle. Yet he was strong enough where it mattered. He . . .

Conn Iggulden

'You are s-sure of the n-name?' he said suddenly, look-ing up and back at her. 'Once I add my s-seal, it cannot be undone. The adoption w-will enter the . . .' He struggled to finish, growing red until he almost spat the word 'record'.

Agrippina leaned closer, letting him enjoy the scent that surrounded her in a cloud. All men knew when she had swept through a room. That oil had been brought from the heart of Egypt, the very one that had touched the throat and thighs of Cleopatra. A single bottle was worth more than its weight in gold, but she loved the musky intensity of it, for its heat and the effect it had on Claudius. He was pharaoh of Egypt that day, after all, just as he was emperor.

Even as she leaned over, pressing against his shoulder, she knew he glanced at the slope of her neck, the way the cloth of the stola shifted to reveal her breasts. She was in her thirties, renowned for her beauty. Claudius had turned sixty that year. He breathed her in and she remained inno-cently unaware of that gaze as she read and nodded.

'It is as you suggested, Claudius. "Nero" . . . after my brother. "Claudius" to honour you, before even my family names. Then "Caesar" for the bloodline, "Augustus" for the family and "Germanicus" for my father. "Nero Claudius Caesar Augustus Germanicus". It is a good name, old and new together.'

'I only h-hope he c-comes to d-deserve it . . .' Claudius stammered.

Said quickly, it might have been a quip, an amusing aside. As it was, he made it a labour and Agrippina had to force herself to smile. Her only son attracted trouble, bringing chaos wherever he set foot. She knew better than the em-peror what a long road lay ahead. Yet she noticed too that Claudius had not appended his name to the sheet. Claudius was an educated man: he needed no ring seal. Yet until he scrawled his name on the white, her son was not part of the imperial family, nor protected by it.

Two senators had come to witness the adoption of her son Lucius Ahenobarbus into the emperor's family. Agrippina sensed their discomfort as she knelt at her husband's side, resting one arm and her chin on his bare thigh as she looked up. She ignored the presence of others, focusing completely on her husband as if the room was empty. Claudius reached out and stroked her hair.

'He will honour Rome – and you, Claudius,' Agrippina said in a low voice.

Still, he did not sign! Would he make her repeat every argument she had brought to bear over the engagement and the first months of marriage? She had worked on Claudius like a sculptor, in bed and out, as a wife, as a mother, whatever he needed from her. She had felt his will sag like a candle in the sun under that assault . . . but again and again he found some reason to delay. She'd wondered at times if Claudius enjoyed having her need something from him. He knew she would do absolutely anything to get her way. Perhaps that pleased him, just a little. Perhaps it made up for her finishing his sentences, or repaid the bills for the huge villa she was building on the coast. Would he prefer she lived in a shack?

She tilted her head a fraction. Her hair brushed his thigh and she knew full well how his imagination would react. She had never thrilled to love, not as men did. Perhaps she had been married too early, or treated too roughly by her first husband, she didn't know. There were times when she enjoyed the sheer physical combat of it, as if she galloped a horse to collapse, sweating and red-faced at the end.

Conn Iggulden

Nothing Claudius wanted was more than a little work — and what she won in return was simply everything. It meant she could endure the grunting noises he made, the way he rocked back and forth until she wanted to push him off, rolling him away like a beetle.

She pressed his thigh, splaying her fingers. It was strange to feel the muscle there. It was not the great shank of her first or second husband. Both those men had ridden and marched from their earliest years, forging legs of rippled strength. Claudius was more slender, but still a man. She sensed him rousing to her touch and saw a deep flush begin on his neck. The emperor half-turned, as if to send the senators away. Yet he had not signed! This was the crisis, she realised. She rose to her feet and took his hand in hers, guiding it to the parchment once more.

'I will *make* him honour you,' she said.

Claudius nodded, thoughts aflame, eyes almost feverish. He scrawled his name and title with a flourish and then watched as the senators came forward to add theirs, scattering sand over the ink to stop it seeping into the sheet.

'You have my g-gratitude, senators,' Claudius said, dismissing the men without breaking from his wife's gaze.

Agrippina let herself settle once more, like a flower as her skirts puffed with air around her. She could see the passion in her husband as the senators hurried out. She was relieved, pleased, exhausted at the battle won. It was time to gallop across the meadow once again. She began to undo her dress, letting it fall from bare shoulders while Claudius watched her greedily. Vulnerable, she stared up at him as he rose from the desk.

'Thank you, Claudius,' she said.

*

Lucius cursed, slapping furiously at himself as he trotted along with his two friends. He'd been stung about a dozen times and he ached with pain. He hated wasps! The things were not mindless like beetles or ants. No, they were spiteful somehow, swimming before his vision as he'd scraped their nest into a cloth. A few of the angry bastards still followed the three boys as he looked back. They were so fast! Their nest had been just some pale and papery thing in the corner of an old shed. He'd thought it might have been abandoned at first, but when he'd poked it with a stick, they'd poured out, looking for a fight. He hated them, honestly. They didn't even give honey, or not that he could see. His tutor said they ate ants, which had interested him for a time. Lucius had wondered if he could build a miniature arena, with panes of clear glass, where wasps and ants might fight for the amusement of his friends.

He grimaced as he wound his way along the track. His tutor would be in the little schoolroom, he had no doubt. Magister Anictetus was always prompt and lectured his young pupils on the civility of arriving early. The man could talk! By the gods, he could lose an hour to any subject Lucius could imagine. Lucius had thought it was his only weakness, that if one of the boys asked the right question, an entire session could be lost to the answer, while they stared and pretended to be fascinated. Of course, he'd found another weakness in the end. That was why it paid to remain alert, to see the world around him as no one else seemed to.

He looked over, to where Otho held the other end of the twisted blanket. His face too was swollen in great pink and yellow patches. His mouth looked like a child's drawing, with one lip swollen to the point of absurdity. Lucius chuckled at the sight, though Otho only rolled his eyes. They had all suffered. It seemed wasps were warlike creatures, more aggressive than the boys had imagined. No one had escaped their wrath, not even the youngest of them, Serenus, who had remained as lookout at the door and been stung on the eyelid for his pains. He stumbled behind the others, still wincing.

The gardens of the imperial estate on the Palatine were tended by a vast number of slaves, too many to learn their names. Lucius and his friends had been all over it, so that they knew a few of the gardeners by sight. Still, there shouldn't have been a wasp nest, even in a tiny shed far out on the edge of a garden clipped and sheared and planted to perfection. That was why Lucius had acted that day – it could have been found and removed at any moment. He rubbed the lumps along his arm again, a cluster of the things. Improvising a plan with a twist of cloth had cost them dearly, but it could still be worth it.

Ahead, the path ended at a bank of herbs, some garden of the imperial kitchen. The scent of bay leaves, garlic, onion and rosemary were thick in the air as the boys pushed through, taking care not to let their burden graze bare skin. Lucius peered at it in fascination. He had seen tiny thorns piercing the cloth as the vicious little beasts tried to sting whatever pressed them. He could almost admire the depth of their rage, the sheer mindless force of it.

Across a strip of tended lawn lay the schoolroom. Before that year, Lucius understood it had been some sort of store. It still had the smell of old grass clippings and sweat. His mother had brought in wooden benches, a table that gleamed with linseed oil and all the slates and chalk her son might need to learn Greek and Latin. He glowered at the thought, imagining Magister Anictetus already pacing up and down, tutting to himself. The man had small feet and a twitching manner, like a dancing tutor or a songbird. They were already late. Even if the boys entered at that moment, they would be made to bend over and striped by the whippy cane he always carried. Lucius had stolen it once, snapping it in two pieces. The magister had brought an identical one the next day and beaten him unmercifully. The fussy little man deserved all he was going to get.

It had been the merest accident that Magister Anictetus had been stung by a single wasp as he used a sheaf of parchment to push it towards the open air. Lucius and Otho had seen him sweat then. His hand had swelled to an extraordinary degree, the fingers like fat figs. They'd said nothing at the time, but an idea had been born. If the teacher reacted like that to just one sting, what would happen if they found a nest and threw it into his schoolroom? Lucius hefted the squirming weight, already grinning in anticipation.

'Ready?' he said softly.

The others nodded. Otho was a year older and wore the toga virilis of a man. He said he'd put his fingers in a local girl, which intrigued the other two as it was something beyond their knowledge. Sitting together on a fallen tree in the park one day, Otho had even let Lucius put his hand inside a girl's dress, slipping down the curve of her buttocks. She'd thought it was Otho's hand at first, until he held her head to kiss her. The result had been shrieking and being chased, but Lucius still remembered the softness of her skin and the feelings it aroused.

On a normal day, without the presence of a distracting

female, Lucius was the one who came up with games and ideas. Denied the area of his adult expertise, Otho was happy to follow Lucius' lead. Bigger than either of the other two, he could also be relied upon to win a fight with boys of the city, if it came to that. They were friends, the three of them. It was summer and life was sweet.

Lucius grinned as they untwisted the wrap of cloth, swinging the weight of the nest between them. The wasps were going mad, the folds surging with horrible movement. He looked up. The open window was some way off the ground. It had to be perfect.

'If it goes wrong, just run,' Lucius hissed. He could not take any more of the angry wasps after him. One way or the other, he'd be sprinting for the hills no matter what happened.

He froze suddenly. His plan, and he had almost ruined it!

'Serenus, the wedge! Have you still got it?'

His friend held it up and Lucius waited for the younger boy to realise he was in the wrong place. With a curse, Serenus ran off, disappearing around the building.

'I'll count to . . . thirty,' Lucius said. 'That's long enough.'

Otho nodded grimly. A few of the wasps had wriggled their way out and were climbing along the cloth towards their hands. Otho watched one reaching his thumb, buzzing wings as if to ease them after its captivity. The main nest was still concealed, but without the twist . . . He heard Lucius yelp as one of them attacked.

'That's long enough,' Lucius snapped. 'Ready? One, two, three!'

They swung cloth and nest together in a great heave. It went in through the window and thumped on the wooden floor inside. A greater buzzing could be heard then, along with the first questioning voice of the magister, followed by anger and horror.

Lucius grinned at his friend, the pain from the stings suddenly forgotten.

'He comes close to see what has arrived through the window,' he murmured. 'He sees the wasps and remembers the last one. He runs . . .'

They heard hammering and began to laugh. One little wooden wedge could jam a door. Serenus had kicked it into place from the outside, holding it shut. The magister yelled in fear as he attacked the wood, but there was no way out. Lucius wondered if he would think of escaping through the window, but the nest had landed there. The wasps would surely bar the way.

A few of the buzzing insects drifted out of the window above. It was the sight of those that made Lucius and Otho move off. They met up with Serenus at the main door and punched one another on the shoulder in a combination of greeting and praise. Just one wasp had given them three days of freedom before. As the boys wandered down the hill to explore the markets, they thought a whole nest would surely win them a week or two, even longer if the magister gave up and went home.

Lucius was snoring when his door slammed open. He had come back to his rooms late and Otho had introduced him to two of the girls he favoured. They'd seemed interested in the heavyset young lad, growing like a weed and already with a shadow on his cheeks, though he had not yet passed his thirteenth birthday. It would be at least a year until he wore the toga of a man instead of a boy's tunic. Yet one of the young women had caught his interest, with tanned

Conn Iggulden

legs, eyes made huge with kohl and a strange way of holding his gaze. Laitha. He had gone to sleep saying her name and it was she who swam through his dreams, shattering into pieces like a thrown pot as he was yanked out of bed by the foot.

Lucius wore a loincloth and a sleeveless tunic – the nights could be cold, with a hundred halls on the Palatine to suck warmth from the air, or never grow warm at all. He felt himself slide and grabbed blankets, dragging them with him so that he hit the ground in a great, roaring bundle of confusion. He was cocooned for a moment, then surged up, panting and ready to fight.

Burrus of the praetorians looked with interest at the dagger in the boy's hand. He had to have reached for it even as he was dragged out of bed. Burrus saw too that Agrippina's son wore a heavy bracelet of gold and polished resin, with snakeskin glittering beneath the surface. That snake had saved his life years before, so it was said, when assassins had come to his home outside the city. Perhaps that was why he still slept with a knife to hand, Burrus thought.

'Put that down, son. Your mother has summoned you.'

'So? You're not prefect of the praetorians, are you?'

Burrus said nothing, though Lucius knew he had scored on him.

'No, not until Rufrius retires. Perhaps not even then. You can't just come in here when I'm sleeping! Get out.'

With wide arms, the boy tried to crowd him out of the room. It might have worked on his younger brother or one of the house slaves. Burrus was reminded of the bravado of a young praetor. That was not a pleasant memory and he reacted more harshly than he would usually have done. With a quick strike, he smacked Lucius' arm, knocking the knife from his grip. It went skittering across the tile and he thought the boy might leap for it.

'The emperor is still up,' Burrus snapped. 'Your father, as he is now. Your *mother* sent me to fetch you to his presence – and I am a praetorian, sworn to obey the orders of the imperial family. I will do that, even if I have to carry you over my shoulder, bawling all the way.'

'What do they want?' Lucius said.

Burrus saw him strangle down the outrage, his eyes narrowing. It wasn't a bad set of reactions to being woken. First a blade, then the self-control an adult male was expected to have at his command. It was not what Burrus had expected from Agrippina's son. He raised his eyebrows.

'Come with me and find out. Put your sandals on. There are sweat stains on that tunic. I'd change first if I were you.'

Lucius waved away the suggestion, then ran fingers through thick black hair. He was a solid boy, Burrus thought, muscular and deeply tanned as if carved from olive wood. His legs were thick with muscle, the inheritance of his true father, perhaps. In another life, he'd have made a decent soldier.

Burrus broke off his examination. The boy's mother would never let him march with a legion, nor be a charioteer like his father. She had some different path in mind. That was the privilege of beautiful women, of course, to do as they pleased.

He saw her son's gaze had come to rest on his maimed hand. Burrus raised it for him to get a good look. He'd hidden it from staring eyes for years, keeping it behind his back whenever he was in public. Little by little, he'd grown furious with himself. These days, he held it where anyone could see.

Conn Iggulden

The little finger and the fourth had been cut away on his left hand. It was not an uncommon injury for a legionary. Burrus hadn't even felt it as he'd taken the wound, fighting in Britannia for the emperor. He was just pleased to have kept the rest of the hand. Legion medics were too quick to hack off entire limbs, set on making their work easy. His praetorian doctor had been a Greek, for which he thanked the gods. That man had tended him for three weeks with bread poultices, hot wine and vinegar, squeezing out pus each day until it ran red.

Burrus turned the claw back and forth. He still had the thumb, that was all that mattered. With a thumb, he could pick up a jug, or grip the strap of a shield. He could have taken a pension and retired from the legion, but he'd stayed on. He was, in the end, a stubborn man.

'Seen enough?'

The boy nodded, though he could not seem to drag his gaze away.

'Did it hurt?' Lucius asked.

Burrus snorted.

'No. Come on now. Your mother is waiting.'

It pleased Burrus that the boy made no more objection, falling in beside him as they strode along the corridors of the palace complex. The praetorian forced a fast pace, but the lad kept up without breathing hard, swinging along as if he hadn't a care. If it was an act, he did it well, Burrus thought.

The boy's sleeping room was a long way from the imperial quarters. Though the world was still dark outside, Burrus could feel something like tension rising in his gut as they drew closer. There were lamps in the corridors around Claudius, low to the floor on ornate stands of bronze and polished wood, burnishing tiles and walls. Praetorians too were there, saluting at every corner and set of doors. Burrus felt the boy watching as he accepted the gestures and returned them, murmuring a word of praise here and there.

'Do you know *all* of them?' Lucius asked.

'I do,' Burrus said. 'I have been a centurion for over twenty years. Long enough to learn a few names.'

'The last praetorian prefect took his own life,' Lucius said. 'And the one before that. Will Prefect Rufrius do the same, do you think?'

Burrus had reached the corridor leading to the emperor's private rooms. He clenched his jaw.

'I'm sure Rufrius will retire in peace to tend his vines,' he muttered. 'Or die of old age, perhaps.'

Lucius grinned at that response.

'Will you lead the praetorians after that?' he asked innocently.

'I have no such ambition,' Burrus said.

'But if the emperor chooses you . . .' Lucius prompted.

'If the gods and the emperor select my name, I will not refuse. Beyond that, I have no desire for anything more.'

'I suppose you might end up taking your own life, then,' Lucius said.

'Perhaps. Or perhaps I'd break the pattern just to spite you, you little shit.'

Lucius didn't have time to reply, though his mouth opened in surprise. As they approached the door, guards to either side suddenly crashed to formal attention, alerting those in the rooms beyond. Slaves drew the doors open and Burrus and the boy went in.

Conn Iggulden

2

Lucius stood with his head slightly bowed, a few paces into the emperor's living rooms. A huge shallow brazier of black iron lent heat and light. Lamps along the walls stood like praetorians. The emperor felt the cold, so he'd heard.

His mother had begun a tirade as he'd entered, voice hard as marble, cadence like the strokes of a whip. Lucius endured. Her anger was real enough, but he felt it was also for everyone else present, almost a performance. She rarely became truly incoherent or speechless with rage. No, his mother poured out anger in a great flood, trying to drown him with words. He'd learned to be a rock when that wave built.

Lucius was aware of Burrus at his side. The praetorian stood to attention, chest puffed out. Lucius had to fight not to grin at the thought of the grizzled old bastard being told off as well.

'I *know* Otho will have been involved!' Agrippina said. 'No, I won't have it! Don't you *dare* deny it! I had his mother in here an hour ago, weeping that her precious son was being led astray. She brought that great clod of a boy with her to show me all the lumps and stings he had taken for this foolishness. The same lumps and stings I see on your arms now!'

Lucius covered one forearm with a hand, trying to hide the worst of it. He saw his stepbrother and stepsister were present across the room. Octavia had her stupid doll with her, though she was too old for it. He felt his scowl deepen. Of course they were still awake. Had he been the only one snoring on the Palatine that evening?

Octavia was a couple of years younger and seemed to take great pleasure in seeing him disgraced. Lucius imagined she had *leaped* at the chance of watching strips torn from him in front of the family. Yes, there was a smile teasing her mouth as she stared. He tried to glare back, to warn her of retribution. She put her tongue out.

His stepbrother looked more upset, but then the nine-year-old usually did. Britannicus was a little whinger who wept over absolutely nothing. Lucius hated him – for his complaints to his father, for the way he followed like a lost pup, for searching Lucius' room for weapons and then giving a box of all he had found to their mother. 'Britannicus' didn't suit him, either. Lucius had invented a number of nicknames and they were all better. His favourite came from a day when he'd accused Britannicus of having no hair down below. Lucius had been referring to him as 'The Bald One' and shrieking with laughter. In rage, Britannicus had shouted that he *did* have hairs there, that he had 'twelve, actually!' The idea that he had counted them had made Lucius laugh until his stomach hurt. Britannicus had been 'Twelve' ever since, though he would cry about that as well. The little baby had only been interesting when he'd

Conn Iggulden

believed whatever wild story Lucius told him. Having been fooled and mocked for it a few times, Britannicus had grown wary – and so less interesting. He couldn't even be a good audience.

Lucius heard his mother's voice growing louder and realised his thoughts had drifted.

'What is *your father* to make of this? Have you any *idea* how furious Claudius is with you?'

For emphasis, Agrippina gestured to where the emperor sat at a desk. The old man blinked and looked up, aware of the sudden focus in his direction. Lucius glowered at him from under lowered brows. He wanted to retort that 'C-C-Claudius' was not his father, though that would earn him a whipping. Nor was it true, at least since the adoption had been accepted by the senate. Lucius was part of the imperial family. He even had a new name, though he had vowed never to use it. He could not stop his mother from punishing him, but that was an oath he could swear, no matter how the woman raged and jabbed with her finger.

'You *swore* to me there would be no more bad behaviour when the *last* tutor left!' Agrippina snapped. She was redfaced, Lucius noted. Strong emotion mottled her skin, like a rash or a fever. He looked for things like that, to hold his interest while she raged.

'I thought you'd learned your *lesson* then, Lucius, on bread and *water* for a week, with your backside striped like beating a *rug*. Then this! How could you ever think you would get away with it . . . how *could* you, Lucius?' She heard herself that time and spat out the alternative. '*Nero!* Your poor tutor is damaged beyond . . . I had to go to the infirmary to see him, to apologise on your behalf. I've never even seen . . .' She took a deep breath, shuddering.

'I *told* the emperor you would make yourself worthy of the new name he gave you. This is how you repay that trust? Well, you have disappointed your father, Nero. Can you not see? The poor man is speechless. By the gods, you have disappointed us both.'

Once more, Agrippina indicated Claudius. The emperor was alert enough that time to nod in silent disapproval. His hands smoothed papers he still read with half an eye. Lucius curled his lip at him. The old man wasn't interested in his wife's son from a previous marriage, not really.

Lucius' *actual* father had been a force of nature – a charioteer for the Greens, not some clerk with a limp and a stammer. Lucius didn't remember Gnaeus Ahenobarbus, or was not sure he did. He could not tell sometimes if a memory was of that man or his mother's second husband. Italus had been a soldier and a good sort. He and Lucius had mended a chariot together, working in silence amidst smells of glue and paint. That was a memory of quiet peace. Lucius summoned it sometimes, on days when his mother was on one of her rants.

He felt his cheeks grow hotter as the stream of accusations continued. With his brother and sister present, and Burrus listening to every word, all he could do was feign carelessness. His mother seemed determined to humiliate him in public. She wanted blood and he could not stop her.

'. . . are you *deaf*? Or just stupid?' she shouted at him. 'I already know Otho was there. Did you drag your brother or sister into this as well? Or that other friend of yours . . . Serenus! Was he there? Was he part of it? I know he was.'

'It was just me,' Lucius said. He had been intending to deny everything, but he was suddenly so angry he didn't care what she did to him. 'I wouldn't ask Octavia or

Conn Iggulden

"Britannicus" to do something like that anyway. They'd go running to tell someone . . .'

His stepsister gasped, though Lucius knew it was all an act. Octavia loved to see him in trouble, that was all. He hated her as well. Some nights, he lay in bed and clenched every muscle and joint until he was shaking with rage, wishing them all into an early grave. He felt better after that, usually.

Before Lucius could continue, he heard guards thump to attention outside, challenging someone trying to enter the emperor's presence. Claudius took that moment to stifle a yawn, though he gestured for the doors to be opened. Lucius looked at the dark sky behind the emperor's desk. Where was the dawn? He'd lost track of time, what with being dragged out of bed. It felt like the longest night of his life.

The one who entered was a member of the imperial staff, though whether slave or freed, Lucius didn't know. Some of the freed ones wore silver rings as a symbol of their status, while slaves wore iron. There had to have been thousands across the entire imperial precinct, working in the kitchens or the laundry, sweeping and cleaning hundreds of rooms in shifts. Lucius imagined they slept in attics or dormitories, piled up like a nest of mice. This one looked Egyptian to his eye, a plain young woman, flushed at the honour of entering the emperor's own rooms. She trotted in as if she'd developed a sudden cramp or her legs had buckled.

Her head bobbed as she came close enough to make out the emperor, without ever really looking at him. She knelt then, dropping too quickly, so that her kneecap made an audible tap on the tile floor.

'Approach,' Claudius said.

He rose from his desk and the young woman came and murmured to him. Lucius watched, pleased at the reprieve. Even his mother had fallen silent, which was a blessing.

The emperor didn't seem to sleep much, Lucius knew that. At any hour of the night or day, Claudius could be found droning on in one of his meetings, planning new taxes and rules. The man loved order, or at least imposing it on others. Lucius made a sour face. In that at least, the emperor and Agrippina were actually well matched. She was never happier than when she was making her son's life harder than it had to be.

The staff woman left, bobbing as she went. Claudius leaned over to Agrippina, repeating a few words while Lucius watched owlishly. They always had plans for him, he'd learned. His mother in particular would talk of the kind of man he might be, what he might accomplish with his life – if only he listened. She always seemed to feature in the years ahead, he noticed. Every daydream or imagining involved her at his side, travelling to see the banks of the Nile, or the great temples of Athens. He wondered sometimes if she would ever let him go.

His mother had managed to grow pale and mottled at the same time. It was as if the blood had drained, leaving only the marks of her previous anger. Lucius raised his eyebrows in suspicion, not trusting any of them. He felt his bottom lip ease out, a childish affectation that Britannicus had dared to mock him for, the little turd. Lucius pulled it back in and waited.

'Your tutor has died, Lucius,' Agrippina said, more softly than anything she'd said before. 'It seems he reacted badly to the stings of the wasps. Some men can bear them,

Conn Iggulden

while others . . . You could not have known. It was a terrible accident.'

She had guessed. Lucius could see the knowledge in her eyes. Otho had told her, or she'd found out from Magister Anictetus himself. Agrippina was bright-eyed as she stared, willing him to understand. He nodded slightly.

'I didn't know,' Lucius said clearly. 'I thought he would just get stung a few times and that would be the end of it. It was just a prank. I had no idea. I'm very sorry.'

He watched his mother breathe in relief. Words meant nothing – and yet they seemed to matter. That was a kind of power, he realised. The right words, at the right time – and it was like sucking poison from a wound.

Agrippina exchanged a glance with her husband. The emperor nodded. It looked like progress. Lucius watched the little scene play out between them. As they were distracted, he took a moment to wink at Octavia. Her little mouth opened in a perfect 'O' of shock.

'The treasury will make good the loss, of course,' Agrippina said. 'The family of poor Anictetus will not be thrown onto the street because of my son's stupidity and carelessness. They will be compensated, with . . . all the wages he would have earned in a lifetime – and more. I will need a blank order on imperial funds, Claudius. I will work out how much it should be and visit them myself.'

The emperor's mouth twisted as if he'd broken a tooth. Yet he nodded, murmuring assent. Lucius remained wary.

'Nero?' his mother said. 'You'll attend the funeral. You'll stand at my side and you'll apologise to the man's wife.'

Lucius began to shake his head, opening his mouth to argue.

'He died, Nero!' his mother said over him. 'If you were

Tyrant

37

not a child, not yet a man in law, you could be brought to trial, do you understand? Be thankful you don't wear the toga virilis this day, or you could be tied to a board to starve, your eyes pecked out by birds. *Wipe that smirk off your face!'*

He scowled, humiliated once more. He hadn't been smirking. His mouth stretched wide when he was nervous and he could feel his mother's ill will gathering like storm clouds. Thus far, it had all been shouting and pointing fingers. He could put up with that for hours if need be. Yet the news of the tutor dying had shaken him. That was a first. He did not know what it would mean.

'Centurion Burrus,' his mother said, addressing the man before her for the first time. 'Thank you for bringing my son to me. You should find two other boys outside by now. Can I depend on you to see all three whipped for what they did? Can I be sure they will understand the seriousness of this?'

Lucius opened his mouth to protest, but the burly praetorian spoke first.

'I'll see to it they do, empress.'

Claudius looked up sharply at that, Lucius noticed. He could almost see the emperor consider it and decide it was not worth the trouble. He sneered then. Claudius had chosen to have her in his bed, in his family. Agrippina was like the sandals of penitents, wearing even stone steps to a bow.

He felt Burrus grip his upper arm and didn't pull away. It was the good hand, Lucius noted, not the chicken foot. He had an idea the legionary's grip wouldn't break, so kept his dignity as he was led out. His heart raced though. It was hard not to fear a whipping, harder still not to show it.

Otho and Serenus waited in the chamber beyond. Their mothers were with them, a cloud of scent and powder. All four rose as the doors closed, blocking the view into the emperor's rooms.

Otho looked pale, his eyebrows raised in question to Lucius. Serenus had clearly been crying, but he wiped his face roughly with one hand. Lucius was there. It would be all right.

'They say the magister died,' Otho muttered. 'Is it true?'

Lucius saw they expected something from him. He frowned. He was still quietly delighted the tutor had died! If he'd been on his own, he would have run and jumped and crowed for the sheer joy of it. That little man would strut and bark and take a strap to them no longer. If the magister had left Rome, that would have been the end. Who cared if his absence was for death, rather than a journey home? He was *gone* – and Lucius had won. That was all that mattered.

Lucius could see his friends were shocked, however. He shrugged, aware of the old soldier listening to every word. Burrus might have dragged him off down the corridor, but he had chosen to wait, giving Lucius a chance to speak. It was uncommonly decent of him, Lucius thought.

'We'll pay his family,' he told Otho. 'Tutors don't earn much, but they'll get a sack of silver instead of his wage. Perhaps we'll have a summer without lessons then, until they find someone else.'

The grip on his arm tightened and Burrus whistled softly. It had been the wrong response, apparently.

'You two are to come with me,' the praetorian said. 'On orders of the empress herself. Killing your tutor deserves a whipping for the ages, one you will not forget.'

'Wasps killed him, not us,' Lucius snapped. 'Who dies from wasps, anyway? He was weak. And I don't forget *anything*,' he went on. 'Or anyone. Enemy or friend. The way I see it – it's up to them.'

It was a half-decent threat. Burrus might have admired it in other circumstances. Instead, he sighed and shook his head.

'Today, it is your mother's will that matters,' he said. 'Come on.'

'I'm past the age,' Otho said. He licked his lips nervously when Burrus glanced at him, but went on. 'I'm fourteen. You can whip a child, but not me.'

Burrus nodded, as if he'd heard a reasonable argument.

'I think your being past the age of manhood has been overlooked,' he said, showing his teeth. 'If I remind the emperor of that, perhaps he'll put you to trial. You can be banished or executed like a grown man then. Is that what you want?'

'No, he doesn't want that,' Otho's mother said quickly. 'He'll take what's coming without saying a word. Won't you, Othy?'

Her son glared with his fists bunched. When Lucius nodded, he did as well.

Burrus had been ignoring the two women present. They were matronly sorts and the wives of senators. Otho's mother in particular was almost as thickset as her son.

'Should we ... wait here?' she added, her voice trembling.

'I don't want to go!' Serenus said, suddenly. 'Don't let him take me!'

'Keep your mouth shut,' Otho snarled. 'Not another word.'

'Othy!' his mother said, shocked at his tone.

Burrus rubbed his jaw with his free hand.

'I'll bring them back to you,' he said at last. 'Though it will be a long wait. The empress has asked me to make a point.'

As he turned to go, he released his grip on Agrippina's son. Did the boy understand there was nowhere to run? Burrus readied himself to knock Lucius on his backside if he tried to escape.

Lucius watched the centurion warily, ready to bolt. After all, what would they do if he ran? Give him another whipping to go with the first? Yet he would have an after-noon in the sun, doing whatever he pleased. The idea tempted him.

'What is going on here?' a voice came.

Burrus glanced over and stood to attention. Lucius too looked up. The prefect of the praetorians was as white-haired as Burrus, but older still, with enormous eyebrows and tufts of yellow hair in his nostrils and ears. He seemed angry about something, Lucius thought, as he bustled up.

'Why was I not summoned?' Prefect Rufrius demanded. 'Why are *you* here, Burrus? Why was I allowed to sleep while the emperor called?'

'I was not aware the emperor sent for you, Prefect Rufrius,' Burrus replied evenly. He had known Rufrius for fourteen years, since the man's appointment to the legion. He thought Rufrius was an idiot, promoted to please sena-tors in his family rather than for any merit Burrus could discern.

'You were "not aware"!' Rufrius said. His mouth was working and spittle showed at the corners. 'No, I see you were not! Perhaps you *should* have been though, Centurion

Burrus! Perhaps you should have wondered why your senior officer was not woken, with half the imperial staff running around like a damned uprising!'

'You are correct, dominus. I should have sent word. I must apologise.'

Lucius was watching the exchange with interest. Once again, he saw the right words steal anger from the senior man. Rufrius seemed to deflate like a wineskin.

'Well, as you say. Exactly. Should have been called. And I see you have the emperor's son in tow.'

To Lucius' horror, the prefect bent down to speak to him, bringing his great nose and eyebrows close enough for Lucius to smell his breath.

'I hear your tutor is very ill, boy.'

'Dead, dominus,' Burrus muttered.

'I see.' The man's eyes gleamed, seeming to grow.

Lucius said nothing. He hadn't actually been asked a question and he didn't want to confirm or deny anything he didn't have to. The silence went on for a moment, and then the prefect took his nose and glittering eyes upright with a grunt.

'He's to be whipped, dominus,' Burrus chose to add. 'With these other two.'

The prefect cast his gaze over Otho and Serenus, the latter beginning to sniff as his nose ran.

'Good. When I am finished in the emperor's presence, I may come to you and take a turn of my own, if my shoulder permits. Boys and the whip must never be strangers, Burrus. Lay it on hard.'

In the imperial suite, Agrippina saw the younger children were yawning. Little Britannicus was swaying as he stood there, resisting the call of his bed. He was a sweet boy, though he cried in the night and wet the mattress, kicking off bedclothes in nightmares about his mother. Agrippina would go to his room then and stroke his brow until he drifted off. Sometimes, she even sang to him. Of course, his actual mother had been a conniving, faithless whore. The empire was better off with Messalina safely in an urn. Claudius certainly was.

More importantly, the slaves and the staff heard all – and some would report to the emperor, without a doubt. Agrippina did not know how many pocketed a second wage to spy for Claudius. Her husband had ledgers he kept locked away from prying eyes. Yet he was said to keep more clients than any dozen senators, all listening and reporting. It was the reason he always seemed to know the mood of the city, how he could predict the price of bread or new fashions for blue stone jewellery. She knew her husband had made fortunes from that sort of knowledge.

Agrippina crossed to Britannicus and kissed the little boy on the top of his head. If Claudius ever asked about her relationship with his two children, he would hear only of kindness and love. That was what mattered.

'You two should either go to bed or wash and change for a new day,' she told both brother and sister. Octavia had brought the doll she loved, Agrippina noticed. It was a creepy little thing, with jointed ivory limbs and human hair glued to its scalp. 'Perhaps your doll wants to sleep.'

Octavia looked scornful at that.

Britannicus yawned hugely, answer enough.

'I'll stay up,' Octavia said firmly.

Agrippina admired the show of will, but suspected the girl would be asleep on a couch before the sun was fully risen. Claudius didn't exactly indulge his children, he just didn't notice them. He expected Agrippina or his imperial staff to feed and keep an eye on them – but if the boy and girl missed a meal or stayed up all night playing in their father's rooms, he didn't mind. Yet they seemed to adore him, without any stroking of foreheads or songs sung. It was a mystery.

Agrippina only wished Nero had the sense to be pleasant to her new husband. Claudius treated him like the boy he was, but there would come a time – rushing down upon them – when her son would wear the toga of a man and be held accountable. She dreaded the gaze of Claudius on him then.

'I will have to get another tutor,' she said. 'Claudius? Would you put aside those papers, my love, just for a moment? Nero is your son as well now. If he's not to disgrace us, I need someone different . . . an ex-soldier, perhaps. Someone who will not run from a fight. I've had two of them walk out and the last one . . .' She shuddered once more, her skin made gooseflesh. The poor man had been fighting to breathe when she visited him, yet still whispering hatred for her son.

She sighed. Why could it not be Otho in trouble, or that slender boy, Serenus? Somehow it was always Lucius – Nero! – who drew the eye, Nero the one who would be caught and then laugh it off. Every tutor she engaged ended up hating him. She'd had to tell the first one to mind his language as he ranted and shrieked about her son. That one had preferred to lose his stipend and the patronage of the imperial household rather than continue one more day.

Her husband was thinking. She could see that internal

gaze of his, when Claudius brought his mind to bear on a problem. He nodded sharply then, a decision made.

'There is one, Agrip-p-pina. He was a soldier, once. A great mind, though perhaps a little in love with the G-Greeks. No, I would say he would be a f-fine m-match.'

'You are not selling him at market, Claudius,' she said. 'What is this man's name?'

'Seneca,' he said. Claudius waited for her eyes to narrow and chuckled. 'Yes. He had an affair with your s-sister, or so it was s-said. Her hah-h-husband wanted the man brought to trial, perhaps executed. I chose to exile him in-stead. N-now that your sister has d-der-d-died, perhaps it is time to b-bring the man back.'

'Are you sure he is even alive?' Agrippina said.

'He writes every m-month, asking to b-be b-brought home. So yes. He would be very grateful, Agrippina. Or . . . is it "Empress Agrip-p-pina" now? I believe that is what Burrus called you.'

She waved a hand, as if it meant nothing.

'I *am* the wife of the emperor,' she said. 'And of the blood-line of Augustus, just as you are. It is just a name, Claudius, as wife is to husband, or niece to uncle, not a formal title.'

'Mm,' he said. He seemed irritated and she knew there was a chance he would work himself into a froth about it.

'I will send for this Seneca,' she said, to head him off. 'He can recruit others. I'll have a school of them.'

'Give them c-canes or horsewhips,' Claudius said sourly. His attention had returned to the papers piled on his desk, news of the empire and a hundred petitions he would approve or deny that very day.

'What?'

'I'd have three or four m-magisters line up and l-let each

of them take a swing as the b-boys enter the s-schoolroom. A new s-st . . .'

'A new start,' Agrippina said, hurrying him along.

The emperor scowled. He hated it when she finished his words. Mulishly, he repeated the phrase, though the stammer worsened.

'A n-n-new . . . *st-start* . . . y-yes!'

'His tutors have beaten him many times, Claudius. It does no more than annoy him. I think he takes it as a challenge.'

The doors opened to admit Prefect Rufrius. The man bowed deeply to the emperor and then to Agrippina. It was hard not to think of the promises she had made to Burrus in that moment. This was the one who stood in the way of redeeming her word. Yet Rufrius kept going somehow, spare of flesh, held together by will and peevish anger. He certainly did not seem close to retiring. She frowned at him.

'Prefect Rufrius? There is no need for you to attend the emperor at this time.'

'With the greatest of respect, dear lady, that is the emperor's decision,' Rufrius said, his voice dripping oil.

Agrippina looked coldly at him. This was one who would never call her 'empress'. Yet Rufrius was a fool to contradict her, especially in front of the children. Claudius was already back reading his reports, running his finger down a page and totting up a column of numbers. Her husband yawned as he did so and, yes, the sun was rising. Claudius was at his most docile just before sleep.

'My husband and I were discussing a trip to bring a man home, Prefect Rufrius. Seneca, who resides this day . . . ?'

She looked to Claudius and he blinked twice.

'Cyrnus,' he said.

'Do you know it?' Agrippina asked Rufrius brightly.

Rufrius suppressed a groan. He had been a praetorian for fourteen years and avoided the sea for longer. His joints swelled in the damp, the food was poor and there was always a risk of drowning to cheer a man up.

'I am not familiar with the island, my lady. However, I can select a few reliable men to bring him to Rome.'

'Thank you, but I would prefer you to oversee this task yourself, Prefect Rufrius. Fetch this Seneca to my presence. Is there anything else you need?'

The prefect eased himself onto one knee. Agrippina waited for him to complete the stiff gesture, then smiled as he straightened.

'Excellent. Then you are dismissed, Prefect Rufrius.'

She watched his eyes flicker to her husband, but he didn't dare try and have Claudius repeat the order. Agrippina smiled as he left. Burrus could be his second, while he was away. 'Acting Prefect' was not what she had promised, but then perhaps the old man would perish on the journey. Travel was a perilous business.

She heard a sound and saw Octavia curl up on one of the couches, already half-asleep. Agrippina went to her and tucked the doll back under one arm, smoothing an errant lock from the little girl's forehead. She returned to where she had stood before, touching her husband on the arm to direct his attention.

'Do you see Octavia?' Agrippina murmured. 'Such a sweet girl. The sleep of the innocent.'

She bent to kiss him. The day had been long and her son had almost ruined it. Perhaps there was hope to be had in the dawn.

'Come, Claudius. Let me walk you to your sleeping room. Perhaps I will join you there for a few hours.'

He nodded, rubbing the bridge of his nose. She put her arm around him as he crossed the floor, knowing how he reacted to touch and warmth. He could be cold, but he was still a man. He just had to be reminded, that was all.

3

Cyrnus was an ancient place, older even than Rome. Most of the island was heavily wooded and mountainous, but there were towns along the eastern coast, where lowlands met the sea. Ancient towers of stones grew through trees, looking over farms and roads. No one knew who had built them. The Greeks had called it the island of sirens, but there were walls and cut stones that went back further than the age of Athens. In summer, the island was a place of fevers and of trade: in copper, silver, iron ore, pine and oak – anything the inhabitants could hunt, dig up, cut down or make. In winter, when the sea was rough, no ships came and the world left them alone.

The trireme from Rome eased into dock in waters that were rougher than the captain preferred. He'd already ordered leather gaskets on the oarlocks, reducing the amount of seawater sloshing onto the rowers. He stood at the prow, guiding his helmsmen and each stroke of the oars. He was a skilled man and the galley reached the mooring without fuss or fanfare.

He glanced back at the praetorians then. They had hardly said a word since stepping on board, especially their commanding officer. That pompous old fool had made it clear he regarded the galley as a mere conveyance. His praetorians waited on deck to disembark, huddled in dark cloaks like gulls.

A breeze had risen, painting white caps on the waves. The day was cold, but the praetorians wore chestplates and kilts of leather and bronze under the cloaks. One or two bore lion skins on their shoulders, giving them a massive, hump-backed appearance. Their helmets sported plumes of crimson bristle, stiff with wax.

Prefect Rufrius didn't thank the trireme captain. The man was not as awed as he should have been to carry praetorians on imperial business. Instead, Rufrius walked to stand where the gangplank would be set. His men were like statues in the sun. Hand-picked from the legions of Rome, they were the elite. Their double pay reflected that status, and there was not one who didn't thank his lucky stars to have won a place – and worked hard with spit and polish to keep it.

Rufrius adjusted his cloak as he waited for ropes to be tied on, running his fingers down a fine weave. The colour was a joy to his eye, a blue so deep it was almost black. Prefect of the praetorians was one of the most powerful positions in Rome, and Rome was the world. He wasn't pleased to be sent to fetch some tutor, nor to have the emperor's wife showing the reach of her authority. Rufrius rolled his eyes at his memory of her expression. A woman of beauty was a dangerous thing, he'd always said. Their husbands never slept well – and men became blushing boys around them.

Conn Iggulden

Claudius could have just taken her to his bed, but no, he'd had to marry her, adopting her brute of a son. Rufrius clenched his jaw. Give him a good, plain girl, with thick legs, strong teeth and a face to please a farmer! His own first wife had been like that, he recalled. He hadn't worried about *her* going off with one of the lads! It was hard to believe she had been taken by fever over thirty years before. Gone like a snuffed candle. He scowled. Life was short. Better these days the ones he could buy for an hour and then head back to the companionship of the barracks. Less fuss, less talk – and no dangerous ambition.

As the gangplank was secured, Rufrius walked down, his men following in a clatter of iron-studded boots. Merchants and fishermen stopped their work to see such glorious birds of Rome. Rufrius allowed himself a smile. No doubt the men of Cyrnus stood in awe at such tall and healthy-looking soldiers. The praetorians were living proof of empire, standing amongst them. These were the very ones who guarded the imperial family, the emperor himself! To such simple folk, it would almost be as if Claudius had come.

With such a spectacle, the entire port seemed to come to a halt, with cargoes left on board and sacks of grain forgotten.

Rufrius squinted at the crowd, eyebrows coming together in a single, bristling line.

'I have business in the Pitch Tar,' he announced, his voice brassy. 'A tavern, or a rooming house of that name. Where is it?'

One of the sailors pointed, his hand rising slowly as if he had no control over it.

'Marvellous. Lead on,' Rufrius ordered.

The man ducked his head and trotted away, accepting the authority of cloaks and plumes. The praetorians set off in step, their expressions cheerful. Though Rufrius glowered as if everything was a personal affront, the trip had the feel of a holiday. The crowds parted quickly rather than be trampled.

Behind them, the trireme captain and first officer descended to the dock. Rufrius glanced back as they began to dicker with a merchant. There was always some exchange of goods when a ship landed. There would be barrels of iron nails or even silver ingots in the hold by dusk, all without the knowledge of the tax collectors. The captain would pay Rufrius his taste as well. Or he'd confiscate the whole lot.

There were half a dozen taverns catering for dock workers and merchant crews. Rufrius strode past them all. He followed the sailor away from the shore and along a side street. Praetorians had no fear of robbery. Rufrius walked with confidence as the man gestured to a door. It was not much different to any other, though the sweetish smell of stale wine was on the air. Rufrius put his head into the gloom and confirmed the name. He tossed a copper coin to the man then and took four praetorians inside. He'd found there were fewer problems when he brought overwhelming force. The rest formed up in the street and for a time the Pitch Tar was the most secure tavern on the island.

Rufrius felt a touch of hunger as he saw a cauldron of stew simmering in the fireplace. The air was thick with smoke and sweat, the entire tavern just someone's home opened up for trade. Three old men were leaning on a bar of wood, watching nervously as the door was blocked by legionaries. Rufrius smiled and took a spot beside them.

'Water of life, is it?' he said.

The owner looked nervous in the presence of soldiers. Rufrius and his four made the room uncomfortably full. The prefect could feel his men's hopes rise, but there were perks to being a senior officer that went beyond a dark cloak. He held up one finger for the drink he wanted.

He wasn't certain how the stuff was made, not exactly. It seemed to involve heating grain and water until there was steam. There would be a big pot of copper or bronze out the back, dribbling from a spout. He licked his lips as a cup of clear liquid was placed before him.

Rufrius knocked it back as he would a cup of wine, then closed his eyes and thumped the bar with his free hand for a time. He could feel warmth spreading through his joints. His usual knee pain faded and he tapped the cup with one finger for it to be refilled. It was as good as he'd been told. Perhaps he could take an amphora or two back to Rome, for the winters. When he spoke, his voice had a rasp, as if his throat had been stripped.

'I am looking for a man who resides here. Name of Lucius Seneca. He would have been on Cyrnus . . . oh, for a few years now.'

'This is a small place, dominus,' the owner replied. 'I've seen Seneca a few times. Is he to be punished?'

The man was cleaning a cup in one hand as he spoke. Rufrius might have told him to mind his manners if the aqua vitae wasn't making him mellow. He drank the second as quickly as the first, tapping the cup again. It was strange. Wine loosened his tongue, but also made him stupid. This? This was a great clarity.

'Not a hair on his head,' Rufrius said. On another day, he would have stopped there, but the man refilled his cup and had not yet said anything about payment. The prefect smiled, feeling expansive. 'He is to be brought home, all honours restored.'

'Your oath on it?' one of the old men said.

Rufrius nodded and tension went out of the room. The praetorian tapped his cup a fourth time. He waited for it to be refilled before he replied.

'On my honour as Rufrius Crispinus, praetor and prefect of the praetorian guard. So. Tell him to come out, would you? Wherever he is hiding.'

The room seemed almost to be melting, but Rufrius had rarely felt better. The stuff was clearly a tonic, good for the blood.

The old men exchanged glances.

'What makes you think he'd be here?' one of them said at last.

Rufrius sighed.

'I'd like to say it was my many years in the praetorians, or that I can track a man across sea or land. The truth, though . . . Seneca puts this tavern as the address whenever he sends a letter to Rome. He isn't hiding. He wants to be found. I must say, this drink is as good as I've been told. Might I have an amphora for the road, to take with me?'

Once again, he didn't offer payment. The owner glanced at the praetorians standing against the wall. There was always threat there. It just never had to be said aloud. He reached beneath the bar and brought out a clay vessel, stopped with wax and cloth.

'The cost is six sesterces,' he ventured.

Rufrius whistled softly, taking it from his hands.

'That is a generous gift. Thank you. The praetorians are grateful.'

Conn Iggulden

He looked around as a man entered from a side room. Rufrius raised his cup in toast as Seneca nodded to him. The philosopher was fifty years of age. They had met in Rome before the exile, though without any liking growing between them.

'It's true then? I'm to come home?' Seneca asked. 'Gods be praised. Was it my last letter? The ode I wrote to Claudius?'

Rufrius shrugged. For all he knew it could well have been. He saw no reason to give Seneca that satisfaction.

'The emperor needs a tutor for his adopted son,' he said. 'That's all. Do you have any other bags, or is that it?'

Seneca shook his head. He had the look of a soldier still, Rufrius noted, certainly the frame of one. Yet Seneca wore a tattered old toga with a hem made dark by dirt and long use. He carried a single leather bag on a strap over his shoulder. It was not much to show for years of exile.

'I live simply,' Seneca said under his scrutiny. 'I've found it a great freedom.'

Rufrius stood, steadying himself when the room tilted suddenly.

'You're not the first poor man to say that,' the praetorian said with a grin. 'Well, you can "live simply" in Rome from now on. Oh, the boy killed his last tutor, so I wish you luck.'

The praetorian waited impatiently as Seneca shook hands with every man in the tavern, murmuring a few words and laughing. Rufrius looked for some exchange of coin to explain their goodwill, but there was no sign of it. Perhaps they were just pleased to see the back of him.

On the way to the ship, the prefect felt the ground had grown a little unsteady. The aqua vitae was much stronger than wine, that was clear. He cradled his amphora like a baby all the way to the docks.

It was irritating how many people called to Seneca. Some of them even asked if he was all right. Rufrius glared at those, surprised at their number. It seemed Seneca was popular on the island, though poor as a mouse and with nothing but a bag to show for his time. Rufrius could not quite explain his irritation, even to himself. Yet it sat like vitriol in his stomach, burning him.

At the foot of the gangplank, the prefect turned to the man he had brought out. The crowds were still milling there. Like country folk, they were apparently able to spend all day just staring.

'I'll be searching that bag,' Rufrius said. 'To make sure there's nothing that doesn't belong to you.'

Seneca grew very still. There was no sign then of the affable man who'd gripped the arms of the tavern-keeper and laughed with him. For a moment, Rufrius wondered if he might refuse. The prefect smiled, showing his teeth. Strong drink still ran in his veins and he thought he would enjoy seeing the man battered. Humility could be taught.

Seneca handed him the bag and Rufrius nodded his victory, breathing through his nose. He opened the latch himself and found a sheaf of vellum, each sheet sanded many times and grey with old ink. The writing was tiny, each word separated by a dot.

'Just this?' Rufrius said. 'Seven or eight years of exile and *this* is all you have to show?'

Seneca shrugged. He had decided he didn't care about the prefect's opinion and so looked up to the galley that would take him home. He wanted to go back to the city that still swam through his dreams, where plays and odes could be performed, where the women were . . . perfumed and lithe and painted. He sighed. He thought age and discipline had mastered his old passions. Yet it all felt closer than it had in years – and that brought pain sharper than a knife.

Rufrius felt spite surge at the lack of response.

'I see you use these specks of ink . . . low, middle, high, to separate your words?' Rufrius said. 'The Alexandrian style? I know it, though only as a curiosity. The great Cicero said a line should finish where *rhythm* demands, as I recall.' He smiled as Seneca's attention came back to him. 'Oh, you thought I was just a soldier, is it? Not good enough to talk to?'

'How old *are* you?' Seneca said suddenly. 'If you remember Cicero . . . what was Caesar like? Is it true he was bald, though all his statues had hair?'

One of the waiting crewmen made a sound like a snort. Rufrius felt himself flush.

'I don't *remember* Cicero,' he said furiously. 'And Caesar died almost a century ago, so I never knew him. I was quoting a great man of letters. One you should respect.'

'Oh I do,' Seneca replied. 'Old Tully Cicero said a wise man rejects pleasures of the moment, to secure greater joys. I've wondered if that might be the master lesson, Prefect Rufrius. To hold back, to command oneself. It is the essence of a man, is it not? The quality that makes us more than just animals of the field?' He glanced at the amphora under the prefect's arm. 'Those who cannot delay their pleasures . . . well, they pay a sad price.'

Rufrius felt his lip curl. The aqua vitae was still making the world blurry around the edges. He waved his hand, half a gesture to board and half in disgust.

'I see you will be well suited as a tutor to boys. I wish you luck of it.'

'Thank you,' Seneca said. He bowed his head and boarded the ship on light feet.

Seneca stood at the galley's prow, straining his eyes for the first glimpse of the port of Ostia. They had been two days at sea and it had given him no great pleasure to have Rufrius ill in his cabin for most of them. The aqua vitae had not sat well in the man's stomach, so it seemed. The prefect had broached his amphora and sampled the contents as they passed into deep waters, where waves made the ship roll. He'd lasted about an hour after that before hanging off the stern and emptying his stomach into the rushing waves. Seneca had kept his thoughts to himself, not yet sure of the man's temper or the loyalty of his soldiers.

The galley slaves rowed against the wind and Seneca closed his eyes as he thought he could smell the port even before it began to appear. With Rome just beyond, Ostia was a vast and busy hub, with food and raw materials brought from all over the empire. In comparison, the island of Cyrnus had been silent for six months of the year. Seneca had walked every hill and path, seen every view and despaired of them all. To come home was a kind of madness, a joy so intense he was forced to examine it. He made himself put it aside, an effort of will great enough to leave him trembling. When one of the praetorians asked if he was pleased to be back, he only nodded, trapping words rather than have them gush like those of a child. Seneca was to be tutor to an emperor's son, he reminded himself. The position would require dignity – and that began from the first hour of the first day.

The drumbeat eased below his feet and the pace slackened, the hiss of waves and the angle of the prow dipping. The great port swam into view and Seneca could almost have wept. Hundreds of ships and boats mingled on docks that stretched even further than he remembered. Had it grown? He knew the places of youth sometimes seemed small to those who came back to them. Ostia seemed even larger – and so full of life he had to work not to grin like a boy.

A boat rushed to meet them, a lone port officer rising from his seat as they came alongside. His official vessel was rowed by four sailors and moved at astonishing speed. The galley captain leaned down to exchange a few words and the officer's manner changed, becoming stern with duty. He pointed to a stone dock that remained clear in all the toing and froing on shore.

Seneca raised his eyebrows as the ship eased closer to land. He saw soldiers waiting there. Praetorians, by their cloaks and plumes. He did not know if they had come to escort their commander, or to arrest the new imperial tutor. He found himself swallowing, his joy dissolving.

Rufrius still looked pale as he came to the railing. He peered at the dock in obvious consternation, which didn't settle Seneca's stomach at all. There had to be a full century of praetorians on that dock, hard men in dark cloaks that moved with the wind.

All Seneca could do was wait and watch as the galley was tied up. Rufrius was first off, the old man heading straight to the waiting soldiers. He halted there and began to argue with one of their number as Seneca made his way down.

The philosopher dipped to one knee. He didn't want

anyone to see and so fussed with a sandal as if it needed to be retied. Yet this was the land he'd feared he would never see again. Cyrnus may have been beautiful, but a prison is still a prison. He patted the ground like a beloved old hound, warm to his touch.

'. . . you have *no* such authority!' Rufrius was saying angrily. 'Oh, without a doubt. You may be certain I will take this up with the emperor!'

The prefect had raised his voice and Seneca could not help overhearing. All he wanted was to find a horse – or march if he had to – to head into the city. He hoped whatever struggle was going on would resolve itself without him, but the praetorians on board tramped down and gathered him up, walking with him until they halted across from their fellows. Seneca found himself at the shoulder of the prefect.

'Welcome home, Seneca,' one of the praetorians said.

The man was around Seneca's age and looked familiar, though it had to be a face he'd known years before. If he imagined dark hair rather than that cropped white fur . . .

'Burrus?' he said, the name dragged out of the past. The man wore a centurion's plume. Seneca remembered him at the same rank, which was surprising.

Burrus grinned.

'I wasn't sure you would know me. We met a few times when you were . . . visiting your friend. You heard she died?'

'I was told,' Seneca said. 'And I was sorry to hear it. Some of the very best are taken young, while others go on and on. There's not much fairness to it.'

'Well, I can confirm, your exile is truly at an end. The senate put it in the record, with honour restored. There's work for you, if you want it.'

Conn Iggulden

Rufrius looked from one to the other in disbelief.

'Have you lost your mind, Burrus? You have made a mistake and I have told you so. I'll have your plume, you arrogant whoreson! I'll break you back to the ranks. No, I'll break you back to citizen for this! To dare tell me I am relieved? It is mutiny – and the penalties are both savage and justified.'

Burrus glanced at the older man.

'Rufrius, I showed you the imperial order. Would you like to see it again? Your authority is denied, your rank withdrawn. I suggest you take it with dignity. What are you, seventy? Your years of service are at an end. You have the gratitude of the city and you are given leave to retire on a good pension, in peace.'

'I am sixty-four – and you are disobeying my direct command. I will see you hang, centurion. I will . . .'

'Prefect,' Burrus interrupted. Rufrius looked at him in confusion and Burrus smiled. 'I am appointed prefect of the praetorians, by the emperor's decree. I understand the news is unexpected. I urge you to summon *praotēs* – control and calm. There is . . .'

'Guards!' Rufrius snapped. 'Take this traitor into custody. Disarm *Centurion* Burrus and hold him for judgement.'

The praetorians who had gone with him to Cyrnus stepped forward. A few of them even drew swords, though they looked uncomfortable.

Burrus held up his hand. He raised his voice to that of the battlefield. With blades bared, anything could happen. Whatever authority he held would be worthless if he was killed 'accidentally' on the docks of Ostia.

'Hold fast!' he roared. 'I rescind that order. I, Sextus Afranius Burrus, have been appointed prefect of the imperial guard. These men with me will affirm. *You* will sheathe your swords and stand down, or I will consider you agents of a hostile power.' He waited for that to sink in, for the soldiers fresh off the ship to consider his words. Burrus gentled his voice. 'Put your swords away, lads.'

Rufrius went even redder, his face darkening almost to the colour of his cloak. He looked poisonous as his men sheathed their weapons, not daring to meet his gaze.

'Very well,' Rufrius said. 'I see this madness will not be so quickly put behind. Did you bring horses, centurion? I would like to get back to Rome – and into the emperor's presence as quickly as possible.'

'No horses, I'm afraid,' Burrus said. He had won the battle and he was polite. 'It's just fifteen miles to the Palatine. We can make that easily enough before dark.'

Rufrius began to sneer, but there was nothing more to be said. Still trembling with fury, he could only nod, falling into place in a line that turned and crashed across the stone of the port. Seneca went with him, shifting the weight of his bag on its strap, caught between dismay and the sheer wonder of being home.

Conn Iggulden

4

Agrippina dared not pace, not as she wanted to. The senators would hear her steps if she did. She clenched her fists. The rules they made! It was all madness. A woman could not enter the senate while they were in session. That was forbidden. Yet there was apparently nothing to prevent an empress raising an enclosure of embroidered silk around a side door, creating a narrow little space where she could stand and listen to every word. They all knew she was there, of course. That was the ridiculous part, the element of farce. As long as they did not actually lay eyes on her, they could not claim the gods were outraged. They could pretend she was not present.

She stood with silk billowing against her face, on a rug she'd brought in to cover cold stones. She could hear the murmurings of senators and the scratching of imperial scribes. They'd been at their labours for most of the morning, recording decisions that would affect the lives of millions. Claudius would get his report in summation, of course, but Agrippina couldn't wait for that. Rufrius had been spotted striding up the steps outside. The man had to be at the rostrum by then, hands on polished wood that had once been part of a Carthaginian prow.

She frowned. Unless that one had been burned in riots, she could not remember. Agrippina strained to hear. There was low murmuring and some laughter in the chamber, but no clear speech. Should she have cut a hole in the tapestry? The idea, of a single eye observing them, suddenly struck her as amusing, made worse by the tension. She had to press a hand over her mouth to stifle any sound. She tried touching her ear to the silk, but it was no good. She actually heard more when she craned upwards, head cocked to the clear air. She could see the ribs of the roof and stood like a bird sensing danger, controlling her breaths. By the gods, she'd almost missed the servant's warning! For three days she'd had eyes on Rufrius and then she'd been bathing when the news came. She'd had to run from the Palatine to the forum, actually run to be there. Her hair was still damp! She'd opened the creaking side door like a spy, instead of just taking a seat with the senators. She was empress! To have to play such games was infuriating. Perhaps Claudius could appoint her to a special role in law, one that would allow . . . She became still as she recognised a voice. Rufrius.

The man walked a blade's edge and she wondered if he knew it. The rule of her brother Caligula was something they would all remember. It was not so very long ago. One word in criticism of the emperor, just *one* Agrippina could report to her husband . . . and Rufrius would be destroyed. She closed her eyes to focus on his speech.

'. . . I am most honoured, consuls, senators, most grateful to have been given this opportunity to describe my mistreatment. I am a man of Rome, gentlemen. I do not wish to change or complain about my fate, merely to have it made part of the record of this august chamber and those who make the laws of the empire. I ask for no redress for injuries I have suffered, nor do I accuse my mentor and dear friend, Emperor Claudius, of anything except the utmost kindness, honour and decency.'

Agrippina rolled her eyes. Her mouth was slightly open as she'd heard the movement of the jaw could improve hearing. Her father had told her that when she was a little girl in Germania. In fact, the memory brought another to the surface. She cupped a hand behind each ear and opened her eyes in shock at the difference it made. Rufrius' voice went from a distant murmur to clear.

'. . . beloved of the gods! No, senators, I suspect there are more sordid and worldly aspects to my loss of position. After all, the man who now holds my post as prefect of the praetorian guard is one who received no promotion for well over a decade. Prefect Burrus . . .' Agrippina smiled at the way he struggled to say name and title. 'Burrus remained a centurion after being implicated in the death of poor Senator Arruntius. That colleague of this house was accused of some petty corruption, though of course nothing was ever proven. There were whispers of ill conduct or impropriety in the manner of his death, but without proof, with the senator's own voice silenced . . . nothing could be brought before the courts. A man's career ran cold, however, a sort of natural justice – until it was picked up and blown upon. I am told a woman's hand is responsible for that ember being nursed back to life. I find that significant, senators. I will not say more until I have been assured my words will bring no spite or attack, no reprisal.

Not everyone understands the, er . . . protected nature of speech in this chamber.'

There was a ripple of laughter across the senate hall. Agrippina narrowed her eyes. She knew they would be nudging one another and pointing to the strange canopy that had appeared amongst them, barring the chamber's side door from view. They could not be certain that she stood there. Yet they would surely suspect.

As they laughed, she wondered if they considered what a sister of Caligula might do to those who mocked or crossed her. Agrippina had seen her mother exiled by men just like these, beaten and blinded, driven from Rome. Agrippina too had known exile, in darkness, in a prison cell. A dark so absolute she had brought some of it home.

She felt tendons rising like wires in her neck as she listened. Her brother Caligula had been too profligate in his violence, lashing out at anyone he saw, terrifying even those set to guard his life. Agrippina knew she was colder than her brother had been, but not less ruthless. The laughter of the senators would haunt them.

She found she was whispering to herself and clamped her mouth shut. Another was speaking and she could not identify the voice, at least at first. One of the consuls, perhaps. Those two men led the senate in all their deliberations, appointed by popular vote each year, yet with powers second only to the emperor. If Rufrius had given way to one of those, it would be important.

'. . . it cannot be a matter for this house to question the emperor's right to appoint whomever he pleases, to any position of the empire. That is a privilege of the imperial estate and beyond our authority.'

Agrippina nodded fiercely, surprised. Perhaps they

would send Rufrius back to his estates after all, red-eared and empty-handed.

'Though I may add my personal sympathy, I cannot therefore allow a vote to overturn the decision. I ask Rufrius Crispinus to withdraw his request, so that it will not be entered on the day record.'

Agrippina took a breath as Rufrius spoke briefly to confirm the withdrawal. What game was this, so warm-voiced and polite, so friendly? It seemed they were denying his request, but Rufrius sounded benign, even cheerful.

The consul spoke again – it could be no other. She could tell he stood on her side of the chamber, closer to her than Rufrius.

'There are, however, matters that do lie within our authority. I propose instead that we recognise long service to the state, that we honour a man who has given decades to imperial service at the highest levels. If my colleagues are agreeable, it is my intention to put Rufrius Crispinus forward as a new member of this senate, with a payment of . . .' He consulted notes. Agrippina could hear the rustling of papers. '. . . one and a half million sesterces from the treasury.'

The cheer that went up was answer enough. Agrippina leaned against the cold wall and thought. They hadn't dared overturn her appointment of Burrus as prefect. It was true she had moved without the explicit permission of Claudius, but the emperor wasn't willing to admit to that, either. Having a wife act on his behalf could be a boon to him, as she'd said a thousand times. It could take some of the terrible weight from his shoulders.

In the end though, it was all just pride. Pride had driven Rufrius into the arms of old colleagues, asking and receiving favours, chuckling all the while. Agrippina didn't doubt the details had been arranged in private meetings as they tried to take the sting out of his foul old temper.

There was pride too in her husband. He could not admit to other men that his young wife had overreached, had taken on some part of his imperial authority. Agrippina was empress, that was beyond dispute. Claudius still thought the word meant no more than 'wife'.

Agrippina didn't wait for the formal vote, slipping out of the side door and away. The senate would not try to reverse her appointment of Burrus, that was all that mattered. Having Rufrius among their number did not trouble her unduly. She had the emperor's ear. If Rufrius moved against her in any way, he could be sent to exile. Men rarely survived such a fate, not as she had. Poor things, their guilt and shame was just too much for them.

As she walked up the Palatine hill, she was hardly aware of the praetorians who formed around her. They bristled at the crowd and so eased her path. More importantly, they reported to Burrus. She wondered if he realised she knew how he felt. She had seen the signs in men before, the sort of mute and private suffering that could come from longing. That was what mattered, more than anything the senate might say, more than all Rufrius' spite and wounded feelings. She considered whether it would be worth taking Burrus to bed for a night, to seal the bargain that had formed between them. Or whether he preferred to see her as untouchable. Perhaps she would consider it, if he ever wavered. The thought was not completely unpleasant.

It was praetorians who had murdered her brother – in the very complex of buildings she faced as she strode up the hill. In the corridors of the Palatine, they had scorned

Conn Iggulden

the gods to kill Caligula, spattering his blood on stone floors. They had found Claudius that same night, the poor man hiding behind a curtain in his terror. There was a lesson there, Agrippina had realised. Whoever controlled the praetorians controlled the emperor. That had been true from the moment of her brother's death – and it was why she had raised Burrus to lead them. After all, if they were loyal to Agrippina, there was nothing she could not do.

Seneca stood in the schoolroom, considering his best course of action. He knew the boys had been told to appear before him at the first hour – and that they had not entered. He listened to his own slight wheeze, controlling each breath. It was not too bad. Today would be a good day, because he needed it to be.

He had been aware of the whispering voices outside for some time. It was almost insulting and he thought they were very innocent not to think he would be listening to everything they did. Placing a leather bucket over the door had tempted him to kick it open at the worst possible moment, to send sprawling whoever climbed a stool to place it there. That sort of thing could come later, he had counselled himself. Like Cicero, he could delay his pleasures.

Instead, he had listened, discerning three voices. Nero spoke more than the other two, which was interesting. The deeper voice was presumably that of Otho. That boy wore the adult toga and came from a good family, but it seemed he was happy to follow Nero. The third . . . well, it had to be Serenus. Nero refused the company of his brother Britannicus, Seneca understood. Prefect Burrus had been exhaustive in his descriptions, giving Seneca all the information he might need. That too was interesting, Seneca thought. Burrus liked the boy and wanted to turn him onto a better path. It suggested there was hope for the emperor's son.

Seneca closed his eyes for a moment in silence. The dawn light was spilling gold along the walls. If Britannicus took a fever or let some foul disease in through a graze, Nero would be heir to the empire. Twenty-eight legions would look to him, both for order and their pay. A vast architecture of scribes and merchant societies, of tax gatherers and builders, would all bend the knee in his presence. Or of course, it might not happen. If Britannicus lived to adulthood and succeeded his father, Nero would be sent to some distant outpost as governor. Britannia, if he didn't mind the rain. Hispania or Greece, if his brother still liked him. The fate of the boy was not yet set in stone and Seneca found himself relishing the challenge.

He had been brought back from exile for this work! That was how seriously the emperor considered the task. Seneca had already sent messengers to summon tutors he trusted. He needed a particular Greek specialist, as well as a Macedonian he knew well. Neither would refuse, Seneca was sure. He could still hardly believe the funds he had been allocated, to spend as he wished. For a man who tried to live as simply as possible, it was a little galling to command the wealth of a town.

Outside, all the whispering had died away. He sighed to himself, glancing at the sun. He had been fair. The hour was truly up and Nero had not set foot in the room.

Seneca crossed to the door, looking up at the bucket they'd balanced. He frowned as he saw the points of nails pressing against the leather. Not just slop water then, or faeces. Iron nails could blind a man, or knock him senseless. It was all something to record in the great ledger of his thoughts.

Seneca stood by the door until he was satisfied he knew where they all were. He breathed deeply, then kicked hard. The bucket of nails dropped as he stepped back and he rushed over it, slamming the door into the burly figure of Otho standing behind.

Otho was strong! There was a corner behind the door and Seneca had expected to jam him into it with his shoulder against the door frame. Instead, Otho grunted and began to push back. Seneca looked up and saw a masked boy, drawing a bow aimed at him.

He stepped towards the single archer, so that Otho found himself with no resistance and crashed the door shut. Seneca reached behind him and heaved the boy to the front with main strength.

The arrow flew, striking Otho. He made a terrible sound and Seneca released him, letting him fall to the garden path. He went forward, smooth and fast as the masked attacker fumbled for another shaft. Seneca reached him before he could and kicked him between the legs with all the power of his outrage.

The archer fell, curling in agony.

Seneca stood for a moment, looking back at where Otho wailed. There was one other . . . Serenus. The boy was gaping from the shrubbery, a wooden stool held like a weapon. No doubt he had been the one to place the bucket. Seneca nodded as if in greeting, then knelt beside Nero.

He took the mask away. Seneca saw two enraged eyes glaring and heard the boy curse as he tried to rise.

The tutor took his tunic in hand, a good bunch of it. With that grip, he dragged Nero along the path towards the schoolroom. Seneca was wheezing by then, each breath coming as if through cloth. He felt fear build and strangled it with anger. His lungs would obey his will!

'I faced real archers in Parthia,' he said as he walked.

Nero began to struggle, so that his sandals scraped the ground. It didn't make any difference to the man pulling him. Seneca smiled in memory.

'To the east. They were . . . fearsome fighters, masters of the horse and bow. As long as we remained in formation, our shields kept us alive. The trouble was, they knew that as well as we did.'

He stepped over the bucket and scattered nails and glanced at Otho. The boy's wound was in his chest, though he had pulled the arrow out and sat up. Otho looked shaken, but there was no great gush of blood. Seneca thought he would live.

'After you, Master Otho,' Seneca said. Despite the wheeze, he spoke calmly.

The boy looked at him in confusion. It was not the reaction they had expected. Otho decided he was not going to die and went in, one hand touching the gash to his toga, stained in blood.

On a whim, Seneca glanced over his shoulder to the last of them.

'Come, Master Serenus. Enter now or never again.'

The boy scurried in. As he passed, Seneca launched a huge kick at him, one that lifted Serenus right into the air and sent him sprawling. Serenus looked back in shock.

'That is for the bucket,' Seneca said.

He dropped Nero at one desk, the boy still sick from his

Conn Iggulden

damaged balls. Seneca waited for Otho to choose a place on a bench and then pointed to another. They would get away with nothing that morning, not after the way they'd chosen to begin. Otho dipped his head and sat where he was told, looking aggrieved. He kept touching his wound in a sort of accusation, as if Seneca was the one responsible.

'The Parthians developed one tactic that worked, though it was costly. They don't seem to mind losing men in battle, not as we do. I suppose they can always breed more.'

Seneca turned to the wall, where a sheet of black slate had been washed and stood ready. With a piece of chalk, he drew a simple legion formation.

'. . . the legion advancing. Note the position of officers, here and here. Front and second lines ready to rotate. Spears ready, shields on the left arm, swords sheathed. The Roman war machine, gentlemen. And facing us, a wild-looking horde of screaming Parthians. Armoured riders – leather and metal, painted dark green for the most part. Helmets, some spears – and those bows. Short little things, like the one you used, Master Nero. Yet with more power. If that had been a Parthian bow, if you had been strong enough to draw one, I dare say we would be telling Otho's father he had lost his oldest son.'

Seneca glanced over at Otho, seeing the surliness still there.

'My regards to your father, Master Otho. The work he did in Illyricum was impressive. Ruthless, but deserved, as far as I can tell.'

Otho mumbled something, flushing.

'I see that is a story that needs telling,' Seneca said. 'This is the very nature of education, gentlemen! The world is full of knowledge, of fascinating things. How did those Parthians create so much power in their bows? I will take you to the imperial record house – there used to be a few of them on the wall there, some old soldier's trophies. If they can be restrung, perhaps we might be allowed to shoot them . . . Where was I? Ah, yes. They raced in, the Parthians. I was standing with my friends in the front rank, shields high as their arrows clattered at us. They could find the gaps, those little bast . . . those determined enemies. They seemed to live in the saddle and their animals could dart back and forth, making them hard to hit. Still, we advanced into their territory. We went in at battle pace – and engaged them. They broke in moments, which I had not seen before. They were running! We gave a great roar . . . Yes, Serenus, what is it?'

'My leg has gone numb, magister. From the kick. It was all right at first, but I don't think I can walk on it.'

'My regards to your father as well, Master Serenus. When you describe the moment to him, please include being lifted clean into the air with the force of my foot alone, would you? A thing worth doing is worth doing well, I believe. I suspect that memory will amuse me for years. Now – the Parthians. They broke, and some of our lads raced forward in chase. You have to understand those horsemen were always just out of reach, killing our sentries, catching our water-carriers at the rivers. A great deal of anger had built over the previous days and weeks – and there they were, milling and crashing into one another, all in panic at Roman force of arms . . .'

He trailed off, looking into the past. The memory was not a happy one. Nero let the silence stretch for as long as he could bear it.

Conn Iggulden

'What happened then?' he asked.

'Hmm? Oh, they did something I'd never seen before. They rode away. We could see their backs and so we knew there would be no arrows from them. Do you see? A man can't shoot a bow when he is facing away from his enemy. Except . . . that was exactly what they did. They turned in the saddle, right round, straining hips and arms. They shot as we broke formation . . . and we lost more men in a few moments than in three months before. We called it the "Parthian shot" after that – and added it to our tally of tactics. We watch for it now, whether they try the false re-treat or not. We even had some of our lads learn the trick, but shooting backwards at full gallop? We never could get the accuracy.'

Seneca stood and paced up and down, glaring at the three boys.

'You seem like good lads, if I ignore the high spirits from before. We can begin each day like this if you wish, or perhaps Masters Otho and Serenus will return with excuses from their fathers, I don't yet know. I will accept them, gentlemen. I have been given the task – the honour – of educating Nero here.'

'Lucius,' the boy muttered.

'No,' Seneca said firmly. 'That was your name before adoption. Your father has all authority in this. You will answer to "Nero" or be flogged every hour. Believe me, son, it is a hard thing to endure. The marks don't heal, do you see?'

On impulse, Seneca drew down one shoulder of his toga, revealing a mass of scars, criss-crossing one another.

'So. I do not have time to waste on what name you wish

to be called! You will answer to "Nero". As for your friends, I see some merit in having them present – ideas flow more freely in conversation. But it is not vital. I have tutors coming from Egypt and Macedonia, to aid me in your studies. We will teach you Greek, of course, as well as rhetoric and geometry, civil law . . . battle tactics, persuasion, the building of physical strength. You should be at least competent in a fight, which we will address in your leisure hours . . . There is a lot to do. I will not ask if you agree. You are a child and these decisions will be made by those with more wisdom and experience than you currently possess. I see you follow the argument. Have you understood, Nero? Have you followed?'

Nero nodded.

'Oaths and agreement must be said aloud, Nero. Always.'

'I understand, magister,' Nero said.

Seneca glanced at the others and they murmured that they too understood. Seneca scowled at them.

'There will come a day when we meet as men. Not merely because you will wear a toga virilis, but because you will have become something more than you are now. I will try to bear in mind that you will stand before me then. That is my oath to you. Nero!'

The boy jumped as his name cracked out.

'I will apply to Emperor Claudius for you to receive the toga virilis early.'

'I am thirteen,' Nero said, adding 'magister' quickly.

'Yes. It is a difficult balance. I do not like breaking imperial rules. They are there to protect us . . . but your actions today could have killed me. In matters of life and death, you should be ready to face the consequences, not hide behind the protection of your youth. No, I will petition your father to have you entered in the rolls before your fourteenth birthday – this week if I can. If you are then involved in anything so mindlessly stupid again, it will mean exile or death. Is that clear?'

Nero squirmed in his seat. The ache in his groin was finally fading, but he didn't like the way the conversation had turned.

'Are you deaf?' Seneca said. 'Why would you have me repeat myself? My time is more valuable.'

'I don't want . . .' Nero began. He could hear the whining tone and took a breath, clamping his mouth shut.

'As was clear from the bucket over the door, your judgement is based on instinct and raw emotion,' Seneca went on. 'It is fortunate, then, that the decision is mine. Now, gentlemen, take your slates from the shelves. I will begin with the poetry of Horace, perhaps the greatest master of letters ever to grace the earth. In turn, the master influenced Virgil. Homer himself would be jealous of either man. They speak to me – and with their voices, I speak to you. You will learn sixty lines of each today – and repeat them to me tomorrow.'

Serenus hobbled to the shelf and passed out slates and sticks of chalk. Seneca made no comment on the leg the boy had claimed was still numb. The tutor smiled in memory and saw Serenus scowl, guessing at his thoughts.

'Begin. Copy this line . . .' Seneca said.

After a while, there was just the scratching of chalk, while the sun rose.

5

Claudius could not quite believe the woman standing at his side. Agrippina intoxicated him, made his senses swim. She talked and talked, words like a river's flow, or the sweep of the golden cloak she wore that day. The weight of it was extraordinary, lined in silk and made from true gold wound around each thread. It represented the work of hundreds of seamstresses and the cost would have beggared a large town. Yet the crowds on the road were awed by it. High on that balcony, Agrippina was the sun come to earth. Claudius merely stood in that reflected light.

For a hundred and sixty days each year, games and feasts of some sort took place in Rome. Perhaps a third of those were spent in prayer and worship, while the rest were given over to some form of entertainment. Everything from Julius Caesar's birthday to the great festivals of Lupercalia and Saturnalia were cause to celebrate. Some of the plebeians simply put down tools and rested, but most gathered their families, eating and drinking whatever treats they had

Conn Iggulden

prepared since the last. Meat was dried in herb-scented garlands and wine laid down to become mellow for those days.

Claudius had added three more to celebrate the conquest of Britain, leaving his own mark on the calendar. He was at his least comfortable on such occasions, though he claimed to understand the need for them. The people lived hard lives, with little pleasure. They worked from sun-up to dark, blessing the gods who kept them in good health. Life was a struggle for them, Claudius knew. They lived for the games and holy days.

Down below, at the foot of the temple to Apollo, Claudius watched as praetorians handed loaves to outstretched hands. That would be happening all over the city, but the crowd on the northern side of the Palatine was thickest. Local people knew to gather there before the sun rose, perhaps to catch a glimpse of the ruling family.

Claudius glanced at his wife and of course Agrippina sensed it, turning to him and lowering her head to his chest. She had to bend her knees just a touch, but all that was covered by the golden cloak. Below, the crowd roared their appreciation.

'You are a good man,' she murmured. 'I hope you know I adore you.'

Claudius smiled. She flattered him. Yet it worked, even as he saw through it. He touched his thumb to the back of her neck, feeling the softness. The way hair curled there, the way her eyes gleamed dark, the touch of her. She turned her head, presenting a slightly open mouth to be kissed. It might have been show for the crowd, but he did as she wanted. They cheered again and Claudius flushed. Let them see a wife who revered her husband, who was not ashamed of him! Let them all see. It had been different when Caligula sat over Rome. Claudius had thought he would never survive the bloodletting, the madness. Even his wife back then had joined in, mocking his stammer and laughing at his expense. Somehow, he had beaten them all. Perhaps Agrippina was his reward.

He had not known love like it before. Agrippina left him wrung out, exhausted. She was like the aqua vitae that had found its way to the city – too strong for the senses, overwhelming. Even her perfume was potent. Yet Claudius could not refuse another cup, not when it touched his lips. He had been dry too long.

The emperor rested one hand on the balcony and waved to the crowds. From that height, he could see loaves being carried off like seeds to feed their children. He felt benign, expansive. *This* was what it meant to be emperor. Not taxes, or warships, or the savagery of tribes. Not even the great markets or opening new mines in the east. No, it was simpler than that. It was the relationship of emperor to his people. Claudius was paterfamilias to a million wives and young women, across a vast empire. He found the thought mildly arousing, which surprised him.

At his back, Nero stepped on the hem of Octavia's dress, sending the girl sprawling. Her squawk turned into a wail and Claudius' smile tightened in irritation. He waited for Agrippina to glare at his children. They seemed to fear her more than they did their father. That was not too surprising, he thought.

'Your t-tutor has made an application for the adult t-toga, on b-behalf of your son, Agrippina, are you aware?'

She turned to him, her gaze very still. She rarely looked away, Claudius realised. When Agrippina focused on a

Conn Iggulden

man, it was as if the rest of the world vanished. It was disconcerting to have someone truly listen, focusing utterly on what he was saying. He'd seen other men reduced to incoherency by that perfect attention. It made his stammer worse, unfortunately.

'I hadn't heard,' Agrippina said. 'I have good reports of his work. Yet he seems rather independent for a mere tutor.'

She turned to see her son wrestling with Britannicus, holding his head under one arm.

'Nero!' she snapped. 'You are in your good clothes. Leave your brother alone.'

They parted, flushed and panting, and she shook her head at them.

'What is this about the toga virilis?'

Nero glowered. The headlock had been quite satisfying. His little brother was already snivelling, though it was nothing! Nero tried to warn the younger boy with a glare, but Britannicus would probably cry anyway.

He glanced quickly at his mother, considering how to answer. Nero had looked into what a man could do that was forbidden to a boy. Some of it was better than just fingering girls in the woods with Otho. To his surprise, he found himself in agreement with his tutor. It had come up more than once in the weeks since their first lesson. Rather than make the argument himself, he repeated Seneca's words, his voice a dull drone.

'Magister Seneca said I should be responsible for my actions, that if I take risks with my life and the lives of others, I should be prepared for proper consequences.'

Agrippina blinked. Nero bowed his head and stood as if abashed while she narrowed her eyes, trying to see what game he was playing. He was thirteen and large for his age.

He had a shadow over his top lip and a sort of heavy strength that reminded her of her first husband, especially when he was in a rage. That was the problem, though. Her son could not control his temper. He flung things around and kicked over tables. He had given Britannicus a black eye and put his foot through a door in the last year alone. Seneca had restored something like order, or given him something to fear, Agrippina wasn't sure. She was pleased at the results, not least because it meant her days weren't filled with dealing with her son or paying compensation.

She glanced at Octavia. And yet . . . if Nero was made a man in law, it would mean more than wearing a toga instead of a tunic. Nero could be betrothed. A betrothal was just a promise, of course, one that could be broken. Still, it would raise her son. Agrippina glared at the boy waiting for her response. She did not trust Nero, nor this Seneca, though the tutor at least seemed competent. There had been no new scenes of chaos and violence for a few weeks. There was that.

'I don't know,' Agrippina said, though she did. 'Claudius, I trust your judgement more than my own. If you think it will help our son . . . if it will temper him, prepare Nero for more responsibility, I will go along. Your will is mine, husband.'

'A year is a l-long t-tuh t-time at that age. He is s-still rather young . . .' Claudius said thoughtfully. 'And it would n-need an order from my own hah-hand, to f-force an exception.'

'I suppose it *might* mature him,' Agrippina said lightly. 'You did appoint the tutor, Claudius. This Seneca sees Nero every day. Should we scorn his judgement? It is hard to say. Either way, the decision is surely yours.'

Conn Iggulden

She was watching her husband closely. Claudius often left gaps as he prepared himself to speak. Agrippina sometimes spoke into them, though she knew she risked annoying him.

'Perhaps it is better not to give the senate another bone to chew,' she added, 'so soon after they made Rufrius one of their own. They are rather full of themselves recently! You know I listen to them, from behind the awning. They are great bags of wine or wind, some of them. Perhaps it is best not to rouse them.'

'Perhaps they should b-be reminded of their p-place,' Claudius said, a little curtly.

'It's up to you, husband,' she said. 'You are the font of all things. I'm sure the senate know it.'

'They should. Yes. I will accept the tutor's p-puh . . .'

'His petition,' Agrippina said, weary of the wait. It was just words that strangled him so! Nothing more than breath and the movement of lips and tongue. It was pitiful that something so weak could stop an emperor's throat.

Octavia had found a piece of twine and was winding tiny flowers into a bouquet. She was eleven years old. An emperor's daughter could be betrothed at any age, but a *son*, an emperor's son, had to wear the toga virilis.

Agrippina smiled at the girl. Nero and Octavia were cousins, which would pass unremarked. They were also brother and sister, which would be the subject of every tavern conversation in Rome. She knew the sort of filthy things they said, even about her marriage to Claudius. No children had come from that union, but they still scrawled their crude jokes. They had their rules and traditions, the people of Rome – things that had to be done by a certain date, things that were forbidden. It was all pitiful, no more than the fears of children! She saw through their little rules, to a place where there were none: no laws, nothing but her will.

She shivered as a memory stole into her concentration. At Saturnalia each year, there was a group of young men who climbed the city wall and ran along the crest – a section between two guard towers. It would have been easy if not for the slight curve of the wall – and the fact that they ran with cloth wrapped around their eyes. One or two fell every year, and yet the numbers taking part only grew. She winced to think of it: running in the dark, never knowing if the next step would be into empty air.

Agrippina looked at the sly smile lighting Nero's features. The boy wore the snakeskin bangle she'd had made, that reminder of how close they had all come to ruin. The best defence – the only one – was to grow, in strength, in power and influence.

She shifted her cloak with a slight grunt of effort. The thing really was heavy – much heavier than she had understood when she'd commissioned it. Servants waited to take it when she was ready. It had become a treasure of the state, the moment it was finished. What mattered was that it drew the sunlight and gleamed. Agrippina was empress in that cloth of gold. The mere ache of shoulders and knees was nothing set against that.

The last of the bread had been given out, though the crowds remained, chanting and singing. From experience, Agrippina knew they would stay as long as the imperial family were visible on the balcony. She glanced at the sun and saw it had passed noon. She muttered a curse then.

'I should be up on the hill, Claudius. I have agreed to meet the head of some "societas publicanorum" there.'

Conn Iggulden

The emperor frowned, bringing his own sort of focus.

'What b-business could you p-possibly have with common tax f-farmers, my dear?'

Agrippina had been about to say that the man had sent her a sapphire ring, huge and polished like a frozen teardrop. She actually wore it on her left hand in that moment – and yet there was something in her husband's tone that stung. She did not raise it up to show him.

'I'm sure I will find out, Claudius. There will be praetorians present, of course. Prefect Burrus himself has vouched for the man.'

'It is . . . beneath the *d-dignity* of my w-wife to discuss trade, especially with m-men of that s-sort.'

Claudius had almost shouted the word 'dignity' when it failed to come out smoothly. Agrippina lowered her gaze. Her husband had a temper and she had no wish to cause a rift between them. She could practically feel Nero bristling. For all his faults, the boy would defend her. She could not allow that.

'I'm sorry,' she said, her voice breaking. There were tears in her eyes when she looked up and Claudius gaped, astonished at the effect of a few angry words.

'I heard he wanted to build a statue in your honour, Claudius. I thought it might work for your birthday. I had no idea it would be the wrong thing . . .'

Her face crumpled and he opened his arms, gathering her to him.

'It's fine, my dear, of course it's fine. Just . . . l-let me know what he suggests, w-would you?'

'You worry about me, I know,' she said tearfully. 'Your praetorians will tell you everything anyway.'

'I should h-hope s-so!' he said.

'Are you sure? I need to find things to do, Claudius! I cannot simply stand and wave to crowds. Yet if you don't want me to see him, I won't.'

Claudius took her hands in his.

'Go. I'm s-sorry I was an . . . an . . .'

'Ass,' she said.

'An . . . *noyed*,' he corrected, frowning.

She kissed him in gratitude, gesturing to her servants to take the cloak. The weight coming off made her feel lighter than air. She walked with more even than her usual grace as she left the emperor's presence, pausing only to twist Nero's ear. He was glaring at the emperor and if Claudius noticed, the boy could still ruin a good day. Nero reached to slap her hand, but she had already let go.

'Come, Nero,' she said as he rubbed the wounded part. It would not do to leave the boy to annoy his father. Not when Claudius was being so sweet.

On the Palatine, Agrippina deposited Nero with a praetorian and swept into the private rooms.

'May I teach the lad to play latrunculi?' the soldier asked.

There was a board cut into the stone bench, to keep visitors entertained while they were made to wait. Each piece had been carved in polished stone, as old as the first buildings on that hill. Agrippina didn't care for games with stone kings or soldiers, but she knew Nero set up a board a dozen times each day with his friends. Only Seneca could beat him, she'd heard. She waved a hand and was gone, leaving her scent on the air.

The man and woman who waited for her were not what she had expected. He rose to his feet, while his companion remained kneeling, bowing almost to the floor. Agrippina looked up at a Roman of her own age, a man with a strong nose and dark curled hair. She felt her womb tighten. She knew there would be colour in her cheeks as the merchant dropped to one knee and bowed his head. She was empress, it was true, in the presence of praetorians watching the strangers for the slightest threatening move. She was also a married woman, and there would be no physical touch between them. In that moment, Agrippina was disappointed.

'I am Cornelius Axilla, empress. Thank you for agreeing to see me. It is a great honour.'

The woman was his slave, Agrippina realised. Close up, she saw perfect skin and black hair bound in silver thread.

'Please rise, Master Axilla,' she said softly.

He reminded her of her first husband, a man who had always shone with physical health. Axilla was not particularly tall, though he would tower over Claudius. No, it was his hands that caught her eye, tanned and strong. She was certain he could carry her, which was an odd thought. Her flush deepened.

'Are you well, empress?' he asked, looking concerned.

She took hold of herself and nodded.

'Please sit, Master Axilla. I'm sure your time is precious. I know mine is. Thank you for the ring . . . it is very beautiful.'

She held up her hand and he smiled at the genuine pleasure in her. Her gaze slid to the nearest guard. He too smiled, an expression that became stone as he saw Agrippina was watching.

Agrippina took a seat opposite the stranger. His slave still knelt, for all the world like a little carved piece herself. Agrippina let a small frown crease between her eyes. The ring had bought him an introduction, but what did he actually want? Her husband's reaction was still with her, colouring her thoughts.

'I am not familiar with your association, Master Axilla. My husband said you were tax farmers?'

It was his turn to flush, though not in pleasure.

'That is how we started, my brothers and I, empress. The imperial state grants licences to collect taxes on their behalf. It can be for a single city, or a dozen, or the whole of Gaul. The sums involved are vast, but of course they are gathered to be returned to the state. We are allowed to keep a small part for the labour. Even that can be . . . rewarding, if you understand me. My brothers still do some of that work, but I would like to move away from it, to begin a new societas. I have funds, but I will need a patron, a friend in the imperial estate. The right name can open doors that would always be closed to me without it.'

Agrippina frowned as she listened. Axilla sat as if he might leap up at any moment, not slumped as her husband usually did. His eyes were dark and he wore a moustache with hints of red or gold in it. She was not sure whether she liked that. It would surely leave her lips reddened if she ever kissed such a brush.

'You have not mentioned what enterprise you wish to begin,' Agrippina said suddenly, realising she had been silent for too long. He blinked in reply. By the gods, the meeting was going in fits and starts, like a hog pissing. His slave's stillness was unnerving, she thought, a statue that breathed.

Cornelius Axilla held out a hand and for the first time the young woman straightened, passing him a long flat box. Agrippina saw the girl blush under her scrutiny. Dark-haired and pale, she was arrestingly beautiful.

The praetorian standing by the wall had also noticed the exchange. He came to stand behind the merchant. Agrippina could not fault his suspicion. A blade could be concealed in that box – and his life would be forfeit if he had missed it.

Agrippina bit her lip, then waved the praetorian back. She could not resist a box! In that moment, she would have risked an assassin just to see inside.

As the guard took a step away, Axilla opened it, revealing a line of gold and silver coins. Delight stole across Agrippina's face as she understood. She edged closer and he held the box out to her, smiling at her reaction.

'There is Claudius – and there am I,' she said in wonder. 'That is me, isn't it?'

'It is, empress. It is just a first attempt, of course. If you would be willing to sit for sketches, I have a man who can make a likeness more worthy of your beauty.'

'I have not seen a coin with two faces on one side before,' she said, peering at each one in turn. 'Not like this. My brother had one made of his three sisters, but you could not tell one of us from another, the figures were so small and thin. No, I see my face there – behind my husband's. It is extraordinary. Is that how the world sees me?'

'Empress, no coin could ever do you justice. Even the gold aureus fails in comparison. I see I will have to whip my sculptor. I believed the man had some talent, but seeing you smile . . . I will have these melted and begin again.'

'No! No, they are beautiful. Claudius will be pleased, I think. He has been all alone on his coins before.' She smiled at that. 'What is this writing, though, Master Axilla? Or should I call you Cornelius?'

'It would be . . . a great honour, empress.'

He continued to use her title, she noticed, not without pleasure. He had some sense of control or delicacy.

'The letters spell out your own name and . . . "Augusta", empress. I know you are of the bloodline of Emperor Augustus. His wife Livia was granted that honour by the senate, after she died. I think it is a title you might claim, that is all. These coins are mere templates, empress, examples of the stamp and the design. They can all be changed, according to your will.'

'I like it,' Agrippina breathed, bringing the coin to her eye. '"Augusta" is a noble name – and I have every right to use it, I am certain.' An awareness stole upon her that she had edged too close to the man, her attention captured by the coins. 'Or . . . well, I will consider it.'

She sat back, suddenly wary. The man was a stranger.

'I cannot deny the craft, the skill . . .' she began.

'Empress, they are only a reflection . . .'

'Interrupt me again,' she said.

He stared, the silence perfect. Agrippina nodded. Being the sister of Caligula had taught hard lessons, but some of them were still useful.

'You come with gifts . . . and flattery,' she said. 'What do you want from me?'

She eased her expression down from a hard glare. Axilla licked his lips, though whether he was nervous or aroused she was not sure. There *could* be some invitation in the words she had used, she supposed. In her experience, some men heard the bedroom's call when she merely enquired about the price of linen.

Conn Iggulden

'I have the craftsmen and the tools to create a new mint in Rome. I have land bought for the purpose, forges and designs like the ones you have seen. More, I have a record of working with the imperial estate – and a family name long proven. Though I am not myself of the nobilitas, empress, I think Rome was made on the labour of men like me. If I could be granted the licence of an official mint, I would produce coins to honour you and your husband, of better quality than any of the poor specimens on the street today.'

He paused, fearful of pushing too far and fast. Yet Agrippina was intrigued.

'How much does it cost to make a gold aureus?' she said.

He leaned close, as if imparting a great secret.

'To mine and refine the metal, to stamp and cut it – a tenth of the eventual value. That includes all my costs. It is a . . . very profitable business. For the emperor as well as the societas I will found if you grant the licence.'

Agrippina frowned. She had no idea how many mints there already were in the city, nor how much profit could reasonably be expected. She had wealth – already more than she could spend in a dozen lifetimes. Yet she liked this man and the way he had chosen to approach her. He still seemed to be suggesting she had the power to grant his request, which was more flattery. She would have to take Claudius to bed to get such a thing, letting him rock back and forth, until he curled up like a tail and slept. Yet it would be worth it. For the name 'Augusta', it would.

'Leave the coins,' she said. 'Though I will sit for your artist if he is as good as you say. I am intrigued, Master Axilla.'

She saw the man's slave was watching, her painted eyes

showing intelligence. Agrippina hesitated. The man had come to her and to that point, he had given little.

'Your slave is very beautiful,' she said.

To his credit, Axilla did not glance at the kneeling woman.

'Empress, Polla is yours. Let her be my gift to you.'

Agrippina nodded, pleased. She had bargained like a merchant and won an advantage. It was oddly satisfying.

'You are generous, Cornelius. Thank you. I will say no more for now, but I am interested.'

Claudius was bright red, panting and weary, but with a smile that said he had seen wonders. Agrippina gasped as he rolled off. It had been a far more passionate exchange than she had expected. At some point in the plunging, lamplit gloom, she had begun thinking of the broad-shouldered merchant. Something had changed after that, until she was as flushed as Claudius. He had sensed that trembling and heard her breathing change. He was de-lighted with himself and began to chuckle as he stared at their ceiling.

'Well!' he said. 'If it matters that m-much to you, I w-will not s-stand in your way. Perhaps that p-pays for your golden cloak! Or does this offering stretch to the m-mint licence as well?'

He laughed and she had to work to keep the satisfied smile on her face. He could not help making comments about her whoring herself to him. Perhaps it was part of what brought him to the bedchamber, the thought that Agrippina needed something – something he could choose to grant or withhold. When Claudius saw she was after something important, it always brought a gleam to his eye.

She could see him planning or imagining what he would ask. He had particular phrases he liked her to say. He seemed to think they would increase her passion, though each one referred to his manhood, or oddly, the amount of his seed. He seemed very proud of the last, as if sheer volume was a factor in her adoration, rather than a nuisance. Still, he was well drained that evening.

'If I meet governors or merchants in your name, Claudius, it is all to your glory – to lessen the burdens you face. I can be your partner in this, trusted as no one else can be. You know that. I'm sure you've heard every word that went on today – and I know you approve, or you would not move a step, no matter how I pleaded. I tell you, you are the sun to my moon, Claudius. My dignity, whatever words men use for me – it is all a reflection of you. I know it – and I have shown you how grateful I am.'

His eyes were closing as sleep drifted down. He was lying on her arm and the limb was already becoming numb.

'All I have is from you, husband,' she said. 'Even "Augusta", though it is from my line as much as yours.'

He grunted and she smiled. Good enough.

6

Seneca stood on the Campus Martius, the great field outside Rome. In Julius Caesar's day it had been vast and
open. A century later, the city encroached, more and more
each year. Temples, tombs and gardens stood where
only meadows had before. The true boundary would be
the Tiber in time, he thought. Perhaps not even the old
river could hold his people in. Perhaps they would burst
even those banks.

Sections of city walls rose in the distance, though they
no longer formed an unbroken ring around Rome. In
places, they had been removed completely, the cleared
ground filled by aqueducts and new wealth – potteries and
baths, or entire districts. Seneca frowned at the thought.
Walls pierced were no longer walls, not as they had been
intended. Change was not always welcome.

It eased his heart to see the Quirinal and Capitoline hills
rising as they had always done, with Mount Pincius in the
distance. Though the last lay outside the city and was not
one of the seven, it was still visible, grand and stern, given

over to gardens and meadows. The Aventine hill lay on his right hand, beyond the great curve of the Tiber river. His home. The land there rose with houses and roads clinging to the slopes, far above the cooking smoke of the city below.

He looked to Nero, Otho and Serenus as they stood there, the boys already dusty and irritable. Seneca exchanged a glance with Burrus.

'Rome is the largest city in the world,' he said. 'The heart of an empire that stretches from the borders of Parthia in the east to the hills of Britannia, from Egypt, all the way west to Hispania, where I was born, with every island, mountain, mine and farm in between. We own the seas, gentlemen. No ship moves on deep waters without paying a tithe or asking our permission. A million people make their homes here, a number so great it is hard to conceive when measured as single lives. Each man or woman of that great host is rising now in the dawn to eat and bathe, yawning as they prepare for the day. Before the sun sets, they will have made roof tiles and cloth, bronze pots, swords, children's toys – a thousand things to sell. They will have copied manuscripts and forged iron nails, slaughtered sheep and swine, sweated and bathed again before this evening. In the senate, men like your fathers will consider plans for the city today – new buildings, new laws, and all the coins of gold and silver that must pay for it all. As the sun sets this evening, they will attend chariot races or the theatre, or gather in groups to drink and talk and laugh. Rome is the heartbeat of the world, gentlemen. It lives today. In you.'

He looked the three boys over, missing nothing. Serenus stifled a yawn under that scrutiny, suggesting he had been up late again. They wore sandals and tunics, with loincloths beneath. The wind was chill and they shivered, looking pitiable. Burrus was in his legion kilt and a sleeveless jerkin, legs bare. The cold didn't seem to touch the praetorian.

'Leave your sandals over there, lads,' Seneca said. 'Your feet should be getting tougher. They'll be like leather in a few more weeks. I think today . . . yes, you can run to the monument to Scipio.'

They groaned. It was five miles to that ancient statue. Once there, they had to recite a passage aloud, stumbling over the lines of verse as quickly as they could get them out, then return. It was always a race, though with no reward beyond Seneca's grudging approval and their own pride. Yet Serenus had won it on four occasions, surprising them all. For a boy who seemed beset by dark moods, those small victories lifted his spirits as nothing else could. Serenus kicked off his sandals first, examining one foot where the skin had split.

'That will go numb after a while,' Nero muttered to him. He raised his own foot, showing a great broken blister under the ball of his big toe. They collected such scuffs and wounds as marks of rank.

'Touch the Scipio monument – and remember to pay your respects to a general of Rome,' Seneca said. 'If Scipio Africanus had not defeated Hannibal, this great city might have remained a forgotten outpost. It would have been Carthage that came to rule the nations of the world. *Carthage*, gentlemen! That will do as our subject today. Recite the first forty lines of the *Aeneid*. "Of arms and the man I sing!" Let your voices ring out – the tale of a Trojan fleet and our first hero. Then fly back to my side. I will test your understanding of circles, with the mysterious fraction of twenty-two over seven.'

'Are you coming with us?' Nero asked.

Seneca cuffed him, knocking his head forward. The boy scowled.

'As you know, Nero, my breath is a poor child, grabbing and catching where it should flow like water. Running makes it worse, above all things. Still, I will consider a wager on strength. When you return, you and I can match one another, lifting the round stones in the gardens of Augustus. A fine suggestion, Nero! Now go – and perhaps this time you might consider trying to beat Serenus. Ah, see him grin, the little wolf! He likes to win, your friend. Otho is content to roll in third, it seems. Perhaps today is time for a change. Put pain aside, gentlemen. Leave weakness in your wake. Go.'

They set off and Seneca watched the first mad scramble settle into a smooth lope. The soles of their feet showed pale for a time until they vanished in dust.

'They are getting better,' Burrus said. He shaded his eyes against the rising sun as Seneca nodded.

'Of course. You remember how Otho vomited at first? He is leaner than before. Nero would be third each day if not for sheer force of will. That is why I need the others. They compete, Burrus, as all men will. No one likes to be last – and I will never say to them, "What does it matter?" No, I will tell them their pride, their honour, their dignity depends on victory! That if they lose, they must train on their own, over and over. That is how we make them men, Burrus! Through their own will.'

'And yours,' Burrus said wryly.

He removed his jerkin, so that he would run

bare-chested. Seneca glanced at him. The praetorian was a serving soldier, with tattoos and two missing fingers to prove it. He already ran each dawn on the Campus. It had seemed natural enough for him to accompany them, especially as Seneca could not. It kept them honest – and it was part of his role to watch over Nero, after all. Burrus wore a legion dagger when he ran with them, always ready to be drawn.

'You enjoy this,' Seneca said.

Burrus stretched his back, legs wide, touching one foot and then the other. He shrugged, but he had learned to trust the other man as well.

'I like seeing how they improve, with you as their tutor. They are already more than they were before. It is only a start, but they sense it as well. Nero in particular.'

The boys were a dust cloud, growing smaller. Seneca saw Burrus was ready to go after them. It was part of their game, to see whether a legionary in his fifties could catch the three. In the beginning, it had always been before they had gone two miles. Seneca knew the praetorian gave them a good start each time, then reeled them in. That too taught character.

'It's why I was brought back to Rome,' Seneca said. 'Though I must admit, it feels like more than that sometimes. Another chance, when I thought I'd used my last one.' He grimaced, as if a cold wind blew. 'I have made mistakes, Burrus. I have more regrets than are good for me – and yes, my breathing is a torment. I am strangled – and I lose my nerve when it is at its worst. I hope . . . for it all to stop, for it to end.'

His voice broke and Burrus looked at him awkwardly. He had not expected such an intimacy.

Conn Iggulden

'I saw you in the schoolroom yesterday . . . with the steam and the cloth over your head. The oils of myrrh and juniper. Is it so bad?'

'Complaining does not make it easier,' Seneca said with a bitter smile. 'But yes. It comes on and steals my breath. I walk with fear then – and I strangle it each day, as it strangles me.'

Burrus shuddered. For the first time, he had a sense of the torment Seneca endured. He'd seen a wheeze come on as if he'd piled wet cloths over his face, every breath a labour. It lasted for hours or even days at its worst, preventing sleep. The tutors he had summoned from Alexandria and Macedonia took over then, droning through the afternoons. All Seneca could do was rock back and forth, straining for air. Yet he rose again the following day. He stood and breathed and went back to work. There were different kinds of courage, Burrus thought.

'Is that why your legion term was cut short?' he asked.

Seneca nodded.

'I managed three years. I was younger then – and I do not think it was as bad. But I passed out often on the march. Can you imagine? The pace is hard enough. The dust raised by five thousand men used to bring on my wheezing, worse than usual. I was whipped for falling out of line more times than I can remember, as if I'd chosen to fall senseless to the road! There was one optio who seemed to think I was making it all up, or doing it just to annoy him. He used to wield the whip himself.' Seneca looked back into the past and curled his lip in remembered anger. 'I am just grateful the legate took pity on me and sent me home. Before that optio or the Parthians killed me.'

Seneca saw Burrus was staring and shook his head, suddenly embarrassed.

'I made a living after that, though poets can starve. I wrote odes and plays and philosophical works. I explored Stoicism, which was easier when I had nothing. After a few years, I opened a school for those who wished to understand. Life was sweet, and in that summer I had an affair with a married woman.' He sighed. 'You know, the Jews tell a tale of a judge, a man of great strength and promise, blinded by his enemies. When he was made to stand between two pillars in a temple, blind as he was, he pushed them apart, destroying both himself and them. It felt a little like that, Burrus. I had my hands on the world – and I brought it all down around my ears.'

The boys were long gone. Burrus would have to half-kill himself to catch them, perhaps not until they were reciting the lines he had set. Yet the prefect was listening and he seemed to understand.

'I've made my own mistakes,' Burrus said. 'It may be the nature of age to see them more clearly, to wish we could undo old knots. And to know we can't.'

'Some men feel like that,' Seneca said. 'Not all. Not many women! They don't seem to consider the past in the same way.'

He bit his lip as he thought of Agrippina. Beauty was a strange thing. It raised a woman, like dryads walking among mortals. Agrippina was extraordinary. He felt his wheeze grow worse and clenched his fists, annoyed with himself.

Burrus smiled.

'Is this your redemption, then? Training these lads?'

'Redemption?' Seneca replied. 'Or one last thing to do before my throat closes for the final time. No, I don't see

Conn Iggulden

redemption. I am not such a fool as that. Though perhaps I can make two or three more good Romans.' He waved a hand, embarrassed. 'You don't know . . .'

Burrus clapped him on the shoulder.

'I think I do,' he said. 'But I will have to start now, or I'll never catch them. I'll be thirsty after, if you want to find a tavern.'

'Yes. I'd like that.'

Seneca watched as the prefect of the praetorians set off at what was practically a sprint to his eye. Burrus ran like a hare, so that he looked slow but covered ground at astonishing speed. Somehow, he knew the man would catch his pupils before they made it back. There was something indomitable in Burrus. They were very different sorts of men, but they understood one another – and they cared about the same things. Seneca realised he was smiling. He'd lost a lot of friends over the years of his disgrace and exile. It seemed he had also found one.

Rufrius welcomed the last man to his home, answering a knock on the outer door. Rome lay to the north and each of them had travelled separately, carefully, drifting in from east and west. No one could be certain they were not overheard in the city. Even so far to the south, Rufrius had dismissed all the house slaves, sending them away. Of course it meant he had to serve food and drink himself to his guests. They understood the need, however. Claudius was a man who paid listeners, that was well known. Even gathering a select little group on the southern coast was fraught with danger. It helped that the men who came there were senators, with estates and mercantile interests far from the capital. It was not so strange that one like

Rufrius might leave Rome for a month to oversee the construction of a home in Herculaneum.

Wealthy families already clustered on that coast, for sea air and good wine, away from the crowds and summer smell of the imperial city. By road, it was a week's hard travel, but by sea, just two days. For those who owned merchant ships or had triremes at their call, it was in reach. The great sharp peak of Vesuvius was the backdrop to a town where senators and noble consuls already came to rest and be entertained. With just a little care, they could meet in secret, bumping into one another as if by accident, choosing to eat or drink wine in private gatherings.

Rufrius had volunteered his new house because it was being rebuilt. The plastered walls were still bare of ornament or colour, with only a few couches and those under cloth. The house had no wife or children to remember men stepping in from the evening gloom, sitting on benches or standing like sentinels.

Rufrius had laid out a few lamps and they spilled light along the polished floors. The atrium would be a grand centrepiece in time, but it was not yet finished. The fountain was still dry and all the plants remained in pots, waiting to be planted. They could speak unheard there.

The secrecy did not seem like an extravagance. Rufrius still remembered Caligula – and Tiberius before him. The wrath of an emperor was a savage thing. No one present wanted to invite that cold gaze into their lives. Just to be there was to take a risk. Dry-mouthed, they drank wine from his new cellar, until Rufrius was red-faced from fetching cups and amphorae.

'That is the last of us,' Rufrius said.

The true host nodded, his youthful features cast gold by

the lamp at his feet. Marcus Junius Silanus had not sat down, but stood wrapped in a dark cloak, like the wings of a crow.

'I am grateful,' he said. 'Thank you, brother Rufrius, for opening your home to us, for letting us gather. The gods will surely bless this enterprise. We share a common cause – one that is decent and honourable. For men like us to have to meet in secret . . . it is not right.'

A murmur of agreement sounded around the room. Rufrius counted twelve present. It did not seem so many, though he knew they commanded fleets and wealth beyond his imaginings. The Silanus family alone was one of the wealthiest in Rome.

'Ours is a bond of trust,' Marcus Silanus went on. 'I do not need to tell you how quickly suspicion can begin. If just one of us weakens, we face ruin, destruction and death. You have made oaths on the gods, on your honour, on the lives of your families. Stay true to those and to your immortal souls.'

He lowered his head reverently and as Rufrius watched, it had the feel of a sacred rite, of an ancient cult. He had not even known these men existed until he had lost the praetorians. In that room, a consul of Rome listened, as well as two praetors and the legates of two legions. He did not think there was one below the rank of senator. Like the aqua vitae he shipped to Rome each month, it lent fumes and strength and warmth – a fellowship.

'Each of us has suffered injury,' Silanus went on. 'You all know my brother was taken from me, breaking the betrothal we worked so hard to bring about. The children of that union with the emperor's daughter would have been just a few steps from the imperial seat. Who knows how far fate might have led us then? Before the emperor took in the viper who sits at his side and shames his noble office. It was her pet praetorian who came to my brother's home, with accusations so monstrous I will not air them here. It was her creature who pressed his knife into my brother's hand, who burned the letter he wrote to me.'

He paused then, crushing old pain.

'It was Agrippina who broke the betrothal of a Silanus to the bloodline of Augustus. A dozen years in the making . . . and she cut the thread.'

They were watching him, Rufrius saw, like wolves in the gloom. Their anger was palpable, as if he could smell it in their sweat.

'We have all suffered from that first sin! How many of you have felt your influence wane, now there will be no Silanus on the Palatine? As with Rufrius here, she has moved against us – and drawn blood. It cannot stand, gentlemen. She grows bold while we do nothing. She strangles poor Claudius in her skirts, squeezing the life out of him. That family! We survived her brother! We endured years of terror, only to fail now? At the hands of his sister? No, it will not be borne. My brother's children may not take the reins of empire, but neither will hers.'

Rufrius tensed as the words were spoken. He had been flattered at first to be approached, wined and fed in taverns almost like a courtship, drawn out in conversation by men he trusted. It had been months before he'd even met the senior Silanus – and understood the current head of that house led a powerful faction in the senate.

Rufrius looked for some hesitation in himself. No, there was none. The emperor was a good man, a trusting man. In his kindness, he had allowed a frozen snake inside his

Conn Iggulden

shirt, like the farmer in the Aesop tale. If they did nothing, Claudius would surely suffer the same fate. Agrippina was a destroyer.

'I asked you here to tell you we have someone close to her now.'

'Not to kill her . . .' one of the others said.

Rufrius recognised the voice of the consul, though the man stood on the edge, in shadows. Marcus Silanus shook his head.

'An empress is brought down in stages, as her mother was. First, she is deceived, then she is ruined. She has come home from exile before. Perhaps this time she will take her own life, just as my brother was made to do.'

'And after that? When she is . . . gone?'

Silanus turned to face the speaker, the planes of his face gleaming as if bronzed.

'The emperor's daughter has no current match. Perhaps another can be found, from amongst our sons. I will not plan so far, with all the gods listening. No, I pledge a life for a life, that is all. A life in vengeance for all that has been taken from us.'

'Who is the one who stands close to her?' the consul asked.

Rufrius saw the younger man frown.

'Don't worry about that,' he said. 'I had to spend fortunes to arrange it. Yet I have said . . . it is not a knife the emperor's wife should fear, but disgrace. I will call for your help, brothers, when the time comes.'

He laid out the bones of a plan then and Rufrius listened with wide eyes. It would work, he was certain. If they held their nerve.

7

Nero felt himself bowed down by hands beating his back and shoulders. There had to be a thousand men and women on the Palatine that day! It reminded him of a wedding. Almost every senator and his wife had come with eldest sons and daughters. Mingling with them were the heads of lesser families, senior officers of the legions, priests and acolytes from every temple in Rome. They had all eaten their fill and drunk from fountains running with wine.

Nero was the centre of it all, in his toga virilis – made a man in law though he was just thirteen years old. He grinned at Otho as he passed by, accepting the congratulations of the noble class of Rome. They cheered him, knowing Emperor Claudius was present and might be flattered through his adopted son.

'Did you see my gifts?' Nero called to Otho.

His friend nodded and rolled his eyes. An entire room had been dedicated just to collecting them. That didn't include the four grey horses and a racing chariot. Those waited for him in a courtyard outside. Nero itched to get out of the crowd and drive the team around the Circus track, but every time he edged away, there was someone else to thank. His mother was watching, he noticed. He smiled and agreed that it was indeed a great honour, that he was lucky and that, yes, he would do his best to show gratitude to his father. His back stung from slaps, his cheeks hurt from smiling and his poor right hand felt crushed, gripped hard too many times.

Music soared over the heads of the vast crowd, some new group striking up a rousing tune as the previous one packed up their instruments. The drunkest partygoers cheered and began to sing, leaning together and attempting harmonies that were only partly successful. After the initial decorum of the ceremony and blessings, the constant supply of wine would see a great debauch before the sun shone again. Otho had told him that, presenting himself as more worldly-wise to such things. The older boy had promised there would be fights and probably sexual liaisons going on in every side room.

Nero was looking forward to seeing some of that. The night before, he had fantasised about joining in. Was he not a man that day – the son of the emperor? His brother Britannicus was too young to appreciate that sort of freedom. Little 'Twelve' would not know what to do with it anyway.

Aware of his mother's glittering gaze, Nero allowed the crowd to move him from one end of the hall to the other. At the halfway point, the music began to clash. The hall was so large, it had a group at each end to entertain the crowd. At the centre point, it was a cacophony. Nero stood entranced for a while, just enjoying the chaos of it. Then he remembered his mother's gaze and moved on, further and further until he stood before the second choir.

One of the theatres had accepted the invitation, sending a group of thirty singers to the emperor's party. Nero watched them in awe, appreciating the soaring harmonies. The notes touched him as nothing else could. They used their hands too as they sang, gesturing, tugging, pushing away. It felt almost as if they had summoned him, pulling him from the crowd like a fish.

One in particular was freckled and large-breasted, her stola dress revealing more than she might have intended as she bobbed in time to the song. Nero found his attention utterly captured by them. Otho said pantomime people were all whores anyway.

The singer had noticed the young man staring. One of her companions nudged her and whispered something. Nero could see her blush, but she did not look away. It was just as Otho had said! The song swelled and he watched her mouth the words. This would be the greatest night of his life, he could feel it.

A great cheer began at the far end, back where he had been before. Nero groaned, certain he would be drawn away from an experience so intense he could hardly breathe. He felt a hand drop to his shoulder, and of course Burrus was there, following his gaze like a hunting dog and grinning to himself.

'Your parents are leaving, lad. You should attend on them.'

'Are you always watching?' Nero said.

The woman was wide-eyed at the sight of a praetorian in uniform. Burrus chuckled.

'Always, yes.'

'Well, you should take an hour off every now and then. It might even start today.'

Caught by surprise, Burrus hesitated. The emperor's wife had sent him – and Agrippina had more pull in that room than her son. Yet it *was* the day the boy became a man, even if Nero was a year or two younger than usual. The praetorian looked over the young woman. She was still watching, he noticed, though she pretended to be talking to her friends.

A troupe of servers wound their way through the crowd, all wearing pale blue tunics. They pressed coins into the hands of those they passed. Burrus held up a hand to wave them around him, then felt the weight of a gold coin pressed into his palm. He let go of Nero's shoulder and whistled softly as he looked at it. Two faces could be seen on one side, with an image of a vase surmounting a column on the reverse. Yet it was the features of Agrippina that caught Burrus' attention. It was true Claudius was first and closer to the eye . . . but the fact that his wife was there at all was new. 'CLAUD • CAES • AUG' ran around the edge, followed by . . .

Burrus swallowed, Nero quite forgotten. 'AGRIPP • AUGUSTA' completed the circle. She had taken a new title. Had the senate approved it? He thought he would have heard if they had. Most of them were present in that hall, learning in that very moment how far she had decided to go. The noise of the crowd had changed to a murmur of awe as they all examined their gifts, whispering to one another.

Burrus looked for Nero, but he'd gone, as had the young woman he'd been eyeing. No doubt he would be showing her his virilis gifts where they were piled. Burrus gave up the idea of searching for him. By order of the emperor himself, Nero was a man that day. It came with the threat of punishment and dishonour, true. Yet if it meant anything, it also meant not being followed around like a child.

On the far side of the hall, Burrus caught sight of Agrippina heading away, arm in arm with her husband. They would retire to more private surroundings while the party ground on, until the guests either left in turn or were rendered insensible. Burrus raised his eyes to the heavens. He was glad Seneca wasn't present to see him scurrying after the empress. His dignity was bound up in hers – and that did not always sit well with him. As a result, he glowered as he crossed the hall. The crowd parted as they saw his expression, moving aside and sweeping back in behind as they drank and cheered and danced.

Agrippina had to stride to keep up with her husband. She could see Claudius was angry about something and she was not a fool. He had been in good spirits for most of the party, before she'd signalled Cornelius Axilla to hand out the coins. The new printing was not yet in general circulation, so they were more in the nature of medallions and keepsakes. Yet Claudius was furious. She could see the way his eyes darted to the young woman who walked at her side, head down and trying to make herself as small as possible. Perhaps the presence of Polla restrained him, Agrippina thought. Though he'd grown up with slaves and could ignore them like furniture. He . . .

'I thought w-we understood one an-nother,' Claudius snapped suddenly. 'Your son is . . .'

'*Our* son,' Agrippina interrupted. She did not like to speak across him, but some things could not be ignored.

'That boy! I p-put my seal to m-making him a man, as y-you, as y-you w-w . . .'

Conn Iggulden

She waited, not daring to speak again so soon. They were striding down a long corridor, the noise of the party fading. The doors to the private rooms opened before them and they swept through. Agrippina looked back as they closed. She stood with her maid, though poor Polla was trembling in terror. Agrippina gestured for her to move to the wall as her husband spun to face her.

'I did as you w-wanted, Agrip-pina! Nero has made p-progress in the last few months. I th-thought I sh-should recognise that, r-reward that. Seneca sp-speaks well of him. I am to take a j-journey to J . . . Judaea, to s-see the legions there. Two m-months away from Rome and I w-would have . . . I m-meant Nero to be left in . . . in c-*command* while I was gone. There! That was to be m-my g-*gift* to you – and to him.'

'I don't understand, Claudius. That was a noble thought, a good thought – typical of the man you are. Nero would be proud, if you allowed it. He has not always felt part of our family, I know. What you describe would heal some part of that hurt, I am certain. I don't see . . .'

'Well, I *won't g-go now*!' he said, deliberately loud so that his voice smothered hers. 'After you give out a coin w-with y-our f-face, with "Augusta" on it? D-did the s-senate grant you that name? I am c-certain I d-did not!'

Agrippina narrowed her eyes. There was a time to rub his temples and ease his passion. This was different. He had gone too far.

'Go or don't go, Claudius. That is up to you. Yet I have been on coins before, when my brother was emperor. My sisters and I can still be found in the markets of Rome on those coins! Did I put my face before your own? No, you know very well that I did not! I am in your shadow on that coin, like a good Roman wife. No one who sees that could think the sort of thoughts that are in you! They see loyalty and love, as I intended them to see. By the gods, Claudius, you've said a thousand times how the weight of the empire bears you down. Yet the very moment I try to lift part of that burden, to take some of the work onto my own shoulders, you speak in anger to me! All I wanted was to help you!'

Tears came to her eyes then, shining, spilling a trail of kohl down one cheek. She could see the way it tugged at knots in him, but she was not finished. As Claudius opened his mouth, she went on.

'And why would you object to "Augusta"? Is the wife of the emperor not noble? Not decent, not worthy of awe? My ancestor was the very same Augustus of your line, uncle! Should I go on bended knee to the senate, to men who will only allow me to sit amongst them when I am hidden behind an awning? *Shit* on their dignity! I won't ask them for anything. *You* are the emperor. You and no one else, Claudius. I reflect you . . . everything I do is *for* you. Can't you see?'

He had calmed as she spoke, worn down by the rush of words. His colour had faded and he was always unmanned in the presence of tears. It was his curse, that he could not shut out her voice. He had to listen, and when she made a point, he could not ignore it.

'I'm sorry . . .' he began. 'I didn't know you f-felt . . .'

'Well I do! And you should know! I've told you a hundred times. Let me take the weight when it is too much. *I am on your side.* Must we dance and test one another, like gladiators? I am your *wife*, Claudius. No one else loves you as I do. Even our children come with outstretched hands,

Conn Iggulden

looking to be fed and clothed, but I ... I am at your shoulder, in your bed. I am yours, in a way no one else can possibly be.'

He nodded, abashed. Agrippina glanced at her new maid and saw Polla was perfectly still, as if carved from ivory.

'You are good to think of Nero, Claudius. You are too generous. He is growing well – at your direction. You are the gardener, the woodsman! I know it. Seneca and Burrus and those Greeks are making a man of him. You know I have rewarded Seneca with property and wealth, though he tries to refuse every time.'

'Seneca has proved his w-worth, yes. He is a g-good m-man,' Claudius said.

He had lost his passion, emptied like an old wineskin by strong emotion. He drowsed in a similar way after she had spent time in his arms. She made a decision.

'Our son should be betrothed, Claudius. He is the oldest son of the imperial family. I know Britannicus is the heir. Nero can be his protector until he is fully grown. Making him a man today is one step on that path – and I have seen affection grow between them. Nero will keep Britannicus safe. If there is lightning, it will strike Nero. Let him be that shield, in honour, Claudius. Raise no other to threaten our wonderful boys.'

'R-raise no other?' Claudius repeated in confusion.

Agrippina nodded.

'You are a strategist, Claudius, I know. You see more deeply than half the senate and all your legion officers. Yet I grew up with vipers. Caligula was my brother, while my mother died in exile. My father and two more of my brothers were murdered. I have learned to look for treachery, Claudius, before it is even there, when it is still just a gleam in the eye. That is why Octavia cannot be betrothed to anyone else. Would you give her to a Fabian, or another Silanus? No matter the name, whoever has her promise will become strong – in power, in influence. Perhaps *too* strong, in time. The children from her womb could stand against our line. In a generation or the next, they will. I know you have seen that, Claudius. Those eyes of yours miss nothing.'

Agrippina clenched her fists behind her back. She had led with her best argument and Claudius had not rejected it out of hand. She watched him as he rubbed his chin, thinking. Would his thoughts turn to the bedroom when he saw she needed something from him? She would run that mile, if he wanted. A dozen times over, dressed as a goddess or a temple priestess if need be.

His thoughts did not seem to be turning that way. Instead, he frowned.

'The p-people would say they are b-brother and s-sister,' he murmured. 'They are!'

Agrippina snorted.

'Then we would tell them the perfect truth, that they are mere cousins. There is no bar in blood to Octavia marrying Nero. No incest. And what if there were? You married me, uncle, though some called out against it. Is an emperor not above such petty things? Above the cheap gossip of the markets? *You* are the fountain of the law, of all authority. There are no chains you cannot break, not if you choose to.'

He liked that, she saw, inclining his head as if she had scored a point. No woman wasted her time in flattering a man, she thought. Not when she wanted something.

'It would raise N-Nero, p-perhaps even above Britannicus. The b-betrothal alone would do that . . .'

Conn Iggulden

'It would keep that strength contained in one we trust – a son of your house,' she replied. 'Or it would be strength lost, the moment you grant her betrothal to another. With Nero, you strengthen the shield over Britannicus. Now that you have brought forth a better man in Nero, Claudius, let him be the boy's protector . . .' She trailed off. Agrippina had been about to mention Romulus and Remus, to compare those twins to Nero and Britannicus. Just in time, she'd remembered Romulus had killed his brother. The city would be called 'Reme' if he hadn't.

Claudius was still in knots, she realised. Agrippina opened her mouth to dismiss Polla for the evening. The private rooms contained robes, costumes and make-up. If Claudius would have her dressing up as Venus, she preferred it not to be in front of witnesses.

His expression cleared.

'It's g-good, Agrippina,' he said. 'I have b-been . . . wrestling with w-what to do about Octavia, ever since young Silanus t-took his life. This m-may be a w-way through.'

'This is exactly the sort of thing I mean!' Agrippina said in exasperation, though her heart leaped. 'Why must you struggle with these burdens alone, husband? You did not marry a fool when you married me. Let me share the weight! Let me take some of it from you, as empress, as your wife. I may have the answer, when no one else has. Is that so strange, so impossible? When all your gruff generals and senators are at a loss, please . . . consider me.'

'And a b-betrothal is not a m-marriage. It can still be b-broken, Agrippina, if I find a better s-suitor for Octavia. But you are right, it will stop the d-dogs sniffing around, all the f-families eyeing her closeness to me.'

Agrippina felt it like the twist of a knife. Her husband wanted something more, she could see. She made herself smile.

'You are emperor, Claudius. You are pharaoh over all Egypt, of the Upper and the Lower Kingdoms. And I am yours.'

'Cleopatra married her b-brother,' he said. 'There was no s-second line then to threaten the throne.'

Agrippina opened her mouth, as if the idea had just occurred to her.

'You see to the heart! That is true. Then Caesar came . . . and fought for her, the strength of Rome entering Egypt. She had herself delivered to him rolled in a carpet – half his age and beautiful enough to madden men. He swept her into his arms.'

Her voice had deepened a touch and when he looked up, she knew she would be fetching the Egyptian princess dress from the other room.

'My pharaoh,' she murmured, kissing him.

'My . . . Cleopatra,' he whispered throatily.

'Gentlemen?' Agrippina announced to the praetorians along the wall. 'Allow the emperor a little privacy, please.'

They didn't wait for Claudius to confirm the order, which pleased her. Of course, they had been listening to every word. They saluted with a crash of arms, then went out. Agrippina smiled like a lazy cat. She stretched and saw how her husband's gaze remained on her.

'Polla?' she said, remembering her presence just in time. 'You may retire. I will not need you again this evening.'

The young woman darted out of the private rooms without looking back, for fear of what she might see.

Conn Iggulden

8

Nero rose with the rest of the crowd as the four teams reached the corner. The effect was a great ripple as tens of thousands stood to cheer their colours. The cheap seats were all on the straights. Nero still had flashes of memory, of sitting there with his father's sister and her lodgers, when he was almost too young to understand all the noise and excitement.

The real drama came when the teams bunched together, when they fought and whipped for space, for just a single opening that would mean victory or disaster. They risked their lives for those gaps, and Nero loved them for their courage.

His friend Otho wore a toga with a green edge that day. Nero envied it. It meant his friend could be the target of rival supporters, but those who loved the Greens would come to his aid. It balanced out, the way Otho told it. Serenus still claimed to support the Reds, though he didn't follow the teams like his friends and didn't dare wear the colour, not in the Green section. In the old days the crowds had mingled, but there had been so many riots, the city vigiles had assigned seats in blocks. Nero doubted Annaeus Serenus could even name the Red driver that day as he galloped past. The man held reins to four horses and balanced on a tiny step of painted wood. As the riders adjusted for a corner, half the crowd leaned with them. It was glorious, the closest thing to flight Nero had ever known.

The great Decimus was leading for the Greens, of course. After a decade of coming second or third, the team had finally brought in a rider able to win. It was his third year in Rome, but he had been a champion in Hispania six times. Nero had heard Decimus wanted to retire, but the Greens hadn't found a replacement and so he rode on.

Of course, if Decimus were ever injured, the Greens would be desperate for a new rider, preferably one without too many years on him. It was hard not to dream of the trainers asking for anyone in the crowd who might take those reins, or seeing their faces when they heard the son of Ahenobarbus would step onto the track. Nero closed his eyes, imagining the crowd rising for him. He had galloped across the Campus a thousand times, but not against ruthless teams. Yet he had the nerve, he was certain. The corners were where death waited, where a single touch of a wheel might smash a man into the ground, great or not. Somehow, he was sure he could throw it all away, could treat death with the contempt it deserved. He could not explain it, but the certainty was there in him.

He knew it was not always one driver's error that sent them tumbling. The mistake of another could cost lives just as easily. That was the sheer wild glory of it, the ivory dice spinning in the air! They risked their lives for pleasure

Conn Iggulden

and the people of Rome. For just an hour or so each week, they were gods walking the earth.

The crowd roared, a sound that shook the benches, the air itself. Two hundred thousand people were more than just part of the city. They were the city. On important race days, the rest of Rome seemed empty, with only vigiles on the streets – and those in a foul mood for getting that duty. Anyone found trying to break into a house on race days was unlikely to see a court. A few bodies were displayed in the forum each month before being taken out of the city and tipped into an unmarked grave. The vigiles kept the peace well enough.

Nero looked left, to the young woman Serenus had brought. He'd seen her first at a party at the Tiber. Some senator had chosen to celebrate his daughter's coming of age on a bridge over the river. Half the crowd had ended up jumping in and of course two of them had drowned. Nero had made it to shore, lying panting next to Serenus and Otho, all three drenched as they looked up at the stars.

Through the blur of wine-soaked memory, Nero still recalled the young woman sitting three careful seats away. Acte was as slender as a wand and so pale she wore wide hats to protect her skin. At the party, she'd come in a dress that left her entire back bare. She'd moved through the crowd like a white flame and his gaze had been drawn. Not the type he had thought he preferred, with laughter and freckles and breasts he could bury his face in. And yet, and yet . . . he had asked about her, looked for her when she'd passed through, vanishing like a dream. Serenus had known her, he'd discovered. Acte was the cousin of some friend of his family. The girl was Greek, when all Nero seemed to be learning about was Athens and Sparta. More, she had been a slave, freed with her parents when their master died. She wore a silver ring that flashed like pale fire in the sun. No man could treat her as a slave, not then or ever again. It intrigued him.

Serenus had asked her to the races, using some pretext of an extra token and a spare seat. Nero was still not certain she understood it was he who truly asked, not his friend. Yet there were moments when Acte looked at him, when he could see her again in that backless sleeve. She was fifteen – a maid of Sparta, strong and lithe. He had learned from his tutors how the Spartan girls ran naked, training with the men. Long-legged Greek nymphs, frolicking. He could imagine the scenes easily enough when he closed his eyes.

On the track, the final dolphin of bronze was turned. The last lap, with Decimus thundering past, neck and neck with the Reds. Nero could see even Serenus taking an interest, drawn to the clash of titans below. He hoped his friend wouldn't shout for the Reds. Blood had been shed for less. Though it might not matter if Decimus won. Half the men there had part of their pay riding on him, clutching clay tokens. They were howling, open-mouthed as Decimus swept around the last corner with his wheels skidding.

The entire crowd rose as if drawn up on strings. Nero's attention was caught between the drama on the track and his constant awareness of the young woman he longed to touch. He could feel Acte like heat on his skin, though Otho and Serenus sat between. That seemed suddenly a very stupid arrangement. He could not think how to move closer without revealing himself as a clumsy, blushing fool.

Conn Iggulden

Decimus held off his rival right to the finishing post and the crowd went berserk. Nero heard Serenus swear at the moment of victory, which caused a few of the chanting, jumping men around him to frown. Most collapsed back into their seats, but some still stood, holding up their fists and cheering as the great Decimus took a more leisurely lap, letting his team cool. The four horses were so perfectly black, Nero could see the salt of their sweat, white lines like waves on shining skin. The seats were excellent, he thought. He could not even see the ones he had known in his first memories, they were so far away.

It always took an age to decant so many people to the street. Nero sat down with his friends, happy to wait in the sun while the crush cleared. Half the Green section was pressing to get out, holding the winning tokens that meant they would go home with silver as well as memories.

With no warning, a burly stranger leaned over to Serenus and grabbed his tunic. The man snarled something and Serenus gripped his fingers and twisted at them, trying to get free. Acte was shoved in the action and cried out.

Nero came forward. He had a knife drawn, though he did not recall how it came to his hand. He stepped past Acte, though even then he knew his leg brushed against her. It felt as if he touched a hot stove.

'Tell me the name of the Green driver, you little shit,' the stranger was saying.

He held Serenus so tightly the boy could hardly have replied. Nero gripped the same arm and rested his blade against the man's cheek. It was not quite a mortal threat, but he froze even so. His gaze turned slowly.

'Put that away,' he growled. 'The lad and I were just having a little discussion. We . . .'

'Shut up and put him down. Or I'll stripe your face for you,' Nero said.

The man tried to gauge if the threat was real or not. Nero smiled and he made a decision, dropping Serenus, giving him a little push at the same time so that he sprawled back.

Freed to move, the burly man looked over Nero and Otho as they faced him. He swayed as he stood there, clearly the worse for drink. A couple of his friends had wandered off, but they were still close by. Nero saw him consider calling to them.

There was a pattern to this sort of confrontation, he knew. It could start and fade to nothing, or swell to something more. Some men felt the excitement of violence. After a scuffle and a bit of shouting, they suddenly found they wanted more. Perhaps it was the presence of Acte, or that he wore the toga virilis, but Nero suddenly relished the idea. Serenus had scrambled up and stood with his hands as fists. They all faced the man, ready to batter him if he moved. Burrus had trained all three for months. They gleamed with health and strength. That confidence shone in their eyes and the way they stood.

Slowly, the man spat on the ground. He waved a hand in disgust, then moved away along the row, leaving them. Nero watched him go, aware once more of Acte's attention.

'I told you not to cheer for the Red team,' he said to Serenus.

His friend nodded, embarrassed. Serenus was the only one of the three who hadn't yet received his toga. In theory, it changed nothing, but the reality was that Otho and Nero had entered an adult world – and Acte looked on Nero with interest she would not have shown before.

Or perhaps it was because Nero was thickset and looked three years older than he was, Serenus didn't know. He felt something between them. After an afternoon worshipping Acte, Serenus felt his heart break a little to see it.

It may have been jealousy that made Serenus reply, rather than take the criticism. He could see Acte staring at his friend and he had never felt younger or weaker than in that moment.

'I hear you are to be congratulated,' he said. 'On your betrothal.'

That broke Acte's gaze, at least. She and Nero both turned sharply.

'Where did you hear that?' Nero demanded.

Serenus stammered and it was Otho who replied first.

'It's all over the city,' he said. 'My father wanted me to ask you if it is true.'

'And what if it is?' Nero snapped. 'I had no say in it! I may not even have to marry her. It's just a betrothal.'

'So it is true, then?' Serenus asked. 'You are betrothed to your sister?'

He felt a little guilty at the way Nero flushed then, going deep red. In Acte's presence, he was quite unable to defend himself.

'She is not my sister! Or she is . . . but not in blood. Octavia is a cousin. There's no law against that. Either way, there may not even be a marriage. By the gods, I may not let them do it to me.'

'If the emperor commands, though . . .' Serenus murmured. 'We all serve as best we can, I suppose.'

'It's just politics, Nero,' Otho said, summoning all the wisdom of his two extra years. 'Your sister is a political prize, so my father says. Whoever marries her will always have the ear of the emperor. If she is betrothed to you, it will stop all the other noble families manoeuvring as she comes of age. Perhaps that's all there is to it.'

Nero frowned.

'No, I think it is real enough. My mother . . .' He grimaced, annoyed with her all over again. 'I was told it was the emperor's decision, that an imperial son has his wife chosen for influence, not love.'

He was unaware that he stood with his lower lip slightly out, head lowered and breathing hard. A year before, he might have raged or kicked the benches. Yet the months of training with Seneca and Burrus had borne fruit. Nero breathed deeply, his eyes clearing. His friends recognised the effort and Serenus gave up his needling.

'I have to walk Acte back,' he said. That snagged Nero's attention fast enough.

'Those men might still be around,' Nero said to her. 'I should probably go with you, to be sure you are safe.'

'You are betrothed, though . . . Is it allowed?' she said. Her accent was wonderfully exotic to his ear. He already knew Acte could converse in Greek as well as Latin. He replied in her language, a little stilted but confident enough. He had a talent for it, so his tutors said.

'The heart is always free,' he said.

Acte smiled and bowed her head, though Serenus snorted, spoiling the moment. Nero scowled at him. He wished suddenly that the drunk man would come back, though the benches were all empty. He wanted to punch someone in the face.

Agrippina had come to look forward to her monthly meeting with Cornelius Axilla. She told herself it was nothing to do with his being handsome, nor her idle fascination with his hands or the moustache he wore. That was still a rare choice in Rome. Most men were either clean-shaven like the emperor, or sported thick beards. Axilla's moustache gleamed richly, she had noticed. It was oiled, or waxed perhaps. She kept wanting to reach out and touch it.

She had known too many men to be some blushing girl in his presence. No woman on her third husband should be wasting time thinking about the great strength in the merchant's shoulders, or the way his hands could bend a gold coin as proof of purity. Not that there was such a thing as a pure aureus, she had discovered. Axilla brought information like water to a dry riverbed, moistening her. That was one reason she looked forward to their meetings.

A coin of honest gold would wear smooth from just the touch of hands, so she had learned. Each aureus had to be mingled with a little silver, durable enough to use, yet still retaining the buttery colour men trusted.

That afternoon, he sat across from her, both chairs placed to catch the sun in a window that overlooked the western city. Outside, birds flew across Rome in a deep blue sky. Agrippina smiled as she sipped at frozen lemon, made from shavings of ice deep beneath the Palatine. Wrapped in cloth, the huge blocks survived a race down from the mountains to make cool drinks all summer. It was an emperor's luxury and it pleased her to let Axilla taste a bowl of the stuff, dipping a silver spoon.

'I will say my husband is more than pleased with the accounts – with the sums you have delivered to the treasury,' she said. 'Claudius says you have a talent, though he does not know if it is for mining or creating wealth.

Either way, he is happy with the arrangement.' She felt a slight colour come to her cheeks as she saw him tasting the lemon ice. 'As am I.'

'The mines in Hispania are still rich,' he said. 'I have certainly driven the slaves hard – Britons for the most part, with a few criminals from Gaul. Good workers, though fevers and injuries do take their toll. We could use another war next year to replenish those numbers, empress.' He smiled and she returned the expression. 'Still, we make progress. Twenty thousand men can dig through a mountain, rock by rock. Though they must all be searched at the end of each shift. I have known them swallow pieces of gold, or put them . . . wherever they think we will not search. It is a hard business, taking gold or silver ore from the earth. Yet the forges there produce bar as good as I have ever seen.'

Agrippina noticed he was tasting every drop of the confection. Axilla put the bowl down with obvious reluctance and smiled when he saw how she looked at him.

'I'm sorry. I haven't had anything like that before, certainly not in summer. The mine workshops are hot places, compared to these heights.'

'Though I hear you are building a new house, almost a palace in its own right.'

He shook his head, suddenly shy.

'It has been a good year, empress. With my small part, I have enough to make a home on the Caelian hill. Like a new nest, it will be ready in the spring. Perhaps I will tempt a beautiful bird to join me there, when it is finished.'

Was it an accident, his meaning? Was she the bird he had in mind? At twenty-eight, Axilla was still unmarried, so Polla had told her. It had taken a flask of wine and an

Conn Iggulden

evening of private conversation to draw that much from the slave girl. Polla had sighed almost in longing while Agrippina teased out the nature of her service. Axilla had never been cruel, though he'd made her rise early and work all day. He had purchased her at the block to keep house for him in Rome. The younger woman had expected the worst, Agrippina understood that much. Axilla had come to the city to make his approach for the mint licence – and succeeded. Polla had been his for just three months before he'd given her away. It meant he was still a mystery in some ways.

Polla had witnessed two mistresses leaving in that short time. They fluttered in and it was true none seemed to stay. Yet when they parted, it was apparently without rancour, which Agrippina found hard to believe. Passion *stung*. It tore apart. Lovers did not part with a kiss and a gentle smile, at least in her experience! She found the idea intriguing. Axilla was a subtle man, but she thought he was not unaware of her.

'I'm sure it will be wonderful,' she said. 'I hope for a chance to come and see it.'

'I would like that,' he said softly.

There was gentleness there, amidst the strength. She noted every darting glance, every twitch of his lips. Yet he was in the presence of the emperor's wife. Praetorians stood along the walls, like blocks of stone but living men with ears and eyes. Her husband surely heard all – and so it had become the most delicate dance between them, so subtle and slow Agrippina was not always certain it existed. The mention of the house had been the closest thing to an invitation in almost a year, but that was natural enough, was it not? Axilla had purchased marble from Athens to make the floors. It would be dangerously grand when it was finished, so she'd heard. Some of the senators' wives already gossiped about it, saying their husbands believed it too fine a home for a mere merchant and tax gatherer.

A frown line appeared between her eyes at that thought.

'I hope it is not . . . too *proud* a building,' she said, struggling for the right words.

As always, he seemed to understand her meaning. Claudius never read her thoughts in such a way. Axilla nodded.

'From the street, there will be a wall like any other, though perhaps longer than some. I know there are jealous eyes in Rome, Agrippina. You . . . it is extraordinary that you might worry for me at all. I am a very private man, you do not need to fear.'

There it was again, the invitation. Despite the ears that listened, she was suddenly certain of it.

'You must let me know when it is ready to be seen,' she said.

His eyes were dark with knowledge as he looked at her. He nodded once and then took up a cup of wine.

'I will have a new business by this time next week,' he said, his voice brisk, 'if the gods allow. That mint licence has opened doors I could not have imagined, not then. Empress, I have only to show that sign of imperial favour and I am made welcome. So I used some of our profits to set up looms, to make clothes. It's a small place as yet, but I have brought in talented weavers and spinners. The quality is excellent. I've had some warnings from the established places, of course. They don't want any new shop bringing the price down. I brought in a few mine guards as well to keep them all honest – paying them extra, though the

Conn Iggulden

labour is more pleasant. Looms are expensive, but when they are set up, the costs are few. I wouldn't be surprised to hear of an accidental fire otherwise. Some men fear competition, empress. I like to think I thrive on it.'

She sat back, just listening to him talk. She liked to hear details of trades, of deals struck or pressures brought to bear. It was all so different from her own experience. This was life, in its struggle and glory. She thought she could listen to his deep voice for ever.

The crash of soldiers standing to attention roused her from a cat-like drowse. Claudius swept into the private rooms, still speaking. Agrippina had thought he was at the east gate, ready to leave on a journey he had already delayed half a dozen times. Just the thought of having her husband away from the city for a few months raised possibilities she hardly dared to think through. She stood and of course Axilla did as well, putting down his cup.

Claudius strode past doors that could never be closed while Agrippina met with another man. She heard her husband halt and clasped her hands behind her back. When the emperor appeared again in the doorway, she was almost sure she didn't look guilty. Agrippina smiled and held out one hand to invite him closer.

'You remembered, Claudius! You are too kind. I wanted to introduce you to Master Axilla, but I thought there would not be time before you left . . .' She realised she was babbling and trailed off.

Axilla went down on one knee as Claudius entered the room. Her husband inclined his head in greeting.

'You may stand,' he said.

A shadow crossed the emperor's face as he realised Axilla was a head taller than him.

'I am most pleased with your work, Master Axilla. Your mint has already made a mark in the city. It is an extraordinary success, with profits to show for it. My man at the treasury tells me the Hispania gold floods in now, half as much again as last year. Your new coins are accepted everywhere.'

'Your Imperial Majesty is too kind, even to notice my work. It is a great honour.'

Agrippina tried to unclench her stomach muscles. Axilla had no idea how delicate the balance could be with her husband. She knew how to work with Claudius, but Axilla was in real danger. As the exchange ended, she began to relax. Then Axilla suddenly went on, his mind always working.

'I *could* arrange for a mint mark, dominus. To indicate which coins are ours – as a sign of quality perhaps.'

Claudius stood still for a beat, then shook his head.

'No, I don't think so. My wife said you had good judgement, Master Axilla! Yet how long would it be before other mints copied your mark? Or if you persevered, how long before your coins were being exchanged at a different rate to the rest? It would create more than one currency, would it not? You see, these things are rarely so simple as they first appear.'

Agrippina could see her husband was delighted to have scored on the younger man. Perhaps it was Axilla's relative youth or the difference in height that made it matter, she didn't know. She accepted Claudius' kiss on her cheek.

'There, my dear. I am glad I managed to see you before I left. I will be away until the new year. An emperor has to be seen in the provinces – in life, as well as on coins.'

He chuckled and Axilla smiled dutifully.

Conn Iggulden

'And Nero?' Agrippina asked.

Claudius became more serious then.

'I have left orders with Burrus and the senate. Nero is in charge, within reason. Don't make me regret it, Agrippina! You said it would be the making of him, that we should reward his progress with his tutors, his new maturity. Well, I will hold you to it – and remember, he wears the toga now. I will show him no mercy if he fails to heed advice.'

He grunted. He suspected Agrippina would be the one in charge, no matter what Nero thought.

'Let the boy preside over cases in law to keep him busy. I have left orders to that effect – minor judgements: theft or disputes over wills. That boy will turn to mischief if he is bored, so I suggest you drive him to utter exhaustion until I return.'

Agrippina leaned in and kissed Claudius on the other cheek. He kept an eye on Axilla as she did so and she feared her husband was noting the man's good looks. She was suddenly sure she would have no freedom in his absence. Perhaps it was lucky Axilla's house was still being built. She could not go there, even to visit. With Claudius away from Rome, there would always be someone watching.

'Come back to me, my love,' she said.

Claudius smiled.

'Is this meeting at an end?' he asked.

Axilla took the hint and bowed out of the room.

Claudius followed him with his gaze, his expression thoughtful.

'These "new men",' he said. 'I'm just not sure what to make of them.'

'He is loyal, Claudius – and he has a talent for gold. You

said legion pay alone was a fortune in silver, each and every month. Twenty-eight legions of five thousand, with almost as many again in support staff. How much silver and gold floods from imperial coffers to pay those men?'

He inclined his head, his interest sharpening.

'Fortunes to beggar Croesus,' he admitted. 'Fair enough. I will look for his new coins when I cross to Egypt and Judaea.' He sighed. 'Pray for calm seas, Agrippina. You know I am no sailor.'

'I will,' she said, nestling her head into his chest, bending her knees just a touch.

9

The day was cold and rain poured down outside, spattering dirt onto the hems of togas and stolas of anyone running across the forum. One year slid into another over gales and frost. Claudius had been gone for almost four months and of course the delay meant the seas had become too rough for travel. Fleets came into safe ports during winter. The entire Roman world grew still.

January was named for a god with two faces, who looked back to the previous year and ahead to the new one. Spring would bring green life and new problems, but in the meantime people ate thick pottage of grains and vegetables; shellfish, boar, mushrooms, whatever could be caught fresh or brought up from deep cellars. Over winter, the city caught up with all the work that had been left undone, while the farms were black and bare.

Nero could see steam rising from the robes of those who had been caught in the rain. He faced the benches as they filled up, swallowing tightly. The entire case might have been heard out on the forum if the weather had held.

When the clouds had opened, they'd all run into the basilica. He could hear a pattering of drops overhead. The air smelled of damp wool.

There was a good chance the emperor would not return now until spring. Nero knew his mother had argued for him to be given greater responsibility, but he thought even her ambitions had spiralled out of control. It was one thing to leave a young man in the semblance of command for a month or two, quite another to leave him to sink or swim for half a year – or even longer if the troubles in Judaea worsened.

In some ways, the results were exactly as Agrippina had dreamed. With Claudius gone from Rome, officers of the courts had come to the Palatine, offering his son a seat in judgement for any of a dozen minor cases.

Nero reached for a cup of watered wine. One-in-six, at least. It would ease his dry throat without stealing his wits. He could see Seneca present at the back, with Burrus beside him. The praetorian wore street clothes and kept his arms folded. Otho and Serenus were two rows closer, in a group of senators' sons – and Nero was raised above them all on a podium seat that always made him feel as if he were the one on trial.

Though he wore a simple white toga, though he had been bathed and oiled, Nero still perspired. He could not remember sleeping the night before, though he supposed he must have done. Exhaustion made his hands tremble, until he clasped them in front of him.

This was no dispute over an old man's will, no broken betrothal or boundary fence between two farms! Those had been his first cases – he'd actually enjoyed sitting in judgement for them. He had given each one the time and

Conn Iggulden

care it deserved, and he was honestly proud of his decisions.

Word had spread of his continuing attendance – and he did not think either Agrippina or Claudius had thought it all the way through. Instead of cases drying up, a flood of litigants had begun to ask for him. At first, Nero worried they might just think him easily fooled, but the truth was something else. Younger senators brought cases forward, but not to earn favour with Claudius. It seemed they were putting down a token for the future – with Nero. By leaving his oldest son in command of the city, Claudius had raised eyebrows all over Rome. Whatever Claudius had intended, Nero was a young man who wore the toga virilis and had the favour of his father.

By the end of the third month, he had ruled on more disputes than he could easily recall. Of course, there were no real prisons in Rome, not beyond a few cells for drunks or those who might flee their trial. The results of a verdict were carried out at once. Fines were the most common outcome, handed out in sums small, or to the value of entire estates. Whippings too were common, delivered at posts not forty paces from where he sat. The crowds loved those and took bets on how many times criminals would cry out.

At the last, the court's authority stretched to an order of death: most often by beheading for free men, or crucifixion for slaves. This case carried that penalty. If the prisoners were found guilty, Nero would stand and watch their execution, either in the forum or on the road out of the city. Seneca said justice had to be witnessed. It was not to be relished, but imposed with dignity and regret, for the most serious of crimes.

Nero swallowed a little more wine and cleared his throat into his fist. Couldn't they see how unready he was? Were they all blind? It was extraordinary the way they could look to him and not see his fear. At any moment, he thought one of them would point and call him an impostor. Yet they just shuffled in, happy to be out of the rain.

Sixty jurors that day would decide guilt or innocence. With them came the law officer ready to be asked any difficult question; the prosecution and defence, and of course the scribes who would record every word, no doubt to be read and condemned by Claudius when he returned. Nero felt fresh sweat break out at that thought. He dabbed his cheeks surreptitiously with the sleeve of his toga. He wore layers beneath, having turned almost blue from cold on a previous day. Yet with so many damp bodies crammed in, the air had begun to warm. He willed himself to be calm, but his breath seemed shallow. He was not ready, not for this.

They came even so. Eight men were prodded in from the back, chained at the hands and with lengths of iron bar between their legs. There were jeers and rumblings of discontent as they shuffled through the seated crowd. Vigiles put them on a bench right under the podium and glared around. They had the authority to keep order. If the crowd became too noisy or Nero gave the command, they could clear the entire room and suspend proceedings.

The senior clerk nodded to Nero and they all rose to pray for wisdom and justice in that place. In a ringing voice, the man dedicated the trial to the goddess Iustitia, introduced by Augustus, with the first temple raised by Tiberius. Lady Justice was a very modern goddess. After that dedication, the clerk asked favour from a dozen other gods, as well as orators and lawmakers from centuries before. He invoked their support in the unending search for truth.

At the last, he dedicated the labour of all men and women present to the honour of 'His Imperial Majesty, Emperor Claudius: Conqueror of Britannia, Pharaoh of Egypt, Beloved of the Gods and King of Kings. His son, Nero Claudius Caesar Augustus Germanicus, to preside.'

The prisoners were called to stand then, one by one, with a few unusual names spelled for the scribes. Nero watched the group closely, looking for any sign of evil or madness. He thought he understood murder, at least could appreciate why it happened. Any man with a temper could do that. In comparison, blasphemy was a strange and twisting thing. Nero wanted to look away from such men, before they invited destruction on them all.

How many stories of Rome and Greece began with a god or goddess slighted or treated with discourtesy? Jupiter or Juno could come in the form of an old man or woman, even a child asking for help. A wrong word, an unwise smile, just a glimpse of them bathing might result in appalling misfortunes falling on the heads of whoever failed to show awe.

Nero nodded to the prosecutor. The man was a member of the Flavian family, still just in his thirties, smooth-shaven and ambitious. Nero assumed he saw prosecuting the trial as another rung on the ladder from equestrian to senate class. According to Seneca, Vespasian was the son of a moneylender and tax gatherer – exactly the sort who might benefit in the absence of Claudius.

'Gentlemen, I could bring a dozen witnesses to the foul blasphemies of these eight,' Vespasian began. 'Instead, I will merely ask them to repeat their words and condemn themselves. When questioned, they are unable . . . or unwilling to remain silent.' He took a deep breath, girding his loins to go on. 'They deny the majesty of Jove, of all the gods who rule us, who grant us life and freedom from conquest and plague. In addition, they reject utterly the authority of the imperium, claiming Emperor Claudius has no power over them.'

That summary brought a shocked murmur from the crowd, while the men in chains gazed impassively. Nero stared down from his podium, seeing more than anyone else. Five of them were visibly foreign: bearded and swarthier than the rest, looking more Syrian than Roman. The three at the end were clearly citizens of empire, from the cut of their hair and clothes, to the simple gold band two of them wore on their left hands. They were listening and . . . yes, one of the citizens murmured a translation. His words brought a tightness to the lips of the others. One of them actually spat on the floor at his feet. Nero frowned, outraged.

Vespasian shook his head. He too had witnessed the act. He raised a hand as if to say, 'What can you do with such men?'

'The empire,' Vespasian went on, warming to his own thought, 'demands no loyalty of the heart, at least not from poor, benighted denizens of far-flung posts and fortresses. We know what children they are, how they worship the sun . . . or false idols of bone and blood. For ourselves, we know the true gods, those who favour us, who call us a chosen people. The proof is all around, to be drawn in like breath, or water to a desert. Yet we are not tyrants, not of the soul. In Britannia, they might talk

Conn Iggulden

of a goddess of the silver wheel, but we do not break them on a wheel for that.' He paused, pleased with the symmetry of his image. 'In Egypt and Judaea, we let them hold their ceremonies and talk of Yahweh and Osiris, of Baal, Dagon, Set – whichever false gods they choose. Yet they understand Roman law stands above all their primitive courts. They observe our days of festival, accept our coins and *bow their heads* in the presence of imperial authority. That is what matters. That is what binds us. These men, these five Jews and their Roman acolytes, they have gone further, with their talk of a messiah. As I lay my case, you will hear of their search for one to lead them in war – and the carpenter these eight claim to have found.'

Vespasian continued in fluent Greek. Nero had to concentrate, but it was the language of civilised men, so his tutors insisted. He saw the heads of the prisoners rise as they suddenly understood.

'This messiah,' the prosecutor said, 'their leader, was crucified outside the walls of Jerusalem, on a hill at Calvary, almost twenty years ago – and all his rabble-rousing died with him.'

One of the prisoners shook his head, his mouth opening as if he might dare to interrupt. Nero saw an officer of the vigiles come to stand alongside, ready to intervene.

The prosecutor too had seen the little moment of tension. He smiled.

'Oh, you will hear that he lives, that this Christ walked out of his own tomb and showed his wounds. These claims are a fever of the mind – and like a fever, it drives them to madness, to throw their lives away. The Gauls and Jews and Egyptians have their gods, but they do not question

Roman law! They seek no new converts from the people. They do not insult the emperor.'

He paused to let the seriousness of the charges sink in before going on.

'These men say Emperor Claudius has no authority over them, that they answer only to this Iesus, this messiah. They have been whipped and beaten before, some of them, told not to preach their lies. Yet they return to the same corners, the same streets, over and over. They hold their meetings in the heart of the empire – and bring others to their side with whispers of secrets. These men are a wound in the body of the state, a corruption. In refusing to accept the order of empire, they surely undermine it. I will call for an example to be made, for this sedition to be cut out and burned. I will ask of the court a sentence of public execution – and they will make my case for me, by speaking their blasphemies aloud.'

The prosecutor bowed to Nero as presiding officer and returned to his seat. The one who would speak for the defence seemed nervous in comparison. He rose like sticks unfolding, tall and thin, his face marked in a rash of spots that was unpleasant to see. Nero thought it was one of those roles younger sons accepted just to lose, as a favour to others, or to have their name on the record. He was glad of it. To deny the authority of Rome was certainly sedition; to refuse to honour the gods was blasphemy. If the prisoners admitted all that, the sentence would not steal any more sleep from him.

'If it please the court,' the defence began, 'I will ask for leniency from the officers, for clients who know little of our laws, nor what punishments they might receive for preaching in the city. I believe the statutes of the Twelve

Conn Iggulden

Tables allow mercy or banishment for those who have no understanding. I will ask for that.'

He sat down abruptly, as if his legs had given way. Nero blinked, aware only that the speech had been short and the man hadn't really tried to defend the prisoners. If his argument was going to be that they were guilty but the court should show mercy, the trial would be over that very hour. He began to relax, breathing more deeply. He'd expected some complex accusations of blasphemy, ones he might have to take advice on even to understand. This was blessedly simple.

Nero glanced to where Seneca sat, leaning forward in his seat as he took in every word. The older man was frowning. Nero had an idea Seneca would favour exile, but then he claimed not to fear any ideas, no matter how strange or dangerous. He said the freedom to argue was the common man's greatest shield against tyrants. However, Seneca was not iudex in that court, nor was he the emperor's son, charged with keeping honour in his father's absence. Nero was.

Nero watched as wax-covered slates were handed out to the sixty jurors, all volunteers that day. Each would be marked with a letter 'C' for 'Condemno' and on the other side 'A' for 'Absolvo'. When they made their final decision, they would rub one side smooth and hand it to the clerks. Nero watched the first of the eight freed from his chains, limping as he came forward to be questioned. If the man responded as the prosecutor said he would, he did not think the jurors would absolve a single one.

Agrippina looked out onto rain falling in sheets and spirals, rattling across the roofs of the city. No one went out in weather like that, not if they didn't have to. She remembered the rain in Britannia, how it would drizzle down all day. This was different. Thunder and lightning cracked and rain poured so hard it could hurt the skin. The streets ran with a great flood in places as streams joined, washing away dirt and emptying drains until the city was made new. Then the sun would return and those stones would gleam, clean and warm. That was rain the way it should be, she thought, not a murmur but a shout.

She was alone, with only her maidservant for company. Agrippina glanced at the younger woman. Polla twisted her iron ring in the other hand, sitting demurely. She was very pretty, dark-haired and youthful, with legs folded underneath. In a white stola, she reminded Agrippina of a little swan. Seeing her turned her thoughts towards Master Axilla, no doubt working in his house on the Caelian. Was it some sign of his common stock that he laboured himself in its creation? Agrippina had sent food to him there, then listened to the messenger's description of a marvellous home, rising from old foundations. Axilla was present more often than not. He mixed lime mortar and cut beams with the carpenters, so she had heard. She could almost picture it. Axilla would wipe his brow in the sun, a smear of dust on his skin . . .

Three times she had met the man since Claudius had left. Each time had been so formal she'd begun to wonder if all her imaginings had been mistaken. She'd known there would be eyes on them, so made the meetings public – beyond reproach. Senators waited and praetorians tramped back and forth as she and Axilla discussed the work of the mint. The imperial household was partner in an enterprise that was growing all the time. She had every right to go over the accounts with him, even the decisions he made. Yet she'd thought somehow that he would find a way to pierce all that formality, to let her know there was something more. Some gleam of the eye or brief touch of his hand, anything! Instead, he had been like a block, as distant as a consul on official business. Had she been wrong? He'd invited her to see his house, had he not? Had that been mere politeness? It was maddening not to know.

She eyed the slave girl. Polla was concentrating on a piece of tapestry, sending needle and thread flying in great, looping stitches. Agrippina allowed her to sell the little coloured patches in the market. That was one lesson she recalled from her own mother. If a slave dreamed of buying themselves free, let them earn it, she had said. Though it might take twenty years, their service in that time would be beyond reproach.

In that moment, in the silence, just watching Polla sew was suddenly stifling. It might have been the rain thundering across the roofs or the thick, damp air, but Agrippina had to get out.

'Pol, dear, put that aside, would you? Bring me my white cloak, the oilcloth one with the cowl . . . You may wear the dark blue one.'

'Are we going out then, in all this?' Polla dared to ask. She preferred the warmth and quiet of the imperial rooms.

Agrippina nodded sharply. She had to see.

'We are,' she said. 'Not another word now. Fetch the cloaks.'

Nero walked up and down on the forum stones. The basilica had a roof that allowed a little shelter if he stayed close. While the jury deliberated, half of those inside had come out and discovered they did not want to go beyond its shadow. Rain still drenched the forum, almost with ferocity. Little streams ran from one side to another and he could see temple acolytes with brooms, trying and failing to keep the water from the sanctums of the gods. He knew the feeling.

No one stood near to him. Those who had been in the steaming, damp hall had an idea of the seriousness of the charges. A grey mood had settled on them, fitting for the weather. Nero stared gloomily into the night and so jumped when Seneca cleared his throat.

'They've handed all the slates in,' Seneca muttered, looking out with him. 'It won't be long now.'

He said nothing more and Nero wondered if this too was a lesson. He had never felt more alone than in that moment. The lives of eight men rested on him – and he was out of his depth. He wanted to ask Seneca what to do, but clamped his mouth shut. The decision was his – and if being a man meant anything, it was making a decision and living with the consequences. That much he could do.

'Tomorrow morning, I will wake up,' Nero said. 'I will drink a little cow's milk and eat. Something light. I have been invited to a lunch, to meet a champion gladiator.'

'Spiculus?' Seneca asked.

'Who else? I imagine that will go on all day. What I am trying to say . . . whatever happens inside, I will go on. The sun will rise and set for me. If the jury condemns those men, they will already be dead.'

Seneca shrugged.

'You could send them to exile, or to be flogged. Some would survive the lash. You have the authority of the emperor in this, Nero. You alone.'

Conn Iggulden

Nero heard a rumble of voices. The jury was returning. He flashed a glance at his tutor and went back in. Seneca frowned, unable to read his pupil.

Inside, Nero climbed to the podium and took his seat. The tablets were piled on the clerks' table. Each one had been counted, checked and recorded in whispered voices. The totals were marked in ink of black gall that could not fade. There would be no confusion allowed.

In silence, the senior clerk handed up a single sheet of papyrus. Nero read the numbers and kept his face like stone. Every eye in the court tried to discern the result. Even those of the eight who spoke no Latin were watching, seeing their fate unfold. He cleared his throat.

'The prisoners will stand,' he said.

The vigiles tapped their arms and they rose, once more chained for the verdict. Nero felt his throat might close.

'You have been found guilty: of blasphemy and sedition, against the lawful authorities of Rome.'

The crowd was noisy for a time then. Nero had to raise his hands and pat the air for them to be quiet. He had been clenching his jaw, he realised. His back teeth ached.

'Before I deliver the sentence, I have a couple of questions.'

He could hear the intake of breath as both clerks and the law officer turned to look at him. The only sound then was the roar of rain across the tiles.

The law officer rose to his feet, half-bent as if embarrassed.

'Dominus, iudex . . . the, er, the time for questions has passed . . .'

Nero shook his head. He had listened to every word spoken, but not said a thing. He had wanted the prosecutor to query half a dozen parts of the testimony, but he had not. One by one, the moments had passed.

'I would like to be satisfied,' Nero said. 'Sit down.'

The man's mouth pinched, but he did as he was told.

Nero turned to the prisoner who had translated for some of the others. He spoke in Latin, knowing his Greek was not yet good enough.

'You are a Roman, are you not?'

'I am a Roman citizen,' the man replied. His smile was wintry. In normal times, that phrase might have kept him safe right across the empire, but not in that courtroom, not that day.

'You are a convert?' Nero went on. 'You know the true gods, but still accept these lies?'

'There is only one truth, dominus. I have heard the words of one who died and rose again.'

Nero blinked. He had not planned to discuss the man's beliefs. Nor did he have any idea whether he reached beyond his authority. He could see Seneca leaning forward again. No, he was the emperor's son. Let them all wait!

'Why do you seek to convert others?' he said. 'There are Jews living in peace under Roman rule. They don't twist the minds of weaker men to their side.'

'Christ said the way to the father is through him, that no one will see God unless they believe in his teachings. It falls to us to bring all men safe, with his truth.'

Nero stared at him.

'If I had a ram brought in – if I handed you a knife, would you make sacrifice to Jupiter, to any of the gods who *truly* watch us? To save your own life?'

The man hesitated. Nero could see he was trembling. The prisoner closed his eyes for a moment and sighed.

Conn Iggulden

'Dominus, there is a fisherman who knew Jesus. His name is Simon Peter and he preaches to this day, alongside another Roman named Paul of Tarsus. I have met them both. Peter claims to be a simple man, while Paul is a great scholar. Dominus, they might have the words to make you understand. I do not.'

'They are not *here*,' Nero snapped. 'And you have not answered. Would you sacrifice the ram or not, to save your life?'

'Peter was the greatest of the followers of Christ, dominus. Yet before the end, Jesus said he would be afraid, that he would deny his friend three times. I have heard Peter describe the terror of that night, when legionaries of Rome came to take his master. Peter tried to hide in the crowds, but he was recognised. They said, "You were with him", "You were one of his followers". He denied it ... .'

'Answer my question, or I will pass sentence this very moment,' Nero said.

'Jesus had said Peter would deny him three times before the cock crew. He was right, dominus. Even Peter was made weak by fear. He did deny him, over and over, until he heard the cock crowing the dawn and his heart ... broke.'

He saw Nero was about to snarl a response and his voice gained strength, echoing in that place.

'No I would not. Did you not hear? Peter *denied* Christ – a lesson he preaches today, so that men like me, lesser men, will not. I would not make your sacrifice to a false god. Just to save my life? No. Have my poor flesh, if you must. There is only one God. My soul is his – and never more of Rome.'

'*Who rules in Rome?*' Nero shouted across the courtroom.

'God and his Son, Jesus Christ,' the man replied.

Nero rose from his seat. For a moment, he was so angry he could not speak.

'Then there is nothing more to say. I condemn you – all of you – to death. The sentence to be carried out this day. You will be taken from here to the road outside the city. You will be crucified there as common slaves, as a warning to others of your foul cult. From this moment, your sedition is proscribed in Rome.'

The crowd erupted in consternation. The law officer was climbing the steps to the podium, trying to make himself heard. Nero ignored the touch of bony fingers on his toga. He knew very well that only slaves were crucified. His sentence went against the law, but he did not regret it. The arrogance of the prisoners felt like a suppurating wound. He met the eyes of the prosecutor and saw the man nod in support. It had to be burned out.

Seneca had misunderstood him before. He was not interested in mercy, in exile or seeing men flogged and set free. They were common men, foreign-born or not – yet they spoke to him as if they were all *equal* in the eyes of their god. His anger only grew at that thought.

Nero ignored the clamour of the clerks and stepped down, ending the session. Seneca had left his seat, he noticed. The tutor would be disappointed. Nero saw the prisoners were embracing. They wept, but it did not seem to be in grief. He wondered if they even understood what lay ahead.

10

The empress was moving. Though lightning flashed and the rain showed no sign of ceasing, Agrippina and her maid hurried down the hill with her praetorians, uniforms all drenched to black. She had not summoned Burrus, but he came even so, leaving a trial in the forum as word reached him. Agrippina saw his white rabbit-pelt hair shining in the gloom. He wore no helmet, though perhaps that was just a soldier's superstition. Agrippina knew some men believed covering their heads in a storm drew the eye of Jupiter down on them. Legionaries had been struck before, bronze armour melted, coins fused into a lump. It was a grim thought and she shuddered as the carriage was brought to the roadside.

Four black horses snorted and stamped in the rain, flicking their heads against the touch of reins. Agrippina frowned at another six praetorians marching alongside, bare legs spattered with mud and who knew what else. She had imagined moving through the city in secrecy, hidden by the storm and hooded cloaks. Instead, a dozen soldiers had been called out in her service – and there was solid Burrus, holding out a hand to help her up the step.

She did not know if the prefect would even let her go alone. That was a loyalty she had not yet tested, not to the full. Burrus commanded the imperial guard, which meant he answered to her husband. Yet Burrus knew Agrippina was the one who had arranged for Rufrius to retire, very much against the other man's will.

Hidden by her cowl, Agrippina glared at the prefect. If Burrus stayed with her, the meeting would be as formal as those she and Axilla endured each month. She shook her head, glancing at Polla.

The slave stood with head bowed. Her blue cloak was meant to be oiled against rain, but Agrippina could already see dark patches appearing. The white one too seemed to be growing heavier. It put her in mind of the cloth of gold she had worn, unless it was guilt that weighed her down. No, it was the rain. She would have a word with the tailors, or perhaps give their contract to Axilla. When he took on a task, he did not fail. That was part of what she admired about him.

Burrus helped Polla climb in beside the empress. The two women sat together like dolls on a shelf. The awning overhead was a construction of wood and oiled linen much like the cloaks. Agrippina sniffed when she saw rain gathering along a seam in fat drops, reaching the seat beside her. If the same blasted societas had made the awning, she really would give their contract to Axilla! What was the point of oilcloth if it did not keep the rain out?

Burrus stepped back to the road and as he did so, Agrippina thought he glanced under Polla's blue hood. She saw the praetorian nod to himself, as if confirming something.

Agrippina frowned. Her prefect was not a fool. The storm and Claudius' absence from the city may have given her cover, but Burrus would see all.

'Prefect Burrus,' she said lightly. 'You are to remain here, on the Palatine. The night is dark and full of omens. I fear some disaster. I want someone I trust to watch over Britannicus and Octavia. Will you look in on them for me?'

'Empress, I . . .' Burrus winced, caught between duty and obedience. If she feared the storm, why leave the safety of the Palatine? Even so, she waited for him to nod.

'Of course, domina,' he said.

Burrus stepped back and saluted. Agrippina saw him exchange a glance with the men who would accompany the empress. Burrus would skin them alive if anything happened to her. She could read that much in his expression as the carriage lurched away.

Cold water splashed from hooves and jogging soldiers. Without having to be asked, Polla tugged the clasps of the awning, letting sides unfold. With that done, the two women rocked along in a dark little box, voices muted in the sound of rain.

'Exactly as I said now, Polla,' Agrippina murmured. She leaned over so that her white cowl touched the blue one. Each could only see the other.

'You will be silent from this moment,' Agrippina said. 'Not a word of anything you see tonight. Do you understand?'

Polla nodded, eyes wide. Agrippina searched her gaze for any hesitation and then leaned back, satisfied. The empress glanced at the awning and the gloom that hid them.

'Take off your cloak,' she whispered.

*

The Caelian hill began barely a thousand yards from the foot of the Palatine. Yet the crest was the longest of the seven, stretching west to east. The remnants of the ancient Servian wall actually crossed it at the peak, swallowed centuries before by the growing city. Agrippina knew Axilla was building his home on the outside of those old stones, two or three thousand paces beyond the first rise of the ground. She could hear the horses labouring as they drew the carriage up the Caelian road. Their burden would be heavier than usual, if the cloaks were any guide.

When they came to a halt at last, she stepped out in the blue cloak Polla had worn. Both women stood with heads bowed against the rain, faces hidden by cowls as well as the storm. Agrippina was a little taller than her slave, so bowed her shoulders and tried not to stand like a free woman. She had lain alongside Polla on more than one cold night, clasped in each other's arms for warmth. Agrippina had whispered a plan to her then, as Octavia still did to her doll.

The empress shuddered as she recalled nights listening to her brother's fears. Those memories were like dreams, sometimes, so that she was never quite sure what had been real and what was just imagined. There was certainly an intimacy in darkness, a closeness that vanished as the sun rose. Not that she had told Polla everything. Agrippina just made sure the young woman knew a slave could speak against her mistress only after torture. The courts of Rome required it as proof for any slave called as witness, whether they were willing to speak or not. Polla had grown dark around the eyes when she'd understood that.

Agrippina remained a step behind as Polla led the way. The house of Axilla really was a huge site, she could tell that at a glance. Some of the building work had been completed and the wall was ready for its gates. Agrippina walked with head bowed, following the white cloak. Praetorians kept pace with them both – and the crisis lay ahead.

When they reached a breach where a gate would stand, Agrippina thought she could hear wood being sawn. She breathed in relief. Somehow she had been certain Axilla would work through the storm. His eyes became fond whenever she asked about his house – not excited, but with simple affection. It was her favourite expression of his.

She held her breath as Polla turned to the soldiers shadowing them. This was the moment it could all fall apart. She had practised with the girl a dozen times, but the reality, actually giving an order, was not easy. Polla was a slave, and a slave did not command soldiers. Agrippina bit her lip, keeping her face hidden as Polla put out her hand.

'You will stay here,' she said, firm and low.

Agrippina watched in pleasure as the praetorian saluted and stood back, taking position on the edge of the road. There was no sign of suspicion in him, not that Agrippina could see. Nor did he ask for an explanation.

It would never have fooled Burrus, of course. Or he would have argued and said she had to be accompanied at all times on strange streets. That was why she'd had to leave him behind.

Agrippina almost went ahead of Polla through the breach, remembering her position just in time. Instead, she followed the white-cowled figure as Polla entered the gardens.

Paths stretched away, gleaming when the moon showed, vanishing under the shadow of rushing clouds. Rain still fell in gusts and dripped from every tree and bush, but the storm had gone on, growling over the city.

Agrippina and Polla made their way gingerly on unseen ground, passing trees that stood in tubs of terracotta, then a fountain still in sections. A fountain on a hill! Agrippina could not imagine what pipes and ingenuity it would take to make fresh water flow. It almost looked as if it was already working, so much rain had gathered in its curves. Yet the spark was missing. The guiding hand had not yet brought it all to life.

With no warning, the rain returned, hammering at them. From instinct, both women ran towards a wooden structure. It was unfinished, but they gasped in relief at reaching even that poor place. Polla went to pull back her cowl and Agrippina touched her hand.

'Not here,' she murmured.

Something crashed over nearby. She could probably have shouted in that gale and still not been overheard. What had seemed a grand adventure in the quiet of a Palatine room felt like madness then. She was half-tempted to go back the way they had come and just head home without ever seeing Axilla.

Agrippina firmed her jaw. She was cold and wet, despite her cloak. The weight of the oilcloth had increased dramatically, but she knew she would never get another chance like this. Every word she had said to the merchant had been in the presence of praetorians and slaves. Tonight, the storm would hide whatever might happen. The thought was a heated iron in her blood, making it seethe and spit. Claudius was away. It was a time of madness, an opportunity she dared not ignore. She was made wild by the wind and rain.

Conn Iggulden

'Go on,' she ordered Polla.

The slave girl ducked her head and rushed into the rain once more. They ran together to walls that would become a great house of Rome, stepping inside.

Agrippina breathed hard. She stood on a mosaic, her cloak spattering rain as if she brought the storm in with her. Should she call out? What if Axilla had retired for the night? Where would a man like the merchant lay his head?

The thought of coming so far only to find he had left was unbearable. She dared not call, not with praetorians close by. Instead she listened. She'd thought she heard sawing before. That had fallen silent, if it had been real at all.

She shivered. On such a night, she could catch some fever and spend a week in bed – or worse. It was insane to risk so much for so little, the sort of bold scheme she might have tried when her sisters and brothers were all very young.

It brought back memories of them to stand there in the dark, head cocked and listening. Agrippina realised she was enjoying herself, even as Polla sneezed and almost made her heart leap out of her chest.

In the darkness, there was suddenly someone there. Agrippina could see him, a tall man who came through a doorway and stood still. The moon was covered in rushing darkness. She supposed only the white cloak could be seen without lamps. Her own dark blue was just a shadow. Even so, Agrippina longed for light. She had never known real passion, not from any of her three husbands. Yet this man had awakened something. To have him standing there, just breathing, was a moment of intensity that astonished her.

'Agrippina?' she heard.

His voice was deep and soft, rubbing like a finger on damp skin. He stepped towards Polla and, before Agrippina could reply, gathered the slave into his arms, crushing her to him, pressing his lips to hers. She heard Polla's gasp smothered by his mouth – and her heart was filled with jealousy, enough to drown them both.

Footsteps sounded, on all sides. Agrippina whirled in consternation, trapped and wary. What was this? Torches or lamps were coming, she could see the gleam. Men appeared out of the night and she was afraid. She drew breath to call for help, then froze. Shock stole over her like cold.

Rufrius was somehow there, his features lit by the lamp he held up. The old man's expression was one of vicious triumph, his teeth showing. Agrippina felt her heart squeeze as she sensed someone behind her.

From the depths of her hood, she recognised Marcus Silanus as he entered. Senator, governor, twice a consul, a family as old as her own. Agrippina blinked, feeling fear surge. His brother had been betrothed to Claudius' daughter, an alliance made before her time, between families of the nobilitas. She had broken it.

In that instant, she understood. Her life was truly in danger and she wished she had not sent Burrus away. He would not have left her side. Where were her praetorians? Waiting on the street like obedient soldiers? She needed their aggression, the threat of unleashed violence. Silanus stood in reach of a dagger in the darkness – and she breathed with death. She could feel it on her skin, a weight like the cloak she wore.

Silanus looked past her, as if she did not exist. His attention was on the white-cloaked figure writhing in Axilla's arms. Agrippina raised a hand to her lips when she understood. It had been such a simple ruse, the sort of caution bred deep in a sister of Caligula. To change cloaks in a covered carriage had been no more than a nod to secrecy, a seed of confusion to throw off any spies of Claudius. As a result, these men clutched at her maid.

Agrippina could see Axilla's face as he held out his hand for a torch. There was cruelty in it, an expression she had never seen before. Silanus went past her and she felt invisible in that place. It was a heady feeling, as if she had somehow died and watched from afar.

In the gardens, she heard the tramp of running men. The praetorians had entered and she breathed shallowly, urging them on. They would have seen the bloom of light in the house, of course. Scales of power tipped in their presence. As Silanus crossed the room, moving away from her, Agrippina began to smile.

'I think the emperor would like to know he married such a faithless whore,' Silanus said.

There was triumph in his voice. Agrippina tried to fix it all in her mind. From childhood on, she had known moments of greatness and disaster. It was rare to understand which was which, until they were long behind. On this night, she knew her enemies had made a terrible mistake. Even in the pain of her disappointment, in the anger and spite of betrayal, she could enjoy it, still unfurling before her.

Axilla accepted the torch and brought the light closer, revealing Polla's terrified expression inside the hood. He jerked back as if he had been stung, but Silanus went on speaking, unaware. He advanced through the half-finished room towards Axilla and the struggling girl.

'If you wish, empress, you may take your life tonight – the same cold choice you gave my brother.'

'It's not her,' Axilla said. 'It is the slave girl, the one who was mine.'

There was horror on his face and he was the first to understand. He jerked round to gaze on the one Silanus had walked past, his mouth agape.

Agrippina shook her head like a dog snapping. She had hoped, against reason and sense, that Axilla was as much a dupe as she had been. Instead, she knew in that moment that he was part of it. She felt fury build, like acid pouring in. In a movement that tore at her hair, she pulled the hood back.

'These witnesses you have brought, Senator Silanus,' she said. 'What do you think they have seen? My slave meeting her merchant lover? Why would I not indulge the girl? A moment of sweetness before I set out to revoke the mint licence, to undo the labours of a year or more? I have work to do, senators. Would you deny me a moment of pleasure before it begins? Before I *set all my enemies in disarray*?'

She was aware of shadows melting away, men throwing down torches and stepping back before she could identify them. Silanus remained, gaping at her. He was their leader, that much was clear. She realised his vengeance had been a possibility ever since the broken betrothal – or perhaps even further back, to the Silanus girl who had married Caligula and died with the child cut out of her.

Agrippina made herself breathe. They had been hovering close for too long. Perhaps she should have watched for Rufrius too, filled as he was with poison and spite. She clenched her jaw, letting rage burn. It felt right, clean and hot so that she could no longer feel the cold. She would find the names of them all, no matter how they tried to vanish.

The praetorians arrived then. They had come to investigate raised voices and light, ignoring her order to stay on the road. That was their duty and she was glad of it.

The atmosphere was one that made them draw swords and spread out, as if there would be violence at any moment. She saw Silanus and Rufrius freeze. The latter knew the danger of those short blades as well as anyone.

'Agrippina,' Axilla said. 'I never meant for this to happen. I was their fool.'

'No,' she said, though her heart broke. 'No, that was me. For trusting you. Let her go now, Master Axilla.'

She felt relief as Axilla released his grip on Polla's arm. Mere caution had made her change cloaks with her maid. It had seemed a fine game and reduced them both to giggles in the carriage. There could be no true danger in Axilla's half-made house! There could be no conspiracy tracking her across Rome in a storm, summoning those who had reason to hate her out of the dark! Yet there they were. Was Axilla truly their creature? The sheer scale of the attempt stole her breath. A playful whim had saved her. No, her life among emperors had saved her. She had survived Tiberius and Caligula, after all. She had endured exile and terror, then married Claudius, wielding his power as her own! It was intoxicating, for all the risks. Tonight, she was the victor.

Polla came to her side, rubbing one arm. Her hood too was down and she looked as pale as milk in the light of fallen torches. Agrippina looked around that place, seeing Axilla and Rufrius and Silanus still standing in shock. The ones with quicker wits had gone, but they would be found.

'Senator Silanus,' she said, raising her head. 'You should leave this place. You should go home and embrace your wife and children. Write what letters you must. Settle your affairs.'

She saw him sag slightly as he understood, ageing before her eyes. No, she would have no sympathy! He had brought witnesses to a tryst that would have destroyed her – and would have left her son without protection. Her only course in that moment, her only possible response, was to harden herself against pity, against regret.

'You should go to a private room and make an honourable ending, Senator Silanus. Or you will find praetorians at your door tomorrow. I can give you the morning, but by the time the sun rises to noon, it will be done, one way or the other.'

'I will appeal to the emperor,' Silanus said softly. Even as he said the words, his eyes were bleak. It would have been one thing to catch the emperor's wife with her lover. To stand revealed in conspiracy against her could not be survived. That awareness grew in him like a weed, strangling all hope.

'I had no part in this,' Axilla said, his voice a plea. 'Agrippina, you cannot believe it of me! The first I knew of their presence was when they came storming in. I thought it was you in that white cloak.'

'Because they *told you I was coming,*' she said. There were tears in her eyes and she brushed angrily at them, annoyed at physical weakness that did not match her mood. She could not accuse him in the words she wanted, not when those words might reveal that he had indeed meant something to her.

Her awareness of the damp and cold suddenly returned. Axilla was sharp enough, if she gave him time to overcome his shock. Could he wriggle free of the hook in him? Her story was only that Polla had come to visit a lover, after all.

She saw something like hope return to the mint master and moved to crush it.

'No, Master Axilla. You said, "It's not her. It's the slave girl." You thought you had taken hold of the empress of Rome, that you had forced your lips against hers, unasked, *unwanted*, in darkness. You and your friends sought my humiliation, or perhaps my life. You stand against the honour of the emperor and for that reason . . . you will not live.'

Senator Rufrius opened his mouth and Agrippina whirled on him.

'Go home, senator. Settle your fine new estates and prepare for a knock on the door. You will not reach a court.'

Rufrius and Silanus shared a bitter glance. Both were armed and for an instant, she *wanted* them to dare, to *try* and reach her before the praetorians at her back could run them through or hack them down. She leaned forward.

Instead, they dropped the last torches and departed, vanishing in the night. Agrippina shook her head. If they had honour, they would die by their own hands. If they had none, the praetorians would make an ending anyway. Perhaps they would even run and be declared criminal, all lands and fortunes confiscated, their families left destitute. She would send men then to hunt them. There was no village, town or forest beyond her reach.

Agrippina looked around, understanding only Axilla

remained. He was brave enough, she thought. Brave and beautiful, with magnificent shoulders. It was just a pity he was such a hollow man.

'Praetorians?' she said, almost as a whisper.

She felt them turning to hear her command, still bristling at the thought of a threat to the empress. They were violent men, she could sense it.

'This man threatened my life,' she said. 'Do what you must.'

They went forward like a pack of wolves, reaching him quickly, gashing and hacking at him. He raised his hands against their swords, but they did not stop.

Claudius returned to a Rome of warm air amid the scents of grass and flowers. Spring had come and all the trials of provinces and protectorates could be left on the dusty trail. He was thinner, darker, a little more bald, weary with the burden of both his authority and the breastplate he wore, but never seemed to suit him. He entered Rome without any great fanfare, but news spread like fire in summer even so, street to street. The people came out to glimpse the man who ruled the world, who had seen places as strange and distant as Jerusalem and Alexandria. Born a thousand miles away in a Gaulish town, Emperor Claudius counted gods in his bloodline.

The result was heaving streets and crowds that cheered, raising his mood. By the time he reached the Palatine, he was flushed and brighter of eye than before. The dust of the road clung to him, but he was home.

Agrippina was there as a dutiful wife to greet him. She dropped to one knee and pressed her cheek against the back of his hand.

'I thank the gods for your safe return, Claudius,' she said. 'It has been a great cruelty without you.'

'I don't . . . What do you m-mean?' he asked.

She told him then of the conspiracy, of a consul and six senators found with wrists opened. There had been a bloodletting in Rome and he paled as he listened.

'I am as-as-t-tonished,' he said. 'Silanus? Why would he b-blame you for his b-brother's death? That poor b-boy took his own l-life, didn't he?'

'There is no sense in their madness, Claudius. They were a boil filled with poison. Even now, I do not know if I have lanced it well, or whether there are still more of them, scheming and plotting against us. I have only waited for your return to complete the marriage between Nero and Octavia. We can do that much at least. That should go ahead immediately.'

Claudius blinked.

'W-why . . . sh . . .'

She went on, unable to control her impatience.

'So our son is safe! The lesson is there, if we can but see it! A betrothal can be broken, but if they are married, per-haps with children, no one will dare threaten either one again. You will close the door.'

Claudius was annoyed she had spoken over him. He nodded, though his reluctance was clear. Still, he was weary. He wanted to bathe and be refreshed, not deal with his wife's fears and conspiracies.

'They are still brother and sister, Agrippina. The p-people will c-cry out.'

Agrippina shrugged.

'Have her adopted by another family, then. What does it matter?'

He looked at her, thinking, before his will suddenly sagged.

'Very w-well, Agrippina. Arrange the . . . w-w . . .'

'The wedding,' she said breathlessly. 'Oh, it will be magnificent. You are right, Claudius, my love, my only love. As soon as we can.'

I I

Nero was furious. He already missed the brief authority he had experienced. With Claudius away from the city and his mother distracted, he had known something like freedom. It had been almost a revelation, a glimpse of adult life that was better than the perks of the toga virilis. Holding fates in his hands was like a cup of Falernian wine. He was convinced he had grown – physically as well as in maturity. Just as he'd developed a taste for Falernian, though a single cup cost a legionary his entire week's salary.

In just a few days, all that had been snatched from his grasp. He remembered some Greek tale of a man taunted in hell . . . tempted? Seneca had said something about grapes dangled in front of him, or water, something like that. Nero could not remember his actual name in that moment, but he certainly felt for the poor bastard. He hadn't missed freedom before he'd had a taste!

Tantalus, that had been his name. He had been 'tantalised' by cool grapes and water, but could never slake his thirst. Nero knew how he felt.

He looked down the aisle, to where Octavia was being brought in like a festival goose. Musicians played and it seemed the entire senate had crammed themselves into the temple of Jupiter on the Palatine. Nero was sweating in toga and tunic. In the distance, he could hear the crowd roaring for the chariot teams. It was typical of his mother to have chosen the champion's day for his wedding. He had fought that like everything else, refusing to cooperate at all, until she'd appointed Burrus to get him to the temple. The legion prefect had not let him out of sight for three full days, ruining all his plans to vanish.

Nero glared at the praetorian, sitting in the front row. He'd thought they had an understanding, the two of them – an agreement not to tread on one another's tails, at least where his mother was concerned. Well, there would be a reckoning for the betrayal, Nero thought. He tried to make Burrus feel the threat through sheer will, as if his glare might be felt like heat on the skin. In return, Burrus looked relaxed. The praetorian nodded to him and Nero looked away in exasperation.

His bride-to-be was trussed and bound in extraordinary colours. As she approached the priests of Jupiter and Juno, the upper half of her face was hidden by a veil of bright orange – the flammeum. Beneath that, he knew Octavia wore a crimson net over her hair. The outline of strange pads rose in lumps from it, looking as if she had sprouted fruit. She wore a simple tunic that left her brown legs bare, cinched at the waist with a double knot of wool. A vast cloak of saffron yellow clasped her at the shoulders and he saw silk shoes in the same colour. There was an iron collar about her throat and the total effect was like nothing he

Conn Iggulden

had ever seen before. Her sour expression survived in the quirk of her lips, however.

Seneca had tried to explain the symbolism of it all. The pads around her head were something to do with Vestal Virgins, he recalled, as was the veil. The ring around her throat was meant to show her obedience to him. Nero thought that was a lie, for a start, judging by the way his mother treated the emperor. He had forgotten all the rest, still too angry to listen.

Octavia reached his side, handed on to him by her new adoptive father. Nero nodded to the man, a complete stranger who beamed in delight as if he had not accepted her into his family just a few weeks previously. Nero knew his mother would have had something to do with that as well. Agrippina loved rules and laws, but only for other people. None of them applied to her.

The priest of Jupiter cleared his throat, raising his eyebrows. Nero flushed and reached towards Octavia to lift her veil. Of course the orange cloth snagged on unseen pins and he had to wrestle with it. Atop that violent orange, she had placed some sort of wreath of myrtle and orange blossom. It was a new fashion for brides, apparently, after a century of dull old verbena and sweet marjoram. Nero hoped he might die, sometimes. He was barely sixteen years old, but he hoped his heart might just give up and fail, in front of them all. It would serve them right, and perhaps for once in her life his mother might realise she had pushed him too far, that she could not make everyone dance to her tune.

He tugged the veil up at last, revealing the face of a young woman he did not love and found neither attractive nor interesting. Octavia's legs were all right, but that was about it.

Her eyes were on him, searching his. He supposed she was looking for some sign of affection, now the ridiculous veil had been removed. Nero forced himself to smile. He saw tears appear along the lines of her lashes, though he did not know if it was joy or fury at him. Some women wept, as far as he could tell, for about a thousand reasons. It was impossible to understand them. He had the constant suspicion they used tears as Otho used his fists, to win arguments. When he looked again at Octavia, the tears had retreated and her attention was on the priest.

'Do you have the ring?' the old man was saying.

Nero tapped his belt, suddenly unsure. That was one thing he remembered from Seneca's lessons. The Egyptians opened up dead men and drew pictures of all the fascinating things they found inside. That had caught his attention well enough! Apparently, there was a nerve that ran from the heart to the fourth finger of the left hand. That was why they put a ring of gold on that finger, as opposed to all the rest. There was more about the perfection of a circle, but that had become a lesson about fractions and circumferences and Nero had lost interest.

'The ring?' the man prompted again.

He too was dressed in heavy robes. Nero doubted he could even bend over. He rubbed his forehead in thought, trying not to panic. He'd had the ring on a chain for the previous few days. In all the rushing about that morning, he had given it . . . He heard a throat cleared and raised his gaze to the timbered ceiling.

His brother Britannicus stood behind Nero and Octavia, holding up a gold ring. The little bastard had grown in

Conn Iggulden

recent months. He stood an inch taller than Nero, which rankled every time they met. Nor could he call him 'Twelve' or 'The Bald One' any longer. Nero had caught a glimpse in the baths and thought his brother had trapped a mouse at the junction of his thighs. He could still beat him in a fight, he thought smugly. Though Britannicus too trained with Burrus every day, there was no real violence in him. In comparison, Nero could dip into a great lake of it, summoning a fierceness and aggression that still frightened the little shit. Nero smiled at Britannicus, taking the ring and handing it over.

The chief priest of Jupiter reached out and took Nero's hand in his, like a warm glove. Nero almost pulled back from the intimacy, but endured. He let the man place it over Octavia's, then stood in strained silence as a white bull was brought in. The congregation was behind them as they knelt. For a time, Nero felt quite abandoned.

The animal had clearly been drugged with something. Even staggering, it still strained the ropes. The acolytes who held it must have been chosen for strength. They were as broad or broader than Otho. Nero watched in interest as they brought the beast to the altar, dragging its head down until the throat could be cut and the belly opened.

The rush of blood and entrails brought a wafting scent of half-digested grass to the temple. Vital parts were collected on golden trays and laid out to be read. The bull sagged to its knees, eyes dark and dying.

Nero felt Octavia's hand trembling in his. She had her head bowed, but he could not look away from the blood that spilled in a lake over polished stone. His mother had found some new auspex apparently, some Gaulish woman named Locusta. She appeared as if summoned, thin and dark with silver rings on each knuckle and dangling from braided hair. She wore a black cloak like raven feathers. Nero saw she carried a sheaf of herbs that smoked, wreathing them in white trails that hung in the still air.

The crowd sat entranced as the auspex poked and prodded – and not even the priests of Jupiter and Juno dared interrupt. If she found disease or some malformation, she would cry out in horror.

Nero wondered if he hoped for it. His marriage would not go ahead if the omens were not good. Not even an emperor's son could ignore the will of the gods. He glanced back to where his mother sat with Claudius. He suspected she would get the outcome she wanted, regardless. He could not be sure. His mother was so sharp in some ways, but she seemed to have a weakness for astrologers, at least until they made the mistake of disappointing her.

'The omens are for . . . long life,' the auspex announced in triumph.

Nero started as the woman came to face him. Locusta held some shining portion of liver, blood dripping down her arm. Octavia drew back, but Nero stared in fascination. This was more like it!

'The gods have spoken,' the auspex said. She gestured to Octavia's womb with the handful of bloody flesh. 'They will bless this marriage and bring forth children.'

She touched her braids then, as if for comfort. If she knew she had smeared blood through them, she did not seem to mind.

After a hush, the moment of tension suddenly vanished. Acolytes cheered and the congregation matched them. Incense was lit in huge braziers to cover the smell of the animal's bowels, still releasing as it was dragged away. Nero knew the bull would appear again at the feast, cut into huge joints and chops and steaks as thick as his thumb. He felt his mouth fill with saliva.

There had been wine, a lot of it. The room still seemed to spin though he rested against a wall. Octavia had shed some layers of her wedding dress and yet did not seem able to relax. Nero had caught an edge of nervousness in her when she looked at him. The shy smile of the service had gone and he suspected she was dreading the wedding chamber. He didn't doubt she was a virgin. The sort of freedoms Nero had enjoyed since receiving the toga virilis would not have extended to his younger sister. He caught himself, shaking his head in irritation. Not his sister! His cousin, adopted by another family entirely. He sighed. His wife.

He wondered if he might be sick, with all the wine and food churning in him. It hadn't helped that his so-called friend Serenus had brought Acte as his guest. Was that spite, some settling of scores? Or just because he had made Serenus persevere in the fiction that he was her companion? Nero supposed it was fair cause for a little resentment. It did not help when he was forced to watch Acte dancing with both Serenus and Otho. The music and the wine tugged at his senses and then, as she whirled, he would meet her eyes. It felt like being punched, almost. There was more passion in a glance from the freed slave than an evening with Octavia.

He glanced at the stairs leading up to a half-floor above. There were rings for a great tapestry that could be drawn across, but that was all the privacy he would get. The guests would expect to hear a cry from Octavia as he made her a woman. He winced at the thought, feeling quite ill. He could imagine Acte writhing beneath him, the Spartan maid who ran naked through his dreams, legs flashing, breasts shining with sweat. Yes . . . that might do.

He accepted another cup of Falernian from a passing slave. It flowed like rain that night, with the emperor and empress present, along with all the noble families of Rome. Nero had been congratulated by hundreds of them, strangers and faces he knew but could not name. Friends and allies as well as those who sought to flatter him, to be remembered for his father's sake. It was worse than his manhood ceremony, with all the winks and sly comments on the night to come. He felt a little like a prize ram, off to service the ewe they had chosen for him. He had certainly not chosen her!

The moon could be glimpsed through the open square of sky over that atrium. Nero took another cup of wine and downed it, though it was suddenly bitter on his tongue. Too much. He turned to where Octavia sat and saw something like fear. He put out his hand to her.

'Come on,' he said. 'They can't leave until they see us go up the stairs.'

'I . . . I d-don't . . .' she began, stammering like her father in her nervousness. 'I-I . . . wanted to . . .'

Nero grimaced.

'Do you think I wanted this? Come on. Let's get this finished. Perhaps afterwards, I might return to the party.'

He looked over, feeling someone's gaze. Acte, of course. She had dressed in a white chiton, with gold straps holding her sandals. Nero looked bleakly at her. He tried to fix the image in his mind. By the gods, what if he couldn't

Conn Iggulden

perform? No, it would be all right. If it was from seeing Acte standing so magnificently before him, that would still serve.

He took Octavia's hand and led her to the stairs. The crowd began to cheer and they both blushed. Nero thought he might actually be ill, so that he had to swallow bitterness.

Agrippina watched her son lead Octavia up the steps. He looked down on them all from the half-floor, drawing the cloth across for some semblance of privacy. Some of the younger children tried to scamper up the steps then. One of them raised the curtain and tried to peer beneath. The child's mother grabbed him and brought him back to the main floor.

Below, the great and good of Rome drank and danced. There was heat in the air, from the braziers, from the awareness of what would be happening on the bed above. Agrippina saw the dancing subtly intensify, drinks thrown back rather than sipped. A senator near her was rolling the edge of a silver cup across a younger woman's cleavage, making her laugh.

Agrippina saw her husband was smiling, enjoying the mood and the contentment. He did not take much pleasure in being emperor, Agrippina had come to realise. Oh, he enjoyed the authority of it well enough. He could order a legion to attack like a thunderbolt, from his word alone. Britannia had been brought into the fold because of Claudius, after all, with thousands of new people using Roman coins. All that had come from his command. Yet the rest – the accounts and discussions, the endless meetings – wore him down. He rose at dawn and worked until the sun set, even in summer. He met governors and shipowners, even the kings of islands and distant lands. The work was a weight, and so she was pleased to see him smile, wide and simple.

'You are drunk,' she said lightly.

Claudius blinked at his wife.

'I don't think so,' he said. 'Perhaps a little. I wasn't sure this was the b-best for them, Agri. I'm still n-not, not really. They are so very young – did you see the way they t-trembled in the temple? I thought Nero would drop the ring.'

He saw Britannicus running by with a group of senator's sons. They were lost in some game of their own devising and Claudius smiled indulgently. Agrippina narrowed her eyes.

'Britannicus is a fine boy,' she said, as if the thought had just occurred to her. 'Though he is still a boy. You and I have forced Nero on: to manhood and having a wife. Yet I fear for them both even now – for Nero and Britannicus. Those senators, Claudius. Silanus and Rufrius, the rest of them. They haunt me still.'

He turned to her.

'They are d-dead, Agrippina.'

'How many others wait in the shadows? You know Nero still wears the bangle I had made for him,' she murmured. 'The one with the snakeskin embedded in the resin. He still wakes at night, you know, though I can't imagine he has any memory of that time.'

'He survived, my dear. That is what m-matters. These things, these threats . . . they are a p-part of our l-life. You have p-proven quite . . . ad-dept at surviving them, have you not?'

Conn Iggulden

It was a long speech from her husband, a man who spent words like hoarded coins, too aware of his stammer to ever enjoy speaking. Perhaps the wine had loosened his tongue a little, she wasn't sure.

'Britannicus is still your heir, Claudius. That puts him in danger from men like those. They will look at him and see just a boy, without guile, without the wit to stop their knives.'

Her husband's expression darkened as if he flushed. The room was a dim gold as Agrippina leaned into him, touching his arm.

'I fear for him, Claudius. I have seen conspiracies whirl and spin in darkness. Men just like Silanus look for champions. They raise one against the other – and destroy all that is good. I wish Silanus had not taken his life, that I could question him tonight! What plots are still there, against our sons? Will some faction threaten Britannicus, or will Nero call the lightning down? It may yet come, without warning.' She moved closer still, breathing on his neck. 'You were there, Claudius, when my brother Caligula was butchered, left in his own blood. He did not see that violence coming. You, Claudius. You must have heard him cry out.'

Claudius took a cup of wine and swallowed deeply, gulping at it.

'I d-don't l-like to sp ... to sp-speak ...' His stammer was suddenly worse, but he shook his head and clamped his mouth over the words.

'Which of our sons is shield for the other?' she asked. 'By the gods, Claudius, if you made Nero the formal heir, Britannicus would not be seen as a threat. He could grow in peace without assassins coming in the night. I know

Nero loves him. Can we not reward that love and make him heir?'

Her lips brushed his ear.

'Nero could draw the lightning, the threats and conspiracies made as men breathe secrets together. Just for a while, perhaps. Britannicus could be restored as heir as soon as he takes his toga, in just a year or two. Until then, he will be safe. He is too innocent, Claudius. Too trusting. I fear for him.'

Her husband was nodding, his senses completely overwhelmed. The touch of her skin on his, the potent wine, the smell of perfume in his nostrils, the music that tugged at his senses all contributed, perhaps even the strange eroticism of the party whirling around them.

'Yes . . . y-yes, I see. Very w-well, Agrippina,' he said. 'Though it w-will put Nero at risk. It is a b-brave thing to c-consider.'

Agrippina looked up as a shriek split the air. It came from behind the awning, high above the drunken crowd. They cheered the sound that pierced even the fog of wine and music, raising their arms and calling ribald comments.

'Let him be his brother's shield,' she said, hiding the exhilaration that soared in her.

She kissed Claudius then on the lips, her hand resting on his inner thigh. He had not come to bed in weeks, not to visit her. Without that intimacy, she feared he would become distant, like ice growing thick. She drifted her hand up and down, feeling his bare skin raise gooseflesh.

'Come, husband. Why should my son be the only one tonight?'

He nodded. Agrippina walked ahead of the emperor and Claudius followed, watching her sway.

*

Conn Iggulden

Hidden by the curtain, Nero peered out, seeing his mother and Claudius making their way through the crowd. He knew that would be the signal for the rest to begin to leave and he nodded, pleased. The sound they'd heard had been from his own throat, pitched high in imitation of a young woman being deflowered.

He turned to Octavia, seeing she was sitting with her legs drawn up. She seemed angry, but then she always did.

'They'll be going soon,' he said. 'Just as I told you they would. You see? All they wanted to hear was a squeal and that's it. We don't need to do anything.'

'They will expect blood on the sheets,' she snapped at him.

He couldn't see why she was angry, but he knew she was right.

'I'll prick my thumb or something. Is there a knife? I didn't bring one with me, not to bed.'

'There is no knife. No. Do your duty, Nero. That is what my father expects.'

Nero flushed, still looking for some fruit knife that would let him continue with his plan.

'You and I . . .' he muttered. 'We are here for obedience, not passion. I don't even . . .'

He looked away as she pulled up her shift and lay back.

'Do what you must. The thing men do,' she said, closing her eyes.

He ignored her. There was fruit on a table. He smiled when he saw the servants had left a little paring knife alongside on the tray.

'Here, I have it,' he said.

The wine blurred his vision and he hesitated, the blade hovering. A quick cut gashed the palm of his left hand, more deeply than he had intended. Blood spattered and he yelped, leaping to the bed to smear the sheets with it.

Octavia shrieked as he got some of it on her.

'They're meant to think I am no longer a virgin, not that there was a murder!'

Nero swore, using the knife to cut a strip of sheet and wrench it away. He wrapped it tightly around the cut. His hand throbbed, making him feel sick.

He was suddenly angry, with himself, with her, with all the guests drinking themselves to oblivion and having more fun than he was. He looked back and groaned. The bed was spotted and smeared, the marks of it already turning brown. Nero scowled in disgust at all the mess he'd made. Octavia saw his appalled expression and pulled sheets up around her, close to tears.

'Go then,' she said. 'Don't worry. I'll tell them you did your duty.'

'I . . .'

She clamped her lips into a thin line, looking away. He'd had enough and he rose from the bed, wrapping his toga around himself in quick, angry gestures, securing it with a silver clasp. That done, he sat on the bed once more.

'You *had* to know this was . . .'

'Just go,' she said.

He rose and stepped through the awning. The guests that were still present all cheered at the sight of him, a great drunken howl that hid the softer sound of sobbing he left behind.

Conn Iggulden

PART TWO

AD 54

I 2

The crowd poured in like excited children, rushing to their seats, pointing in awe at the sheer strangeness of the arena that day. Nero and his friends had come in a side door from the street, reaching the box by way of private stairs. As he'd come into the sun and taken his seat, he'd been aware of the noise of the crowd like the murmuring of wasps, waiting to enter. Horns had sounded to open all the street doors at the same time across the vast arena.

Nero leaned back, raising his face to summer warmth. A cloth awning of black and gold was tied up. Slaves stood ready to adjust it, while others waited to the rear of the little enclosure, tending tables laid with cool drinks, food, cushions, anything he and his friends might need.

Compared to Nero, Otho was hollow-eyed, munching idly on a bit of flatbread laced with olives. He clearly wasn't tasting it and his gaze never settled in one place. Nero smiled. Otho's father was the one who had decided to celebrate the emperor's birthday with a naumachia in the heart of Rome. In normal times, a busy market would have been taking place on the waste ground between the Caelian and Esquiline hills. The traders had rioted, but vigiles had driven them off with long sticks. It hadn't changed the outcome.

Over four months, a vast new arena had risen – and continued to rise. It had become a wonder of the city before it was even complete. Guards patrolled it night and day, paid to keep it safe from vengeful arson or just the local children who saw its possibilities as a playground. Nero glanced to where Acte sat, on the other side of Serenus. Just a few years before, he and his friends would have been those urchins, dodging vigiles or climbing through the cross-beams beneath the seats. It all seemed a long time ago.

Acte sensed his interest, the young woman always very aware of him. She bent her head a little and he knew she was thinking of nights they had spent together. The first time had been not long after his marriage to Octavia, in the open air. The Tiber had been close by and he'd heard the rush of water while he moved with her. He still thought of it sometimes, as an evening touched by glory, or just her flame paleness under moonlight.

Serenus suddenly noticed their silent focus, scowling as he turned left and right. He looked away quickly then, but the moment was spoiled. Nero tried not to be annoyed with his friend, but it was hard. He had spent so long in Acte's company that it was difficult to remember the truth sometimes. He was married; she was with Serenus. That was what they let the world believe. Nero frowned. No, that was what they let his mother believe. He knew keeping the secret was hard on Serenus, harder still on Acte. There were moments when Nero would have given anything just to take her hand or kiss her, with all the crowd watching.

Yet he feared his mother's response. Acte may have been a freedwoman, but there was no class, no group in Rome his mother feared to cross. Nero knew that as well as anyone. If consuls or senators had to watch how they bowed to the empress, what chance did Acte have? At least while they pretended she was with Serenus, they were free of that cold judgement. Nero did not want to invite it into his life any more than he had to.

'Change seats with me, Serenus,' Acte said suddenly.

His friend blinked.

'Are you . . . sure?'

She looked at him. Serenus shrugged and stood, letting her edge past. Nero felt her thigh touch his and wondered what she thought she was doing. They were not alone! The box may have been reserved, but there were seats for sixty thousand stretching in arcs right around the arena. According to Otho, every last one had been taken up for the next ten days. Of course, the tokens were free, so it was not so surprising. Yet by the end, practically the entire city would see the sea battles arranged for them, assuming Otho's father and his backers didn't run out of funds, or British slaves. According to Otho, that last was a very real possibility.

The consortium of senators had known the cost of constructing an arena. Flooding it had brought an entirely new set of problems. Gold had flowed away like the waters that sank into the earth. Nero heard the engineers wore lucky charms and offered sacrifices at the temples of Vulcan each morning.

He distracted himself from the touch of Acte's bare leg

by looking out over an artificial lake in the centre of Rome. The benches rose in layers around it, the rake of them so sharp he felt he might almost topple in. Otho had described each part of the process over the previous months, until Nero thought he could have managed one of the construction teams. Twelve groups of a thousand men could design and build anything, it seemed. It had been no surprise to find the senators had called in legion engineers from all over the empire. Legions built bridges, roads and aqueducts wherever they were.

In many ways, the arena was just a vast ship. The entire floor had been made of overlapping cedar, nailed together and sealed with runners of pitch like strands of a web. It had looked perfect – and it had leaked like a sieve, draining from full to a muddy slurry in two days.

Nero glanced over to where the aqueduct still stood like an unfinished temple. Entire neighbourhoods had to walk a mile for fresh water because Otho's father had diverted their usual supply. His workers had built new columns and arches with tens of thousands of bricks, sealing off the old course with lead sheets. Water that came from a lake fifty miles away had been made to fill the bowl.

Nero shook his head in honest wonder. It was all temporary! When the celebration was over, when Emperor Claudius had thanked his consuls and the senate for this profession of love and awe, it would all be taken down, plank by plank, brick by brick. There was talk of making a permanent arena in marble, a truly colossal ring to serve the city. The legion men said it could be done. Yet this one would be taken down, the lake broken up and made rubble for thousands of homes and shops. An entire new district would rise from those foundations – and if Otho's father

Conn Iggulden

profited from the sale of streets and bath-houses, theatres and gymnasia then, that was surely only right.

Acte tapped his knee. The gesture was perfectly innocent, but Nero glanced around to where Burrus stood, apparently staring at nothing. The prefect of the praetorians was on duty that day, impressive in his uniform and cloak while he waited for the emperor and empress. Nero knew it was best to be cautious. Burrus missed nothing.

'We are in public,' he hissed at Acte, his lips hardly moving. Her eyes flashed and he knew he would pay for it later. Yet she knew the rules. There had to *be* rules!

'Perhaps I should go,' she said. 'I feel a little faint, Serenus. It might be best if you took me home.'

His friend began to rise and Nero leaned across Acte to take his arm. To his irritation, Serenus shook him off. The younger man was prickly around Acte, ever since Serenus had been given his own toga virilis. He may have thought he hid his interest, but he was like a pup with its master, the way his eyes followed her.

Loyalty between friends could be fragile over such things. With tears already shining in Acte's eyes, Nero suspected Serenus would be willing to offer comfort. It was too easy to imagine her embracing him in her weeping, her lips somehow finding his . . . Nero glowered. A weeping woman was one who ended up in bed. That was a rule of life and one he had used once or twice himself.

'If you leave now,' he said to them both, 'I will be sitting next to empty seats, with the rows all packed. You'll embarrass me – and Otho's father. Stay, Acte, please. I'm sure Serenus would like to see the battle.'

It helped that there was movement on the waters. At a dozen points around the huge ring, craft of every size and description were being winched down on ropes and pulleys. One of them was barely a dozen paces from where they all sat and Nero found himself looking down onto a deck. He could see every tiny detail, like a bireme at half-size. In its own way, it was a beautiful construction, a warship reduced to the basics. No mast or sail, however. The wind would not reach a sheltered bay like the arena lake.

Acte settled back, sulking. Nero relaxed, craning from his seat to see the ship. There would be betting and he trusted his judgement. There were places for rowers in the hold, he noted, a dozen a side, in two rows of six. Yet the work was skilled. If they could handle oars, the narrow hull would be a dagger on the water. He grimaced. The reality would be more like chaos. British slaves were bulls on a plough: strong enough, but they didn't work well together.

Acte pouted still. Nero ached to kiss her, but he made himself concentrate instead. There were different ships being readied. They varied in type, but one was huge, a full-size trireme with a deck and masts. If they gave that one a crew to match . . . He frowned. Across the arena, the craft settled. Winch arms were pulled back in and the ropes were drawn out, dripping in great loops.

'See that?' Otho said. He was breathing in relief. 'They had to bring in navy men to lower them. No one else could do it. We sank two ships in practice when one end dropped faster than the other. Three men had an arm crushed. See there though! They float.'

Nero and the others looked where he pointed. The arena had filled with tens of thousands, creating its own sound. Nero realised he could smell fried food and . . . yes, the sea.

'Is it salt water?' he asked in astonishment.

Conn Iggulden

Otho nodded without looking away.

'We tried fresh at first, but all the fish and squid died. I thought my father was going to have a spasm like my uncle. Remember him? You met him. The one with a face sagging on one side. We had to bring seawater from Ostia, a thousand barrels a day, then add it to the fresh water. Half-drained and refilled. It isn't fully salt even now, but . . . there! Look.'

He pointed to a dark shape swimming across the centre. Thousands of the crowd saw it too and pointed it out to their friends. There were big fish in the water, moving from side to side and in sudden darts.

'I wanted eels or those ones with teeth, but no one could catch one. We had one huge octopus wash up dead at Ostia. My father thought we might float it as a hazard, but it was full of maggots and rotting. The squid are useless, except to scare anyone who falls in.'

Otho pointed to where painted lines showed the level of the water. He actually smiled then, relief visible in him.

'I think my father is thin for the first time in his life. For a while it looked as if half of Rome would be made into a swamp because we couldn't keep the water in the arena.'

'How did you fill it then?' Acte asked.

Otho chuckled, smugly proud of his father.

'Mortar. We used a light coating, right across the bottom. There is a mix of ash and lime that dries hard. It can be moulded, smoothed, anything we want. Better still, it can be painted.' He gestured to the dark blue waters, an illusion of depth. Waves rippled across the surface. 'That colour is the final coat. It works – better still, it actually looks like the sea.' He laughed with such genuine pleasure that Acte joined him.

Nero raised his eyes. She was doing it for him, laughing with his friends to show she didn't need his attention. He was suddenly sure of it.

He looked up at movement and swore under his breath. His brother had come. Nero felt a ripple of cold pass through. Had Britannicus brought Octavia as well? She'd said she had taken too much sun and was feeling ill. Nero had invited Acte and Serenus as a result, but if she came now . . . He caught his breath. There she was. His wife.

Octavia's gaze reminded him of his mother as she swept in. Otho, Serenus and Acte all stood out of respect. Nero remained seated, making a point. His wife's expression tightened, her lips pinching to a single rosebud. Nero leaned back. Perhaps his wife would understand she was not welcome and find another place to sulk and bicker. Was it too much to ask? One afternoon with his friends, without his wife's constant awareness? He dared not even look at Acte. Octavia was not an idiot. She would suspect, or be jealous, he was sure. Acte was lithe where she was heavy, her hair loose black curls where Octavia's were pinned and singed like a Roman matron. Acte was just a swan, Nero thought. A beauty, to a poor dull bird.

'Why, husband, do you have no greeting for me?' Octavia said.

Of course she would force the issue. Nero stood, pecking at one cheek and then the other. She turned her head as he went for the second, so their lips met. Half the city were watching and some of them cheered that public affection, or whatever they believed it to be.

'I thought you were ill,' he said, irritated with her.

Octavia shrugged.

'Britannicus said this would be a wonder. I thought I'd give up a day resting to see something extraordinary.'

She looked for an empty place and Acte and Serenus moved to the edge of the box, leaving her a spot by her husband. Nero narrowed his eyes at Britannicus, hovering. His little brother would have been behind it. He should have known that from the outset.

'Well?' Nero challenged him. 'You've brought her. Why don't you go home now? Or you can sit with the emperor when he comes.'

Britannicus looked mulish.

'I'm happy here, thank you,' he said.

The only seat left was on the shorter bench behind, so he settled himself there. Nero could feel him breathing and shifting. He still wet the bed sometimes. He wanted to strangle the little bastard for ruining his day.

Legion trumpets sounded as Claudius and Agrippina finally arrived. Otho breathed in relief and wiped perspiration from his forehead. His father would be near collapse somewhere in the wings, Nero realised. If the emperor had not come, word would have spread faster than a fire. It would have turned triumph into disaster for anyone linked to it.

Nero scowled as his mother and Claudius took their seats under another awning, not a dozen paces away. He frowned further at the sight of the two women with her. Her maid held his mother's cloak so she could sit, but then stood back. She seemed respectful, but Nero didn't like the closeness Polla and Agrippina shared. They looked at him sometimes, whispering comments and apparently close to infuriating laughter.

Yet another woman took a seat in the same row, like a

guest. Locusta. Nero remembered the woman's mad intensity from the marriage ceremony. The auspex was pale and wore dark braids, like many of her people. Nero wondered if her sight was weak. Locusta leaned close whenever they met, as if to examine him. As a fellow native of Gaul, Claudius was said to have accepted her presence on his wife's staff. Still, on instinct alone, Nero did not like either woman. His mother was meant to be sharp, he reminded himself. If she had developed a weakness for mystics and servants, it forced him to be more protective of her.

The heat of the midday sun would not reach his parents or their tame mystic as the games began. The crowd too were kept to a respectful distance by rows of praetorians. Some of that legion stood at the very edge of the seats, backs to the arena to watch for assassins. They would see nothing of the action on the water.

Nero glanced back at Britannicus, clenching one fist in his lap. They were not friends, he'd told him that. Only the accident of their parents marrying had made them brothers! Nero had explained it to him and heard weeping afterwards. Well, the truth could be a cold thing. Yet for all his efforts, Britannicus still followed like a lost dog, caught between adoration and spite. For all he idolised his older brother, it seemed he was also always listening, ready to report anything that might cause trouble.

'Seriously, brother,' Nero said with sickly sweetness, 'why don't you go and sit with my mother?'

Britannicus glared. He knew very well he wasn't wanted there, but he would not move.

'This is a good seat.' He gathered his courage then. Nero could see him doing it, like a cockerel puffing up. 'Why don't *you* move, if you want?'

His mistress and wife were both watching, while Otho and Serenus pretended not to be aware of every word. Nero closed his mouth. Britannicus brought out a childish spite in him. In that moment, he wanted to put the little shit in a headlock and rub his ears until they were bright red. Only the presence of women kept him from doing it.

Nero was grateful when the arena slaves appeared. The crowd roared in excitement as they came out of the gloom at last, driven into the light from some lower section. Whips lashed anyone who hesitated and legionaries made free with kicks and blows. The British ones were sun-burned, most of them, their skin pale and obviously raw. They wore chains around their ankles and could only shuffle along. Yet they looked strong enough. Ignoring his brother, Nero watched the closest ones jingling up a ramp to the deck. They gaped as they stared around.

'Twelve oars to a side,' Otho confirmed, pointing. 'Only two boats like that one. They have a good chance of making a fight of it if they can get the sweeps going.'

He was nervous with the emperor present. Nero just watched, feeling excitement grow. He could not imagine how that crowd would appear to such men. The emperor of Rome had brought legions and elephants to conquer their miserable island. Now they stood in the heart of that very empire, the people of Rome craning to see them.

More men came out, some even bigger and hairier than the ones before. A few of those were chained at ankle and wrist, he noted. Legion men kept swords drawn as they were freed and driven back to stand at the prow. The legionaries left a pile of swords and shields on the deck, ready to be snatched up.

Some of the Britons stared like sacrificial calves. Others

darted forward, grabbing weapons and hefting them. The boat rocked at the motion, making them freeze. Some pieces of armour had also been left, so they began to resemble gladiators as they tied them on. Others looked at the waters, judging the depth and pointing to whatever swam in it. The same actions were repeated across the arena, though Nero saw one group were made to swim to a raft, anchored below with weapons piled on the wood.

The sun was high, casting no shadows as it made the waters glitter. Horns blew, a blare of notes that fired the blood. On the decks, the slaves spun in fear at the sound, wondering what it would mean.

The entire crowd stood to chant dedications to Jupiter, Neptune and Mars – and to wish the emperor and empress good health and long life. Claudius and Agrippina raised their hands and the people clapped and shouted in a great thunder, roaring their names, expressing thanks for something they would tell their grandchildren they had seen.

Caractacus stood on the deck of a boat that rocked gently. The grim-faced navy men untied the last rope holding them to the ramp. One of them pushed the boat away with his foot, saluting ironically. Caractacus glowered, unsure. He hadn't wanted to step on board. For one who could not swim, it was another sort of cell. The chance of escape receded like the edge of the arena.

He looked around, seeing what he had to work with. A few of his Catuvellauni stood with him, men who knew his name and line. The rest were strangers – even some of the Brigantes from the north. He was not sure if he had gentle words for those. It had been their queen

Conn Iggulden

who'd had him taken in the night, handing him over to the Romans. Perhaps she'd thought it would win her some special favour, he neither knew nor cared. Her people had seen the shame of it, at least. They'd rebelled against her rule and shed the blood of her lords and brothers.

Caractacus eyed the bearded men of that tribe. The trouble was, he didn't know if they were good Brigantes or bad ones. He had been a king once – and demanded fealty from all the tribes. That didn't seem to mean much to them.

Without men at the oars, the boat began to turn, drifting. Caractacus swore to himself.

'Has anyone rowed before?' Only two said they had and he groaned. 'You two can give the orders, then. We'll need a dozen of us each side. Those who aren't fighters. Come on! Move, you idle bastards. Jump down. You two – tell the others how to bite the water, would you? The faster we can respond to orders, the better.'

They began to move and he nodded. The moment of frozen panic faded, as it tended to with a red-faced king bawling orders as fast as he could draw breath. Caractacus had picked up a short sword he liked. Hadn't had to kill anyone, either.

'There will be only one winner today, lads. If we take the Romans at their word.'

There was a growl at that, but the rest of them lost their stupor, their sense of helplessness. They were overawed, of course. Most of them spoke no Latin, not as he did. Caractacus had a gift for language. He had spent three years working in a silver mine before they'd dragged him out for this. He'd learned the tongue of his enemy. It had meant the difference between dying and living in the mine, and he was grateful for it. It had always been a trick of his, to learn the words men used. On a good day, he could even speak Welsh.

Of course, the Romans hadn't let them train. Caractacus and a few thousand other prisoners had been taken from deep seams in their chains and made to walk for weeks, with barely enough food to live. They had lice and fleas, most of them, with skin so marked in bites and scratches, they looked like a map. And at the end of that walk had been the city itself, the font of all his troubles . . . and at its heart, a sea. They'd built themselves a sea in miniature, with ships and oars and wonders. He told himself they were just ordinary men, but as he looked across the open waters and saw fish swimming beneath the surface, it was hard to believe it.

He'd asked for a few weeks to train a crew, but the slave masters had beaten anyone who tried to speak up. Caractacus and the others had been whipped back to the pens around the lake on three different days when something had gone wrong. One time, water had come rushing in until it was almost waist height. The rest of the slaves had started yelling then. Their chains were bolted to the floor and they feared drowning. Caractacus had stayed silent. He'd fought long enough and if it came, it came. He'd been the calmest when the ones they called praetorians had come rushing in. Fit-looking bastards, all of them. The one with white hair seemed to see everything, even the Briton watching him and waiting for a chance to get a loop around his neck. That chance hadn't come. Instead, they'd been dragged out while the water level dropped to reveal dead fish and shining muck.

Conn Iggulden

Caractacus had spent time looking at one of the ships then, staring at the oars plunged into mud. The Romans loved workings of wood and bronze and iron. It had honestly looked like magic to him once, but he'd fought them and learned from them. The elephants they'd brought to land along his coast were just animals, like bulls or horses. One of them had died and been left to rot. He'd gone out and prodded the thing in the darkness, its corpse swollen with gases. He could not imagine the sort of land that had produced such beasts, but they were not gods or sorcerous creatures, just big brutes, brought to his land to make men afraid. He'd seen another with a man riding its neck, using a whip like a farmer with an ox. That had been a moment of wonder for him. They were only men, all of them. Trained and skilful, there was no doubt about that. Not gods, though.

Below, the ones on the oars rattled them out. Of course, one of them was lost and floated away. Caractacus heard its owner swearing. He rubbed his jaw. There were eight boats on the waters, two rafts – and a promise of freedom for the victor. His crew of thin and mangy slaves would not inspire anyone, but he supposed the others were just the same. He raised the gladius he had taken up, a good weight in his hands.

'I am Caractatus, king of the Catuvell . . .' He caught himself. 'I was a king once. Even so, I find myself here. No man can stand too high for long. You heard the promise of freedom? If we are the last crew, we will be let go.'

'You can't trust them,' one of the others said with a shrug.

Brigante, he noted. Short and wiry, but unbelievably aggressive in battle. He needed the man – and the group of his mates who stood near him. They had all taken up weapons, he noticed.

'The ones who *lose* won't get a chance to find out,' Caractacus said.

He had no time to be challenged and he exchanged glances with those closest to him. The other vessels were beginning to move. One of the smaller ones was darting around, already looking for targets.

They'd all heard the oath, read to them by some fat slaver and repeated in a dozen tongues. If they won, they would live. If they pleased the emperor, they might even go free. Caractacus glared at the motley crew he had been given. There was a mountain to climb.

'I need someone to stand in the trench and pass orders to the oarsmen. He can have a shield but no sword, at least to start.'

A skinny fellow held up his left hand. The other arm ended in a stump, a recent wound or punishment.

'Adoc,' the man said. 'I'm no fighter, not now. I'll take that spot.'

'Good man. We need straight lines – forward and back. Another man at the steering oar, someone who has fished at sea, perhaps. Yes: you, if you know the work. A third at the prow. Give your sword to another. Then keep it, you cunt, if you can fight!'

One by one, they went where he told them. The Brigantes remained with a dozen others. Caractacus saw only half of them had blades.

'We'll get more swords and axes, lads. That is the first task. We need weapons and that means we have to pick some weak fish and gut it.'

He stared into the distance. One of the larger ships was turning on itself, spinning slowly like a piece of wood in a gyre. Its crew milled with long spears. Caractacus showed his teeth. They were already drifting closer, fifty or sixty paces away.

'There it is, lads. Our little fish.'

'Why should you give orders though?' one of the others said.

Caractacus blinked. The man spoke halting Latin. He was dark and very thin, his beard laced through with beads of amber and blue.

'Where are you from?' Caractacus asked.

'Parthia. My name is Ormaz. I was not a king, but I was a free man before they captured me.'

His skin looked like puckered leather, Caractacus noted, as if he'd scarred himself with the tip of a hot knife. The man's shoulders were wide, making his head look smaller than it really was. He had some anger in him, that was clear. Enough for three.

Caractacus stared in frustration for a moment. He'd already *said* he was a king. That was clearly not enough for all of them. He sensed hesitation in a few more. A couple were as dark as the Parthian and they looked to Ormaz in kinship. Caractacus wondered if they'd understood a word he'd said. Perhaps they didn't even have kings where they came from. By the gods, he'd been given savages! He didn't have time to impress every pock-marked whoreson, not while their fate was being decided. Instead, he jabbed his sword in the air, miming a cut against a kneeling captive. The threat was clear enough, he hoped.

'Ormaz, was it? If we hesitate, we die. If we fight, *maybe* we die.' He mimed the blade passing across his throat to make that clear. The Parthians muttered to themselves. 'If we win, maybe we go free.' He blinked then, not sure what gesture could convey his meaning. In the end, he fluttered his hand like a bird, raising it up and away. The Parthians looked at him as if he'd gone mad. The one who spoke Latin nodded.

'We'll fight,' he said. 'But we are better with bows than swords. Find us bows and we will strike our enemies.'

Caractacus squinted to where the emperor was sitting with his wife. They were too far to fear a thrown spear, but an archer would be a real threat. He wondered if the Romans had thought of that.

The gently spinning ship had drifted closer. Caractacus pointed to it.

'They are the target. Tell our rowers we need a dozen strokes in a straight line . . . Take up swords and shields, lads. Watch me for orders – and stay out of the water if you can.'

The ship lurched and he almost went over the side. The crowd behind them roared in appreciation. They liked to see aggression, he realised, aggression and blood. Well, he could give them that.

Conn Iggulden

13

They took the first ship before the men there really knew what was going on. Caractacus had made a crew out of those he'd been given – a crew with factions of Catuvellauni, Brigantes and Parthians it was true, but at least one willing to fight. More importantly, he had oarsmen plunging away below deck, giving them some control over the boat. To board another vessel, they needed order and discipline – and a little trust. In normal times, such things took years to build. Here, they had to leap and hope.

The crew they faced had not done so well in the time they'd been given. Half the Britons there were still on deck, milling and shouting. More of them actually fought one another in the hold, leaving their craft effectively helpless.

Caractacus boarded in a tight group of a dozen, carrying shields and short swords. His violent crew hacked through anything like armed resistance in the first moments. After that, the rest were scrambling to get away. Some had fought in grim desperation, but long spears were useless in close quarters and those who had swords didn't seem to know how to use them.

Every moment required new orders, but that was what a king did in battle – and Caractacus had not lied. He had seen the Roman war machine three times and lived. It was his voice heard above all, directing the assault. When the main deck was clear, Caractacus set burly Brigantes to heaving the wounded and the dead overboard. The rest of them jumped down to the hold, slaughtering the ones who tried to hide down there.

In the waters, living men began to shriek in horror. Caractacus peered over the edge at them. His Catuvellauni formed behind him, still wary of the savage Brigantes. Some of those men had gone wild with the violence. Blood coated their hair and beards, making their eyes look oddly bright.

Risking a glance down, Caractacus saw men thrashing. He thought at first it was just because they could not swim. Yet some of them were working arms and legs, trying to get back to the ship. They had to know it was hopeless. The waters around were already blooming in red clouds as corpses rolled, wounds gaping. Above them all, the crowd roared their appreciation. Coins glittered through the air, disappearing into the water in silver trails.

Caractacus saw one of the howling men was tangled in long strands of white across his face and shoulders. He opened his mouth in clear agony, drawing in salt water and sinking. Caractacus saw it then, a great white thing like an upturned bowl. It tipped and rocked as men kicked desperately at it, seeming to follow their movements for all their thrashing. Caractacus had never seen such a creature.

Conn Iggulden

Moments later, he saw another – and then two more. The waters were full of them. Their touch seemed to burn, judging by the yells.

So much of this day was strange, Caractacus felt he could not bear it. He stood very still, until one of the Brigantes darted round his men and clapped a hand on his shoulder. Caractacus whirled, his sword rising. He saw it blocked and realised the man had found himself a bracer.

'Peace!' the Brigante said, grinning, slicking back red hair. 'We should go. The rest of the ships are moving.' He raised an axe. 'We all have iron now.'

Caractacus stepped in from the edge, his thoughts sharpening. He had to survive. After three years digging in the dark, he'd never have another chance like this, that was clear enough. Yet to live would take more than just hacking at prisoners as desperate as himself. He needed a plan, before he met some bigger fish and was destroyed without one. He had two ships, though one was bare of crew. Perhaps he could tow it behind . . .

He felt the deck lurch and heard a cheer from below. There was a roaring sound and the Parthians came scrambling up, Ormaz leading, all three soaked to the skin and pleased with themselves.

'Get back to the first boat,' Caractacus snapped.

They'd smashed through the hull! The craft was already sinking and he was furious with them for making the decision without asking him. The deck leaned and he ran uphill to the edge, judging the distance and kicking off. He made it, though he had to scramble to stay on his feet. The ship he left rolled right over and some of his own men went into the water. Caractacus counted those who had made it and swore as the shrieking began. By the gods, he had to lead. He *had* to, or none of them would survive.

Nero called the betting slave over. The man was owned by a gambling societas, a consortium of wealth backed by dozens of senators. Famously, they would take a bet on anything at all, with stories of entire estates being wagered on a single cockfight, or which dog would bring back a hare. He hefted a pouch in his hands, still deciding where the bet should go. The coins were gold and he had drawn them from the imperial treasury, adding his name to a ledger that would come due at the end of the month. If he could double or triple the money before then, the profit would buy him a small house, perhaps one he could give to Acte. Her family was not wealthy, not like his. Even his tutor Seneca had been given a palace! For what, Nero was not even sure. The man lived like a Greek hermit, washing his own loincloth, eating little and complaining about his lungs like an old woman. The luxury of life in Rome seemed to embarrass him.

Nero wanted to do something like that for Acte, but it could not be official, not when his mother was in the habit of checking every sesterce that crossed his hand. Control, always control, he thought. The slave was waiting and Nero hesitated, watching the action on the water. He had to admit, it was going well. The crowd already had their favourites and followed each triumph or disaster with howls and roars. Otho had explained it, he recalled. People liked a simple race, of course, with a victor and the vanquished. More than that, they loved a story. A little boat overcoming a larger one, a team saving themselves in the last moments before disaster. Learning

Conn Iggulden

to row and crew and fight like brothers? To betray and befriend? It was a magnificent spectacle. The crowd was gripped by it and Nero thought Otho's father would be the man of the hour.

Nero knew he would get better odds if he placed the wager early on. If he waited until there were just a few contenders, he wouldn't win half as much. Of course, if he went too early, he might see his chosen crew wiped out and lose it all. He didn't like to think what would happen then, when it became due. Claudius was usually angry at him anyway. Something like that would keep the old man going for days.

He shook his head, forcing a decision. He didn't want to choose the crew he favoured just because they were closest to where he sat, but they did seem better organised than some. They'd already sunk a larger ship and pillaged their weapons. Otho was delighted by them and called encouragement as Nero hesitated. The steering oar was painted black and yellow, like a wasp. That could have been a sign as well, the sort his mother's auspex would declare in awe. And yet . . . they caught his eye.

'What are the odds on the yellow-and-black?' he asked.

The slave glanced at his master and the man came forward immediately, bowing so deeply it looked like he might tumble down the seats.

Nero repeated his question and the man glanced at the action, calculating.

'For the imperial house, we can offer four to one on that boat, dominus.'

'And on the big one? The blue-and-white stripe?' Serenus asked.

The man squinted into the distance, but it was just to

give him time. He knew the young men in that box had wealth enough to raise his interest. It merely had to be tempted out of them.

'Ah, a fine choice. That is the largest of the vessels, dominus. I would give evens – match each coin – for anyone else. On the emperor's birthday . . . two to one, dominus. A fair exchange for the risk, I believe. They began with a hundred men – and look, they despatch another.'

They all craned to see. Nero frowned as he watched an eight-oar back away from two enemies converging on them. Their desperate attempt to escape took them under the bows of the largest ship on the waters. Screams and cries of fear were hidden in the roar of the crowd, the boat ground into pieces by the great prow.

'I'll put six aurei on the big beast,' Serenus said.

It was a sizeable sum and Nero wondered if he was trying to impress Acte. In reply, he tossed the heavy pouch at the betting slave, who made it disappear.

'That much more on the wasp,' Nero said, waving a hand as if it was nothing to him.

The slave counted the coins within and his master beamed, greasy in his pleasure as he bowed away.

Serenus leaned forward, watching the action. Otho's gaze had never wavered and Nero too was focused. It mattered. He was not certain why it mattered, but what happened on the water suddenly meant the world to them.

Octavia pursed her lips so tightly they almost disappeared. She had been overlooked and had to wave to catch the betting slave's attention once more. She put a silver sesterce on a boat that had survived the initial clashes. Britannicus had not brought any coins with him, so she gave him another to bet. After a lot of thought, he wagered it

Conn Iggulden

on the big one, the ship Serenus called the beast. Nero didn't even look at him, though his jaw clenched.

The breeze built as the rowers found a rhythm they could maintain. Caractacus actually felt cooler, desperately welcome in the still air of a Roman summer. Their boat skimmed around the edge, away from a group battling it out in the middle. Two more sat outside that maelstrom, blood marking their decks. Everyone had fought. Two hulls had rolled right over and they had sunk the third themselves. Bodies of men bobbed in the waters and the afternoon sun was slanting across the arena so that men covered their eyes with a flat hand.

'Look at the speed we're making!' one of the Brigantes said, cackling. 'We should ram someone.'

Bloodthirsty little wight, Caractacus thought. Of course, he needed some of that. He needed men who liked to fight, or failing that, those who would do it anyway.

'Shut up,' Caractacus snapped. 'I need to think.'

The Brigante blinked and would have replied, but his mate was a few years older and a little wiser. He put a hand across his chest and shook his head.

'Listen to him,' the other Brigante said.

He was so smeared in blood he looked like a butcher's carcass, but Caractacus was grateful. The older Brigante nodded and Caractacus returned the gesture. The young one just glared, barely in check.

It helped that men had offered fealty before, a thousand times. Caractacus knew they looked for kings. Leading men was a heavy stone for some. He thought sometimes that kings were just the rare few, the ones who actually liked the weight.

Caractacus held the young one's gaze until the Brigante gave up and looked away. It was strange. The wiry little bastard would fight anyone, but confronted with power and authority, he was abashed.

'The big ship has the most men,' Caractacus said. 'On deck and below. They're going to be the victors, unless we stop them. They might be weakened by the others. I'm hoping they lose some of their fighting men . . . but we can't do it alone. We need a pact with another boat.'

'There can only be one winner, though,' one of his own Catuvellauni said. The big man stood uncomfortably, unwilling to argue with Brigantes listening.

Caractacus nodded.

'And if we do nothing, that will be the big ship with the blue-and-white steering oars. We have . . . fourteen fighters and a couple of dozen below deck, men of lesser quality. We might arm our rowers, but we can't stand against eighty or ninety. I don't think we can even board easily, from a lower deck.'

'What about tempting a few to board us?' the Parthian Ormaz said. 'If we came close, they might jump across. We could slaughter them a few at a time.'

Caractacus shook his head. They looked to him for the right decision. The truth was, there might not be one. It was possible they would all die, drowned or cut to pieces.

'No. They'll see what we are doing. We need to make an alliance.' As he spoke, he searched the waters for what he wanted. One of the vessels caught his eye. 'See that boat? It stays out of trouble. Look how well they row. That's their tactic, to let the rest of us break our teeth and then hope to beat weakened crews.'

'Aye, and that's a good plan,' one of the Brigantes said.

Conn Iggulden

Caractacus shook his head.

'Not against the big ship. The Romans didn't bring just one to my coast, Brigante. They brought a fleet.'

He called to the one-armed man who stood in the trench and guided the rowers. Another leaned on a tiller bar at the rear. Caractacus knew almost nothing about ships, so he pointed.

'Adoc! See that boat? The one with the red steering oar? Take us close enough to shout, but no closer.'

He eyed one of the long spears they had captured. The Romans held banners in the air when they marched to war. He gestured to one of the Parthians.

'Take your tunic off,' he ordered.

'I will not! Why should . . . ?'

The man yelped as two of the Brigantes grabbed him and ripped him out of the garment. He stood naked and furious on the deck as they held it up.

'What is this? Why is my man treated so?' Ormaz shouted, pushing forward. He too looked furious, though wary of Brigantes marked in blood.

'Carac is king,' one of the Brigantes said. It was the one who had nodded to Caractacus before. 'And we'd like to get home. So tell your man to shut his mouth, or he goes overboard. You too if you want. All right?'

Ormaz subsided, not looking at his companion. That man took a shield from another and stood with it covering him.

'Put the spearhead through the tunic,' Caractacus said. The rowers below were working hard, sweeping them closer to the boat he wanted. 'And wave it. We need to let them know it's not an attack.'

Around them, above and across the whole vast space, the crowd suddenly roared, standing in their seats and making a sound of a great storm. It shook the air itself, like a stunning blow. One of the other boats had survived a boarding, fighting their way clear though men clung to it like ants. The watching Romans cheered courage and survival against the odds, delighted in the ebb and flow of action.

Nero felt a line of sweat inch down his brow. He wiped at it and signalled for the awning to be brought further across. The afternoon sun had moved and he sipped peach juice and water, wishing it were cooler. The tickets may have been free, he realised, but the food and drink was not. He wondered how much Otho's father stood to make at the end of the festival. Sixty thousand citizens a day for ten days could spend a fortune. Of course the real profit lay in the land beneath their feet. Otho had mentioned entire new districts, all to be built by the consortium that sponsored the games. That would make Otho's family as rich as Crassus by the time they were finished. He eyed his friend, feeling irritation surge. Otho didn't have to risk his father's wrath betting borrowed gold, just to have enough to entertain a mistress! His friend seemed to have a bottomless purse. Though he was generous with it, Nero envied him the freedom. Claudius and his mother thought they could control him through the funds they allowed. It would not stand, he realised.

'Otho . . .' he began.

His friend froze suddenly, tapping him on the arm.

'Wait. Watch that ship there. See how they row close? You'll love this. All of you! Keep an eye on that boat – the one with green and white on the steering oar.'

Nero leaned forward, though he could not see anything special. The boat was perhaps a dozen yards long, one of

Conn Iggulden

the smaller vessels on the water. Its crew had fought off two attempts to board, or perhaps the ones who rowed it were more skilled than most. That would be an advantage for a time, though he did not think it would save them.

They were slipping around the edge of the arena towards a larger craft. Perhaps that one had lost too many of its men, but it was slow and lumbering compared to its pursuer. Nero felt his pulse beat faster as he saw they would reach one another almost below his feet. He rose with hundreds more in that section, all trying to see.

'The one they chase . . .' he said.

Otho nodded, laughing.

'Yes, it's a trap. They think they have found a weak one, but I've seen it work once already. All the fighters are hidden below deck, ready to spring out. Watch, though.'

He was indecently proud, as if he had created it. Nero watched even so, his breath caught. The fast little boat drew up and, just as they manoeuvred to board, a great roar sounded and some thirty armed men surged out. They spilled over to the attacking deck and blood sprayed as they cut men down. It was carnage for a time. Nero watched in fascination as slaves hacked each other to pieces.

At the stern of the first boat, two remained. Their stillness caught Nero's eye and he frowned. They had not taken part and just stood, though they looked like hard men. As the boarders advanced in a tight group, the crowd called to them to jump overboard.

'Watch,' Otho murmured once again. He was grinning in some private delight Nero could not understand.

The two men on the boat looked at one another, then one of them heaved a bar over. Nero assumed it was some part of the steering, but the result was astonishing.

The deck fell away, a whole central section dropping on hinges. Men who had been advancing in feral anticipation suddenly vanished into waters below. The crowd howled shock. Otho yelled in crowing victory.

Not all of the boarders had been caught. Perhaps a dozen had grabbed for something and held on. Others surfaced as swimmers, already trying to get back on board. The two at the stern exchanged a look and dived off, swimming for the edge of the arena.

'Our people,' Otho confirmed, beaming. 'We had the boat made for the contest.'

'Why didn't it sink?' Britannicus asked. His eyes were wide with awe and excitement.

Nero caught a waft of urine from him and grimaced. Did he not know? The day was hot. By the gods, the little sod embarrassed him just by existing! Nero felt a strange sort of responsibility for him, though they shared no blood, not really. Still, his brother could annoy him even in his sleep.

Otho shrugged.

'Navy engineers made it. I asked the same question. The . . . sides of the drop touch the water. That makes a difference, apparently.'

On the waters, more bodies had begun to surface around the smaller vessel. As many floated face down as struggled. The two legionaries who had triggered the mechanism had reached the edge and been winched up. Those they left behind watched them make it to safety, their expressions grim. The crowd threw coins, though whether to hurt or show their appreciation, it was hard to say.

14

Caractacus waved the spear. The crew they approached had to expect a trick, but they would surely be a little curious. That was all he hoped. They were still withdrawing, but the white froth at their prow began to drop as their speed eased.

'That's it . . . that's it. Trust me,' he murmured, as if they might hear him. 'They're slowing!' he bellowed. 'Bring me close enough to shout across.'

One-armed Adoc raised and dipped his head, giving commands to the men sweating on the oars. The helmsman helped with a stream of description. Caractacus rubbed his jaw in wonder at it all. In just a short time, they had learned to make a ship move. Of course, their lives had depended on it.

The worst crews had already been slaughtered, picked off, one by one. Those that remained moved well over the waters. They had survived the first raids and battles. Blood ran on their decks and scars stood out on the wood. They roamed the arena like wolves as the sun began to set – and there were no more weak fish.

The biggest one was still holding the centre. Caractacus had to keep glancing across, in case the vessel made a sudden lunge. They had oars and men enough. He could swear it was almost a full-size warship, though perhaps of shallow draught. Even with his lighter weight, it could run his boat down, he was sure. He still hadn't come up with a plan to take it.

The boat he pursued came to a stop, oars held out as if to fend off enemies. Caractacus saw some twenty men coming to his side of their deck, waiting to hear whatever the madman with the flag wanted.

Caractacus pointed to the centre of the arena. Men fought and died there still, thrown into the water.

'They will win – and they will be the ones to go free. Unless we make a pact.'

'Come nearer,' a man yelled on the other boat. He was a brutish-looking fellow. Dark-haired and scarred. He looked like a pit fighter or a king's guard. 'How do we know we can trust you?'

Caractacus walked back to his helmsman.

'Get me close, but give the rowers word to pull for their lives if I yell. If they try something, I'll want to get clear and then circle back to attack.'

His orders were passed on and he assumed something similar was being discussed on the other boat. He just hoped the man who led the other crew wasn't an idiot. Neither of them could take the big ship alone. Together, or with a third, even . . . it would be hard, but it was possible.

'If you're a Briton, I've led you before,' Caractacus called across the gap.

Conn Iggulden

The man peered at him.

'I know my own,' he shouted. 'You're not Iceni.'

'Catuvellauni, though the Iceni marched with me.'

'Ah. And died with you,' the man said. 'I remember you, I think. We ran, twice. I was on the Thames bank.'

Caractacus said nothing. Those were dark memories and he did not want to revisit them.

'I stand with Brigantes here,' he said at last. 'Though their queen sold me to the Romans. What does any of that matter in this place? With these people watching? I just want to get out. If I could have one day of freedom, I would use it to walk home, perhaps to spend one night with my wife.'

'Good-looking, is she?' the man called.

Caractacus shrugged. His mind went to the woman he loved and he nodded.

'Like a summer's day,' he said. 'If you had your freedom, what would you do?'

'I would visit your wife as well, I think.'

Caractacus blinked.

'Fuck off,' he said.

The man's glower split into a grin, slapping his leg in amusement.

'I am Senovara of the Iceni. Prasutagus is my king. But I'll fight in truce against the big boy, at least until we two are left. Give me your oath, Caractacus. I'll take your word on it.'

'You have it, on my honour.'

'Come near and take my hand,' Senovara said.

There was a challenge there, for Caractacus to prove his good intentions. Yet it had to be done. Caractacus knew there was danger, that it could be a trap. He nodded to the one-armed man peering up from the deck trench.

'Take us alongside. Warn the rowers on the right to pull their oars in. We'll be helpless if those are broken.'

With orders shouted back and forth, little by little the boats eased together. Someone on Senovara's craft had a single rope and threw it between them. Brigantes grinned as they hauled, drawing the hulls to touching.

Caractacus waited on deck, unsure whether he should step across or whether his new ally would make the leap. Before he could decide, Senovara jumped the gap and held out his hand. He shrugged when Brigantes bristled at him, noting the blood that coated them.

'Sometimes, we have to take a risk,' he said.

Caractacus gripped his hand, feeling strength there. As he did so, the Brigantes suddenly recognised some of his crew. They went leaping across, roaring to men they'd thought were lost for ever.

'I have twenty fighters,' Senovara said, watching the re-union. 'Brigantes for the most part, but a few Catuvellauni, six Iceni and some strange buggers who might be Jews or Syrians. I can't honestly understand them, but they fight well.'

Caractacus rubbed his jaw.

'It isn't enough to take the big ship. We'll need a third.'

'All right. I see you have shields, though. I'll take any you can spare. Perhaps you should have a couple of my Brigantes as well, to even up the crews.' Senovara leaned in so that their heads almost touched. 'To be honest, they're all trouble. I wouldn't borrow a coin or a woman from any of them, but they're good lads.'

'Fine,' Caractacus replied. 'You have swords for them?'

'More than we have hands to hold them. Swords, bows, a dozen quivers of arrows. None of my lads can use those.'

Caractacus felt his eyebrows rise. Ormaz and his Parthians were in their little group on the far side of the deck, looking around suspiciously at these developments and not liking any of them. They would be delighted.

'I have three who say they can. I'll send them to you.'

He looked over at the big ship, rowing through a skin of wreckage as it waited in the centre. The fighting there was dying down as it broke the crews, one after another. Caractacus had excellent vision over distance, but he could see only the big trireme and two others still afloat. The sun was setting and even as he had the thought, iron bowls of oil and charcoal sprang aflame, one after the other, a line of rippling gold around the arena.

The sight stopped them all, even those who fought. A *lake*, made by the labours of men, ringed in fire that reflected and doubled on the rippling surface . . . it was like nothing anyone had seen before. The crowd clapped appreciation, a storm like pigeon wings.

Caractacus felt tired. He was battered and wrenched and sick of being the entertainment. He could feel the end coming, whatever that might mean.

Over on Senovara's deck, there was a sudden commotion. One of the men pointed over the side and another held up a hand for a spear.

'Man in the water,' Senovara said with a shrug. 'Some of them can swim.'

Caractacus took a sharp breath. That was the edge, the thing he needed.

'Let him on,' he ordered. 'We need more men, don't we? What does it matter where they come from?'

'Can we trust them though?' Senovara said doubtfully.

Again, Caractacus felt the frustration of his position.

The crewman was ready to spear the swimmer. There just wasn't time to build a bond.

'You took my hand,' he snapped. 'Now do as I tell you.'

Senovara began to react in anger. Then he caught himself and the moment was gone.

'Let him on board,' Senovara ordered. He did not take his eyes from Caractacus, seeking acknowledgement. It came with a slight nod and all was right between them.

'There must be a hundred in the water,' Caractacus said. 'Get someone on the prow. Seek them out. There is another. Throw that rope to him!'

Across the arena, the big ship was attacking another boat, the prow breaking through part of their deck. Men swarmed across then. The waters were dark and the shadows were as much blood as failing light.

Caractacus reached for a medallion he had once worn, looking for luck. His fingers closed on nothing. It had been taken from him in the mine, he recalled. The goddess of the silver wheel was on someone else's neck that day.

The sun set slowly in a Roman summer, he knew that much. Not that there would be true dark, not on water lit all around by golden braziers. They could not hide from the big ship. Caractacus saw men being drawn on board, clutching spears or the single rope. They were exhausted, but perhaps they were still his people.

The two boats were close enough for all the men to hear him.

'I have a plan,' he called to them.

Senovara looked up sharply, hearing a note that had been missing before. He seemed satisfied. Caractacus was a king.

'Understand me,' Caractacus said. 'It's not clever, or

Conn Iggulden

some ruse to fool them. We collect as many men as we can pick up alive. We arm them as best we can and we fill the holds. They won't know how many we have. Then we hit them from both sides at the same time.'

Senovara dipped his head in thought.

'And if we win?' he murmured. 'What then?'

Caractacus didn't answer immediately. The Romans had said one crew might be freed – if they fought well. He wondered if they would even honour that promise.

'I don't know,' he said.

Senovara blinked, then clapped him on the arm.

'It's a good plan. Who wants to get old, anyway?'

They picked up more and more men as they eased into the centre. Some of them were half-drowned, so they could do little more than lie on their backs and pant. Caractacus hoped they would recover before the fight began.

The big ship waited at the midpoint, oars still. There were no currents in those man-made waters, but it turned on massive steering oars alone, keeping the great prow towards the approaching boats. Caractacus could see men lining the dark deck, clashing swords on shields and clearly relishing the prospect of final victory. The crowd too sensed the climax coming. They had risen to their feet and they were chanting and singing together, some dirge they all knew. The sound was like battle. It fired the blood.

'They don't look very afraid,' Senovara said. He had found himself a Roman helmet from somewhere, jamming it over the mass of hair so that it stuck out oddly beneath the rim. He carried a shield on his left arm and a gladius in his right fist.

'You've fought before?' Caractacus said.

'A few times as a gladiator.' Senovara shrugged. 'I killed a guard. They flogged me, so I killed the one who held the whip. I was waiting to be executed when the call came for this. Funny how things work out.'

Caractacus grinned but there was not much humour in it. He had fought and stood all day and he was no longer young. His joints ached. One of his teeth was hot and sore, the beginnings of a pain that would grow and grow until the thing was yanked out. If he could even find pincers of iron and a smith to wield them. In the meantime, he was sick of this place, with the roaring crowd and his own people trying to kill him.

One of the Brigantes brought him a shield and sword. Caractacus exchanged a glance with Senovara.

'Aren't you going over to your boat?' Caractacus asked.

Senovara looked abashed for a moment.

'I'll stay here, if that's all right.'

Caractacus nodded. King's magic.

The two boats swept in together, barely out of range of each other's oars. They could see every detail of the big ship. It was turning gold in the setting sun and it looked strong. Caractacus knew he could die trying to take it. The alternative was going back to working in the dark like some forgotten creature. No, this was better.

'We're not going back to the mines, lads,' he called to the crew of both decks. Men nodded as they understood, growling assent. 'Better here. Better to die today.'

Senovara patted him twice on the arm. They all knew death stood with them on that deck. It smiled on them all and Caractacus feared if he turned his head, he would see the goddess – and know he was done.

At the right moment, men heaved against the steering

oars, sending the boats either side of the big ship. It was well done for crews who had never helmed or rowed before. On one side of each one, oars were dragged in with desperate speed. A great crash and rattle sounded from the hold and Caractacus felt the way coming off as the big ship began to slide past. He faced a line of roaring men with shield and swords, waiting in gleeful anticipation for him.

'Catuvellauni!' he roared at them. *'Fight for your king!'*

His voice was a battlefield blast and it stunned the ones waiting. His crews began to scramble across on both sides, battering men back. Caractacus didn't look down as he leaped to the other deck. It was higher than he had expected and his foot slipped. He might have dropped between the ships if Senovara hadn't heaved him on board.

Caractacus had picked his spot well. Three men gaped at him. Just moments before they'd been howling with battle rage, waiting to batter anyone who tried to come on board. He'd seen their shock at his words and in that moment, he knew them. His people.

'It *is* the king,' one of them said in astonishment. 'It's him.'

'To me, Britons!' Caractacus roared.

A dozen more raced across the deck to kill him. It was the three he faced who suddenly turned and raised shields, killing two while the rest yelled in shock and rage.

Senovara was using sword and shield with horrible skill. Not many of the men on either side were trained, not as he was. He knocked huge blows aside and despatched men with a sort of neatness. Nor did he seem to tire. Caractacus stood with him and for a while the slaughter was relentless and bloody. There could be only one victorious crew. They all knew this was the end and so fought without quarter or mercy. Men stood with a hand pressed against some terrible wound, life leaching out of them, but *still* raising a bit of jagged metal or a club. They bit, punched, kicked and strangled – and died.

The oarsmen joined the fight, swarming on board from both sides. Weary as they were, they carried anything that served as a weapon. Perhaps three hundred men fought for their lives on the central deck. The first clashes were brutal enough, but the following minutes took life after life, ruining limbs and hope together. The wood was slippery with blood and scores of dead men lay underfoot, shifting with the tilt of the deck.

Caractacus felt himself driven back as the crew of the big ship rallied and brought a shield wall to bear on his position. They'd marked him as a leader, but the men of his own tribe had all been cut down. Brigantes were still fighting nearby, but he did not call to them. They fought for their lives and freedom and they would not listen, not to some king of the Catuvellauni.

He could not see the deck of Senovara's boat, nor be sure how the fight was going. It had been a key part of the plan to hit both sides at once. He'd understood that much from the start, when the enemy darted back and forth, desperate to defend both sides. A disciplined crew could have set teams, perhaps with a third to plug gaps and breaches. Yet like him, the men on the big ship had been mine slaves a few months before.

Despite the scores Caractacus and Senovara had dragged from the waters, despite the twin attack on the big ship, or even the brief advantage Caractacus had won calling his own tribe out of the enemy, they were still losing. If Senovara had not been there, Caractacus did not think

Conn Iggulden

he would have lived that long. Spit was thick in his mouth and his face burned. He could not quite take a breath and knew he had been cut two or three times.

Perhaps thirty men remained from the boarding crews. Sixty faced them, veterans all. They too were panting, but they grinned as well, knowing they had the victory. In that moment, Caractacus saw it was not enough. He had played every piece he had. He felt anger surge and kicked out in fury as a stranger ran at him. The man slipped and fell into the blood. Caractacus took out his frustration then, hitting him over and over until he was still.

Caractacus glanced at the ship he'd come from. The gap had widened. He thought he might still make it in a great leap, but the chances were he'd slip and drown. He almost welcomed it. To come so close only to fail was like bitter gall in his stomach.

The lull was not real. He faced six or eight men, panting and spitting blood, and the fighting was still going on. His Brigantes were good at what they did and they did not give ground, even as they were killed.

He could see right across the deck, he realised. The numbers had thinned to the point where he could see Senovara's boat. There were still some men on the deck there. They carried the bows he'd sent them to collect. Caractacus felt cold ripple through him as he watched them bend.

'Drop!' he shouted. He and Senovara crashed to the deck together.

Arrows whirred. Caractacus could hear them, though his heart thundered in his ears and his breath wheezed. They were like wasps, until they struck in a hammer's blow. More men fell and he thought at first that they followed his example. When he looked, he saw they had arrows in them, through them, sometimes more than one. And still the Parthians loosed the whining, buzzing things, until the quivers were all empty.

When Caractacus rose to his feet, the last of the big ship's crew were down. He raised his hands slowly and around him the survivors did the same, jabbing the air with iron and roaring. The Brigantes made wolf howls echo around the arena and the crowd erupted, louder than before, stamping until ripples showed on the waters. There were suddenly tears in Caractacus' eyes and he rubbed at them.

He turned to Senovara and there was something odd in the way the man stood. Caractacus put out his hand, but the other did not take it. He narrowed his eyes.

'Will we fight now?' Senovara said.

He hefted the sword in his hand and though it had taken a battering, it was still a wicked thing. Caractacus glowered at him. Barely twenty men still stood, some mingling of crews and tribes. He did not think the Romans would know one group from another.

'There's just one crew now,' he said firmly. 'The victors. My boat is there – ours. Step back with me and I'll take your hand as a friend.'

Caractacus waited for the other man to accept his authority. Senovara may have been a slave like the rest of them, but he had been born free. Caractacus could not turn his back on him until he was sure.

It helped that they were all exhausted. The will to resist, to be a mule, is lost with youth and strength, as Caractacus knew only too well. He saw Senovara dip his head, then go to one knee. Whether the gesture was in fealty or exhaustion was impossible to know.

Conn Iggulden

Caractacus stood and looked around at the citizens of Rome, at more people than he had ever seen in one place.

'All this, and they still wanted our huts?' he said in wonder.

Nero watched as the surviving boat was brought to the edge of the arena. One of the ramps was set in place and tied on so the exhausted crew could climb up. Their vessel had a black-and-yellow steering oar, like a wasp, Nero noted with some pleasure. The betting slave looked sour when he glanced back. Even the presence of Octavia and Britannicus couldn't dent his mood then. He had won a bet that would buy Acte a little place with a garden, somewhere he could visit.

Praetorians halted the weary crew with drawn swords. They removed both armour and weapons of any description. Only when Burrus was completely satisfied were they allowed to progress. Imperial guards lined the aisle then, all the way from the water's edge to the emperor and empress of Rome.

Nero saw battered men cheered by the crowd as they made their way up the steps. They lost some of their upright bearing as they were swallowed in the mob, he noticed. The experience had to be the strangest of all their lives.

There were not many. Over six hundred men had begun the naumachia that day. Nero counted around twenty survivors as they were made to kneel for the emperor. Claudius rose from his seat and silence fell then, right around the arena. It was not even at his command, but because the crowd strained to hear. Those slaves had fought well and bravely. There was hardly a man or woman present who didn't feel they had earned some reward.

'Who is your captain?' Claudius called.

One man rose to his feet and Nero thought he recalled him from the heart of the last action, leaping onto the big ship.

'I am Caractacus,' the man said. His Latin was clear, his voice strong.

'Why should I spare your life?' Claudius asked.

Caractacus was silent for a long moment. Just as Nero thought he would refuse to speak, he raised his head.

'In another year, I might have entered Rome with honours, as a king of my people. You would not have refused to meet me then. I had horses, men, swords and land. I fought your people when they came – and lost. Yet there was glory in the action . . . and it was a close-run thing. Your honour is the greater because of how we fought. That day and today. The choice is yours, I know it. No matter what was said before, your word will decide. Yet you should spare our lives . . . you should grant us freedom, because your honour demands it.'

He stepped back and Nero was not sure how his step-father would react. Claudius did not appreciate noble savages, or wondrous feats of arms. Of all the crowd, he doubted his father had enjoyed the battles they had witnessed. Yet this Caractacus had spoken well and without fear.

'For your honour, then – and yes, perhaps also for mine,' Claudius began, 'I declare you victors this day. From this moment, by my word alone, you are free men.'

Not all those with Caractacus understood the language of their captors. The Briton repeated it in a strange tongue

Conn Iggulden

and their faces lit with hope. One of them wept and was cuffed on the back of the head by another.

Nero turned to his friends and saw his brother Britannicus up on his toes, practically wetting himself with excitement. He had been named for those lice-bitten tribesmen, of course. He could not even see he was an embarrassment. Nero rolled his eyes and gestured for the betting slave to approach and settle his debt. Otho sat as if he had been knocked out, looking shattered. It had been a good day.

'I've been stuck in my seat for hours,' Nero announced, rising and stretching.

The Britons were being led away, still under guard though he assumed they were now free to starve on the streets. The crowds too were rising to leave and Nero rubbed the small of his back as he did the same.

'The track at the Circus will be empty at this hour,' he said, raising his eyebrows. Otho and Serenus perked up, guessing where he was going. 'We could take my team out for a run.'

'I'll come,' Britannicus said.

Nero wanted to hit him. He'd spent all day with his brother, with the sun making him scratchy and hot. Could he not have a few hours alone? Perhaps with Acte watching as he showed his skill with a chariot? Was that really too much to ask?

'No, you should take Octavia home,' he said curtly.

Britannicus clenched his jaw, looking stubborn. Nero smiled at him. The betting slave was counting out a pile of gold coins, a huge sum. It was a shame to have to give any of it back. Did he actually have to return the original stake? What would happen to him, really?

'Come on,' Nero said to his friends.

Otho and Serenus were keen enough. Acte would come with Serenus, of course. There would surely be a chance for Nero to grab hold of her, after a day under his wife's cold gaze.

'I'm coming as well,' Britannicus said again.

Nero took hold of the front of his tunic, bunching the cloth in his fist.

'No,' he said. The single word was a threat. He turned to leave then. He would have swept right out if Octavia hadn't leaned in to be kissed. Nero clenched his jaw, but pecked her cheeks and left, heading for the city beyond.

Out on the water, small boats were being lowered to collect dead fish, bodies and broken oars. A new crowd would enter the following afternoon, with another fleet of boats and fresh slaves to crew them. It all had to be cleared away before then.

15

Nero closed his eyes, running his hand down the flank of a pale horse. The Circus was empty at night. After all the noise and madness of the naumachia, it seemed even larger, echoing, cool and still.

They had it completely to themselves, Serenus and Acte and Otho all watching. They'd purchased wine on the walk over, stretching their legs and enjoying the quiet streets. Nero felt he needed to bathe, but that would wait until he had galloped a few laps. There was a bath-house on the street outside and he'd left word to keep it open, the waters steaming hot. There were advantages to being the emperor's son, but also to having a pouch of aurei gold coins. He checked the reins and bits were all secure, a routine that calmed him. Acte liked it when he smelled of horses anyway. She said it was a clean scent on his skin.

The moon was almost full, making the track silvery grey as it stretched into the distance. Nero supposed he could have asked the nightwatchman to light the torches, but that might have attracted visitors and gawkers – or the vigiles who patrolled the night streets. For just a while, he and his friends were alone. He raised a wineskin and directed the flow to his mouth. Falernian, of course. The best. Otho claimed to prefer some red from Pompeii, grown on the slopes of Mount Vesuvius. He said the slaves of Spartacus had tended vines there while they hid from the legions. Nero shook his head. Falernian had no story. It was just the best wine in the empire.

'You should go home,' he heard Otho say behind him.

Nero turned and froze as he recognised the quick, darting gestures of his brother. There was something about Britannicus that brought anger to the surface, some talent to infuriate. Nero groaned as Britannicus came out of the shadows and onto the track.

'I just want to see!' his brother was saying. 'It's a public track, isn't it? Let me stay and watch, Nero. I won't say a word, I promise.'

Nero glared at him in the silver light. Britannicus didn't know about his relationship with Acte. His presence ruined the evening completely. Nero couldn't put his arm around the girl, nor get drunk or relax in her presence. Britannicus loved his sister, after all! He would tell Octavia anything he saw, claiming some higher duty.

Nero began to breathe harder, fury rising. The little prick would probably tell their mother as well. Agrippina had already lectured him on providing an heir. If she heard he was distracted, his seed spilt with another, Acte's family would surely suffer. It was maddening.

'This isn't a game for babies and little children,' Nero growled at his brother. '*Watch those hooves*, you fool! *Never* walk behind a horse you don't know! If my team sense a weak hand like yours, they'll kick your chest in. As much as

Conn Iggulden

that would make me laugh, I don't want to have to explain it to father afterwards. Just go home, would you? These are my friends, not yours. You don't even have friends.'

'I'm not a baby or a child, not any more,' Britannicus said.

His voice was rising as if he wanted the others to hear. Nero seriously considered punching him, knocking him down. There would be trouble later, but at least he would run home. By the time retribution came, Nero would have finished his laps – and kissed Acte goodnight, aroused by snorting, stamping beasts.

'Father said you should look after me,' Britannicus went on. 'I don't want to tell him you sent me away, but I will . . .'

'You're still a child,' Nero interrupted. 'Or you'd see you have no business here. This is the real track, Britannicus. This is a racing team. I could put them up against the Greens themselves and have a chance.'

'Maybe,' Britannicus said, moved to spite. 'Father says you are the son of a charioteer, the ones who stand behind. The horses do all the running, though.'

Nero blinked.

'The horses . . .' he repeated in disbelief. 'You have no idea. There is more skill in this than anything we saw today. The horses . . . ! You would not last a lap behind a team like this, little Twelve.'

Britannicus put out his lower lip, his mouth twisting in dislike. It was an expression he had learned from Nero himself and it made him look about as stubborn.

'I could. It doesn't look hard.'

'Twelve? Take the reins. I'll watch.'

In a temper, Nero threw the reins to his brother, whipping them through the air. The horses shifted nervously and he touched the closest on its neck, calming it.

Britannicus gaped, then set his jaw, stepping onto the small step and raising the straps. Otho called out some question or warning from the seats. Nero ignored him, his expression fatally cold.

'Go on then, little soldier. Whip up and see what happens.'

His younger brother glared for a long time, long enough for Nero to think he would not do it. Then he snapped the reins, up and down with a crack like a plate breaking.

Britannicus almost tumbled off as the team sprang into motion. Only his grip on the reins saved him.

He dared to snap them again, sawing air as he lost his balance. Nero watched in mounting concern as the team took his brother down the silvery track, hooves kicking up clods of ash.

Otho and the others came running up, still drunk and wild.

'What is he doing?' Otho demanded. 'By Mars, Nero! What have you done? He'll be killed!'

Nero nodded. He hadn't planned it, he hadn't. He was almost sure it was Britannicus who had taken the reins from him.

'He said he could do it,' he said, as if tasting the words. 'He just jumped on. He took the reins from me and . . . went.'

'What will happen?' Acte asked. 'Can he stay on?'

'On the straights, perhaps,' Serenus replied. He was drunk. They were all drunk. 'Not the corners. He's not strong enough. No, he's finished.'

An awareness seemed to steal over them. It was as if the evening cold found a way in, despite the wine, despite the dwindling sound of a racing chariot hammering away down the straight. Nero was the official heir to the empire. If Britannicus was killed that night, they were in the presence of the next emperor.

Britannicus was terrified and exhilarated, all at the same time. He hadn't any room for more emotion. He was too full. Even the air that rushed past seemed to push into his lungs, making him tight.

He'd long passed the point where he might have jumped off. That had come and gone in a few heartbeats, when he'd still been tangled in the reins. If it had existed at all, given the way those horses could run. Nero had not lied about them, he realised. They were no country mounts, fit for a noble son. These were true racers, hardly tame at all.

He hadn't appreciated how *high* charioteers stood. Britannicus swallowed his fear. He was looking down on the horses from the step, with clear air all around and nothing to brace himself against. He had to shift his weight constantly and he felt he might go flying off and break his neck at any moment. The speed itself was a danger, so that all his senses shrieked he was going to die.

A point came on the straight where he suddenly found his balance, where the reins seemed to fit his hands and he could stand and actually look ahead. It was an instant of wonder and he felt his breath catch. His legs began to tremble then, thigh muscles fluttering. He could feel the moment torn from him as sight and sound returned. All he could see were the plunging heads of the four greys, running at speeds to make the world blur. He dared not look at the ground. The wind made his eyes stream. Only when he squinted to the far end of the track could he see anything clear at all.

He swallowed, panic rising so that he sipped the air to breathe. The straight was one thing. As long as he could stand on a step no bigger than a dinner plate, with wheels ready to snatch his fingers or snap bones whirring alongside ... as long as he didn't tire, if he just balanced and didn't fall, he might live.

The corner was coming. Britannicus had never galloped a quadriga chariot before, never mind guided a racing team around the first of two ends. The Circus Maximus was a simple enough track – two long straights with two wide corners. Britannicus saw death in the shadows that surrounded it. In desperation, he leaned, heaving on the reins.

Nothing changed. The horses plunged in rhythm together, as if they would run right into the wall at the end and not make the corner at all. He looked in terror at ground rushing past. He would be killed if he jumped, he was certain. Even if he cleared the wheel and was not dragged along, the ground would break him. Why were these mad horses not slowing?

He heaved again, then dropped one rein and put all his effort and weight onto the other. The team responded slowly, the horses snorting almost in anger. The wall was coming! He could see the deeper darkness looming, with no more sight of track beyond. There was not enough room and though he shouted in fear and put all his strength into it, the horses were pulling against one another, panicking under a hand they did not know. Two of them pulled left, but the other two tried to drive on mindlessly.

The chariot tipped. Britannicus heard the noise change before he understood. One of the wheels lifted into the air and spun there. The horses felt the wrongness of it and shrieked. He would make it, he thought. With no one else on the track, he had the whole width to get round. He could do this. He would never again tell Nero it was an easy thing, but . . . no, if he survived, he would say exactly that. He could see his brother's face even then, before him, full of spite and jealousy that he had managed it.

Britannicus leaned hard from instinct, trying to bring the raised wheel back down. As he did so, one of the horses stumbled. It might have been the loose rein trodden under a hoof or the tightening angle as he tried to force the corner at full gallop. There was a moment almost of stillness as something caught and then the wheel bit and jammed – and the world went white.

The chariot slammed right over. One of the wheels shattered as it was suddenly made to stop. Britannicus hit the ground with the chariot crushing him. He did not see Nero running down the track, nor his friends. He didn't see the fear and worry in their faces as they loomed over him, asking questions.

The rooms and corridors around were very quiet, kept so by an emperor's rage. Across the entire Palatine complex, perhaps even the whole city, free citizens and slaves hurried to work or home with their heads down, fearing some nameless wrath or retribution. Vigiles watched, ready for violence to erupt, ready to respond with force if need be.

In the imperial precinct, praetorians guarded the door and a single figure had been laid out on clean sheets. Two women in black robes were dipping fresh cloths into bowls of water, cleaning the emperor's son. As Claudius entered once more, they rose and bowed, trooping out like crows.

The temples across Rome were closed to the citizens. Inside, priests and acolytes lit thousands of candles and prayed Britannicus would live. The god Asclepius was invoked for healing, along with his father Apollo. Their love of life and youth could be harnessed for the right cause. Down on the river Tiber, Christians gathered to baptise new converts. They too prayed the emperor's son would be saved, for fear of what might happen if he was not.

Two days had passed since the crash and Britannicus had not woken since that time. There was a lump like an egg on his temple, scabbed over, though it had leaked blood and water for an entire day. One of his eyes had turned completely red, but he did not blink when the priests snapped fingers close enough to touch the lashes. There was no response at all.

For all the incense and prayers said, there had been no change since he'd been laid out and washed clean of blood and filth. His arm had been set, but that was nothing compared to the silence in him.

As a legion man, the emperor's doctor knew how to splint a broken bone. In many ways, Britannicus had taken a battle wound. There was nothing Imperial Physician Albicius had not seen before in a wounded soldier. Even the fact that Britannicus sweated in beads, or the way his urine stank – it was all known.

The doctor had slapped his face and twisted a testicle, hoping to shock Britannicus awake. Nothing had changed and his expression had turned hopeless. Sometimes, men who had been hit that hard just faded away. They could not eat while they slept, so grew weak. The doctor's Greek servants wet the boy's lips and tried to dribble water down his throat, but he just choked without coming awake, his chest spasming. Britannicus was strong and very fit. He might last as long as a week if he did not wake. Beyond that, no one could say.

Claudius had spent the first morning being told there was nothing he could do, that all the powers at his command could not bring one boy out of a stupor. On the second day, his wife's auspex had come, appearing in a bustle of equipment and strange odours. When she had argued with his own physician, Claudius had nearly had the Gaulish woman dragged out and flogged for failing to show proper respect. Agrippina had stayed his hand, though it had not taken more than a sharp word, not really. In his desperation, she knew he would try anything.

Agrippina herself took Physician Albicius out to calm down. She rubbed one hand on his arm, soothing his dignity and nodding while he complained. In the room, Claudius stayed, wincing as Locusta burned ibis feathers with a smell like death and bad meat. The auspex had to reach into the days ahead, of course, using her gift to see whether death or life awaited. He understood that much. Claudius stood with a face like sour milk while the Gaul chanted in a trance, her hands scrabbling in a bowl of livers until the fingers were all brown with juice.

Locusta sat in that way for another hour, then read the patterns in the bowl. She pronounced herself satisfied then, even hopeful. Claudius felt helpless as the woman peered under his son's eyelids and pressed grimy fingers into armpit and groin, looking for swellings. At the same time, Locusta poured powders into shallow bowls and lit them, seeking the exact mix that would bring Britannicus back from wherever he had gone. It was as much art as knowledge, she explained. Words poured out of her like an incantation as she worked.

'I have seen this before, Majesty, in two men,' Locusta said at last. She sat hunched over, her energy entirely spent. 'One died and the other lived – the one I was allowed to treat. Your son wanders the banks of the Styx at this moment. He has no coin . . . and the boatman waits.'

Locusta held her hand over Britannicus' forehead. Her eyes widened as a frown appeared.

'There, Majesty! Did you see that? He is confused. If we put a coin in his hands now, I think he would feel it – and cross.'

She reached for a pouch on her belt and Claudius snapped out an arm, holding her tight.

'No! He must not cross. Bring him b-back – if you can. He is my t-true son.'

'Majesty, it is not his time, I swear it. I was only looking for a paste I have used before, a foul-tasting thing of myrrh and gall. It might help anchor him to our world.'

Claudius nodded and watched as the auspex used her bloodstained hands to push gritty brown muck under Britannicus' lips, rubbing more onto his tongue. The result could be seen in redness and swelling, wherever she had touched. Britannicus began to sweat and then cough. His hand twitched on the covers and Locusta seemed pleased. She leaned in and once again Claudius took her bony arm. The emperor could not quite explain the distaste he felt, but it surged in him.

'Imperator,' Locusta whispered. 'Let me try.'

Claudius let her go and the Gaul bent to hiss a flood of words into his son's ear, a horrible intimacy.

The eyes opened, suddenly and without warning. One was as red as polished agate, yet it blinked and turned. Locusta made a sound of joy, falling to her knees at the

Conn Iggulden

side of the bed. Claudius too cried out in shock, taking his son's hand.

'Thank the gods!' he breathed. 'Britannicus, can you understand me? Are you awake? Talk if you can, please.'

'What am I doing here? Where is this place?' Britannicus said weakly. His voice was hoarse and the auspex passed him a cup of liquid. It was not water and Britannicus eyed it suspiciously.

'She brought you b-back,' his father muttered. 'Drink it. You have slept for t-two days. I thought . . . It does not m-matter now. Drink.'

He guided the cup to his son's lips and watched as Britannicus swallowed. Confusion wrestled with pain in him.

'I remember the naumachia, the boats fighting . . . nothing more after that. Was I . . .'

Britannicus winced and tried to sit up. Locusta shoved cushions behind him. Outside, the word was already going out, two or three runners doing their duty. Agrippina would return soon, Claudius realised. Perhaps Nero as well.

For two days, he had put everything else aside. He had not spoken to his wife or her son, beyond getting a brief explanation from Nero about events at the track. His grief and fear for Britannicus had left no room for anything else. Claudius yawned, suddenly exhausted. He had not slept for two days, he was reasonably sure. Instead, he had stayed in that room, willing Britannicus to wake, bowing his head to prayers and doctors as they'd examined every inch of his son's battered body.

Britannicus winced as he struggled up. He yelped when he tried to lean on the broken arm, pulling back with a hiss of pain.

'It is splinted,' Claudius said. 'A clean b-break, I'm told.

You may have a f-few cracked ribs as well – and the b-bruising looks appalling. Your chest is p-purple and gold, lad, a very f-fetching colour.'

Britannicus nodded, though he still looked confused.

'It was a chariot,' Claudius said. 'Nero's t-team on the racetrack. He should n-never have let you take them out.'

'I . . . I don't remember,' Britannicus said, almost in wonder. 'Are you sure? I remember leaving the naumachia. Octavia was there . . . no, there is nothing after that.'

'Majesty, I have had some success with bringing mem-ories back,' Locusta said. 'On the edge of sleep, men can be made to remember things they have forgotten, at least in the hands of a skilled doctor.'

Perhaps she wanted to remind them of her triumph, Claudius thought. She had some crowing rights to that. Agrippina too would be pleased her favourite had brought Britannicus back to the world. The thought fed his anger, like a fire kept banked for too long.

'I think if the memories are bad . . . perhaps it's best to forget them,' Britannicus said slowly.

Claudius nodded.

'You must eat and d-drink, Britannicus, as much as you c-can,' he said. 'I will leave Locusta here to t-tend you.'

He turned his attention to the young Gaulish woman, rubbing one finger along his jaw.

'You have sh-*shown* your w-worth. I will appoint you . . . imperial physician to m-my family.'

'Majesty, what of the other man, who left so red-faced?' she asked.

Claudius thought of him and scowled.

'Albicius? He did n-nothing. You'll take his p-place.'

Locusta dropped and pressed her head to the emperor's

sandal, wiping her hair across it. Tears glittered in her eyes. Claudius pulled away and left her to her gratitude as he went out. He had waited long enough to see Agrippina and her son. Having Britannicus hover on the threshold between life and death had stolen his wits for a time. That was at an end.

Claudius felt his will return as he strode away to the private rooms. Like fire fed with coal, he grew stronger and more sure with every step. He was the furnace. He would make both mother and son feel all the fear he had known.

16

Agrippina turned as the doors opened. The emperor entered without slowing and for an instant, Claudius thought he saw nervousness in his wife. It pleased him.

He halted by his great table, still laid out with manuscripts and bound books, maps and ink and scrolls of papyrus. He stroked a pile with splayed fingers, touching items like talismans, finding reassurance in the scholar's clutter. His normal life lay there, exactly as he had left it.

Beyond that imperial desk, a window looked out on Rome from the height of the Palatine. The night was clear, with stars shining across the dark and not a cloud to be seen. The sun would rise again, but in that moment, the world was cold and very still.

That room was the heart of his administration, where Claudius worked all the hours he could steal from sleep. It was comfortable enough, with couches and rugs on a floor of polished stone. He did not have to glance to see the huge shallow brazier was lit. He could feel the warmth of it, already easing his bones.

Conn Iggulden

'You have news,' Agrippina said.

She feared he might say Britannicus was dead, that her son was responsible. The very possibility made fury rise like salt in his blood. Claudius felt a sort of bitterness spreading as he stood there. He weighed words in his mouth, readying them.

Despite his anger, Claudius' gaze flickered along the walls, taking in the slaves and praetorians in attendance. On a normal day, they were almost like furniture. If he needed something, they were simply there, appearing at his whim. He did not often notice their presence, not as he did then.

'Leave us, all of y-you,' Claudius said.

The praetorians met his gaze to be sure he spoke to them, then filed out in silence. A dozen slaves went with them, appearing from side doors and alcoves like mice. Claudius watched them close the doors. He was alone with his wife. When he looked up, he saw Agrippina was trembling.

'So, will you tell me?' she said.

Claudius nodded. He hated to speak. Words boiled like smoke, but when he tried to say them, they stuck to his lips. He wanted to tear them from his mouth and throw them at her, but he could not. Even his son's name was a trial.

'B-Brit . . . tannicus has w-woken,' he said. 'Your d-doctor, your au . . . au . . . the *auspex* brought him b-back.'

Agrippina reacted as if she was about to faint. He saw her sag and yet he did not move to hold her. She looked at him in confusion.

'Why are you so angry, Claudius? Isn't that wonderful news? If my auspex helped, why do you look at me like that?'

'T-two days, Agrip-pina! T-two d-days while I wondered if my s-son would live. Or if . . . N-Nero had k-killed him.'

Agrippina rounded on him then, bristling in defence of her son.

'You are exhausted, husband, or you've gone mad. You know very well that is not what happened. You forget, I was there when you questioned them! I too spoke to Otho and Serenus, as well as Nero! While you watched over Britannicus, I brought them all in, over and over. Even that Greek girl with Serenus. They all said it was an accident.' She realised he was withdrawing from her anger. That was not what she wanted and she took a step closer, gentling her voice. She reached to touch his arm. 'What good is it now to torment yourself, Claudius? Rejoice instead that Britannicus lives! It is all that matters.'

'No,' he said clearly, pleased the word had come out whole. 'I've h-had t-two days to think, Agrippina. To s-see I have ind-dulged you . . . and your s-son. Th-this is the r-result of my . . . *my w-weakness*!'

He shouted the final words to force them out. Agrippina paled.

'*Our* son,' she said quickly. 'You always call Nero mine when you are angry with him, but he *is* ours, by adoption – and tradition! And he is becoming a fine young man, you have said so yourself, many times. You shouldn't take this so much to heart, Claudius . . .'

She would have continued, but he raised his hand sharply, his colour deepening. In that too, she could in-furiate him. He had to choose and prepare his words. If she wanted, she could rattle on and on and never let him speak.

Conn Iggulden

'You w-wanted men to call you empress. I d-didn't m-mind. You wanted the t-title of "Augusta" and I s-said v-very w-well.'

'Claudius, please . . .' she interrupted.

He continued over her, louder.

'You w-wanted your f-*face* on coins, alongside mine. I l-let you stamp them in gold and m-meet a common tax g-gatherer in these r-rooms. I adopted your s-son and g-gave him my n-name, Agrippina. I d-did all . . . th-that, for y-you.'

'Have I not shown my gratitude, husband? Is that the source of this anger towards me, to your wife who has done you no wrong? Should I kneel like a slave when my magnificent husband comes into the room, or sing praises whenever you address me? I am your *wife*, Claudius, so I *am* empress. I am of the line of Augustus, so I have the right to that name. You mention coins to me? Coins that have your face before my own? As for Nero, my son is *our* son – and he took part of his name to honour you. Nero "Claudius" Caesar, remember? Tell me, where were you wronged in this? Where have I overreached or done anything but honour you in all ways?'

Even in her indignation, by the gods, she was arresting, a nymph brought to life. Claudius could see the perfection of her even as he remembered how still his son had been just a little while before. He had prepared himself to lose the boy – and that coldness sustained him.

'No,' he said again, delighting in the word. 'You will not twist this to s-suit you. I made N-N . . .'

'Nero, your son!' she snapped.

'*Yes, Nero!*' he roared, stunning her. 'I m-made him my heir. Y-you said he w-would be a sh . . . shield to

B-Britani-c-cus . . .' His eyes dared her to interrupt again. Agrippina glared at him, but didn't speak as he struggled. 'Th-that . . . th-that was a lie! That sh-shield almost got him k-killed. Well, I w-withdraw it. He w-will not b-be heir, not any m-more. Brit . . . B-Brit . . .'

Agrippina's eyes narrowed.

'Nero is older than Britannicus,' she said over him, her voice hoarse. 'And he is a married man. If you had never made him heir, that would be one thing. Claudius? If you take it from him now, it will be a blow struck. You will hurt our son: in the eyes of the city, in the senate, with his friends. He may never forgive you, do you understand? You will do more damage than you know.'

Claudius set his jaw, choosing the words he would speak, willing them to come out as if drawn on a single thread of silk. She had interrupted him again, showing the impatience he hated above all things. He drew himself up, summoning the dignity of an emperor.

'I g-gave you the b-betrothal you wanted for him, to Octavia. H-he will always b-be a son of this house. B-but he is too w-wild! Too . . . full of sp-spite. Brit-tanicus is my heir. There, it is decided. I w-will let the senate know my d-decision.'

She could only stand as he walked quickly around the desk, almost as if he sought to get away from her. Agrippina watched as Claudius sat at his favourite chair. No slave was present to mix his ink or set out a fresh vellum page. He grunted in irritation, though the habits were old. His hands fell to the inkstone. He held it in one palm and saw the little jug was dry. With a grimace, he spat on the surface, sweeping a scraper back and forth until there was a paste. Two of his fingertips had blackened in the process. He peered at them in irritation, all the while ignoring his wife. Agrippina stood there radiating fury.

'Your will is law,' she said.

Claudius looked up, almost flinching as she came close and rested one hip on the table's edge. She took his ink-stained hand in hers.

'I know it! You are the emperor, Claudius, paterfamilias to nations. It is your right to choose any heir you want, of course. Do you think I haven't spent the last two days in terror? That I didn't fear what you would do if Britannicus died?'

Tears appeared in her eyes, spilling down her cheeks. She rubbed at them, smearing the kohl. Claudius almost rose to embrace her, but resisted the urge. Slowly, with force, he took back his hand. It was like waking from a dream, he realised. For the first time in an age, he truly saw her.

Agrippina frowned, unsure of herself. Claudius usually hated to see her weep, would do anything to reassure her when tears flowed. They were just one of her arrows, where a man might have swung a mere fist to less effect.

'Britannicus lives, Claudius,' she whispered. 'It was a terrible accident and he was hurt, but that is the end of it. He lives. You know Nero isn't responsible! Britannicus took the reins from him, they have all confirmed that. What he was thinking I don't know.'

'He doesn't remember the c-crash,' Claudius muttered.

Agrippina nodded, hiding her relief.

'That doesn't matter now! Britannicus will heal and grow strong once again. Seneca says his arm has been well set. What are a few bruises? He will have a story to tell, that is all. Of galloping a team down the racetrack under moonlight.'

'If he had d-died . . .' Claudius closed his eyes for a moment. The fear and pain was too recent, still cruel in him. 'N-Nero would be emperor after m-me. Th-that was what I understood. Y-you said he w-would be a sh-shield and I wanted to p-please you, but the t-truth . . . When I s-saw it, with B-Britann . . . icus so still and p-pale, I knew it was not what I w-wanted. I vowed, Agrippina, to the gods. If Bri . . . t-tannicus lived, I w-would m-make him heir once m-more.'

Something like tension flowed out of Agrippina then. She understood he would not be moved. Gently, she reached down and kissed him on his forehead.

'You must, then. I understand,' she breathed. 'If it is already sworn, if it truly means so much to you, I will not say another word. You are my husband, Claudius. Your will is mine.'

He nodded, pleased to have won an argument for once. His hand trembled as he reached for a reed pen and examined the edge. A tiny blade lay alongside it, though there was no slave to sharpen the tip. Claudius busied himself, feeling worry vanish in the old routines. He had been an author and scholar in the reign of Caligula, after all. These were his tools.

Agrippina watched him for a little while, then swept from the room. He breathed more deeply in her absence, feeling a weight lift. He had been blind, for too long.

There was a Christian preaching in Rome, a Roman citizen. Claudius had set spies to listen and report on him. Rome had always attracted such characters, of course. That was to be expected, in the heart of the world. Yet

Conn Iggulden

Claudius remembered one thing he had said. This Paul talked of scales falling from his eyes on the road to Damascus. For him, it had been some twist of faith that led him to give up his persecution of others. For Claudius, it was the closeness of death, the prospect of having Nero rule in Rome after him.

He smiled as he wrote orders for the senate and consuls. One by one, the folded sheets piled up at his elbow, ovals sealed in ink and wax. Claudius paused only to suck the end of the reed, tasting its bitterness. He would have a black mark on his lips, he realised. An old, old taste for him. Yet it was right. He had been blind; now he could see.

Agrippina walked quickly through the corridors of the Palatine. She knew where she was going, though not exactly what she would do. She remembered something her brother had said, before madness consumed him. Some people thought the Greek word 'crisis' meant a disaster, a catastrophe. It didn't, Caligula had whispered in the small hours. It meant a choice. It was still dark outside as she passed open windows and gardens. Half the city was asleep, while she remained awake like the Sphinx, unable to rest. If she had her way, the sun would not rise. This was the night. This was the crisis.

Praetorians stood to attention as she reached the room where Britannicus had lain for two days. She went through the door they held open, entering a suite that still smelled of illness. On into the private room and there was Britannicus, sitting up, pale as candle wax, his hair unbound. Her auspex stood at his side, bathing him from a bowl so that his skin shone wet.

Agrippina stopped as Britannicus looked up at her,

surprised at the strength of her relief. She had made her-self cold to deal with Claudius, but to see Britannicus awake stole fear. She felt her knees buckle slightly, as if her strength failed.

'Thank the gods,' she said, crossing to him and taking his hand. It was warm under hers. 'You're so pale, Britan-nicus. We were all worried for you, more than you know.'

There were dark circles under his eyes and one of them was filled with blood still. He looked exhausted, but he managed to smile.

'Locusta here is looking after me,' he said, his voice hoarse. 'I have her to thank for my recovery, so my father said.'

'It was Locusta I came to see.'

The Gaul bowed at her name and Agrippina nodded.

'You should rest now, Britannicus,' she said. 'The sun will be up in a few hours – you should try to sleep. Would you like me to leave a lamp burning?'

'Yes, please,' he murmured. She bent to kiss him on the cheek and felt again a wave of relief. He really was her son, wound through her affections like a curling vine. It had happened without her even noticing.

'Good boy,' she said.

She rested her palm on his forehead for a moment, until he closed his eyes. Agrippina rose, taking the auspex by the arm and walking her out of the room. In silence, Agrip-pina closed the door behind them.

The outer chambers were empty. For once she had a spot where no one listened to report to her husband. It was just a reality of her life that she expected to be over-heard, wherever she was. This night was different. She spent a moment to check the room. The outer door had praetorians on guard. She knew she would hear them stand to attention if her husband returned. For once, she and Locusta were truly alone.

She took the Gaul by the hand and moved her to the window, looking out on darkness. Agrippina had chosen this woman, had raised her and bound her to service. Locusta was hers, but what Agrippina would ask . . . would put a life in her hands. She hesitated and Locusta frowned, worried by her elaborate care. Agrippina's hands trembled on hers and she could feel it.

'Locusta,' she began, her voice a whisper. 'Tonight . . .' By the gods, she was getting as bad as Claudius with her stumbling! 'Tonight, the emperor will eat a final meal. I will prepare the food – your hands will not be part of it, I promise. I just need foxglove powder from your bag. It must be potent. I don't have anything like that in reach, not in the next hour. Do you understand?'

The Gaulish woman nodded, mute, her eyes very wide.

'My husband is an old man, Locusta – and all reigns end. My son will be emperor tomorrow morning, if I act tonight. Ask me anything, dearest Locusta, in return for your trust and your silence.'

In the stillness, Agrippina thought she could hear her own heart beating.

'Foxglove is too fast,' Locusta whispered suddenly. 'Belladonna is better. You'll want him to take ill and fade over a few days.'

Agrippina closed her eyes, feeling tension flow away. The auspex had thrown in with her. Women like Locusta had always walked with death. They used poison on babies mothers did not want, rubbing gums with a finger, sending them back. Some of them visited the very old and gave them peace. It was a vital part of their trade, and yet Agrippina had been afraid she would refuse. She felt dizzy with relief.

'Fast is best tonight,' she said. 'There are matters I do not want to reach the light. This has to be settled before the sun rises. Do you have what I need?'

Locusta reached into the bag she carried over her shoulder, long fingers searching through tiny folds and packets. She grew suddenly still then, looking up.

'I want a palace, with slaves . . . and an income, for life.'

Agrippina raised an eyebrow, but the woman was emboldened, going on in a rush. 'And I would like to be the official physician to the imperial family. Your husband promised me that much already. I would like it honoured.'

'Very well. You have my word,' Agrippina said, holding out her hand.

It was Locusta's turn to tremble as she handed over a tiny bag. The empress looked inside and was satisfied. Foxglove flowers were pretty, speckled things when they grew in a garden. Dried and ground, they were as deadly as aconite.

'Thank you,' she said. 'Will you be staying here, to watch over my son?'

'Unless you need me, yes,' Locusta said, bowing her head.

The Gaul was still awed at what they had discussed. Agrippina was already looking ahead. She touched the woman on her arm and saw her awareness.

'Be ready. I will call for you when the emperor falls ill,' she said. 'If you try to save him . . . and fail, you will have your palace.'

'And the title,' Locusta whispered. 'And the slaves.'

Agrippina smiled.

'All of it. Now, I must go. Remain here, Locusta. Do nothing until I send for you.'

Claudius stood before the great brazier when she entered the room. Agrippina bore a tray with a steaming drink and a collection of cold meats and bread. He realised he was hungry, that grief and fear for his son had made him ravenous.

'You always th-think of me,' he said.

He saw the marks of crying were still on her. He had poured out all his rage into the orders he had written. He felt quite empty and winced at the sight of Agrippina downcast. She laid the little tray on his desk and he came back, feeling the air cool as he left the brazier.

'I'm . . . s-sorry about what I s-said before. My a-anger.'

She nodded and he wondered how he had ever seen her as an enemy. She looked so small, so abashed.

Claudius sipped the drink and smiled at how much honey she had put in. Almost too much, though that was a message in itself. She knew he liked sweetness and was trying to make amends between them. Hunger made his stomach growl and he chuckled. The pork flavoured with rosemary was also a favourite. She had to have raided the kitchens for things he liked the most. He ate a few of the slices, chewing.

An ache began in his chest. He didn't notice it at first, not really. Claudius suffered at times with a gripe of his gut. Cow's milk eased him then. He rubbed a spot with one thumb as he continued to eat, a point between his ribs that had begun to pain him. He held a hand to his fore-head and felt sweat there. Claudius tutted to himself.

'I always know w-when I haven't h-had enough s-sleep.

It's the . . . s-sweat! Honestly, I don't th-think I have slept for t-two days, I was so worried about Britannicus.' His son's name came out as one word and he smiled, pleased.

Without warning, the ache swelled into a great pulse. All his muscles grew tight and he staggered.

'What is it?' Agrippina said. 'What's wrong?'

Claudius vomited, suddenly and violently. Yellow bile and scraps of meat spattered onto the carpet. He gestured for the hot drink and she handed it over.

'Let me call Locusta,' she said. 'You are ill. You have pushed yourself too hard in your grief.'

She was already heading to the door. Claudius shook his head.

'Fetch my own physician. Albicius knows me best.'

His eyes were already clearing, she realised in horror. Claudius was gulping air and rubbing his chest, but he had vomited most of the poison on the rug. He was not a fool, she realised. If he lived, if he understood what she had done, he would tear her apart.

She put her head out of the door, addressing the prae-torians there.

'The emperor has fallen ill,' she said. 'Fetch the auspex, Locusta. She is still with Britannicus. Run!'

The sound of footsteps clattered through the open door as she turned back to Claudius. She helped him to a chair. His lips were a little blue, but he was breathing deeply, frowning to himself. He rubbed the same point on his chest. She took the cup of sweetened wine and held it to his lips. The honey hid the bitterness well enough.

'Drink, my love,' she urged him. 'The doctor is coming.'

Conn Iggulden

17

Locusta entered with her bag on her shoulder. She looked about as pale and sweaty as the emperor. Her eyes darted to Claudius and then Agrippina, over and over. Her mouth worked as if in prayer.

Agrippina grabbed her by the arm. She gripped flesh as hard as she could, wanting to squeeze calm into the woman. Locusta didn't seem to feel it and only gaped at the emperor.

Two praetorians entered with her and Agrippina felt their scrutiny fray her temper further.

'Fetch Prefect Burrus,' she snapped at one of them. 'You! Guard the outer door against any other.'

The second man hesitated, shifting his weight. His entire purpose was to guard the life of the emperor, and now the man was blowing and choking and he was helpless.

'Well? There is nothing you can do here!' Agrippina said, her voice tight and cold. 'Close that door! Do you think my husband wants the whole world watching?'

It was a delicate balance, but she heard the soldier leave.

'He vomited,' she told Locusta. 'I think it is a spasm. I gave him honey in wine to drink.'

The woman nodded, understanding all. Before she could reply, Claudius opened his eyes very wide.

'Oh gods . . . I need a pot,' he said.

With a heave and a terrible groan, he rose from his seat and staggered into the private room beyond. Locusta went with him, but Claudius raised a hand in Agrippina's face, preventing her from coming in. Even then, some rag of his authority remained.

Agrippina was suddenly alone, walking back and forth, hands opening and closing. She heard her husband emptying his bowels, the sounds appalling. She could hear Claudius cursing and it did not sound like the cries and groans of a dying man. She thought her own heart would stop then. If Claudius somehow purged the poison from his body, if he lived . . . everything she had made would be ashes. She remembered her brother Caligula and shuddered. Claudius had witnessed that reign of horrors, just as she had. He would make it his inspiration.

'I need help in here,' Locusta called from the inner room.

Agrippina didn't hesitate a second time. She went in.

The room was gloomy and filled with a thick stench that made her want to gag. Her husband lay on his side on the little bed he kept there, paler and weaker than before, but still clearly alive. She dared not peer into the pot that held his emptyings. What lay within was black and foul, the very essence of death.

'What can I do?' Agrippina said desperately. Burrus would be coming at the run. Yet her husband lived! Claudius still lived!

254   *Conn Iggulden*

'The emperor must try to empty his stomach once more,' Locusta said. 'He may be too weak, but I have a feather to put down his throat that will help.'

She rose then, so that she stood between Agrippina and her husband. The empress looked down and saw Locusta held out an empty hand.

She still had the little bag. Most of the powder had gone into the honey drink, but there was still some left. She took it from a pouch in her dress and Locusta nodded grimly.

Claudius groaned on the bed, opening his eyes.

'Please help him,' Agrippina said loudly. 'Do whatever you have to.'

Locusta nodded. She watched the woman pour the last of the foxglove powder into her open palm. Locusta drew a long white feather from some hidden sleeve and ran it through the powder, coating the vanes.

'Empress, I cannot give you orders, but if you could fetch another pot, I will help your husband empty himself further.'

Agrippina went out. She could hear running steps, she realised, the rattle of legionary boots on marble. There was nothing like a chamber pot in the outer room and she didn't know if Locusta had truly meant the request or just wanted her safely outside. Her gaze swept across Claudius' desk and suddenly snagged.

A pile of folded documents rested there, all sealed by her husband, waiting for the morning. In one swift move, Agrippina grabbed them up and crossed to the great brazier, dropping them onto the coals.

A flare of yellow flame sprang up as Burrus came in. The imperial physician was with him, clutching a bag with his hair wild. It was clear he had been dragged from his bed and was still unsure what was going on.

The praetorian took in her tear-stained face and dropped to one knee.

'Empress, I came as soon as I heard. Does the emperor still live?'

Agrippina touched tears in each eye, nodding.

'Claudius has been taken ill,' she said. 'Locusta is with him. He has . . . emptied his bowels and vomited. It may yet be a passing thing. I pray it is.'

The prefect of the praetorians looked as if he'd been on parade when the call came, as neatly turned out as ever. She saw Burrus watching her, judging every word and turn of her head. He was not a fool, but he had no reason to suspect.

'I should go in,' the physician said.

She nodded, suddenly close to tears once more, so that she touched the back of one hand to her lips.

She looked back at the brazier as Burrus and the doctor went into her husband's private room. Ashes lay there, the lettering all gone. The cup of honeyed wine still rested on her husband's desk and she swept that up as well, throwing the contents in so that the stones sizzled. She put it back then, turning sharply as Burrus entered once more.

Slowly, he dropped to one knee.

'The emperor has . . . He is dead,' he said, his voice choked. 'I'm sorry. The . . . lady with him says it was a spasm of the heart, after too long without sleep. Physician Albicius is examining him now.'

He rose, seeing how she trembled still, like an aspen leaf. Agrippina shook her head and raised a hand, as if she could hold back the full truth of it.

Conn Iggulden

'No,' she whispered. 'No, it can't be. I must see him.' She saw Burrus might prevent her from entering the private room. Men had some odd ideas about dignity, sometimes. She made her voice harder. 'I *will* see my husband, Prefect Burrus. Stand out of my way.'

He bowed his head to a direct order and stood back.

Agrippina entered to find a very different room from before. Someone had removed the noisome pot. The room smelled a little better. More, Locusta or Claudius' own doctor had laid the emperor out on his bed, pulling blankets up to his chest. Discarded sheets lay crumpled in a corner and a water jug had been spilled in patches on one of the rugs, but apart from that, it was a peaceful scene. Life was hard to wrench away, Agrippina thought. Yet once it was gone, there was only stillness.

She sat on the edge of the bed, looking down on her husband. Claudius looked so peaceful she felt a twinge of panic he might open his eyes. Gently, very gently, she reached out and brushed his hair from his temple. His skin had a fine tracery of wrinkles, she saw, like very good cloth.

The physician hovered at her elbow.

'The emperor went without much pain,' he said.

He was lying, of course, but perhaps he wanted her to believe it. Agrippina raised her eyes to heaven. She had seen men die before. It was a time for reflection, to recall the good memories. She thought sometimes it was when she really loved them, perhaps the only time she did.

Locusta was packing up her bag. Agrippina crossed to her and drew her into an embrace.

'Give me the feather,' she whispered.

She held out her hand and saw the younger woman hesitate. It was why she had asked for it, of course. With all the letters burned and the drink made into steam, there was no other proof of what they had done. Agrippina accepted the damp feather with a grimace, sliding it into a sleeve. Only then did she relax.

'Prefect Burrus!' she called.

The man turned from the emperor's bedside, still looking stunned. She wondered if he feared some punishment. Perhaps the head of the praetorians expected to be dismissed on such a night, she didn't know. Tradition could be a very powerful thing, once it had men in its grip. She was lucky not to feel the tug of it.

'Burrus, my son is heir – and emperor from this moment. Have him woken and brought to me. There will be unrest in the morning, when people hear poor Claudius is dead. I remember when my brother was killed. There were riots then, violence and murder and fires in the streets. Rouse the praetorians you command, Burrus. Have them on duty at every corner, with the vigiles. I will not allow disorder in my husband's name.' She paused in thought, pacing back and forth. 'Pass word to the heralds and have them come to me for the announcement.' She glanced at the night still visible outside. 'I'll have something to read out in a little while.'

Agrippina saw Locusta was standing with her mouth open. The Gaul was still stunned by all that had happened, and presumably the part she had played in it. She had been a fine conspirator while her hands were busy, but clearly needed more to do. Agrippina could see it eating at the woman, fear slowly uncoiling.

'Locusta!' she said sharply.

The Gaul startled, looking at her like a beaten hound.

'I need to know the right hour to announce my son as

emperor. Cast your bones. Have the staff bring you what-ever you need, do you understand? There is a moment in the day to come when the gods will look most kindly on our great enterprise, when they will sing of grief and passing – but also rebirth. Find me that moment.'

The truth of her words was dawning on her as well, even as she spoke them aloud. Claudius was dead. His vast shadow no longer fell on her. Even as she looked on him, she saw how reduced he was. Where was all his strength, the threat and snap and anger of him? It had all gone. She was alone, but it seemed a glorious isolation.

Burrus was still there, hesitating. Had the man lost his wits?

'What is it?' she said curtly.

'Empress . . . which son do you mean?' he said.

Agrippina blinked in surprise.

'My husband's heir,' she said. 'Nero Claudius Caesar. Wake him gently, Burrus. He sleeps only lightly at the best of times. Nero has been consumed with worry for his younger brother. He will fear the worst – and this news will wound him deeply. He adored my husband, as you know.'

Burrus dropped to one knee again before he left. Others were entering that sacred space, Agrippina realised. The moment of stillness had come and gone. Her husband's slaves were weeping, of course, telling the gods a great man had passed. The news would be going out like spar-rows across the Palatine, across the city and the world. Twenty-eight legions would have to be told, kings and satraps and governors of Judaea and Egypt would learn an emperor had fallen. She imagined it as ripples, all spread-ing from that single room.

'Wake the senate,' she ordered, sending servants running out as fast as they came in. 'They will want to come to the Palatine, to pay their respects. Summon the consuls to this bedside, that they may pray for a noble soul. As Jupiter is my witness, the glass is broken; my husband is gone.'

No one dared question her orders. Her husband's staff moved smoothly into routines they had planned and prepared. They could have handled the death of a foreign king or an outbreak of plague with equal aplomb. Agrippina watched, weeping softly to herself as senior men and women of the imperial staff entered those chambers and took command. What had been private became slowly public; chaos was pushed back. The crumpled sheets vanished, the shutters were pinned open, ready for dawn. Even Agrippina had to leave the room for a time while women came in to clean and prepare the emperor's body.

By the time she returned, the air was sweet with perfume and someone had brushed her husband's hair. Claudius had been laid out, slightly raised on cushions, looking at peace. The mortician stood nearby with bowed head. He had glued the emperor's mouth shut, she noticed. She had seen that before, to stop the jaw sagging open. She could see a silvery line of gum between his lips as it dried.

The sun was rising, at last. Agrippina could only stand and stare as light returned to those rooms. There had been times when she'd thought she would never see it again, that her actions had doomed her to eternal night. She shook her head, ridding herself of childish fears. She could hear her son's voice. Not yet seventeen, Nero would need his mother.

'There he is. He comes. Let him in,' Agrippina called to the soldiers on the door. 'Let my son in.'

Unlike Burrus, Nero looked as if he'd been dragged from sleep. His hair was wild and damp, so that he tried to slick it down as he entered, running his fingers through thick locks. The sense of noise and bustle was growing every moment. The Palatine had a staff of thousands and they were drawn to that place as word flew beyond. All over Rome, the households of senators were being woken. Horses were riding out of the imperial stables, heralds bearing the grim news.

Through the crowd, Nero strode in. Agrippina had not been sure how he would react to the news. He could be mulish or aggressive when he was crossed, she knew. In that, he was his first father's son, more than any child of Claudius. As he entered, she could almost see the shadow of Gnaeus Ahenobarbus in the way he swung his arms.

Burrus stood with him, his face somehow darker, as if he held his breath. Nero looked from one to the other, trying to judge the mood to take. Agrippina grasped his hand.

'Your father is dead, Nero. I'm so sorry. He was not a young man and he has not been sleeping well for months. It was swift, I can tell you that. He was talking and laughing and then . . . there was a great spasm. He's gone.'

Nero only stared at his mother. He had never liked Claudius, though she supposed he had some grudging respect for him. Claudius was simply not the sort of man Nero admired and he had never really taken to his stepfather, despite all her efforts to bring them close.

'I'm sorry,' he said at last. 'You must be . . . torn apart.

He was old though, mother. What was it, sixty-four? Sixty-five? That is a good life, especially for one of our family.'

She saw he would not be shedding tears and wanted to hit him. Senators were already entering the room, waiting to show their respects. They would see Nero's coldness and perhaps some of them would wonder at it. She buried her head in both hands then, sobbing.

Nero came forward, unsure of himself, but drawn by instinct to give comfort to his weeping mother. She rested her head on his shoulder. He had grown, she realised, in strength and height. She was glad of it. Still sixteen for another couple of months! He may have been a married man and heir to the empire, but he would need her counsel.

'You are the heir, Nero,' she said. 'I have set Locusta to finding the right hour to announce it, after sunrise. The empire cannot be left without a hand, not even for a day. Do you understand? You are emperor, from the moment of your father's death.'

'Not Britannicus?' he said. He took a step away from his mother to look at her, his eyes searching.

'Claudius made *you* the heir, Nero. You are the oldest and he loved you. It was his will that you inherit the empire, that is all that matters now.'

She thought for a moment before going on.

'You are overwhelmed, I understand. Yet I know the traditions, the names of the senators and consuls. I have been at your father's side for years. We ruled together, Nero, at times! As I did for him, I will be there to guide you, I swear it. I retain all my titles, by blood and marriage, after all. You will *never* be left alone, I promise. I will be

Conn Iggulden

there, at your right hand. If there is chaos at first, we will face it together.'

She reached to embrace him again, but he turned slightly, looking to the room beyond, where Claudius still lay.

'I should go in,' he said.

He was reluctant and she took his hand. For once, he let her. There had been years when she'd thought him the most stubborn, bull-headed young man in Rome, but he let her lead him to the body of Claudius.

The crowd parted before them. One of the consuls had arrived and he stood back to let the dowager empress and her son pay their respects. Agrippina felt the crackle of the feather in her sleeve and hoped it would not scratch her skin. Perspiration broke out on her brow at the thought and she dabbed at her face with a square of silk.

Nero knelt by the little bed, his head bowed. Agrippina felt the gaze of dozens on her from the other room and so did the same. She led her son in prayers to Jupiter and Apollo, to the souls of their family gone before – to her father Germanicus and the emperors Caligula, Tiberius and Augustus. They would see the soul was not lost, that Claudius found his way to Elysium. In the end, though her throat choked almost closed, she prayed to Claudius him-self. She thanked him for the honour he had given, and the trust he had placed in her – to see Nero was a good emperor.

'You're sure?' her son whispered.

Agrippina could hear Octavia outside, the young wom-an's voice unmistakable amidst the public grief. They would all come, like flies to honey, she realised. Yet her son was the only one that mattered. The reality of it soared in her. Nero would be emperor! She hugged herself, making her dress crackle and shift.

'It is what Claudius wanted. I will never leave your side, Nero. Fear nothing while I am with you.'

He nodded and for once he seemed like the little boy she had known, without guile or anger. On impulse, she bent to kiss Claudius on his lips. She could smell the spirit gum that held them closed. She would never hear his stammer again. It was hard not to smile at that, though tears shone in her eyes.

'Thank you, Claudius,' she said. 'I promise you . . . he will be a great emperor, because I will be there to guide him.'

At noon, on the fourteenth day of October, the doors to the imperial complex were thrown open. A huge crowd had gathered as news spread, coming in their thousands to witness a young man of the Augustan line declared emperor.

Nero came out, flanked by Prefect Burrus of the praetorians and the dowager empress. His wife Octavia stood one pace behind, her arm entwined with one of the senior Greek freedmen who formed the backbone of the imperial staff. Octavia was made small by shock and loss, still visibly weeping for her father. Fresh from grief, they all wore dark cloaks and did not smile as the crowd chanted prayers for the dead.

Otho and Serenus had been summoned, standing on either side of Seneca. Their tutor had put on a fresh white toga for the occasion, spending a few coins of the vast fortune his work had brought him. Nero's friends stood in a sort of stunned wonder, still unable to comprehend the change in all their fortunes. Being the official heir was a

Conn Iggulden

title that could always be removed. After the crash at the track, they'd half-expected the sky to fall on them in some form or other. Yet Nero had moved beyond all that in a single night. He was emperor – and if the senate and the praetorians had yet to confirm their support, the citizens clearly felt no reluctance.

Agrippina read their mood well enough. She ushered her son forward with his wife, raising their arms with hers. The crowd cheered the three of them until the priest of Jupiter called for formal prayers. They stood then, heads bowed for the passing of an emperor.

'Even great lamps burn low,' the priest said. 'A man who stands across the world is still a man, for all his power and his glory. Yet Emperor Claudius was no ordinary dust, not as we are dust. He was of the line of Gaius Julius Caesar, made divine; of Augustus Caesar, made divine. As chief priest of the temple of Jupiter, I will seek the counsel of the gods to confirm what some of us surely know already. Claudius was no mere man, but immortal, wise: divine.'

The crowd had swelled to fill every street in that part of the city, swirling and flowing like wine. They roared approval at the priest's words and Nero could only blink in confusion to his mother. He was out of his depth and completely overwhelmed. Divine, as in a god? The fussy little man who had stammered and walked with a limp? It was true that neither Tiberius nor Caligula had been granted the honour. No one who had known either man would have dared to mock the pantheon in such a way. Still, were the gods so flawed and petty they would grant one like Claudius entrance?

'Bow your head,' his mother hissed to him.

He and Octavia both did so, though Nero did not see

why he couldn't look over the city. Burrus was watching and Seneca too had come. Nero felt their gaze on him, their expectation. He clenched his jaw. They all looked to him in a sort of awe, as if they saw the future. Well, he would not let them down.

Horses and carriages appeared, marched into place by praetorians in black cloaks. Nero looked to Burrus, raising his eyebrows.

'You must visit the barracks,' Burrus said, 'to be acclaimed by your legion. After that, it will not matter what the senate say.'

'The senate won't dare say a word,' Agrippina said. 'Nero is emperor. I stand with him as second. That is all that matters.'

'Second?' Nero said lightly. He was still watching the carriages, ready for Burrus to signal the moment to go down to them.

'As Claudius' wife and your mother, of course,' Agrippina said, a little sharply.

He inclined his head in reply, accepting it.

'Where is Britannicus?' Nero said suddenly. 'I'd like him to see . . . all this.'

'He is still too weak,' Agrippina said. She felt her mouth tighten at the thought and tried to smile. The result was not pleasant. 'He grieves, Nero, for his poor father, as do we all.'

'Of course,' Nero said. 'Of course. I'll go and see him this evening.' He turned back to the crowd and smiled as he waved to them. The sun was high, the sky a cloudless blue. Winter lay ahead, but it felt like summer that day. 'Lead on then, Burrus. I would like to hear my praetorians take an oath of loyalty to me. That would be a fine thing.'

Conn Iggulden

He paused for a moment, his brow furrowing. He was very aware of all the eyes on him, watching and judging.

'I could tell them to come to me, could I not, Burrus? If they are to take an oath of loyalty?'

'You could,' Burrus said.

His voice was utterly colourless and Nero heard the message and understood.

'But I will go to them, to show humility before the gods.'

Burrus bowed his head, hiding his smile of approval.

PART THREE

AD 55

18

Everything had changed: in a month, in a single hour. Nero looked across the heads of the senate as he stood before them. Those white-haired old men did not shift in their seats or whisper behind hands, not then. It was as if he had put on a strange new cloak, some symbol that changed him subtly and permanently in their eyes. Their eyes! He felt them watching now, wherever he went. He could not visit the baths or the track, or watch gladiators train, not without half the city peering at him. He had been unknown once, and therefore private, but now . . . By the gods, his people were a curious breed. It seemed they tried to fix his image in their minds, as if Nero were a painting they might never see again.

He cleared his throat, feeling sweat trickle down his ribs under the toga. He would need to bathe again, after. His mother had told him to count to two in his head whenever he came to a natural pause. She said it would seem like eternity, but when the heart raced, his sense of time would alter. He could not help glancing to where the awning still obscured the side door. He saw air flapping the panels there, as if it took a breath. Was she present, listening to her son? He thought it likely.

'It is my intention, senators, as I stand here before you, to establish forms of rule closer to those of Augustus than Tiberius, or even my beloved father, Claudius. The authority of this senate has been weakened over the last century. Power has been collected instead on the Palatine, and in the emperor's hands.'

One . . . two.

'I give you my oath, I will respect the consuls and august members of this house, involving them in the exercise of government. More, I pledge an end to trials held in secret. Justice has to be seen to be known.'

He touched a finger to his lips and counted in his head once more. It was rather dry stuff, he realised. Seneca had written it, of course. Nero had seen the tutor biting a thumbnail as he forged those very lines, pacing up and down in lamplight night after night. Yet his insight was something Nero had come to respect. The man knew everything, just about.

He looked up again. The senators seemed pleased at what they were hearing – and he wanted to honour Seneca. The man was not a father to him! He scorned the very idea. Perhaps, though . . . with Burrus to train them, with his friends Otho and Serenus, perhaps he had a group he could trust. He did not know if that was what a father was. He could not remember one, not really.

He'd paused too long. More sweat trickled as he looked down at the parchment, at Seneca's neat printed letters. Had he missed a line? The page swam before him for a moment. No, he found his place.

Conn Iggulden

'I pledge a life of service and honour. To the gods, to the consuls and the senate, to the people. Whether my years be long or short, I will seek wisdom and learn the humility of power. My ancestor Augustus said he found Rome in clay – and left her in marble. He was granted a rule of forty years. If I am given even a quarter of that time, I will devote my life to this city and her influence. Before the gods, I give you that oath, as you have given oath to me. Thank you.'

He left the lectern and went to sit among them. As he did so, the entire senate rose and clapped. Hands pounded him on the back and he saw Otho's father shouting his name, the single word taken up in a chant by all the rest. Everything had changed. Everything was new. He could not help grinning as they cheered him. Whether his mother listened behind her awning or not, it didn't matter. He was emperor.

He had planned to take lunch in Otho's new house on the Caelian, purchased for almost nothing from some failed tax collector. The gardens were splendid, Nero had been told. More importantly, he would be able to dine there with Acte – and without watching eyes.

One of the consuls was patting the air for quiet. In the front row, Nero could hear the man's call for order. The senators chose to remain on their feet a little longer, making their approval clear. He sought out Seneca along the edge. The man was smiling. It seemed he had done well.

At last, the senators took their seats. Nero remained standing, very aware of how they stared. Even there, they looked to him as if he were made of some different clay. It was extraordinary. He glanced at a bar of shadow on the floor and saw it was past noon. They would meet in that place for another hour or two, but his friends would already be serving wine and food on the Caelian. He bit his lip and made a decision, inclining his head to the consul.

The man realised Nero was leaving. He spluttered for a moment, then gave way.

'Rise, gentlemen, for the emperor,' he said.

They stood once more and Nero felt himself grow hot as he walked across the floor, heading out to the winter sun. He heard steps hurrying behind and glanced back to see Seneca too had taken the opportunity to leave.

Nero looked at his tutor, trying to read the man's mood as praetorians brought his horse. He had refused the closed carriages Claudius had used. They had an old-man smell and he loved to ride. Prefect Burrus was there, of course, looking about as uncomfortable on horseback as a child. The praetorian sat like a sack of wheat – and what good he'd be if an assassin struck was not clear. Still, the man had been loyal when loyalty mattered.

'What did you think?' Nero asked Seneca.

To his surprise, he thought he saw a line of brightness like tears in the man's eyes. From one who prided himself on control, who revered the Stoics of ancient Athens, it was shocking.

'It was a good start,' Seneca said.

Nero smiled at the simple praise. That was more like it. Yet he blushed even so, pleased.

'We'll do more,' he said.

Seneca nodded and Nero mounted with an ease that made both Burrus and Seneca regret lost youth. Nero looked back through the door to the senate house, the seat of power in Rome. He hoped his mother was still there, ear pressed to the cloth, straining to hear. The thought made him grin as he dug in his heels and sent the horse

Conn Iggulden

cantering in the direction of the Caelian hill. Praetorians rode alongside him and the crowds stood back, cheering and watching the young emperor of Rome.

Agrippina walked with hands clasped behind her back, Britannicus and Octavia on either side. The day was a little colder than she liked, but the sun was out and the gardens on the Palatine were still beautiful. Rowan trees lined the path where she walked with her children. Even in winter, they bore clusters of red fruit that attracted pigeons. Those fat and stupid birds clung upside down to branches, flapping as they gorged themselves. A memory came of her first husband, of him saying he preferred wild places to gardens like those. She shook her head, smiling. No. Agrippina loved the tended paths, where nature bent to the will of men . . . and women.

Britannicus had healed like a young dog, of course. He still wore a cloth sling, though he used the arm more and more. Burrus had been worried he might grow weak if he didn't, so made the lad lift stones each day. It showed in the breadth of his shoulders, Agrippina thought, the easy way he moved. Britannicus wore the toga virilis, but he was a man regardless.

The mark on his temple had lingered for weeks in gorgeous shades of gold and purple, but even that had faded. He still said he didn't remember anything of the crash, which she thought was for the best. Nero had told her Britannicus had spoken strangely, though his body lay broken. It was a mercy not to remember that.

Agrippina knew he'd been given a glimpse of death, in the midst of careless youth. A sight like that had clearly made him thoughtful. Britannicus had come back without some of his confidence, smiling less. Yet she liked the man he had become, was still becoming.

Octavia stopped to look at one of the pigeons, the bird retreating from their presence and still eyeing them, in case they had breadcrumbs. Agrippina shooed the bird away with a sharp gesture, but it didn't go far.

'The gardeners have been feeding them again, though I told them not to,' she said. 'I should pay a boy to come out here with a sling.'

Octavia looked at the woman who still insisted on being called 'empress'.

'He's only hungry,' she said.

Agrippina returned her gaze.

'You are not a child, Octavia, not any more. Try that sentimental tone on your husband. It does not work on me.'

'It doesn't work on Nero either,' she muttered.

Agrippina firmed her mouth.

'Then you should use whatever does. You need a child growing in that womb. Should I send Britannicus further down the path so we can speak in private? I'll tell you how to bring the horse to you. I'll tell you what men like, if you wish.'

Britannicus was already close to bolting, it looked like. Octavia went a deep colour and shook her head.

'No . . . well, not now. I might like to hear at some point.'

She chuckled and Agrippina was pleased to see it. There was not much laughter in the girl's marriage, as far as she could tell. Nero was busy with the sheer excitement of his new role. He had little time for his wife.

'Another day then, I promise. I have had three husbands, my dear. I know what makes them breathe and paw the ground.'

'I like hearing you call me "my dear",' Octavia said.

'Nero says I cannot call you "mother" any more, since the adoption. I know it was to make things right for my marriage, but . . . it makes me feel a little lost sometimes.'

'He's quite right,' Agrippina said firmly. 'If I call you daughter, it will sound like incest. You and Nero are barely cousins. There is nothing to prevent you bearing six squalling babies if you want. That you and he were brother and sister for a time is just a crumb for gossip-mongers. They are like those pigeons, Octavia, always hungry. We should not encourage them.'

'*I* can call you mother, though,' Britannicus said into the pause. 'And I will call Octavia my sister, no matter what. You two are the only family I have, since . . .'

It did not need to be said and Agrippina felt a twinge of guilt. She had known Britannicus first as a rival to Nero, an obstacle in the way of her ambition. Oh, she had been pleasant enough to him, usually for Claudius' benefit. She supposed he had grown to love her over the years. That was what children did, usually.

Now that he had been overlooked, now that Nero ruled as emperor, she found she could talk to him without that shadow. To her surprise, she thought Britannicus better company than the son she'd raised to greatness. The walks had become a regular thing between them, with Agrippina discussing meetings and people she met, almost as if they were her advisers. It took some of the sting from the way Nero ignored them all.

Agrippina unclasped her hands and linked her arms in theirs, so that all three walked together. The path was not quite wide enough and Octavia trod on neatly trimmed grass.

'Nero is your family too, you know,' Agrippina said.

Britannicus shook his head.

'He hates me. Oh, don't look like that. He always has. I used to try to speak like him, I admired him so. That just made him angry.' He sighed. 'I know there are bonds in families, deeper than friendships. I never thought they could be broken between brothers. I was wrong, that's all. He doesn't feel it, or he just doesn't like me, I don't know. I'm a nuisance, an embarrassment to him. Did you hear about his friend Serenus?'

Agrippina shook her head. She could see the pain in the young man and she was not sure whether to be firm with him or let it pour out. Some men needed to talk and Britannicus did not seem to guard his words, at least with her. She learned more from him sometimes than listening in the senate.

'He has been appointed head of the vigiles, for all Rome. Nero did that. And Otho? He is to be made quaestor, with some responsibility for the imperial treasury. Nero sacked some fellow by the name of Pallas and put Otho . . .'

'Marcus Pallas?' Agrippina interrupted.

He nodded and she bit her lip. Pallas had been one of her favoured clients, doing well after a promotion to run the mint. He had been an ally, the sort of relationship she had once wanted with Axilla, before his betrayal. To learn of the man's dismissal from Britannicus was a serious blow – not just the news itself, but hearing it from him before her own sources. She thought of the new coins Pallas had shown her just a week before. She and Nero faced one another in gold, mother and son to rule in Rome. Had that been the problem? She scratched one eyebrow with her nails as she thought, hard enough to redden the skin.

Britannicus was still talking, too lost in his own troubles to see her eyes become distant. Octavia noticed, though. The girl was sharp enough for both of them.

'Nero has offered me nothing,' Britannicus said. 'Not governor of a province, though I would accept that; not praetor, nor quaestor, not even a seat in the senate. I am a spare part, Agrippina, one he does not need.'

'You have a fine house in Rome, with gardens at least the equal of these,' she reminded him gently. 'Another on the sea at Herculaneum, with a galley at your beck and call, whenever you want it. You have slaves and wealth beyond the dreams of most men, Britannicus.'

'I hate being idle!' he said. 'I can be useful, if he could see it.'

Agrippina nodded, wanting him to lower his voice.

'Nero knows that, of course. He will find you a role, I do not doubt. You are of the bloodline, just as he is.'

She made herself stop there, walking them through a row of bare cherry trees. The branches were dark that day, but they would be reborn in spring. She wondered if she should mention them, or whether the point would be too obvious.

Agrippina did not want Britannicus or Octavia thinking of the succession, not then, not ever. It was true Britannicus was next in line, at least until Nero warmed the womb of his little wife. If Nero fell from his horse or suffered a fever and died, it would be Britannicus who addressed the senate and ruled in Rome.

She shook her head, irritated even at the thought. She had done terrible things to make Nero first among his peers. It was her life's ambition made real, and the fact that he now ignored her advice, that he cancelled meetings she had set up, undermining her authority . . . None of that should matter. Yet it did. Her ungrateful son should have raised statues to *her*, not Claudius! Her husband was safely in the tomb of emperors out on the Campus Martius. What did he care whether pigeons sat on some bronze image of him? He was already divine.

Agrippina frowned as she walked. Nero should have devoted himself to making the senate accept his mother as divine! Julius Caesar had been granted the right to be worshipped while he still lived. *That* would be a task worthy of a son, given all she had done for him. By the gods, was it not enough? Instead, she had to hear the latest appointments from poor Britannicus.

She clenched her jaw and tried to smile. In promoting his friends, in sacking men she favoured, Nero was trying to reduce her influence, something she had wielded since he'd sucked a tit for milk. She could feel him doing it, tugging at her, trying to find weakness. His ingratitude was her burden. She wondered if all mothers felt the same way.

'I heard about poor Silanus,' Britannicus said.

He was watching Agrippina for a response and caught her by surprise. He saw the sharp glance and nodded to himself, as if she had answered a question.

'They are a troubled family . . .' Agrippina said.

She bit her lip once more. Could she discuss such a thing with Britannicus and his sister? Octavia would surely report anything interesting back to Nero. The poor girl was desperate for his affection, after all. Agrippina shrugged. It might not hurt to remind Nero she could not easily be swept from the board.

'The first Silanus was engaged to your sister for a time, Britannicus. Poor man, he was prone to madness, as I

Conn Iggulden

heard it. He began an affair with his own sister and took his life when it was discovered. A terrible loss.'

They were both listening and she pressed on, gripping Octavia's arm tightly.

'Your father betrothed you then to Nero, but the head of the Silanus family saw my hand in it. He started a little club of men with reason to dislike me. One of them came quite close . . .' She sighed, remembering a glorious male, safely in her past. 'That Silanus took his own life as well. He realised he had gone too far in the things he had said, the accusations he made. His guilt bore him down, as I heard it.'

'And the son?' Octavia asked.

Agrippina raised one hand to her throat, drifting the backs of her fingers over soft skin for a beat of time.

'Killed in the street, poor man,' she said. 'Some sort of failed robbery. Rome is a violent city, especially after dark. I think the Silanus family is cursed. Octavia, you were lucky not to be part of it. Instead, you are the wife of the emperor himself.'

They all turned at the sound of approaching steps, perhaps a little nervously given the topic of conversation. Britannicus relaxed when he saw a herald's tunic, but the man was still stopped some twenty paces off. Praetorians stepped into his path and halted him before he could get close to the emperor's wife and mother.

Agrippina watched as the man was searched and then allowed to approach. He looked flushed and irritated, his composure ruined. She smiled as he dropped to one knee.

'Empress, I am to say the emperor requires your presence,' the man said.

'Well, that is good timing,' Agrippina replied. She unhitched her arms from Britannicus and Octavia, touching them lightly on the shoulders. 'I hope we can do this again, very soon. I enjoy these walks more than you know.' She said it out of politeness, but to her surprise, she realised it was also true. For once, she felt flustered and spoke on. 'I can . . . take the opportunity to discuss a posting for you, Britannicus.'

'I don't think there is much point,' he murmured. Seeing her hurt, he relented. 'But if it please you, yes. He might listen to you.'

The herald was shifting from foot to foot.

'Ah . . .' He rubbed his lip as he thought. 'Domina, the message was for Empress Octavia, I'm sorry.'

The full power of Agrippina's gaze turned on him and he shrivelled like a worm in the sun.

'I see,' she said.

Octavia could not hide her pleasure, of course. Agrippina hardly had the heart to tell her Nero had surely arranged it to humiliate his mother. She doubted he even had anything to say to Octavia.

'Go then, my dear,' Agrippina said sweetly. 'You must not keep my son waiting.'

Octavia hitched up her dress and followed the herald back down the path. She went with a very light step. Agrippina exchanged a glance with Britannicus.

'He will have to see me eventually,' she said. 'I *will* raise your position with him, Britannicus, I promise. Your father would have wanted you as governor, perhaps of Gaul.'

There it was again, that strange sense of discomfort! Agrippina knew what guilt was, how it could sting. She accepted it as a cost of achievement and prided herself on never looking back. Still it could surprise her, like a knife between the ribs, making her gasp.

Conn Iggulden

19

Nero watched the gladiators battle back and forth. He ate an apple as the great Spiculus unbalanced an opponent, shoulder-charging him at the perfect moment. He stood over the fallen man and if it had been a match to the death, that would have been it. On the training ground, Spiculus held out his hand with a grin. His opponent took it and raised himself up.

'Well done,' Otho called.

Spiculus bowed in his direction, then gestured.

'Would you like to try a bout?' he said. 'I hear Burrus has been training you.'

Otho shook his head, laughing.

'Against you? No, Spiculus. You are the master. I would look like a child.'

Spiculus seemed to have been carved from teak. There were ripples and veins in him that did not show on most men. He had been drawn from a legion line when a senior quaestor had spotted his potential. He'd earned fortunes since, for his sponsor as well as himself. The odds were often terrible, but Nero too had won a dozen bets on him.

'I will not bear a sword, if you wish,' Spiculus said, smiling.

The expression was not particularly gentle and Nero's attention sharpened. He knew the gladiator loved to win. It was said he loved to kill as well, but Nero had forbidden matches to the death as soon as he became emperor. He wanted to see skill and courage, not dead men dragged away.

Otho understood there was a real challenge in the other man. Yet he was fast and strong – fitter than he had ever been as well. It was hard not to feel he might have a small chance.

'I'll have a sword . . . but you won't? To first blood? It sounds like something I cannot lose, Spiculus.'

'It does,' the man said.

He smiled wider and Otho understood suddenly that if he refused, he would be mocked or shamed for it. He glowered then, irritated with games and challenges.

They stood on the private training ground of a gladiator school, near the Viminal hill. North of the Palatine and the Circus, it was far enough from their usual haunts to give Nero some sense of ease.

Otho looked at Serenus. His friend was over by Acte, wearing his usual sour expression. Though he was the new head of vigiles in Rome, Otho knew he was sick of pretending Acte was his lover. It may have protected Nero from the gaze of his wife and mother, but it was no role for a man, not really. Despite his new title, Serenus would never be able to find a wife of his own, not with Acte always on his arm. Otho thought it would end in chaos

Conn Iggulden

eventually. Either Acte would grow tired of the pretence or Serenus would. They shaped their lives around Nero, he realised – and always had.

He looked at Spiculus, the grizzled fighter still watching, eyebrows raised in question. There were days since Nero had become emperor when Otho just wanted to hit something.

'Very well,' he said. 'For the honour of saying I stood against you with steel in my hand, just once.'

Spiculus tossed him a sword and Otho managed to snatch it out of the air without losing any fingers, though he swore in shock. Some of the other gladiators chuckled at that and he found he was angry. Spiculus was not a pleasant man, no matter how some people admired him. In all ways, the big bastard liked to humiliate those he faced – at least in front of Nero. Perhaps the gladiator thought it pleased the emperor, he didn't know. When Spiculus fought for real, he crushed those he faced, battered them bloody and still, so that they could not rise to bow and offer thanks. He was always the only one standing at the end, no matter what rules were set.

Yet Otho was eighteen and the weight of the gladius felt good in his hand. Burrus had drilled them with sword and shield over a thousand days and more, saying it built fitness better even than running. Otho grinned, feeling the confidence of his own strength.

Spiculus beckoned him closer, his hands like clubs. Otho made himself breathe and stepped into range. He watched as Spiculus scraped a line in the sand with the toe of a boot. He stepped back then, arms loose and ready.

'Cross that line if you have the nerve,' Spiculus said. 'All right?'

Otho nodded – and charged him. He hoped to catch the gladiator by surprise. Someone cried out behind him – Acte? – but Spiculus just stepped aside from his rush, seeming almost to vanish from view. Otho kept his balance and swung behind him. He was disappointed as Spiculus remained out of reach, looking completely relaxed. The big man chuckled at his frustration.

'You can run all day, I suppose,' Otho said.

Spiculus frowned. He didn't like the suggestion, even with the way he had stacked the odds already.

'Run? I don't do that, son.' He looked to where he had drawn a line, scuffed now by Otho's sandals. 'I'll keep one foot there, if it makes you more willing to face me. Is that enough for you, or should I wear a blindfold as well?'

His cronies all laughed at that and Otho did as well, though he felt no amusement. He watched Spiculus put one toe very obviously on the line. In turn, Otho faced him, sword ready. Nero and Serenus had grown still, as had Acte. They understood there was real risk in what Spiculus was doing, or real arrogance. Otho showed his teeth, hoping the man had overreached. He had a short sword in his right hand and he was quick. All he needed was to cut him once – and he'd have something to tell his friends for the rest of his life.

'When you're ready, then,' Spiculus said. He swayed as he stood there and he was still smiling, though his eyes were cruel.

Otho faked one blow and then another, making the gladiator shift to react. He swung for the neck then with all his strength. Spiculus slipped it, leaning away from the blade. Otho reversed as fast as he could to sweep back at waist height. There was no way to dodge that and instead

286   Conn Iggulden

Spiculus rapped the blade with his forearm, knocking it away.

Otho leaned in and hardly saw the fist that struck his nose. White light flashed and he took a step back, quite unable to go on. Tears made him blind and he could feel blood dripping into his throat. A jab. Spiculus had not said he would be allowed to punch, but of course he had not said he wouldn't either. Otho gripped the bridge of his nose and handed back the sword, scowling.

'Well done,' Nero called.

Otho would have said something sharp, but he saw a thin line of red on Spiculus' forearm. The gladiator hadn't even noticed it, but it was there. A slow smile spread across Otho's face.

'To first blood, wasn't it?' he said. He pointed to the wound and Spiculus looked at it in dismay.

'That's where I blocked the blade,' he said. 'I did that to myself.'

'Still,' Otho said, 'it was before you struck me, wasn't it? That's how I remember it. What do you think?'

Two of the other gladiators had come across to see what the fuss was about. Nero too came close, his presence bringing a new tension to that group as they tried to stand respectfully.

'I think he had you, Spiculus,' Nero said.

The gladiator did not look pleased about it, but he had to bow his head and say that it was so. Otho beamed at them all.

'What a day,' he said.

'I'm happy to go again, if you wish,' Spiculus said.

It was deliberately light, but Otho's nose was still bleeding and beginning to swell up. He was very aware of the spite simmering in Spiculus, so shook his head.

'I'd better have one of the trainers look at this,' he said. 'Thank you, though.'

Otho had plugs shoved up each nostril while Nero arranged for a lunch and wine to be brought to the gladiator ground. He always treated them well and they cheered the news. Otho had heard they ate twice the amount of other men, training like fighting dogs, seeking a perfection that was always out of reach.

On the street outside, praetorians fell in around Nero and his friends. They were a constant presence in his life and both Otho and Serenus had complained in private about them since Nero had become emperor. It was not that they wanted Nero to be in danger, but neither did they want grim-faced soldiers listening to every word.

They walked, as crowds thickened around that street. The people did not have too many opportunities to see the emperor. News spread of his presence on the voices of children, running inside to bring parents from their looms and shops. They came out brushing dust or flecks of metal from their hands, leaving making a living for a chance to see Nero, to feel the youthful excitement in him. To have an emperor of just seventeen was somehow glorious. It felt like a rebirth for the city, with new ideas and new fashions every day.

Nero walked a mile through the streets, gaining a great tail of cheering citizens. He had increased the allowance of free grain to many of them and they blessed his generosity. More, they'd heard he was excavating three new lakes around the city, so that they would always have clean water, even at the height of summer. Thousands had family members engaged in those great works, paid good silver

Conn Iggulden

each day. They called his name as a result and prayed to the gods on his behalf, wishing him good fortune and long life.

He heard them, of course. He pretended he did not, that he just talked to Serenus and Acte about a party he was going to throw on the Palatine, but Nero was aware of individual voices and pleased by them. He was emperor and they were his people. It lifted him, like dandelion seeds on the breeze.

An arch loomed at the entrance to the imperial estate. The praetorians formed a line across the opening and the crowd were not allowed to advance beyond that point. Nero walked with Serenus, Otho and Acte, from the midst of the crowd into clear space, as if they had been spat out. He grinned, waving to his people. They doubled their volume then, pleased to be acknowledged, to be seen.

'Where was all this when we were running the Campus with Burrus? Or when you were thrown out of that tavern last year?' Serenus murmured. 'Do they love you, or just whoever is emperor?'

Nero didn't like that and frowned at his friend. Serenus had taken on a bitter edge for months and he was not sure of the cause. He'd put his friend in charge of the vigiles, giving him power and wealth at a stroke. Serenus had only grown darker since then, so it seemed.

'Perhaps it is a little of both,' he said.

They walked on together, leaving the tumult of the crowd behind. It was a relief, like coming out of the light into cool shade. Nero strode up the Palatine and the others went with him.

Nero glanced at the sun. It was past noon and he was starving.

'Come on. The cooks have promised a delicacy. New

wines from the north, roasted squid and anchovies in oil
and vinegar, all brought from the coast this morning.
Honey cakes afterwards – as fresh as anything you will
ever taste.'

Even Serenus cheered up at that, while Otho was practically salivating. His nose had stopped bleeding, but it
looked sore and swollen and his eyes were already growing
dark with blood under the skin. Nero laughed to see his
friend's expression. In reply, Otho pointed ahead.

Nero's mother was there, walking alone in the imperial
complex, the spring breeze ruffling her hair. Agrippina
had seen her son first and Nero could only stand still and
wait for her to reach him.

'Perhaps you should go ahead,' he muttered to his
friends. 'She will not let me pass without a word, I'm sure.'

'Do you want us to stay?' Otho asked.

Nero shook his head. His mother could twist words and
conversations to suit her, apparently with ease. He was
stronger without ears listening.

'I'll come as soon as I can. I'm sorry, Acte. I'd hoped for
more time with you.'

His Greek mistress said nothing, but she took Serenus
by the hand as they left. Nero wondered about that.

'Where have you been?' Agrippina said as she reached him.

'Good day, mother. I'm not sure it is any . . .'

'Your tutor was looking for you. He expected you at
some theatre or other on the Campus.'

Nero swore under his breath. He had forgotten about
that. Irritably, he waved a hand.

'I was called away. Seneca will understand.'

'So you weren't just amusing yourself watching gladiators,
then? You were on important business for the imperium?'

He stared. She had more eyes in the city than Claudius, he sometimes thought. The ordinary crowds were bad enough, but the idea of his mother's clients and servants all watching him as well . . . it was too much.

'You have no right to have me followed,' he snapped. 'And what I do is not your concern.'

'Not my concern? My own son?' she said in amazement. 'The city my husband broke his heart to rule, all held in trust for you? I was empress here when you were just a fat little boy, Nero. How dare you tell me what is or is not my business.'

Tears came to her eyes and he shook his head.

'Don't bother weeping for me, mother. Not today. I know the tricks you play. I'm not Claudius. Weep away! It changes nothing.'

'You are wrong,' she hissed, her anger made visible. 'You think you know absolutely everything, where all I see is a frightened boy, wearing clothes that are too big for him!'

He glared then, driven to real dislike.

'You'd like that, I know,' he said. 'A boy you could command and control. Instead, I *am* emperor, a married man. Where does that leave you, mother? Be careful now. When I said I was not Claudius, I have his title, all his authority. I have his name.'

'You poor fool,' she said, almost sadly. 'You remind me of your father when you speak like this, all anger and yet understanding nothing. You would have been a fine charioteer, as he was. This? Perhaps it is the fate of men in our family. They reach too far.'

She hurt him with that, worse than she knew. Nero felt a great wave of grief pass through. There was spite enough in her to drown him and he hadn't known the depth of it, not really – not until he had crossed her. He fumbled for a way to hurt her in return.

'I have seen those new coins of yours,' he said. 'The ones where you face me like an equal? I will have them restruck. You have no authority in Rome, perhaps we can agree on that. All your titles and airs came from Claudius . . . and he is gone. Otho will command the mint now, as quaestor. He will answer only to me and what new coins there are will not have your face on them. "Agrippina Augusta"? It is obscene.'

'I knew you had dismissed Pallas,' she said. 'You wear your pettiness too openly, Nero. That has always been your problem. When you were very young, I could protect you, as I did with your tutors. Now, though? Look at the arrogance in you, at the way you speak to your own *mother*.'

'You don't want a son! I see it in you! You just want authority, for men to bow and scrape. As soon as they actually stand up to you, you have no further use for them. I should warn Britannicus, mother. He should know the way you are.'

'You will say nothing to him,' she said, closing her fists. 'He is a good and honourable young man, without all these games and vicious entertainments you enjoy. He has no whore, no freed slave, pretending to be with Serenus!'

It was like a blow over the heart, to understand she had somehow learned of Acte's role. He winced at the implications, at what she might now say to Octavia. Slowly, he raised his head. She had played a powerful piece, but only when he'd attacked Britannicus. She sought to divert him.

'I think I've heard enough from you today, mother,' he said with a terrible lightness that was somehow worse than rage. 'I have a lunch planned and then a party tonight, with

Conn Iggulden

half the senate in attendance. Don't feel you must come. I'd really prefer it if you didn't. After that, I don't suppose I need to tell you all my work next week, not if you have spies watching me. I tell you again: be careful. I will not stand for this.'

'You *will not stand for it*? Poor cockerel, to puff your chest in such a way. I survived Tiberius, boy – and my brother Caligula!' She raised one finger and prodded Nero in the chest with it. 'I *raised* you to the purple – you should re-member that. I swear, if you ever threaten me again, you will regret it. I could dash you down just as quickly. Do you understand?' Her finger was like bone, poking at him. She advanced, and he stepped back. 'The gods hear when a son is cruel to his mother, when he scorns her advice. Go – eat, drink, play with your whore while your wife goes unplanted. When you realise you should have listened to me, I will still be here. I will still be your mother. That is my burden.'

She walked on, stiff and visibly upset. The child in him wanted to rush after her, to say whatever was needed to soothe the hurt. Yet she had stung him as well, he reminded himself. Worse than a bloody wasp.

Rome was never really still, but steps echoed more at night. As the woman entered, Nero tried to see the vaulted room through her eyes. She certainly looked around in awe, as he had intended. To be so deep in the Palatine, actually under the palace of Augustus, but still see a domed ceiling decor-ated in mosaic, well, there was nothing else like it. She had descended a hundred narrow steps, then walked into an open space like a temple. Lamps flickered on all sides, re-vealing an eagle in the ceiling, glittering in ceaseless vigil.

Nero rose from his couch and came across the tiles to greet her. They were truly alone, in a place that had no alcoves for slaves, nor side rooms. Everything had to be brought down those stairs and through the single entrance. He didn't think his mother even knew of the place. He had found he could hold private meetings there, as almost nowhere else in Rome.

The young woman knelt, becoming very small. He smiled and took her by the hand, raising her up.

'Please. You are my guest,' he said. 'Have no fear in my presence, not here. Do you know where you are?'

'No, Dominus,' Locusta said softly.

'This is the Lupercal, the cave of the wolf. It was here that Romulus and Remus survived their first winter. My ancestor Augustus built his palace above the very spot where Rome began. You were born in Gaul, I believe. Did you hear the story there?'

She shook her head and he saw her glance at the entrance. He chuckled, raising one arm to guide her further in.

'It was open to the wind then, of course, a cave in the Palatine hillside. Two abandoned brothers – sons of an ancient king – were saved in this place by a she-wolf. She let them suckle, and so they survived the cold. Please – that couch is for you.'

Locusta sat down, legs drawn in tightly, her ankles touching. The table held a dozen dishes, gleaming as they began to congeal. Nero poured wine, filling two cups, one after another. Her eyes watched him almost feverishly.

'When they were fully grown, they argued over which hill was best to begin a city. Romulus loved the Palatine. He wanted to build there, safe from raids. When Remus refused, they fought. Romulus killed his brother with a stone – and so we are in Rome, named for him.'

He let his smile drop away. He knew his face settled into an expression Serenus and Otho said was stern. His hair was very thick, his head almost leonine, large and imposing over broad shoulders. In that place, with the mantle of his authority, he knew he was terrifying. He studied the effect on the young woman.

'Rome was made in wolf's milk and a brother's blood, Locusta. We were bred strong, from the very first. That is why we rule Greece and Britannia, Hispania and Gaul . . . Judaea and Egypt and all the rest. Like Romulus, we see what has to be done and we do it, without regret.'

Locusta bowed her head again. She feared she was in some fever dream, brought on by her own powders and oils. The single chamber glittered, the tiles of some stone that reflected the lamps like mica, seeming almost alive. She felt as if she had entered a stone womb, deep in the Palatine. The story of wolves and murderous sons only added to the feeling of strangeness.

Her eyes flickered again to the entrance. There was no chance of escape, she knew that. She had never felt so helpless in her life – and part of her wondered if that was exactly what this man, this emperor, wanted her to feel.

'You were with Claudius when he died, Locusta,' Nero said, his voice barely a breath. In that chamber of rock, even a whisper could be heard.

She hesitated before replying, nodding before she spoke. Had Agrippina shared her secrets with her son? It was possible. Locusta swallowed nervously. She walked on broken stones in that place, her feet bare.

'It was a dark day,' she whispered. When Nero did not

answer, she found herself babbling on, words drawn out by his silence. 'I hope never to see such things again, dominus . . . You must know I am an auspex, a midwife, a physician . . . I have been all those things. I have seen death come, many times. Both in the bones and entrails and then again, in life. It is . . . a hard path to walk, dominus.'

'I am sure it is,' he said. 'Though perhaps there is mercy in your work as well. When pain is too great, perhaps, or a child is born with twisted limbs.'

He did not wait for her to reply, though he saw knowledge in her eyes, knowledge and a little fear.

'Some men have fate happen to them, Locusta. I believe Claudius was one of those. He . . .' Nero broke off. The woman had flinched at his words, as if he accused her. He felt his heart beat faster and stumbled on. 'H-he . . . He was witness to the death of Caligula in halls above our heads, did you know that? Claudius did not make himself emperor. It was forced on him, by praetorians with bloody knives. He was Romulus in his own story, Locusta. I wonder, though . . . if he was Remus at the end.'

He saw she was trembling. By the gods, what had his mother done? He had found a thread, something to tug and worry at until his fingers were sore.

'Emperor Augustus thought of calling himself Romulus, did you ever hear that? To show his faith in a city on a hill, a city of the dawn. I might take the name myself, now I am emperor. I see what must be done – and I will *see* it done, no matter what. Do you understand?'

She nodded, though there were tears in her eyes and her nose was running. He looked on her in fascination, as if he'd opened an oyster for the first time. By the gods, what

Conn Iggulden

had he found? With a twist of the knife, what else might he learn?

'A secret can be a great burden, Locusta,' he whispered, leaning in.

With one hand, he drew his couch closer underneath him, scraping it across the floor. His legs were bare and massively muscled as he lifted the weight. He frightened her with that display of strength. She was trapped with him and it showed in her nervous gestures, the way she raised her open palms as if to fend him off.

'What did my mother make you do?' he said.

He knew, in that moment, what it had been. He had summoned the auspex to that place to ask her for some of the unguents and herbs she used in her work. He had hoped to disguise his true intention in a long list of ingredients, some real and some to be thrown away. Now, though, he felt the hair on the back of his neck rising, like a dog's hackles. Or like a wolf's, perhaps.

'She . . . she wanted foxglove powder . . .' Locusta said. 'In small doses, it can ease pain in the heart, dominus. I swear, I never believed it was to be used . . . for anything more.'

'And you still have this . . . powder?' he asked. 'I would like to see it.'

She produced a leather bag from under her dress, warm from her skin. Nero shuddered slightly at the thought, but then watched with bright eyes as she opened it and picked through packets and folds. She handed over a little cloth bag, plump as he moved it between finger and thumb. In something like awe, he opened it and dipped a fingertip. He brought it close to examine the dust and she reached out like a snake striking, gripping his wrist.

'Do not taste it, dominus. It will kill you.'

He shook himself free, repelled by her.

'I was just looking. You gave this to my mother? And then the emperor died . . . It is not proof, is it?'

'She promised me a palace, dominus,' the woman muttered.

Nero blinked at her. Did she think a broken promise held any sway with him, while they discussed murders? The woman was . . . He caught himself. Locusta was both petty and spiteful in her frustration. Perhaps she did hope to cause trouble for his mother. Yet she had knowledge . . . and more importantly, she was his. She may have been a free woman, but she was his slave from that moment, whether she knew it or not.

'Your life hangs at my word, Locusta, do you understand? All I have to do is call a praetorian down the steps.'

'Your mother would fall then, when I tell what happened,' she said, raising her chin in defiance.

Ah, that was it, he realised. She thought she was made safe by his loyalty to Agrippina. He smiled slowly. It was almost amusing to watch her fear return.

'I have other plans for her, Locusta. She is the dowager empress, after all. If she could accept my reins, my iron bit in her mouth, she might yet be useful. You, though? Some Gaulish witch who chants over old bones? I could cut your throat myself and no one would care.'

He reached over and tapped her on the forehead, knowing exactly how frightening he could be.

'Your value to me lies in what you know.'

He sat back then, seeing she was shaking almost violently. He did not want to terrify her into drowning herself in the Tiber. Young women were fished out of its waters every year, often pale and pregnant.

Conn Iggulden

'I take it you didn't get what you were promised?'

She shook her head, eyes huge. Nero chuckled. His mother had made a mistake there.

He thought of the little house he had given Acte. It had six rooms and a pleasant garden. Acte scorned it now she shared an emperor's bed. She had a new mansion on the Caelian, so the old place lay empty.

'I may have a house for you, my dear, close to me, where I can call on you. Better than you will have known before, I imagine. That is . . . if you are mine, Locusta. You kept my mother's secrets, before.' He held up the little bag, turning it in the light. 'If you keep mine in turn, you will know an emperor's gratitude.'

In reply, she dropped to the floor. Weeping in relief, she touched her hair to his sandals, over and over. Nero looked up at the eagle in the mosaic – and in his mind's eye, right through it, to the palaces and city above.

20

Agrippina sipped at a tisane, enjoying the scent of rosemary and mint. Britannicus too had accepted a cup, though he sweetened his with honey. Her guest though, was on wine and water. Aulus Didius had waved away the idea of a hot drink, his distaste poorly hidden.

She looked at him over the lip of the cup as he talked, judging the man more than his words. Didius was round-faced, with cheeks she could almost imagine apart from him, perhaps as quivering cuts on the butcher's slab. She shuddered at the image, wondering where it had come from. They did have a life of their own, shaking and moving as he gestured.

'How long have you been in post, Governor Didius?'

'Aulus, Majesty, please! I'm honoured just to be received here, in these surroundings. When I asked for an audience, I thought it was a chance in a thousand. My leave was almost up and . . . well, I am grateful.'

'Very well,' Agrippina said. 'Aulus.' She smiled and he

Conn Iggulden

grew flustered, overawed by her as much as the room on the Palatine.

'Three years, Majesty. It feels much longer. I do not wish to seem ungrateful, if you understand me. Britannia is a fine step in a man's service to Rome, I don't doubt it. Emperor Claudius certainly looked kindly on me when he sent me to replace Governor Scapula. I came direct from Sicilia, heading to my new appointment without the usual months of furlough. Oh, if you could see . . .'

'Yes, you said,' Agrippina broke in. She exchanged a quick glance with Britannicus, hoping the man would not launch into another description of the island's rugged beauty.

Governor Didius squirmed in his seat. He knew it was the height of bad manners to ask for a different post before his five years were up. He also knew he had the chance of a lifetime to do so, if he could just find the right words. The tension of the struggle was killing him as he sat there. He drank another cup of watered wine to the dregs, only vaguely aware of it being refilled. Passing slaves dipped and departed, all unnoticed.

'If I had known what awaited me in Britannia, I would have asked to stay where I was, Majesty. The rain alone! In my second year, I saw perhaps a month of summer, with snow in March and hail the next month. I saw legionaries rattle as tiny chips of ice struck them in a storm that went on for hours. Britannia is almost never warm and always wet. In comparison to Sicilia . . . All I ask is the chance to petition your son, Majesty. There will be others who would love that bitter place. The er . . . hills are very green with all the rain, of course. They can be quite attractive when the clouds part.'

He saw his description was not making much headway with the dowager empress and changed tack.

'In truth, much of my work there is done. I have built a city in the west, on the coast. The natives call it Caer Didius, if you will forgive a little vanity. The tribes there still raid and attack our forts, but we have new roads and stone walls.'

'You don't go out to challenge them?' Britannicus said.

Agrippina turned subtly to watch. He had listened, it seemed, until he was ready to speak. How different to Nero he was.

Aulus Didius was not certain of the young man's rank, nor his right to question him. Britannicus held no formal post, as far as he knew. Yet the governor depended on goodwill in that place. He put aside his pride.

'I believe they will grow used to our presence in a few more years. It has been my policy to hold what we have won, not risk legion lives looking for more. My men have enough work building bridges, towns, forts in the hills – connecting them all with good stone roads. The tribes fight all the time, usually some dispute between their small kings. They have learned not to challenge us while we work, however. I don't allow that, you may be sure.'

The man looked bleak as he saw his words didn't please Agrippina or her son.

'Majesty, it will be winter by the time I get back. Six months or longer without seeing the sun, not as it is in Rome. Rain and bitter wind, or storms and sleet and endless nights. It's not for me. If I could pass my governor's staff to another, perhaps whoever has my old post in Sicilia, I would never leave those shores again, I swear. I have no more ambition than that, Majesty. I would work to my dying day for Rome, without a word of complaint. Or Syria, perhaps, or Judaea! Anywhere a man can feel sun on his face, where his limbs work, where the food isn't terrible and damp. Majesty, I beseech and implore . . .'

Agrippina looked again at Britannicus. He nodded to her, accepting.

'Aulus, I believe there is something to be done here. I don't know yet if the position in Sicilia will come free this year, but if all you want is a warmer post, I don't see why . . .'

She heard the clack of legion sandals approaching and broke off. Aulus was enough of an old soldier to recognise the danger of an interruption. He spoke quickly, risking offending the empress in doing so.

'I am very grateful, Majesty. If you could intervene on my behalf, I would be forever yours.'

'What is it?' Agrippina said.

The approaching praetorian came to attention and saluted.

'The emperor requires your presence, domina. With Britannicus.'

'Very well. When I am finished here, I will . . .'

The soldier's mouth twisted. He dared to interrupt her, so that Agrippina broke off in shock.

'I was told to bring you to him now,' he said. 'I am not to allow any delays. The emperor's orders were very clear.'

Agrippina rose to her feet. Britannicus and the governor of Britannia stood with her so that all three faced the praetorian. He regarded the little group impassively.

'*My* orders,' Agrippina said, 'are for you to go back to

the emperor, *my son*, and tell him I will attend when I am ready.'

'This meeting is at an end,' the praetorian said, his voice louder. He didn't seem embarrassed to be saying such things. It looked like Nero had picked a young man who might even enjoy such a task. The praetorian almost leered as he spoke, well aware of her shock and relishing it.

Agrippina turned in frustration to the governor. Didius gaped at her, out of his depth and unsure what to say. Her influence with him had crumbled – exactly as Nero had intended, no doubt. She clenched her jaw, remembering some of the things that had been said between them. She regretted losing her temper with her son, for the damage she had done. He seemed determined still to remind her where power lay.

Agrippina rubbed a finger over a spot on her temple where a headache had begun. She had carved out a place for herself in the administration, at least during the years where Claudius ruled. Little by little, her own son was intent on undoing all of it.

'Governor Aulus, I will do what I can,' she said. 'I am certain your petition has merit. Leave it with me.'

The praetorian began to shift his weight, looking for another chance to interrupt and humiliate her further. This was the sort of man Nero kept around him?

'As for *you*,' Agrippina said. 'What is your name?'

He flushed a little at that, understanding the threat. It was just a moment of doubt, though. He was in the emperor's favour.

'Marcus Publius, domina,' he said. He avoided the word 'empress', giving her the term he might have used to any noble lady.

Conn Iggulden

'It is noted,' she said, smiling sweetly. 'You may recall I appointed your Prefect Burrus to his post. I will be having a word with him this evening about your manner.'

She thanked the gods that barb seemed to strike home. The emperor may have been the font of all authority, but Burrus was still the praetorian's commanding officer – and Agrippina's most loyal man. She watched the little cockerel deflate as he considered his position.

'Lead on then,' she said lightly. Agrippina had controlled her anger by then, hiding it beneath a cold facade. 'Let us see what could possibly be urgent enough to interrupt me in this way.'

The crestfallen praetorian led them through the corridors of the imperial complex, towards the wing she knew best. Agrippina and Britannicus passed the door to what had been Claudius' office and private rooms. She knew Nero rarely went in and there were no legionaries on guard. As a result, that part seemed lifeless, forgotten. The furniture within was draped in sheets to keep dust from gathering. She did not need to look inside to be sure the huge open brazier was no longer lit. Nero didn't need to warm old bones, not as Claudius once had.

Britannicus walked alongside her, frowning to himself. He had no reason to welcome being summoned to his brother's presence. Agrippina's heart went out to the young man, but she could not speak to reassure him, not with ears listening. The praetorian had already revealed himself as a little tyrant and she could not bring herself to ask where they were going. She had the feeling he would remain silent, his revenge for the threat to report him to Burrus.

After an age, the legionary halted where two of his colleagues waited, impassive and utterly still. They faded back to either side, opening doors to one of the smaller banquet rooms.

Agrippina saw Nero rising to his feet from a long couch. He wore imperial purple, a toga of rich, dark cloth. That was a sign, of course. She had not raised a particularly subtle son.

Octavia too was there, on a couch close to her husband's. It looked an intimate setting to Agrippina's eye. As she entered, she thought the young woman seemed pinched and nervous. The poor thing had never been a beauty, Agrippina thought. That did not mean she was unfertile soil, however.

'Thank you for coming, mother – and dear Britannicus,' Nero said. He embraced her, holding her tightly, then took his brother by the hand in brisk fashion.

Agrippina glanced behind, but the doors were already closing. Serving slaves stood along the wall, between the torches. Besides those, they were alone. She bit her lip, unable to read her son's mood. Nero could be so quick to anger, she was never sure how far to push him for apologies or redemption. Having Britannicus there meant she could not just let it go, however.

'The praetorian you sent was most rude, Nero. He interrupted a meeting with the British governor, Aulus Didius, then would not wait, even for a moment.'

'I'm sorry, mother. I may have been too urgent with him when I gave the orders. I just wanted you here – Britannicus too. The way we talked . . . the way we argued before. It has weighed on me ever since. I arranged this meal for just the four of us, to make things right again.'

Agrippina looked at a table already set with lit candles and small dishes. She felt a slight, cold place open within. She almost stumbled as her son took her arm and drew her towards another couch. As she settled herself, her mind flickered like pages, wondering what he was doing. She had survived Caligula, she reminded herself – and Tiberius. She had survived Claudius too. Agrippina swallowed, her throat suddenly dry.

Nero watched like a proud parent as his mother, wife and brother took places on separate couches around the central table. He resumed his own then, leaning on one elbow, sighing with what looked like satisfaction. He glanced at the cups and one of the slaves filled them with wine that could only be Falernian. Agrippina stared at hers, thinking of Claudius.

'I have ground to make up with you all,' Nero said. 'I know it! I see now that I have been too concerned with affairs of state, with the senate and the thousand things I've had to learn since I put on the purple. I cannot undo all my selfishness in a single night, but I can show willing. I can promise to listen to all of you, from this night on.'

He indicated his cup and Agrippina watched as one of the slaves raised it to his own lips and took a sip. There was a pregnant silence in the room then, as the man narrowed his eyes. After an age, he nodded and replaced the cup.

One by one, the taster did the same for the three guests. Nero watched their reactions, a slight smile playing about his mouth.

'The Egyptian court insists on such things, you know. There have been rumours, just whispers really . . . but still. Of poisons put in food. Horrible idea, but I want you to be comfortable in my presence. You are my only family now, all of you.' He raised a cup, showing it to each of them in turn. 'My wife . . . my brother . . . and my mother. Your health. May you live a thousand years.'

They drank and Agrippina felt the wine warm her stomach, easing her wits from where they stood frozen.

'Are you well, Octavia?' she asked faintly, seeking some start to the conversation.

The young woman nodded, but it was Nero who replied. There was bitterness in his tone.

'Her menses began today, after another fruitless month of trying. Even in the blood, I plough that field, but no green crops grow, not yet.'

Octavia looked stricken and Agrippina was appalled to have her son speak in such a way before them all. Her gaze flickered to the tasting slave, but he was blank-faced, almost as if he had gone deaf.

'Such things take time,' Agrippina said firmly to Octavia. 'I was eight years married before I became pregnant with Nero. I thought I would surely never conceive – and never did again. Such things are secrets of the gods; there is no rushing them, no commanding them.'

Octavia nodded and seemed appeased. Nero looked rather sourly on them both.

'You get on so well, don't you?' he said. 'All three of you, really. I think sometimes you would be happier if I were not here at all.'

'That is not true, Nero,' Agrippina said. 'As you know very well. You are my son – and there were years when there was no one else. I cannot say I don't love Britannicus and Octavia – my dear, whether you were adopted by another house or not, you will always be my daughter. Yet you are your father's son, Nero. I raised you and I am proud of you. In fact, why don't you tell us all of your labours! I have to rely on gossip in the markets these days. I don't know half of what goes on.'

Nero looked at her so coldly, she wondered if he had misheard. Then he seemed to come to himself and smiled, warming up.

'I have three lakes being dug – and another in the process of being drained for farmland. Seneca says the fields there will be rich enough to provide grain for the whole city, just about. There is a new theatre under construction. That will be finished in time for a festival of Aeschylus and Euripides, perhaps with a tragedy by Seneca, I have not decided.'

He signalled for the first course and they all kept their eyes on him as the taster dipped a spoon into every bowl. For his part, Nero gestured more aggressively as his enthusiasm grew.

'I have joined a choir – and I have engaged a master musician to help me with my lyre work. There is a soothing quality to music, mother. I will have to play for you some evening. I have a talent, it seems. One you never tried to find in me.'

'That is wonderful,' Agrippina said. 'I wish your father Gnaeus could hear you talk. He always said he was about as musical as a stone. You must get that from my side of the family. You know, Britannicus here . . .'

'In a moment, mother. I have not told you yet of the Parthians. There may be an agreement coming, at least a trade pact. In Judaea though, there is talk of yet another revolt. I may even have to go out there, unless I can appoint a man for the task. All I want is quiet for our people! Is it too much to ask? They can work and know peace under my rule. There is no *need* for protests and rebellions. To what end, when I am father to them? Please eat. I talk and talk, I know. There is so much to tell.'

The dish was two small chops of lamb, with fresh mint from the gardens. Agrippina eyed the tiny bite already taken from hers with some distaste. Still, Nero watched as she nibbled at the bone. She had no appetite at all.

'I worry you take on too much,' she said. 'Claudius had trusted men around him to carry the weight. Even I played my part at times.'

'Yes, I heard about that,' Nero said.

He emptied his wine as if he hardly tasted it. His eyes were growing glassy, she noted. Worry bloomed in her. Nero sober could be decent and humorous. Nero drunk was one who made her afraid.

'Whom should I trust?' Nero said, his voice slightly too hard for the question.

'Your brother, for one,' Agrippina replied. 'Britannicus wears his toga virilis. He wants to serve – perhaps in the territory for which he was named. The governor there is unhappy with the post. He says . . .'

'Why not?' Nero said. He raised his cup in toast and they all had to wait while the rest were refilled and tasted. The taster too was looking a little worse for wear, Agrippina saw.

She raised her cup and Nero waved his at them all, sitting up and belching.

'If it is your wish, Britannicus, I will grant an order for you to govern Britannia in my name. It will be a five-year term.'

'Thank you,' Britannicus said. Like his mother, he was

Conn Iggulden

still looking for the sting, or the joke at his expense. He had learned to be wary a long time before.

Agrippina spoke to break the tension,

'I know Governor Didius is desperate to find somewhere warmer. If you need a man in Judaea, he might be suitable.'

Nero waved a hand, scowling.

'There is always something else, isn't there? I give so much . . . and your response is always to ask for more.'

'I didn't mean to offend you, Nero. I have been on the Palatine for most of my life. I have seen three emperors ruling here before you. Is it so strange that I would want to help my own son?'

She put down her wine cup, feeling she'd had enough. It loosened the tongue and she did not want to argue with him, not when he was trying to make amends.

Nero gestured and the plates were swept away, hardly touched in her case. Slaves moved like a dance to replace finger cloths and add spoons as bowls of soup were placed before them.

They all sat up then. The lounging position was fine for conversation and comfort. Soup was a different matter. Agrippina watched the taster dip his spoon into each bowl, sipping and considering.

'A speciality,' Nero muttered when he was done. 'Leek and dried peas, a little dill for flavour.'

He was watching Britannicus, eyes slightly narrowed. Agrippina wondered if they would ever be friends. Perhaps a few years away from Rome would be good for the younger man. She did not like to think it, but she had survived the court of Caligula in part because she had been banished from it. In the same way, a posting to Britannia might keep its namesake safe.

'Mine is very hot,' Britannicus said. He was wincing as he blew on a spoonful.

Agrippina could see steam rising. Nero frowned, gesturing to one of the slaves around them.

'Bring a little cold water,' he said.

It appeared in moments, a tiny jug Britannicus poured in himself.

'Did you say a new tragedy by Seneca?' Octavia asked suddenly. 'Is it *Medea*? My friends were talking about it.'

Nero turned slowly to look at his wife, his expression already scornful.

'A woman's rage at her faithless husband . . .' he said. 'Yes, I can see how that might appeal to the ones you call friends. Though you would never murder your children, Octavia, if you ever manage to bring them into the world. You long for them so.'

She blinked back tears and replaced her spoon, sitting with her head down. Nero returned his attention to his mother and brother.

'What?' he demanded.

Agrippina took a deep breath.

'You should not speak so coldly to Octavia, Nero! Look at her now.'

She put her own spoon down with a tap and Britannicus did the same, sitting back. Nero looked furious.

'You should embrace her – and apologise, Nero. Honestly, you should.'

'Oh very well,' he said. He rose and did as she asked, holding Octavia briefly. His wife's tears overflowed, though she smiled and wiped at them.

'There – do I not listen? Though perhaps I will avoid that play of Aeschylus ... *Agamemnon*? The one where Clytemnestra murders her husband. I think the Greeks liked to play with fire, sometimes. I should ask Seneca to write a comedy, something light for the reign of a new emperor.'

'He may not be the right man for that,' Agrippina said. 'I have never heard him joke about anything. I have pressed enough wealth on him to buy a nation, but it has not brought a smile to that stern face, not once.'

Britannicus was rubbing his throat. He made a growling sound as he tried to clear it, then touched his other hand against his chest. His eyes widened as sharpness swelled there.

'Britannicus?' Agrippina said. 'What is it?'

'It is just a fit,' Nero said softly. 'They come on him sometimes, since his accident. It will pass.'

'No, he is in pain! Can you speak, Britannicus? Nero, would you please call a doctor? Your brother is choking, look!'

Agrippina rose and thumped Britannicus on his back. He grew red and then very pale. His fingers scrabbled at his chest, tearing his toga open, as if trying to pull whatever hurt him into the open air.

With a great kick, Britannicus sent the table flying, along with everything on it. Slaves rushed in and cleared, heads down and concentrating on their work like creatures of spirit.

Agrippina stared at the little jug that lay on the floor. She looked up into Nero's eyes – and knew.

'What have you done?' she whispered.

Octavia was on her feet, shrieking. The slaves were

making the mess disappear, but Britannicus still twitched and writhed, his face bulging. He fell limp then, sliding to the floor. His eyes were open. Agrippina couldn't speak, couldn't do anything to save him. She dropped, taking him in her arms as she sobbed.

'It will pass,' she heard Nero say again. 'It's just one of his fits. Come back to the table, mother. I have another course of lemon ice and mint leaves. Please, take a seat. I order it. You too, Octavia. Sit, I command you.'

Agrippina heard the edge in his voice and did as she was told, though her touch lingered on the fingers of Britannicus. She sat upright, hands clasped in her lap. She didn't dare look at the body on the floor, nor Octavia as she sat on the couch across from her.

Slaves served lemon ices and the taster stepped in once again with his little spoon. He was as impassive as ever, though Britannicus lay dead and both women streamed with tears. Octavia was sobbing as she ate.

'It is a tragedy,' Nero said after a time. His voice was almost a whisper. 'How fragile we are. In just a moment, it can all be snatched away. Everything. By the gods, if that had been me, Britannicus would have risen from this very table as emperor! With you at his side, mother, you might have remade the city in your image. He loved you, after all. Now though . . . I am alone. It is for the best, perhaps. Seneca has said so, many times. A man must bear his burdens alone.'

Agrippina said nothing. He had demonstrated the reach of his power and she was still reeling from it. The body of a son she loved lay at her feet and she dared not look at him. The brother who had killed him dipped a spoon into his dessert – and smiled at the sweetness.

PART FOUR

AD 56

2 1

The heat of the day had been brutal, the air still. A storm was surely due but it had not come and the three friends were sweating and out of sorts.

Nero didn't wear imperial purple that evening, though it would have matched the sunset. The light had become a glorious twilight, shading through lilacs and carmines so subtly he knew he would be surprised by the dark. He looked at Serenus and Otho, the two he trusted more than anyone. They had history together – and perhaps there were still debts between them. Nero did not like feeling he owed another man. It was an itch he could not reach. He smiled at Serenus as his friend kicked a stone at a dead dog, the corpse lying in the gutter. The head of the vigiles in Rome had a position of power and wealth – enough to thank a man for the pretence with Acte for years.

Nero watched as Serenus retrieved the stone and kicked it back towards the dog. He missed again, so Otho collected it and set it on the same spot.

'An aureus you cannot hit it twice in three shots . . .' he said.

Serenus chuckled. They had all been drinking, but only Otho had been sick. The other two were still at the stage of the evening where the air was sweet and all the world was theirs. Which in Nero's case, was essentially true.

Both Otho and Nero watched as Serenus missed all three attempts, the last in a sudden temper. The stone clacked against a shopfront, skipping down the road. With a grunt, Serenus opened a pouch and tossed a gold coin through the air. Otho took it with a grin.

'What about that murder case on the Quirinal – any progress?' he said. 'My sister was asking.'

Serenus shrugged, still annoyed with himself for accepting the wager.

'Daughter of a magistrate. Wealthy family. Her father offered me a fortune to find whoever did it and bring them to him before the courts.'

'And will you?' Otho said.

'Probably. Silver runs in the veins of this city, Otho, as you know very well. Just today, I told another man there are costs involved in finding a killer. He too had lost a daughter, but you know, there are only so many hours in the day! My vigiles can break fingers and get men to talk, but it all takes time. So I asked him: of the two, which murder will get my full attention? He understood. He was weeping, but he understood.'

'Was that it then, for his daughter?'

'Unless he sells his house and comes back tomorrow with the proceeds, I should think so. If I'm honest, we will probably find some poor bastard who was in the area and have him tied to a board for the crows. Whoever was really

Conn Iggulden

responsible might heed the warning, but probably not. There will always be crime and fires set, my friend. I had no idea there was so much of it when Nero gave me this post. I thought it would mean the right to go anywhere and take a seat at all the high tables! Instead, I have weeping fathers threatening to talk to a consul. Everyone claims to have friends in power when they are in trouble, did you know that? Pitiful.'

'What of you, Otho?' Nero said.

He would not have had to ask when they were tormenting tutors together. They'd been as close as brothers then! Now though, he realised it had been over a month since the three of them had last been out together. They had taken on responsibilities of work and family, and somehow life had become less simple. He missed the boys they'd been. Where once they would have done a dozen things on a summer's evening then slept for an entire day, something had changed. If he looked back on the previous week, he could hardly remember what he had achieved.

'Otho here is engaged,' Serenus said, his bitterness obvious to the other two. 'Did you not hear? Poppaea Sabina – a rare beauty and seven years older than us! Great tits as well.'

Otho took a swipe at the younger man. Serenus ducked and almost fell into the gutter, staggering three steps and pressing one hand against a wall as they passed.

'You've kept that secret,' Nero said. 'When will you introduce me?'

His friend blushed.

'I wasn't sure how it was going in the beginning – honestly. Serenus hears everything first these days, with all the informants he pays.'

'How would I find thieves otherwise, and tax whatever they stole?' Serenus demanded. 'The vigiles must be paid – or there would be chaos in these streets. Chaos!'

He took a moment to swig from a wineskin, palpating the swelling in a lascivious manner and then laughing so hard he was in danger of choking. He pulled himself together and it was Nero who caught his attention. He handed over the wineskin.

'And you, Nero?' Serenus asked. His voice had an edge his friends could hear as he went on. 'You have us, you have Acte. You stand across the world. Is it all you hoped it would be?'

Nero considered as he walked. The sun was fading. The shops were beginning to close, but there were still people looking through the offerings, choosing clothes or food or some implement he could not name. He should have felt the beat of the city's heart, he thought. He *did* stand at the centre! Yet he could taste sourness, and it was more than just wine.

'I sent my mother away from the city, a few days ago,' he said.

Serenus would have responded with a joke, but Otho took him by the arm, distracting him. Nero smiled, suddenly weary.

'Not exile. I just told her to go to the summer villa, to remain there until I call for her. The emperor's word, lads! It has power enough.'

'Why did you send her away?' Serenus said, shaking free of Otho's grip. 'I thought I had a meeting with her next week. So . . . that's not happening, clearly.'

'You'll work it out, I'm sure,' Nero said. 'I think it was part of her games to make me feel she could not be replaced. She filled every day with meetings and notes and scribes copying everything three times over – questions that had to be asked or researched, as if it was all vital and urgent and not a thing could be left undone. For example! Why did you have a meeting with her?'

'It was about fire equipment,' Serenus said. 'She has some senator whose house was lost on her side. He is willing to pay for wall hooks and sand, or barrels of water, I forget. To be stored on city corners. Something like that. She asked me about it first a few months ago. I was meant to have answers next week. To be honest, I was dreading having to say I hadn't done anything.'

He beamed at the reprieve and Nero chuckled.

'You see? Meetings upon meetings, records written and copied out, given to scribes and senators – anyone who wanted. She wasted time better than anyone I know, but at the heart of it, there she was still, watching me . . . judging me.'

Serenus raised his eyebrows and made an 'O' shape with his mouth. He took the wineskin back and upended it, spilling a fair amount down his toga.

'But not today,' Nero said. 'Today, she is gone from the city and can have her meetings with gulls and fishermen.' He laughed at that. 'No more disappointed stares. Let the people of Misenum enjoy her!'

He saw his friends exchange a glance and suddenly scowled. He knew they avoided some subjects. Octavia's empty womb, for one. Agrippina, for a second. Nothing had been right since Britannicus had died! Nothing. His mother had turned cold towards him, as if he were just another official. He'd expected some response, of course. He'd even waited for it, night after night, wondering if she might bring half the imperial complex down in vengeance.

He sighed. In his childhood, she'd always been given to great flaring rages, over as quickly as they began. His mistake had been in thinking this too would be a passing thing, that it would not settle into a more measured and enduring state. Instead, he had begun to feel her enmity as a weight, one that increased each month until he could not bear it.

He wondered if he'd ever know the extent of her campaign against him, he thought sourly. It had surely begun with the suicide of one of his praetors. That had him scrambling to replace a key man, while a fleet of merchant ships remained in port and wheat crops rotted in the fields. Agrippina seemed to know exactly where pulling a single stone would bring a whole wall crashing down.

If she had taken some of the burden of imperial business from Claudius, Nero had the sense she made it worse for him. He was certainly besieged night and day by petitioners and senators, no matter how angrily he sent them away. He'd seen too the hurt and shock on their faces, enough to damage his reputation. That would also be something she had planned, he didn't doubt. Agrippina knew everyone. She was too subtle for him, so that he spun and whirled and never knew when to react and when to ignore.

He had retaliated, of course, hoping to warn her off, at least long enough for her temper to cool. He'd removed her personal bodyguards and had her followed, openly. Why should he not show his anger in turn? He was her true son, not Britannicus! The relief he'd felt at his brother's funeral showed how right he had been to pull that thorn. In fact, Agrippina's spite showed him how correct he had been! With just one act, he had removed the single greatest threat to him. If that had cost him the support of a mother and wife, well it was still a cost worth paying.

A group of young men came running along the street, laughing and shoving one another. As they reached Nero, they swerved, buffeting Serenus. He drew a knife and would have striped a hand or cheek if not for Otho's grip on him. Once again, he shook Otho away.

'Leave it!' Serenus snapped. 'I would have taught them a lesson, that's all.'

'To what end?' Otho retorted. 'Drunk and angry, we'd have had to fight them all.'

Nero lowered his head, relishing the prospect. He looked down the road, but the group had gone.

'I would have liked that,' he growled. 'We had enough fights in the past, didn't we? You remember? It all feels a lifetime ago.'

'We could rob some of these shops,' Serenus said.

Otho's mouth opened.

'No we couldn't. Give me that wineskin. I think you've had enough, *prefect of the vigiles*!'

Nero grinned suddenly, showing his teeth. He was almost nineteen and lightly drunk with his friends – on a day when his mother no longer held court on the Palatine. It felt like clouds parting and he thought Serenus had the right idea.

'Why not? Give me the knife,' he said, holding out his hand.

'*There* is the Nero I used to know!' Serenus cried.

Nero crossed to a wine merchant and kicked open the door, breaking it. There was a shout of alarm from inside and Otho only stared.

'Poor boy, what are you going to do?' Serenus asked him in scorn. 'Call the vigiles?'

He followed Nero into the gloomy interior and there was a great crashing and yelling from within. Otho swallowed nervously. Nero would surely remember if he remained apart. Yet his father would hear of this – and Otho's father was not one he wanted to cross. The dilemma kept him in the street for a moment, as other shop owners came out to see what was happening. Otho swore then and followed his friends inside.

The wineshop owner looked in disbelief at the young men menacing him with knives.

'Give us Falernian,' Serenus was slurring. 'And . . . any silver you have.'

'I don't have Falernian!' the man replied. 'We don't stock it.'

He raised his voice then and began to yell for help. Serenus darted in and hit him. The man fell across a display of clay amphorae, breaking half a dozen. Wine poured and two younger men came out of the back, waving cudgels. One of them struck Serenus hard, beating him about the shoulders. The other menaced Nero, driving him back to the door as Otho came in.

'Get out! Get out!' the man's sons shouted.

The bigger one stepped too close and Nero jabbed a knife into his side. It happened in an instant and the son gasped. The father yelled and Nero suddenly felt sober and afraid. He pulled the knife out and saw bright blood on it. Otho gaped at him in horror. The shop owner's son fell back and Nero reached to grab Serenus as he flailed, almost getting himself cut in the process.

'Help!' the owner was yelling, over and over.

Nero hesitated. He reached into his belt, where he kept coins in tiny sewn pockets. He tossed two of them through the air, where they struck the ground by the young man. The shopkeeper's son sagged against sacks of grain, hand pressed to his wound.

The coins landed with a dull clink and then Nero felt a hand on his collar. He and Otho were yanked out into the street. Nero twisted around desperately, trying to fight whoever assailed him.

He stopped when he saw it was Burrus. The praetorian let him go and Nero stood panting.

'There's a man hurt in there,' Nero said, trying to pull himself together. 'An accident. I've left them enough to pay a doctor to attend.'

Serenus strolled out then. His friend stood with a swollen eye and bloody nose, but an unopened amphora of wine tucked under one arm. He looked rebellious and triumphant, though Burrus glared at him.

'I think you've had enough for the evening,' Burrus said.

'Do you?' Serenus replied lightly. 'I disagree. What do you think, Nero? Have we had enough?'

Nero recalled the expression of fear in the young man's eyes inside the shop. He winced.

'He's right, Serenus. I'm tired. I should get some rest.'

Serenus made a snorting sound and began wandering off, his staggering path taking him from one side of the road to the other. Burrus made a gesture and two men followed him, their uniforms covered by brown cloaks. They would keep him safe from the vengeance of shopkeepers, Nero realised. That was the usual justice meted out in Rome, after all.

A wailing went up inside the shop, no doubt as the owner discovered his son's wound. Nero hoped he wouldn't die. He felt slightly sick about it and could still feel the knife going in.

'What happened in there?' Burrus said.

'I was defending myself,' Nero replied.

His lower lip stuck out and he was feeling stubborn. Burrus was not his mother. He smiled bitterly. Burrus still wanted him to be a good man, for a start. His actual mother wanted nothing to do with him.

'I sent her away, Burrus,' Nero said. 'Did you know?'

For the prefect of the praetorians, he didn't need to say whom he meant. Burrus nodded.

'A dozen of my best men went with her, to keep her safe on the roads. You know, the villa at Misenum is not too far. If you wish her to return, a messenger might do it in a day or two.'

'Wish her to return?' Nero asked in disbelief. 'Not having my mother in Rome is like the sun coming out. I am free, Burrus, from all her disappointment and spite. Perhaps for the first time since becoming emperor, I am free. I swear, if I had not sent her away, I do not know what I would have done.'

'As you wish, Majesty,' Burrus said, a safe response. He bowed his head, seeing the young emperor was swaying as he tried to focus. Nero was in a dangerous mood, where wine could speak for him.

'Majesty, your personal staff wished me to mention the governor of Hispania Lusitania has entered Rome and hopes to be granted an audience tomorrow dawn. Shall I say you are occupied with matters of state?'

Nero blinked slowly, the words sinking in. He could

Conn Iggulden

hear raised voices coming closer and squinted down the street, looking for the source. He smiled when he saw Serenus was back, a woman on one arm and his stolen amphora swinging.

'I've found a whore,' Serenus announced, his voice too loud.

Some of the shopkeepers stepped forward with clubs. Flustered-looking praetorians came rushing up, dropping hands to sword hilts to warn them against trying anything.

'I'm going with Serenus,' Nero said. He scowled at the thought of what his mother would say and then remembered, brightening. 'Tell the governor I'll be along tomorrow evening, or the day after. Tell him that.'

'Majesty . . . I will tell him, but he controls a vast territory for Rome. He is a key ally of that region. And he has come far to speak to you.'

For a moment, Nero hesitated. He knew he had to apply himself to his work. He had already missed important events and offended allies, if they could even still be called allies. He had never quite appreciated how much his mother had organised the administration of the city. With her working against him, things had begun to tear themselves apart. Bills went unpaid – and no one seemed to know who was responsible. Tax revenues had dropped. Corruption had grown like a curling vine and there was nothing he could do about it. Even Serenus expected to be bribed to do his job. Without pay, all the workers complained and had to be flogged. It felt like a campaign against him, a sort of woman's war.

He snorted, wiping his nose with his wrist. Without his mother handling his appointments, he had no idea whom he was meant to see, or who needed gold, grain, soldiers marching. It felt as if he had thrown a sword high into the air and had no idea where it would fall, nor what the damage would be.

He smiled, though it was a sickly expression. He knew he was drunk. He rarely vomited, so he did not fear humiliating himself, but he could still sense Burrus' hope in him.

'I . . . no, he'll have to wait, Burrus. Do what you can to keep him happy, all right? My friends and I are going out for the evening. That's if I have your permission?'

Burrus bowed his head rather than reply. Nero could sense the man's displeasure. Well, perhaps that too was a burden he could put aside. Perhaps he should start looking for another prefect of the praetorians, someone who would owe him proper loyalty! He considered for a moment. No, he was not quite ready for that. He clapped Burrus on the shoulder and set off with Serenus and the woman he had found. Otho fell in beside them, still pale and unsteady.

Seneca was writing at his desk, squinting as the light failed. It was dark outside and he knew he should replenish the oil. Too lost in the words, he just leaned closer to the paper like an old scribe. His eyes were not as sharp as they had been and his breathing could worsen at any time. He felt the closeness of death sometimes. Anyone whose breath could be stolen knew the feeling.

He heard Burrus coming before he saw him. The prefect of the praetorians walked more heavily when he was in a bad mood. His steps thumped on the wooden floor of the old schoolroom.

Conn Iggulden

Seneca sighed and put aside the reed he was using. He rubbed a point between his eyes.

'Good evening, old friend,' he said. 'I take it he refused to come back?'

Burrus made a disgusted sound and sat on one of the chairs, his legs massive in the gloom.

'If it wouldn't cause a crisis, I could strangle the stupid . . .' he said. 'The cocksure arrogance of him!'

'You've forgotten being that young,' Seneca said. He waved a sheet of papyrus in the air like a fan, drying the ink. 'Did you never avoid responsibility, or get drunk with your friends?'

'Perhaps, but I didn't have a city looking to me for a steady hand, did I?'

'He was made emperor at sixteen, Burrus. We knew there would be storms. Our task – yours and mine – is to guide him through the worst years, so that something good and true comes out. I did not expect it to be the labour of a season.'

'He stabbed someone,' Burrus said.

Seneca froze for a beat.

'Killed them?'

'The doctor says he'll live, but the boy is lucky. Some son of a wineshop owner.'

'Well then. When I was fourteen or so, I waved a knife at a group of lads. If they hadn't backed down, I could easily have stuck one. I might have ruined his life and mine in a single moment! That is the nature of youth, Burrus. It does not think, or plan. It acts – and old men like us just stand back in awe at what it can achieve.'

Burrus made a snorting sound. There was a jug of wine on the table and a couple of clay cups, glazed in red. The praetorian's gaze rested on them and Seneca waved a hand. It had been a long day and the two men were weary. Burrus filled the cups and they touched them together.

Burrus looked around at the little schoolroom.

'This is you standing back in awe, is it? I thought you had a great mansion now, as well as the rooms on the Palatine. Yet I find you here, straining your eyes with that tiny lamp.'

'I am more comfortable in this room,' Seneca muttered. 'With hard wood and cheap wine. Wealth weakens a man, Burrus.'

'I would allow it to weaken me a little, just to see if I agreed with you.'

Seneca smiled. He liked the praetorian.

'You too have prospered, my friend. Yet you have a discipline that is rare in men, at least the ones I've known. I would love to think we could pass that to Nero, along with his Greek verbs.'

'For the sake of Rome, I hope so too. In fact, I will raise a cup to that,' Burrus said, refilling. They drank in silence for a time then, thinking of the young man they wanted so desperately to succeed.

Conn Iggulden

22

Agrippina looked out of a window, high on the cliffs. In the distance, she could see the outline of the island of Prochyta. On the clearest days, she could see its bigger neighbour of Aenaria, or even Capreae, miles off across the bay. It was not a prison cell, not as she had known once. In another life, that great villa might have been a glimpse almost of Elysium. The sea breeze eased the summer's heat, while the shore was sheltered from storms. The house had been a favourite of Tiberius, before he took up residence on Capreae. It contained its own rock cavern for water, so still and deep it gave her chills to look into it. More, it had gardens that stretched right over the face of the rock, with statues by master sculptors and every flower that could be made to grow in the salt air.

She could not say Nero had treated her with cruelty, for all she'd felt his dismissal like a lash. Her son had come like a summer storm, blustering and shaking the shutters, ordering her maid Polla to fill bags for a trip to the coast.

Agrippina bit her lip as she thought back. She had

pushed Nero beyond endurance, at least as he saw it. He'd made that clear, with his talk of failing things and spies watching, always watching. If she had loved him, Agrippina might have eased his pain, soothed the hurt and fear. Yet that had died, along with Britannicus.

She shuddered. The memory of the poisoning was vivid still. Oh, there were days, months even, when she hardly thought of it, but something had withered in that little room, with Octavia and Nero looking on. Perhaps it was hope, or the expectation that somehow Nero would be a better man than his father.

Some things could not be taken back, could not be undone. She knew that better than most. Claudius had been a vengeful old man, standing at a height he had never truly deserved. His death had been a mercy, almost. Britannicus was a different kind of sin – a life unlived; stolen before it could unfurl. It was not regret she felt, exactly. There was no point in looking back, she'd known that from childhood. It was more a cold dislike – for her own misjudgements, for the spoiled boy she had raised. It was strange. There had been a time when she'd thought a mother's love unbreakable. She'd learned it could turn to thick curds, souring and swelling within, until there was no more room for anything good.

Her maid Polla entered, bringing with her a young man Agrippina had met a few times at gatherings in Rome. She'd sent the entire staff away for the day, watching them troop down to the town below the cliffs. More than a hundred had left at her explicit order, and even then she'd searched the house for anyone left behind. One boy had been sleeping in the stables and she'd let him snore on.

There were different kinds of prisons, she thought, as

Conn Iggulden

her guest knelt on the stone. Tiberius had loved grandeur all around. His floor was of some dark blue stone, polished to reflect. She felt as if she stood in a palace. Yet in that moment, she still wondered if she was being watched. That was what Nero had brought about, she realised. A constant, nagging worry that he would see and hear.

She smiled. Her brother Caligula had employed half of Rome to watch the other half. Criticism of the emperor would always lead to reprisal, never mind actually acting against him. She wondered how many senators had taken advantage of such a mood of fear over the dark years, having their enemies denounced and removed. That would be a dangerous game, as was her own. Yet she could remember Britannicus' fear, could *see* it, the understanding in his eyes that he was truly dying. She had watched hope crushed, and so she stood in that place and took a young man's hand.

'Thank you for coming, senator – is it "Senator" Rubellius? I heard you accepted a seat but don't attend.'

'Empress, the senate is a place of corruption and depravity, all wind and bribes. I prefer to live quietly on my own estates. Politics is a sewer, as you know.'

He spoke with certainty, as if there could be no alternative to his belief. She felt a pang then for some of the men she had known. They were all so sure they were right! Perhaps she even loved that about them.

'Come,' she said. 'Walk with me in the gardens.'

Rubellius looked for servants and found only the one maid, waiting with her head bowed. Agrippina followed the sweep of his nose, which was a rather protruding thing. With slightly wet eyes, mere youth did not mean he was handsome.

Tyrant

'I keep a very small staff,' she lied. 'Pol, you may retire. I won't need you till this evening.'

Agrippina led her guest through a large open door. He looked appreciatively at the great horizon, sea and sky together.

'The beauty of nature has no rival,' Rubellius said, breathing out. 'Majesty, I see the people building in Rome every day, but they make nothing like this.'

'So you do come to the city, Rubellius, despite all the corruption and depravity?'

She regretted the jab when she saw his eyes narrow. He nodded stiffly.

'I have a number of trade concerns. Without my eye on them, my factors and foremen would rob me blind, I am certain. I assure you, I kick the dust of the city from my sandals whenever I pass the gate to my fields. I keep an older Rome there, one where I am master. Older than Augustus, even. Certainly older than Tiberius or Caligula . . . older than the divine Claudius.'

Agrippina raised her eyes without him seeing. She noticed he didn't quite dare to name her son. Rubellius was a bit of a bore, she realised. Still, what was that in comparison to some of the men she had known? Boredom had to be preferable to constant strain, or the fear of soldiers coming at any moment to take her away.

'Yours is an old fortune, Rubellius,' she said. 'I did a little research in the archives on the Palatine a few years back. I noticed your name then, appearing in the lists. You are descended from famous men – Mark Antony, for one.'

Rubellius sniffed and inclined his head as if granting a favour. They were walking along a path lined with ancient pines. The surface had been swept by the house

Conn Iggulden

staff, needles and cones all taken from sight and burned. Agrippina saw just two, fallen after she sent the servants away. She picked one up, feeling the rough wooden leaves of it.

'I do count Mark Antony in my line,' Rubellius said. 'He was a noble Roman and I see no shame in that.'

'Nor I, Rubellius! He mourned Julius Caesar, rousing the mob against his assassins. And he loved Cleopatra, though it cost him everything. We can agree he was a great man. You know, I saw too a connection to Augustus. And, of course, through him . . .'

'To Caesar himself, yes,' Rubellius finished.

Agrippina halted and he took a couple of steps before he realised and came back.

'You are the very last,' Agrippina said. 'Though you have children, do you not?'

'I do. Two sons and two daughters, Majesty.'

'You are proven then, unlike my poor son. No child has come from Nero these last years.'

'Oh, well . . .' The young nobleman was flustered as he began to fear the direction the conversation had taken. 'I'm sure that will come in time. I have been blessed to have my little brood, of course. All spared so far, thank the gods. You know, my oldest boy is as sharp as a knife. Just the other day, he asked . . .'

'It's strange to think, is it not,' Agrippina went on, 'that you share the same bloodline as my son? If no children come from him, yours might one day be emperors.'

Rubellius froze as if he had been struck.

'Majesty, I do not wish to invite disaster, not even in light talk. I know you speak in jest or as an exercise of the mind, but if such things were ever repeated, if those words reached the ear of the emperor, your son might believe the worst. He might fear, where no fear can ever be.'

Agrippina took him gently by the arm and walked on.

'I understand. Of course, whatever is said here is just sea breeze – forgotten the moment it is spoken. You have my word.'

'Majesty . . . a woman's word is never stone, not in my experience. It is . . .'

'Can you feel the wind, Rubellius? It feels as if it is changing, don't you think? I am no sailor, but such things are known to happen. My brother Caligula thought he might rule for fifty years, after all. My son believes the same, I'm sure. Yet the gods laugh at all our plans, Rubellius, just as they laugh at the thought of safety.' She halted and turned to face him. 'None of us are safe. Not in these times. A single hour – a drink sweetened with honey, even – can tear us from life.'

There were tears in her eyes and he was quite unsure how to react to them.

'Majesty, I . . .'

She laid a hand on his chest, seeing him blush at her touch.

'I can feel a heart beating, Rubellius Plautus. In those veins is the blood of Caesars, of emperors.'

She took a slow breath. She did not want to threaten him, but he had not come to her filled with bile or envy, as she had hoped. Men like that were ones she could measure and cut to length. This rural cousin seemed all too content with his life – and that was the destruction of her hopes. Her hand on his chest clenched, tightening on the cloth.

'In the veins of your sons and daughters too, Rubellius. Of course, I only need one. Or none, if you betray me.

You will never see those knives coming, Rubellius, not if you whisper my name to my son. You will destroy me if you do – and months will pass, perhaps years. Then one day, you will look for them . . . and one will be lying still. You will weep and rage and bury them deep – and months will pass again, before another will be found, cold. Perhaps you will wonder then if you should have listened this day. *But it will be too late.*'

His eyes showed white around the dark irises. Agrippina smiled, though there was no softness in it and she did not look away. She had no one watching his children, but as long as he believed it, that was all that mattered.

Rubellius swallowed. He wanted to run, but remained, his eyes beaten.

'Majesty, *please* . . . I take no part in plots and schemes. I keep away from such things and that has always kept me safe.'

'They have found you anyway,' she said. 'Your blood calls, Rubellius. The blood of men who ruled Rome, once. As you will again, when my son falls.'

Even in the gardens, he looked sharply around, fearing some slave who stood in silence. There was no one and he could only shake his head.

'I want no part in this, I swear. If it is some test of my loyalty, you need have no fear. I have no ambitions of the sort you describe! Please. I ask nothing more than to return to my home. I will not visit Rome again, if you wish.'

'Your ancestors may test you, but I do not,' she said.

She stepped closer to him, so that they breathed the same breath. He flinched before her, his hands trembling.

'My brother Caligula was killed by his own praetorians, Rubellius. Do you recall? Claudius pardoned them, because they did what had to be done, when Caligula would have destroyed everything your ancestors built.'

She paused, letting the fever of her intensity subside. She reached out and smoothed a curl of hair from his brow.

'Do you know who leads the praetorians now, Rubellius?'

'Prefect Burrus,' he whispered.

She nodded, patting his cheek.

'A man I appointed. One who stands with the emperor every day, whose sword and loyalty I command completely. So ask yourself this, Rubellius Plautus, descendant of Caesars: if the emperor falls, will you honour your line? Will your children wear purple? Will you rule . . . with me at your side?'

'To say such a thing . . . is to pronounce my own death. *Please*, Majesty, I don't want any part of such madness.'

'Whether you want it or not, the choice . . . the crisis, is come. Choose, Rubellius. Rise, or know more grief than you thought existed in the world. I sat at a table and watched a son die of poison. Shall I describe it to you?'

'No . . . no. Very well.' He looked grey, sick and older than when he had entered, as if she had pressed ten years into his eyes.

'Good man,' she said, which felt strangely true. Rubellius was neither strong-willed nor brave, as far as she could tell. Nor was he attractive, with that nose. Yet she could marry him, when the time came.

Otho was giving a speech, honouring his new bride. Poppaea Sabina stood before him, with Nero at her back in a state of confusion and arousal. He had been flirted with before, as the noble daughters of Rome sought his favour.

Conn Iggulden

He might have assumed it was his fine shoulders or dark eyes, if not for the fact that he had been almost invisible before becoming emperor. They did not see *him* when they fluttered and blushed, holding his gaze a little too long. He felt sometimes like the only cockerel in the field – and he had acted on it more than once, tumbling some daughter of a grand house while Serenus and Otho kept the husband occupied with drink and laughter.

He had never had an actual bride take such an interest, however. Poppaea had been demure enough on their first meeting, but she'd been pressing him or brushing him whenever they passed one another. He had not been certain at first, for the longest time. Surely her hand had lingered in innocence on his arm, or slid in jest around his waist? Perhaps she was just one of those who touched all others and thought nothing of it. He had danced with her and it had been a formal thing, though he felt the heat of her skin next to his cheek. He wondered if women knew when a man found them attractive. Of course, it was usually a safe assumption.

Poppaea was indeed a fine-figured woman, as Serenus had described. She resembled the prow of a warship in her wedding dress and Nero could not help wondering what lay beneath all the embroidered cloth.

Otho was thanking his father for his support and the new house the senator had bought the married couple. Nero cheered and raised a cup with the rest. Poppaea stood just in front of him, the happy crowd pressing all around. He could see fine curls on her neck, where the mass of her hair had been raised and pinned. He liked the style for what it revealed.

A man's neck served only to connect his head, Nero

thought. A woman's though, could be a slender thing, like a fine mare. It was somehow an intimacy to see it.

He looked at his cup and grinned to himself. Falernian – with all the warmth of some lost summer's sun captured in the depths. He could almost smell the rich earth – and he had kept his taster busy that afternoon. The poor man would have to call his second if he swayed any further, Nero thought. That was what a wedding was about, not some mad idea of flirtatious brides. It had to be his imagination.

He felt the lightest of touches at his waist and glanced down. The crowd was clustered thick where he stood, before the raised stage. Poppaea stood just in front of him, cup raised to her new husband. Hidden by folds of her dress, her fingers reached for Nero. He felt himself stiffen in surprise. If she was trying to take him by the hand, she was making a poor job of it.

'And to my friend, the emperor,' Otho was saying, looking in his direction.

Nero felt his cheeks burn as he nodded awkward acknowledgement. Still her hand moved! He could neither retreat nor go forward, so reached down and gripped her wrist, holding her still. He heard her gasp and prayed Otho would not call him up to stand before the crowd. He'd have to fake a fit rather than reveal what she had done to him.

Otho continued to speak and Nero raised his cup, draining it to the dregs. His taster approached with an amphora and Nero was able to step away from Poppaea. Not once had she turned round. The experience left him dazed and sensitive to touch.

He had been considering offering command of a legion

to Otho, as a wedding gift. Sending him away from Rome for a year or two would mean his new wife would be lonely. He knew it was madness, but he felt inflamed. Acte had turned cold to him over the previous few months. Nor had she grown large with child, any more than Octavia had. Perhaps he needed new ground to break. Just the thought of that ship's prow, bursting free of its ties . . .

He stood, slightly hunched as the taster went through his routine. The man took his work seriously and, for once, Nero was grateful for any delay. He looked around the room, at the sons and daughters of a hundred senators. This was a new generation, all watching him. They had been just children when Tiberius sat the imperial throne. They were the sons and daughters of empire and he could see confidence in them, in the way they stood.

On the edge, Serenus was dipping his head to speak to someone. Otho had been looking for him before and Nero wondered what would keep his friend from celebrating new love, or whatever it was. He shook his head. Being an emperor had its perks, but he had never been fondled at a wedding before, at least not by the bride. In private, he wished Otho luck with that one.

Serenus showed no sign of the laughter and song in the rest of the crowd. He came through them with gentle force and his expression alone made people step back.

'Nero,' Serenus said when he was close. 'You should hear this.'

The emperor followed him to the edge of the room. A boy waited there, shifting from foot to foot.

'Argeus here accepts a few sesterces each month to report anything interesting out at Misenum.'

Nero looked sharply at him and Serenus shrugged.

'I am head of the vigiles. It's my job to keep you safe.'

'No, it's not that. I have a dozen of my own on her staff – and I haven't heard anything.'

'The lady sent the servants into town,' the boy said.

He remembered too late that he was speaking to the emperor of Rome and tried to drop to one knee. Serenus held him up, so that he sagged.

'Just tell my friend what you told me,' Serenus sighed.

'I was working in the stables and so I didn't go out with the others. The whole house was empty, so I went up on the roof. I go there sometimes to eat. There's a spot between two slopes where I can sit in peace and no one bothers me.'

'Cut to it,' Serenus said. The boy was babbling, over-awed in Nero's presence.

'Yes, dominus, sorry. I saw the lady talking to a man.'

'What did she say?' Nero asked. His focus was complete and the boy stammered.

'I-I couldn't get close enough to hear the words what they said, dominus, I'm sorry. I tried, but they walked out into the gardens and if I followed, they would have seen. He had horses and servants, though. And three gold rings on his left hand.'

'On these fingers?' Serenus said, holding up his own hand. The boy nodded, wide-eyed, and Serenus grunted. 'That's Rubellius Plautus. Country senator not much given to warming his senate seat. That said . . .'

He frowned and Nero waited for him. His friend knew more about the nobilitas of Rome than anyone. He'd already stretched the authority Nero had given him to a position where even old families bowed and hoped he would not stop to talk.

Conn Iggulden

Serenus shook his head. He looked seriously at Nero and then tossed a small pouch to the boy.

'Head straight back with that, Argeus. I need you in place now, more than ever. If I hear you dallied for girls or drink – and I will hear – I will make you regret it. Understand?'

The boy nodded and bowed deeply to them both, taking his spoils with him.

Serenus leaned in, too close for anyone else to hear.

'How much does your mother actually dislike you, Nero? How far would she go?'

'What do you mean?'

'Holding a meeting with just one man – that could just be a tryst, an affair. But that Rubellius is your cousin, if I remember rightly. I'll check the archives, but I think he's bloodline.'

'She wouldn't dare,' Nero snapped. He knew that wasn't true even as he said it. There was nothing his mother wouldn't dare to do.

'Are you certain? Because she has survived three emperors before you.'

Nero swept a cup from a passing tray. His taster hovered, but he waved him off. No one could have known he would take that drink and his throat had gone very dry.

'Her father was killed, did you know that?' Nero said faintly. 'Her mother was exiled, blinded and starved on some island. Her two older brothers were murdered, both of them. Her sisters died when I was still a child, taken by fevers. And of course, there was Caligula, the brother who lived. My father was the only good man she ever knew, I think.'

Serenus took a cup of his own and drank it. The bride

was dancing with her husband and the crowd was cheering.

'At least Otho looks happy,' he said.

'One of us should be,' Nero said bitterly. 'I want to hear everything she does, Serenus. I cannot move against my own mother, I can't. Perhaps she can be warned off, before she goes too far.'

'Perhaps,' Serenus said. He did not look convinced. 'If she has considered a cousin in your place, Nero, that is the greatest sin of all – and she has already gone too far.'

'Just watch her. Do nothing else, Serenus! Your oath on it. I will not move until I am sure.'

Serenus was very much the head of the vigiles in that moment. He had grown into a role where each night could be packed with violence and its aftermath.

'Nero?' he said in a murmur. 'I've uncovered what could be a plot against you. If it was anyone else, I would have Agrippina taken to be questioned – without mercy, so nothing remains unknown. The fact that she is your mother is her only shield at this moment, but I will not let you be harmed, not when I could have stopped it. So I'm going to ask you for permission to do whatever I have to. I will pull Rubellius in and heat knives for him. He'll confess everything, don't worry about that.'

'Is it so serious?' Nero said.

'You know it is. Do you think Claudius would have ignored a threat of this sort, or even the whisper of one? Perhaps he did – and now you are emperor in his place.'

The two young men looked at one another, sharing the same thoughts. Yet only Nero could give permission and Serenus had to wait for him to speak.

'It's my mother,' Nero said.

Conn Iggulden

'. . . who threatens you,' Serenus finished for him.

He reached out and tapped the bangle Nero had worn from childhood, tight on his wrist. Snakeskin shimmered in golden resin, catching the light as Serenus raised Nero's hand.

'You survived assassins once, Nero. I won't let them try again. Turn me loose.'

Nero almost nodded, but then shook his head.

'No. Do nothing. Bring me a plan of action, but don't take a single step unless I agree it. Is that understood, Serenus? If you move against her without my permission, I will call that treason. She is empress and Augusta. I must be sure.'

'Then I will double your personal guard – and have Burrus pick each man himself,' Serenus said. He looked around the gathered crowd. 'It could be anyone, Nero. She has been on the Palatine for many years. You can't know who to trust, who she can reach.'

Nero clapped Serenus on the arm, touched by his concern.

'You are a good friend.'

'I enjoy this sweet life too much to throw it away, that's all,' Serenus said. He was pleased though, that Nero had understood.

23

Burrus did not enjoy riding. Horses seemed to him to be very stupid animals, with a will of their own that did not always match what he wanted to do. He was not even sure he needed one. When was speed so important, really? In his youth, he had marched twenty-five miles a day for weeks at a time. He'd only grown stronger.

He'd always enjoyed the legion life, he thought, the sense of purpose. Transferring to the praetorians had been a challenge to himself. They took only the best – and Burrus could not be satisfied with anything less. He knew he could have risen to lead any other legion, with a little good fortune. The gods rewarded talent and over decades he had learned everything there was to know about tactics and men. Burrus knew he had made himself a good leader – and then grown into the role he had created. His men saw a grim and distant statue of a man, without any of their weaknesses. He let them believe he was made of different stone, because they loved him for it. The only seasoning he allowed came in flashes of wit, as rare as

Conn Iggulden

falling stars. They relished his gruff replies to fools, repeating the better ones amongst themselves. Some of the older men had known him as a centurion, but not a single praetorian thought Burrus had bought his way into the post, or been given it for his connections. He had none – until Agrippina. Without her favour, he knew he would have remained a centurion under Rufrius until he was put out to pasture, his knees and back gone.

Burrus bent low as the wind blew in gusts. A storm was on the way and grit spattered against his face and hands as he trotted down the road. The animal was already panting, showing big yellow teeth as he rode. He reined back rather than risk being thrown, or the beast dying under him. The next inn was only a few miles off. He remembered one close to the lakes at Nemi. He would show his legate's seal and pick up another mount, perhaps on the way back. He rubbed the horse's ears as it breathed better.

His back was aching, along with his hips. His hands were yellow and crimped from the pressure of holding reins too tight and too long. Burrus had been told he rode badly, but he knew his balance was good. That mattered, when he bounced on a hard road. His legs flapped and he was pleased none of his men were there. Even his dignity would take a beating if they saw that, he thought grimly. He would walk the last mile when he returned to Rome. Or the whole way if his back didn't start to ease. At that moment, it felt like something sharp was digging in each passing moment.

Nemi was surrounded by rocky crags, with ancient villages nestling in some of the high places. Wild strawberries grew in profusion around there. Tiny, red and sweet, he could see them in bushes as the road climbed. He passed a cart with a local family cutting figs and wild branches thick and green. He did not know what purpose they would be put to, only that they watched him pass, standing in suspicious silence.

Burrus slowed further as the horse began to make a coughing sound. Its head dipped. He was unsure whether he should beat the animal. Nemi was only a dozen miles south and east of Rome. On another day, he could have run the distance. Or another year, perhaps. He grimaced at that. He fought the passage of time with everything he had – and lost, of course. All men lost. He just held on as best he could.

The wide road turned away from the lake and he dismounted to lead the panting horse to a ridge that looked down across open water. The lake was not deserted, though the day was still and the air pure at that height. As well as a source of fresh water for Rome, Nemi was where the navy tested ships and new devices. Burrus had seen deck weapons that turned on bronze balls trapped between circles of wood, the whole thing smooth as oil. Seneca understood how it worked, how they were forged. Burrus was in awe of men who designed such things. Roman power was enforced at sea, he understood that much. Nemi was where they trained.

A series of locks led from one shore right to the coast. He had been told to head down to them and he led his drooping horse, choosing a track. The message had been cryptic, though in plain language. He supposed it could have been intercepted. Yet he had not been followed, he was certain of that. Just the thought of being watched, of being suspected, made his sweat run cold. Before Agrippina, he had survived in Rome by avoiding all

Conn Iggulden

plots and secrets, by taking no one's side. Then she had raised him up. He knew he owed her his life's ambition. It was a debt he could never repay and he wondered if she even knew how much it mattered to him.

The track reached the bottom of the lake and turned in both directions around it. He supposed navy crews ran circuits there in the mornings. His horse nibbled at a clump of ferns and he looked around for any other sign of life. Out on the water, two triremes rowed in the distance, making good speed. There was a battered old hulk anchored almost in the middle of the lake. It looked as if they were going to ram it.

Burrus stood with one hand over his eyes, soaking in the quiet. The scrape of a foot interrupted his reverie. He had a sword drawn and the reins loose in an instant, turning to face the threat. He found a terrified maidservant, her hands raised against being struck.

'It's Polla!' she said, blushing furiously.

He grunted as he put away his sword.

'Well, don't come creeping up on a man, Polla. That is my advice to you. Where is your mistress?'

'O-over there . . .' she said, still trembling. She hadn't crept anywhere. He'd been lost in his thoughts and watching triremes, oblivious to her until the last moment. She didn't like to suggest his hearing wasn't as sharp as it had once been. The reflexes were still there. She had almost lost her bladder when he'd turned like a wolf snapping, going from stillness to deadly threat between heartbeats.

Burrus walked his horse behind her, to the spot a little way from the lake where Agrippina waited. She wore a dress of pale yellow and sat with her legs curled under her. Food was laid out in tiny baskets, with a wineskin and two cups.

Agrippina rose and Burrus dropped to one knee. His joints protested, but he made no sound, any more than he would have done in the legion barracks. Let them think age did not have a hold on him, as it did on other men! What they didn't know they couldn't judge.

'You look a little stiff, Burrus,' Agrippina said. 'Are you all right?'

He chuckled at his own vanity. He'd almost forgotten how little this one missed.

'I prefer to run, empress. Horses and I have never got on, not really.'

She watched as he wrapped the reins around a sapling and left the animal to crop grass and rest.

'Sit by me, would you?' she said. 'It is a perfect day and the lake is beautiful. If we are very still, Burrus, dragonflies flit back and forth through this clearing – like jewels.'

'Don't they bite?' Burrus asked. He was a city boy and he did not really enjoy wild creatures that might sting or suck his blood.

'I don't think so,' she said.

He took a seat and accepted a cup of wine, though it was early in the day to drink. The maid appeared to have vanished, he noticed. The little spot felt suddenly rather intimate. He was grateful when Agrippina poured water as well to thin the wine.

'There. You have been served by an empress of Rome, Burrus. Not many men can say that.'

He could think of a few, but it would have been bad manners to say so. Deep in thought, he sipped his wine.

'I received your note, empress. As you see, I came. I cannot stay for long, though. Your son knows I train every day for a few hours. Beyond that, my absence might be reported. I do not want him to wonder where I vanished to, empress.'

'Agrippina, please,' she said. 'The same is true for me, or even more so. Not in exile, but forbidden to return to the city? I am watched, like a prisoner almost. For one who stood at the right hand of an emperor, it is an insult. Or a tragedy in the making.'

She put her hand over his. It seemed such a casual thing, but he felt the warmth of her skin and her complete attention. He steeled himself, remembering the fate of those who crossed her. She looked an innocent when tears sparkled and she seemed helpless. All men wanted to put an arm around her, to rub a thumb along those tears. The truth was something else entirely.

'Majesty . . . Agrippina. I cannot stay,' he said.

He saw her mouth firm and looked away from her, through the trees to where the triremes trained. There were dragonflies in the air there, he realised. Blue and green and red, they danced together. Agrippina's focus was on him and she did not notice them.

'I trust very few men in the world, Burrus. You more than any other. Did you know that?'

'If you wish me to speak to your son on your behalf, I will try. I know how much I owe you.'

'Yes. I saw you when no one else did,' she said. 'I raised you to the one thing you wanted above all others, to lead men as you believe they should be led. The praetorians are better now than they have ever been. Everyone says that, Burrus. You had your dream from my hand . . . while I am kept prisoner, kept from all I have built in Rome. By my faithless son, Burrus. A boy I raised, whose bloody knees I cleaned, whose wife I picked for him. A stubborn boy made emperor because of me, when *all he had would have been taken from him!*'

Burrus leaned back from her anger. He did not understand all that lay behind it, but he had never seen such a depth to her fury before.

'What would you have me do?' he asked. 'No games – I am not made for them. If I am your man, tell me your will and let me decide.'

He watched the emotion smooth away. She breathed and took his hand once more.

'My brother Caligula was killed by his praetorians, Burrus. And it was right, because he had gone mad.' Even she hesitated, but her nerve was iron. Though a pulse showed in her throat, she went on. 'I need you to be the blade, Burrus.' He might have spoken as his eyes widened, but she went on, relentless. 'I have another to be emperor, one who will not refuse my counsel, who will not scorn the knowledge and wisdom of serving three emperors at the heart of Rome. I have earned my place, Burrus, just as you earned yours. As you once went to the house of Junius Silanus, do this for me.'

He looked at her then, his face utterly still. Though Agrippina was close and touched his hand, she could not read him. Her heart fluttered in her chest and she was breathing too fast. His secret was that he loved her. He thought it was a private thing, but she knew it, as she had always learned to know. She had seen that in the beginning – and raised him for it.

'For you,' he breathed. 'I think . . . I could do it for you.'

'It cannot be a blade,' she said. 'You would not survive him for long. And all his food is tasted. I have thought on it, Burrus, every day of my imprisonment here. Take him riding – and when he dismounts, you could break his neck.

Conn Iggulden

It would be as if he fell, do you see? Rome will mourn a wasted life and I will return. It will be as it was when Claudius came to the throne! I was recalled from exile once. I can be again.' She leaned against him, so that he could rest his chin on the top of her head. 'If you love me, you will do this last – because though I hate it, I am responsible for Rome. Though he is my son and my heart breaks, this is right. Do you see?'

'Yes,' he whispered. He could imagine her turning her head to look up at him. He thought he might kiss her if she did. The moment came and went as she waited for his answer.

'Very well, Agrippina.'

The sun was setting by the time Burrus reached the city walls and dismounted in aching relief, passing his mount into the hands of praetorians there. He had left the first animal back at a tavern close to Nemi, swapping it for a younger gelding that wanted to run and didn't like being held back. He had wrestled with the sprightly animal for a dozen miles and was exhausted as he finally stepped down, trying not to hobble in front of his men.

To loosen up, Burrus walked through the city. Night was coming and vigiles were out on the street corners, their presence a warning to drunks or thieves, or anyone else tempted to use darkness to hide their sins. Burrus bought two wineskins of Sicilian red and tucked them under his arms. He wasn't challenged as he made his way up the Aventine hill. He knew where he was going and as the road rose, the houses grew in wealth and size. On the very top, he stopped at a door in a wall and rang a small bell that hung there.

He'd half-expected a servant, but it was Seneca himself who peered down from the wall at him.

'Burrus? Is that you? Come in.'

'I have wine,' Burrus said, yawning.

Seneca nodded.

'Well, I have cups. Come in.'

The door opened and Burrus walked a path towards a huge home. It sprawled across a plot that stretched for acres in the evening gloom. Burrus found himself smiling tiredly as Seneca went ahead. The man's hand lamp was the only light and the house had a sense of being shuttered. He followed the tutor through vast echoing rooms with furniture hidden under linen sheets, then through an internal garden where crickets chirped and a pigeon erupted in panic at their presence, climbing madly to the night sky.

'How much of this place do you actually use?' Burrus said.

Seneca shrugged and gestured to their destination.

'I only need one room!'

He set his lamp down and lit another, now that he had company. Burrus saw a thin palliasse on the floor where Seneca slept. Beyond that, there was just a table and a couple of stools, with piles of books and papers all around.

'Don't knock *anything* over,' Seneca said. 'There is a bench here, if I move these piles. I know where everything is, don't you worry.'

Burrus sat down as the space was cleared. He could not help smiling at the man he considered his friend. Just having Seneca fussing around was like a balm on the wounds he had taken that day. He felt some part of him begin to ease as he filled two cups and they clinked them together.

'There are men in Rome who would kill for a house like

Conn Iggulden

this – and they would say a hundred slaves or more would be needed. Yet you live alone and it is wasted on you.'

'It's not wasted, not really. I enjoy the gardens, though they are rather overgrown. I write in the evenings here, when I am not at the theatre.'

'Is it not lonely?' Burrus asked.

'A little. My wife kept a busy house, with all the people she would invite. I miss that sometimes, the bustle and talk. I miss her. But here I am, with my plays and my poems. It is not a bad life. She and I met a little late . . . but that's the way it is, sometimes. If I'd known I would have her for just a few years, I wouldn't change it.' He waved a hand, embarrassed. 'What brings you to me this evening? You look troubled. And two wineskins? I'm not much of a drinker, which you already know. So either you intend to flatten both, which would be unlike you, or you think I will join you when you have said whatever you wish to say. Come, you know me well. Tell me whatever it is.'

'Some things are hard to say aloud,' Burrus said. 'Even alone, even to a friend. They come with danger.'

'Danger to me? Just by hearing a few words?' Seneca's expression darkened. 'There are not many subjects that come with such a burden, my friend. Yet I trust your judgement, do you understand? If you need me to hear, to give my advice, I will do what I can.'

The praetorian emptied his cup and slowly refilled it. Seneca took up the second skin and directed the flow into his own, waiting. In the silence, like a creaking door, Burrus began to speak.

24

Nero had reopened the rooms Claudius had used. Without his mother's stern eye on him, the action came more easily. They had a view over Rome that was unparalleled and when the nights were cold, he actually appreciated the great brazier of black iron, as wide across as two men. More than any of that, it was a sign of his right to rule in that place. The suite of rooms was the heart of the Palatine, the emperor's private wing. Somehow, that had remained true even as Nero slept in other parts of the imperial complex.

He rose from his seat as Serenus entered. His friend's presence had been signalled by praetorians on the door and Serenus had been searched. He may have been head of the vigiles, but no one reached the emperor's side wearing a blade. It did not matter if they were governor of Gaul or king of a small nation, they came before him in wool and leather, with praetorians watching every move, hands on the hilts of swords.

Nero saw his friend's dark expression. Serenus nodded.

Conn Iggulden

'In private, if you wouldn't mind,' Serenus said.

The emperor waved his hand and the slaves trooped out.

Serenus waited with his head slightly bowed. He was not certain every last pair of eyes had gone, of course. Nero could easily keep a couple of praetorians in the other room for him to call. He was the sort who believed in precautions, as Serenus knew very well.

'How is Otho doing?' Serenus asked while the doors were still open.

'Very well, as I've heard it. He sends reports of great labours, with costs incurred, of course. I . . . don't question those.'

'No, I suppose not.'

Serenus knew Poppaea Sabina had spent a number of nights in those very rooms. It was possible she waited in the private part at that very moment. He didn't approve of Nero sharing a bed with Otho's wife, nor the affection he saw growing between them. Rather than come to blows, Nero had posted his friend to Lusitania, to the western edge of empire and about as far from Rome as he could find. It would lead to trouble when Otho discovered his wife's affair, Serenus was sure. In that area, Nero was dead to reason, however. His relationship with Acte had cooled when she had remained as slim as a willow stem. Octavia too received only his cold glares. Serenus hoped Poppaea would prove more fertile. From the way she draped herself on Nero in public, she seemed to know the stakes were all or nothing.

The doors closed and Nero turned to him.

'So? What brings you here at this hour? I was just going to bed.'

'You said to report anything your mother did. Well, she disappeared yesterday. She ordered her servants to remain behind and took just one maid with her, out into the wilderness.'

'You had them followed?' Nero demanded.

'How could I? None of my people were allowed to go with her. She rode out alone. I could have the maid taken up, perhaps. My men could make her talk.'

'No, they are always together, like sisters. My mother would know we had tripped the snare.'

'What if she did? Just that warning might stop whatever she is planning.'

'Couldn't it yet be something innocent? Some trip to buy dresses or jewellery? I never told her she couldn't leave the house at Misenum, only that she couldn't enter Rome without my permission. It isn't exile, Serenus! Perhaps I made that too clear to her, left her too much freedom.'

'There is nothing *innocent* about any of it,' Serenus said. 'She meets your cousin Rubellius in secret, then vanishes for an entire day? She is a threat, Nero. That is my judgement, and if you'll forgive me, it should be yours as well. By the gods, do you think I want to say any of this? She is Caligula's sister! She has half of Rome in her hand.' He took a deep breath. 'There were rumours about the way Claudius died. He was in good health and then . . . he was puking and purging, dead before the sun rose. She may be more dangerous than you know.'

'Claudius was an old man,' Nero muttered, thinking of Locusta. 'And old men can be swept away by a single cold night, everyone knows that. No, I looked into it, Serenus. I am satisfied.'

'Britannicus, then!' Serenus snapped. 'Do you not wonder? Agrippina was at that table with you. Britannicus choked to death in front of you all.'

Conn Iggulden

Nero shook his head, his expression darkening.

'That was a fit, nothing more.'

'Perhaps,' Serenus said grimly. 'But even if you're right about all of that, she *did* meet in secret with Rubellius Plautus, your blood cousin. She *did* disappear for an entire day. She is plotting, Nero. My job – part of it – is to make sure there are no threats on the horizon. Agrippina is a threat – tomorrow or in a month, I don't know. As your friend, I ask you: give me the order.'

'I'm not killing my mother, Serenus! Is there a worse sin? The people would rise up if they heard.'

'Then we'll make sure they don't hear. If you saw a snake on your bed, you would cut its head off before it strikes, wouldn't you? *Before* it strikes!'

'They would say I am a monster,' Nero murmured. He looked stricken, his eyes blank.

'You are emperor. Your enemies will say that anyway. Have you read the walls of any brothel in Rome recently? Your name is usually there. Mine too, in a couple.' Serenus smiled, but it was habit more than humour. 'I even added a few lines myself.'

'No. A sin like that cries out. It's my *mother*!'

'There never was one like her – except Medea, who killed all her children.'

They stopped the furious back-and-forth between them when the praetorians came to attention outside the door.

'Who else comes at this hour?' Serenus muttered.

Nero said nothing and they both waited as the doors opened.

Burrus entered, in the formal uniform of a prefect of the praetorians. His legs were bare under a kilt of leather and cloth. He carried his plumed helmet under one arm and his expression was like flint as he surveyed two of the young men he had trained from boyhood. They were not the same selfish, wilful urchins who had thrown a wasp nest into the schoolroom. Those boys were as dead as the wasps, dried up and carried away on a summer's gale. He had shaped two young men from them, gleaming with health and unmarked skin. He halted before the table.

'What is it, Burrus?' Nero asked.

Agrippina had been right, of course, as she was always right. There was only one man in Rome who could stand next to the emperor and keep his weapons. Burrus reached to his left hip and drew his gladius from the sheath, the sound very loud in that place.

The shore at Misenum was far below the house on the cliff. Agrippina saw torches lit on the dark sea as a boat approached, its deck a gold moth passing across the waters. That light was taken up as the vessel reached the dock below – a new construction from the time of Tiberius, to allow stores and men to land there.

Agrippina had come to the balcony of the house, looking down to where the sea showed white, hissing over sand and stones. She and Polla watched the lights bobbing as they were carried up the cliff path. Agrippina lost no time then.

'Fetch me the stola in white,' she said. 'And my cloak of forest green. It will be cold on the water.'

She thought rather wistfully of the cloth of gold she had worn once. That would be proof against any sea breeze. Yet it remained in Rome, a treasure of the city.

Agrippina dressed with the greatest of care, returning to the balcony at intervals to watch the progress of the lights. Polla piled up her hair with long gold pins, resting a veil on it that added to her height and stretched as gauze to her fingertips. Agrippina put her foot into slender golden sandals, open in the Egyptian style. Her toenails were painted and her eyes made large with kohl. Gold gleamed at her ears, her throat and her wrists, drawing the eye. Polla touched a great glass orb to her skin, dipping it in the perfume Cleopatra had known. Her cloak was last, resting on the veil and her hair as she wrapped it around herself. They both heard the tramp of legionary boots coming closer on marble floors.

Polla could feel her mistress trembling, then, in a moment, the slight shake ceased as if it had never been. She blinked at the level of control or courage, wondering at it.

Agrippina rose from her seat, turning to face soldiers of Rome. She had known they would be praetorians. They too wore cloaks as well as kilts and helmets, the effect both dark and frightening in the torchlight. It was hard not to think of them as death, come to that place.

It was a small victory to see the centurion hesitate. Perhaps he had expected a woman called from bed and wrapped in a sleeping shift, her hair in disarray. Agrippina stood before him as the dowager empress, and his manner gentled before the art.

'My lady . . .'

'Now now, centurion! Have I not earned my titles? Were they not granted to me by the senate and the consuls, speaking in Rome and signed into law?'

She was not sure how he would react to being interrupted. It depended on his orders, but it helped her to remain calm. She had sent men before into the night, to the homes of others. She knew what it could mean. A few words spoken was a way to put off the moment she would learn her fate.

He inclined his head, as if accepting a point of debate.

'Empress Agrippina Augusta,' he said. 'My name is Marcus Junius Pera, first cohort, first century of the praetorian guard. I have been sent to summon you to the emperor's presence. He commands it. Is there . . . anything you would like to take with you? My orders are to return immediately.'

'To where, Centurion Pera?' Agrippina asked. Her heart was beating again, where she thought it had surely stopped.

'Just a little way along the coast, empress. The town of Baiae.'

'I know it,' she breathed.

Could she trust his word? She was not sure. Yet she felt hope kindle. If he lied, he gave no sign – nor could she think of a reason for him to do so. It seemed her destination was not to be Pandateria, where her mother had died in exile. Nor the island of Pontia, where Agrippina had known a dark so absolute she carried it still. She gestured to the door, where cloaked and armoured soldiers stood in silence.

'Very well, Centurion Pera. Polla dear, bring my bag. Lead me down, centurion. I wish to see what the night has in store. Whatever it is, I will rush towards it!'

Her maid picked up a large satchel, carrying it with both hands. The praetorian glanced at her, but he did not ask Polla to turn it out, not then. Agrippina was dowager empress and Augusta – and his prisoner – as men fell in before and behind. Agrippina understood that last part very well.

Titles were just gilded words, after all; sending men with iron in the night was the reality of power.

The praetorians touched lit torches to dark ones and light spread amongst their number once more. The path down grew sandy as the slope increased. Agrippina could not shake the sense of unreality. Since her arrival in that place, she had walked it scores of times, yet never in the dark, with the sea like a silvered lake. The sound of gentle waves was comforting and she realised she would miss the house on the bluffs if she did not see it again. She had only visited Baiae once or twice. She knew Nero loved the city of Neapolis – and Neapolis was mother to the towns along that shore. If he yet lived, if he waited for her there, it meant . . . She blinked, not wanting tears to spoil her make-up. Polla could undo a little damage, but not work miracles.

Between torches, the night hid her fears. Agrippina breathed deeply, settling herself, summoning her will. If it was to be exile, she would go to it with dignity. If death . . . No, she could not bear the thought of that.

She and Polla made their way to the end of the wooden dock. The boat that waited was smaller than she had expected, a slender thing compared to the massive bulk of a trireme. The centurion gestured for her to step across and took the hand she held out. Agrippina smiled thanks in the torchlight and noted how he watched her. Everything mattered, when her life was the stake.

She was intrigued to see a couch on the narrow deck. It might have been taken from some fine room in Rome, carried across land and sea to that place. She and Polla seated themselves and Agrippina wrapped veil and cloak around her. The breeze was cold, just as she had thought.

Below deck, unseen rowers unstrapped their oars and slid them out. Someone pushed them away from the dock and they were floating, rocking in a way that brought back dark memories. Even a trireme was more stable, she thought. Agrippina could hear Polla praying to Neptune for safe passage and joined her in her own thoughts for a few moments.

'No silver oars, centurion?' she said then.

The man had stayed close, a dark sentinel under the stars. His torches had all been extinguished and the helmsman was taking them away from the danger of rocks on an unseen shore, out into deep waters. The town of Baiae was to the north, deep in the bay that ended with her house at Misenum. It couldn't be more than an hour before she had land underneath her feet once more. Agrippina shuddered and told herself it was just the wind.

'Silver oars, Majesty?' the centurion said after a time. The curiosity of men was boundless and she smiled.

'Cleopatra's barge had them. As I heard it. When she came to take Julius Caesar on board. The oars were dipped in silver somehow, so that they shone as they swept through the water. He wrote about it, described it all. Her sail was a glorious purple. It must have been magnificent.'

'Yes. I would like to have seen that, Majesty,' the centurion said.

He fell silent and Agrippina realised, almost for the first time in her life, there was nothing more she could do. Her fate was in the hands of others. She closed her eyes, hearing the hiss of water under the prow, the rhythmic grunts of labouring men below deck. The smothered sobbing of her maid.

Agrippina reached out and drew the young woman

closer on the couch, the bag still clutched in her arms like a child. They were both shivering. Polla's teeth chattered together. The wind was cold, Agrippina told herself. That was all it was.

The prow turned back towards the distant shore, to where the town of Baiae was celebrating the feast of Minerva. Lights danced along the beach there like fireflies. Agrippina could hear the sound of laughter and song as they swept the dark waters and skimmed in alone.

25

Minerva was a goddess of justice and the arts, perhaps even of war when the factors aligned and there was no alternative. The Greeks called her Athena – and of course, they were the ones who had first seeded the city in Neapolis, when Rome was just a dream on seven hills.

Agrippina had never seen Minerva as a patron goddess, worthy of particular reverence. She had made her own small offering earlier that evening, in the little shrine at Misenum. A light burned for the goddess there – it was never a good idea to risk one of the pantheon taking offence. Yet Agrippina preferred the clean burn of Apollo, the youth of sun and fire. The Spartans had loved him, she recalled. His wrath was a furnace, as immortal as the god.

Agrippina and Polla waited on the couch as the boat was rowed in, coming at last against a bigger dock than the one at Misenum. Full-size triremes rocked there, making her craft look fragile in comparison. The stars were bright in a clear sky and she could smell damp and seaweed, along with old fish. Sentries kept watch, she noticed, though the docks were quiet. The main crews would be on leave, adding mirth and violence to parties in the town. Neapolis lay just a few miles to the east along the coast, secure in its reputation as a place for the young. Noble sons and daughters of Rome could escape stifling rules there, or just the watchful eyes of their families. Agrippina could imagine Nero visiting Neapolis. For a young emperor, it was a place of wine, women and song, of tastes sweet and new.

There was no hesitation in the centurion, she noticed. Marcus Pera took her by the hand and helped her climb a slippery ladder set into the dock. He even took the bag from Polla and hefted it as she followed her mistress up the rungs.

'I will have to look through this, Majesty, I'm afraid.'

'Of course! Though there is nothing but women's things inside. Things your own mother would know – paints and brushes and certain items of clothing.'

Those last words made him blush. The centurion gave the contents no more than a quick fumbling before handing it back to Polla. Agrippina smiled as he led them on. He had missed the tiny knife, as well as the vial of foxglove powder pressed into a jar of rouge.

The presence of armed legionaries had not gone unnoticed, of course. Half the town seemed to be awake and about for the festival. At that late hour, most of them were drunk and singing arm in arm. The sudden presence of uniformed praetorians was like cold water dashed into their faces. Beaming smiles turned to scowls; voices called insults from out of the darkness. Agrippina saw a few gestures she remembered from legion camps of her childhood. Pushing the tip of the thumb between the second and third knuckles was an old favourite, as were the horns of a cuckold. Yet they were aimed at the soldiers, not the women they escorted.

The centurion clearly thought so. When one group of laughing men stood in their way, he gripped his sword hilt in unmistakable threat. He called no warning, but went from peace to fighting stance in an instant. The group scattered and he lost the prickling stillness as if it had not come about.

A dozen paces later, a drunk was too slow or too aggressive to move. The centurion straight-armed him and he went down like a wall, wailing as praetorians trudged over him. No one stopped the imperial guard from going about their business, Agrippina recalled. No one.

In the dark, she had to scramble not to step on the man. Polla looked down at him and then at her mistress, visibly afraid of what lay ahead. Agrippina could only keep a tight smile, though it had become a skull-like thing and her cheeks ached.

'Is it much further, centurion?' Agrippina asked. Her feet were beginning to hurt. 'I would have worn boots if I'd known we would be marching like this.'

Centurion Pera slowed. In a hostile crowd, he and his colleagues had fallen into their ordinary marching pace. He bowed his head.

'My apologies, empress. We are nearly there – the house of Consul Barcellus. My duty is at an end.'

'That is never true,' Agrippina said.

He considered her words before nodding.

'I believe you are correct, empress.'

It was a moment of understanding. She reached out and touched him on the arm to mark it in his mind.

The entrance to the consul's house revealed a

butter-gold light inside. It was entered by a flight of steps in white stone, washed by that colour. Centurion Pera exchanged passwords with another praetorian she did not know, saluting Agrippina as she was passed into the care of a different group and ascended, moving through outer doors to the light within.

Agrippina entered a great hall with Polla at her side. She heard the maid's half-stifled gasp and came close to making the same sound herself. Dozens of oil lamps hung from a vast, domed ceiling. The curve had been painted with gold leaf and so reflected and doubled the light. The floor too was as highly polished as she had ever seen. It was as if Agrippina and Polla walked on a golden lake.

It might have been a peaceful summer's evening if not for the praetorian escort, in two files of six. Those men did not look up at wonders above, Agrippina noticed. No, they kept their eyes on the end, on another set of doors there.

As the pace increased, Agrippina found herself breathing faster, almost panting with the strain. She did not know for certain who stood beyond those doors, nor where her fate would take her. Whoever it was had power, or they would not have been able to send praetorians. Perhaps six men in Rome could have fetched her to that place. She could have named them all, but only one truly mattered. She did not know in that moment if her son lived or not.

The twin files of praetorians halted before the doors, turning on the spot so that they faced back the way they had come. Agrippina saw some of them glance upwards then. For all their armour and dark cloaks, they were still men.

The doors opened and she went forward, Polla clutching the big bag almost as protection against whatever awaited them. Agrippina filled her lungs with cool air, feeling light to the point of dizziness.

Inside, three men rose from where they had been sitting. Agrippina stepped onto a woven rug and was grateful for the softness and the way it muffled clacking heels.

Her son was watching, weighing her in his judgement as if she sat beneath a scrying glass and he could not quite read the lettering it revealed. Agrippina let her gaze sweep across him, all she could bear in that moment. He did not seem triumphant, she thought.

Serenus was one she knew, though she had never liked him. Perhaps that was a mother's luxury, to feel her son's friends were not a good influence, were not right for him. He, Nero and Otho had been inseparable for a dozen years or so. She knew Serenus used the vigiles like his own personal guard, taking on authority that had no clear ending. Like her son, he was a dangerous man.

The third was the one who made something break within her, as if a glass had been wrapped in cloth and then pressed until it shattered. It was just a little pain, as a knife going in might have been.

Burrus stood with his head slightly bowed, watching Agrippina from under lowered brows. His hair gleamed white in the lamplight and in that instant, she understood he had chosen Nero over her. Agrippina's life hung in the balance, or was already lost. She smiled then.

'Come in, mother,' Nero said. 'There are a few things that must be said, as I think you know.'

Agrippina left the doors behind as she approached. Polla followed at her heels, head down and clearly wishing she could just vanish into the floor. The maid still clutched the bag as the two women took seats where Nero gestured.

One by one, the three men sat. Wine was brought and tasted, then passed to each of them. Agrippina waved hers away.

'There's nothing in it, mother,' Nero said, suddenly irritable.

She had to trust him and so accepted the cup as it was offered again. Though it cost her, she sipped at it.

'The presence of Burrus, armed and at my side, should tell you most of what you need to know,' Nero went on. 'He came to me on the Palatine – and drew his sword in my presence. There was a moment . . . well, it does not matter. He knelt and offered me his sword's hilt. He put it to his own throat when I accepted it. Do you understand? You thought he was your man, mother, but Burrus serves the imperium. His oath was to the emperor. Like the man himself, that word, that *loyalty* is iron – and mine.'

He paused, but Agrippina said nothing. The game had begun and she had very few pieces left on her side. Nero had Burrus and Serenus and all the praetorians waiting. Yet he had not had her killed, not as she would have done. She lived – and that meant she had some value to him, or that he thought she did. She inclined her head, letting beauty remain silent for a little longer.

'So, Burrus told me of your plan,' Nero said. 'I knew you were a cold woman, but still . . . it astonishes me that you would consider such a thing. You would make yourself Medea, mother? Scorned and outcast for killing your own son? Half of Rome would sign an order for your death if they learned of that! They would seal that order for treason, for conspiracy – and sleep like an innocent child after, knowing they had rid the world of a dark and sinful woman. You would not see the sun rise again. Do you understand? If I gave the word, you would be dragged out of here by my praetorians. It could happen this very night, with your bones on a beach pyre before dawn. Are you listening?'

'I am, of course,' she said.

He searched her face for some shred of guilt and found none. It was as if a statue looked back at him, with black eyes and lips the colour of blood.

'Do you like stories, mother?' he said at last. 'You used to read them to me sometimes, when I was young. Do you remember the last days of Augustus?'

'Some of it,' Agrippina replied.

Nero nodded.

'He was worried about Tiberius, do you recall? Rightly as it turned out. Tiberius had grown old waiting for Augustus to die, waiting to be emperor. He had not quite become the man he would be, but Augustus always looked on him as the future of Rome – and saw he fell short. I do not know if Augustus saw the depths of his depravity, his love of cruelty and control. Tiberius is the one who had your brother Caligula on his island, all to himself. He broke your brother, didn't he? He sent him mad.' Nero leaned forward, his eyes bright and fascinated. 'Who knows what you both saw in those years? Your father was murdered, your mother blinded. Yet you survived, mother, somehow. If you were hardened by it, perhaps your beauty hid it from the rest of us.'

Agrippina dipped her head, but said nothing. Words poured out of her son and she saw him as a man almost for the first time, even as an emperor. Nero looked weary, but there was no petty triumph in him. He spoke well, as one trained by Seneca might speak.

Conn Iggulden

'Augustus' daughter Julia had raised a son – Marcus Agrippa. A grandson of the emperor by blood! Yet Agrippa was lazy, cruel and obsessed with violence. That young man broke laws of decency and order, doing whatever he pleased to whomever he pleased, until Augustus had him banished to an island – Planasia. You know, mother, it lies not too far from where my men picked you up this evening.'

Nero emptied his wine cup and saw it tasted and refilled. Agrippina could only wait and sip at hers. Her son loved theatre, she recalled. He had even talked of taking on masked parts as an actor. This was all a performance in a way, the outcome decided. She was not sure if she was the audience, or whether he spoke for Burrus and Serenus. Her fate was already written, she was certain. She knew the story he told. She knew the ending.

Agrippina gripped the wine cup, placing her free hand over it as a servant tried to refill the contents.

'When Augustus was very old,' Nero said, 'he feared he had made a terrible mistake. He went to see this Marcus Agrippa in his exile, to judge whether he had been right to raise Tiberius over him. The emperor went inside and spoke to his grandson alone in his prison cell. He was in there for hours, and when he came out, he ordered his guard to go in and kill the young man. Do you remember the story, mother?'

'I remember,' she said softly.

'Right or wrong, he could not leave his grandson alive to threaten Tiberius, to undermine his right to rule. That was the decision of an emperor. I imagine it broke his heart.'

He gestured expansively, more sure of himself.

'And so . . . here I am tonight, with a choice to make. The question I have been asking is whether there is any point to this. I can show you how loyal Burrus has been to me. I can tell you how Rubellius Plautus has been swept up in my nets, along with his four delightful children. I have not yet decided their fates. Like poor, long-dead Marcus Agrippa, they are of my blood. The same ancestors gave children to the world, and they had children – and there it is. I could burn my line from the world tonight, if I chose to.'

'Is your wife with child?' Agrippina asked. Her son's smile tightened, becoming a snarl. 'Or your mistress?'

'No, mother. Perhaps it would be rash of me to touch a burning brand to the last of my line until I have sons of my own. Yet the world is large. I can send them east, to cities where Rome is just a legend. I might do that . . . if you gave me reason.'

Agrippina refused to let herself hope. The moment a leaf pushed through the blackness of her thoughts, she tore it out, root and all. Her son would give her nothing, she was almost certain. Almost.

'What do you mean?' she said.

'I wanted to let you see there is no hope for what you were planning. Rubellius Plautus will not see Rome again in his lifetime. He is gone. Burrus is loyal – and you have no one else who could come so close, who could strike at me. At your own son! You are my *mother*! I don't want to give an order to . . .' He forced himself to say it. 'To have you killed! No matter how well deserved. Can you understand? I asked you here to talk of peace between us, not vengeance. Please. Tell me you will give up these plots, that you will live quietly and never again dare to move against the imperial estate. That you will support *your son*.'

374   *Conn Iggulden*

There was memory in the way he looked at her. Decades sat heavy between them, unknown to either Burrus or Serenus. Those men could not see the days of laughter and tears, or the affection. Such things mattered, sitting like a stone.

'All I wanted . . .' Agrippina began. 'I found myself on a path I did not choose, or at least not as a single choice. It *twisted*, somewhere back along the line – and I did not mean it to. I had power when I was the wife of an emperor, do you see? I walked with kings and they listened. I made decisions and the world changed. Then . . . Claudius died and Burrus and I raised you over Britannicus. You were the heir, as I had begged Claudius to grant. You were held up on our hands – and we threw open the doors of the Palatine and declared for you.'

She closed her eyes. A tear broke from her lashes, washing a line of kohl down her cheek.

'I lost as much as you gained that day, Nero . . . Lucius. Can you understand? Perhaps I grew angry, yes, I will speak the truth. I *was* angry with you. I felt you overlooked all I had done. To see poor Britannicus die . . .'

She bowed her head and Nero spoke over her. There were some things he did not want discussed, not while there were others to hear.

'We have both known hurt,' he said. 'Is there a way back? If I offered you some of your old influence, some role in the city, would it all grow like a weed to attack me again? Or would you be satisfied? Can you ever be satisfied?'

'I could,' she said. 'What is the point of the passing years if we learn nothing? I have made mistakes, Nero – but my son is emperor. I know your father would be proud of you, and perhaps of me. Yet I am no longer the girl I was when I knew him, nor the young mother! I can hardly even remember what once seemed so important. Life is simpler now. The cares and tangles smooth away. I give you my word. I *can* live simply, in Rome or out, in something like retirement. If you will allow me a small staff, I might yet be some help to you. My forty years in the world have answered some of the great questions. I have known emperors and served them. Perhaps that will be of use, I cannot say. But if you offer to forgive me, to put our sins aside and start again, I will accept. I will take your hand and kiss it, as when you were a small boy.'

He stood then and held out both hands to her. Agrippina rose from her couch and knelt before him, pressing lips to his trembling fingers as she shook with sobs.

'You are a better man, a better emperor than I knew,' she said. 'Thank you for this mercy, Nero. I will call this the first day – and I will never let you down again. I swear it on Apollo – and Minerva, as it is her feast.'

'Very well,' he said. 'Just know, there will be no other chance after this. You are my mother and so I honour you above all other women. Go now, that I may think and pray. Serenus will take you back to the house on Misenum. On the . . . first day of next month, I will see you in Rome. We'll break bread and discuss what role you can play. Less than before, mother, but still useful. That is all I can offer.'

'Then that is all I want,' she said, pressing her cheek against his hand.

She stood then and accepted a cloth from Polla to dab her eyes. The young woman kept her head down as if she stood in a thunderstorm, terrified of a bolt from the dark.

Serenus extended an arm in the direction of the doors

and Agrippina nodded to him. She saw Polla had taken up the great bag and Agrippina knelt once more to her son, the emperor. She backed three paces and turned. In that moment, she caught a flicker of motion.

Serenus was watching her son still. Agrippina saw Nero tap two fingers on the bracelet that had always adorned his wrist, a bracelet she had made for him. She gave no sign she had seen and left the room with her maid and her son's friend.

Without praetorians to stamp and crash alongside, her steps seemed to echo in the domed hall, click-clacking back from the ceiling and walls. Agrippina frowned in thought, concentrating. She could hear Polla's breathing as the poor girl gasped, just relieved to be out of the emperor's presence and away from stakes she could not really understand.

On the steps outside, Centurion Pera and his praetorians fell in beside them. The group left the consul's home and walked down to the docks. Agrippina said nothing. Serenus was a stiff and unbending presence, offering no light talk or reassurance, though he had heard all that had been said. The streets were still busy with revellers, but they fell back from the armed men as they made their way to the boat.

Polla gave the bag to one of the soldiers and he climbed down with it. The maid turned to Agrippina then, but she waved her on board.

'A moment, Serenus, if you wouldn't mind,' Agrippina said.

The young man turned to her with a questioning expression and she made herself smile.

'As I left, I noticed my son tap his fingers on a bracelet I had made, when he was very small.'

The head of the vigiles in Rome only waited, saying nothing. Agrippina could feel her heart racing as she stood there, hard enough to hurt.

'The signal he gave . . . it was for you, I think. As with the young man Augustus once went to see. So . . . was it for me to live, or to die?'

Serenus inclined his head, impressed.

'It was for you to live,' he said.

The world swam for a moment and she almost reached out to him to steady herself.

'Thank the gods,' she whispered. 'I should make Minerva my patron. Perhaps I shall.'

She found the tightness in her chest easing, each breath coming more easily.

'He is my only son, but a lion. Do you know that story?'

'I don't believe I do,' Serenus said, looking over the docks. He gestured for her to descend the ladder to the boat that waited. She took hold of the rungs, but remained.

'It is an old one, by Aesop. A vixen had a great litter of fox pups, a lioness just one. The vixen mocked the lioness for it. The lioness shrugged and said, "Only one . . . but a lion." Do you understand? Only one, but he is a lion.'

Agrippina climbed down to the deck, where Polla waited. Serenus looked up at the stars, clear and bright, before he followed.

26

The waters were dark as they passed beneath. The sky was clear and stars shone in great abundance, casting silver light on the waves. Only the oars lent movement. The speed of the prow brought its own breeze and Agrippina drew the cloak around her shoulders as she and Polla sat on the couch for the return trip. She trembled even so, though it was part in relief. The sight of Burrus standing with her son had been a dagger's blow. In that moment, Agrippina had known the praetorian would cut her down if Nero ordered it. That he had not meant Nero had become the emperor she had always dreamed. Seneca and Burrus had been part of that change, she realised – just as she had. She grimaced, unseen on the dark deck.

Perhaps Tiberius *had* damaged her family. He had broken and twisted her parents, her brothers and sisters . . . herself. Yet it seemed Nero had escaped the darkness that stalked them all over the years. His reign might match that of Augustus, a golden age.

Could she forgive him for Britannicus? Agrippina

worried at her lip as she sat there, borne along by rowers across a hissing sea. The boy had been an innocent, but she had known emperors and their fears. Britannicus had been a full son to Claudius, and Nero's brother. Though the heavens cried out at his end, if he had lived, he would surely have become a threat. Whether he wanted it or not, others would have raised him up. She closed her eyes for a moment, putting pain aside and drawing in the cold night air.

The shore lights of Baiae retreated and the boat turned, orders called from the helmsman to the rowers. Agrippina felt Polla shivering and drew her into an embrace as speed built once more, taking them back to the house at Misenum.

Serenus was just a shadow in the darkness as he walked past the pair, clutching one another for warmth. Agrippina thought he might speak, but he said nothing as he made his way to the stern. A frown touched her features then. If Nero had forgiven her, she did not think Serenus had. With his vigiles, he was a powerful man and hard to reach. She wondered . . . Agrippina caught herself. No. She had promised Nero she would not plot or seek advantage. She had sworn it on Apollo and Minerva.

Her eyes followed her son's friend as he made his way to the helmsman at the stern. The crew were not working too hard that night. Misenum was just a little way along the coast from Baiae, after all. She looked for the lamps of the home dock, but the land was dark, darker than the night sky.

Agrippina watched as Serenus exchanged a few words with his crewman under starlight. He looked at her then, she was almost sure. His face was in shadow, but she thought he stared across the deck to where she sat. Agrippina frowned as another of the men came forward, clambering down through a hatch. The way came off the boat, the sound of movement dying away. Stillness descended. Agrippina felt sudden fear take her in its grip.

'Polla?' she whispered. 'Go and see what . . .'

At the stern, shadows writhed. Serenus made a huge movement, wrenching at some bar or beam she had not seen. Agrippina heard his grunt of effort. She felt the world tilt – and the deck under the couch suddenly dropped into the sea.

Polla vanished into black water, her terrified scream cut short. Agrippina had thrown her arms wide in panic and only one of her legs plunged beneath the surface. Somehow, in the darkness, the couch had jammed the opening. Had they struck a rock? She clung to wet cloth in terror and confusion, shrieking for Polla to hold on. She could not see her maid anywhere. Waves crashed up somehow from below and Agrippina slipped. She found herself almost upside down, holding on for dear life as waves seemed to leap and plunge over her. She drew some of it in and choked, raising her head and looking into blackness.

It had to be a rock. Agrippina could see almost nothing, but there were wet wooden walls on all sides, too slick to allow her to grip and hold on. Only the couch had stopped her dropping into the sea and that was creaking ominously as she clung to it. Would it give way? She dared not move.

'Over here!' she shouted.

The rowers no longer swept, she realised. The boat rocked alone. She could hear Serenus shouting orders, but there was no sense to it.

'Get to the rail and tip the boat!' he roared at his men.

'Then back, to the other side! That damned couch has jammed the deck.'

Agrippina felt a new coldness enter as she understood he was not trying to save her. The deck leaned at a sickening angle as half his crew rushed to one side of the boat. The couch shifted, one corner skidding on wet wood. Agrippina looked again at the water. She had grown up in army camps in Germania, with three brothers and two sisters. She had learned to swim there. It had been a lifetime before, and she wondered if Serenus knew. She tore at her cloak and veil, yanking at the pins in her hair. There was chaos on the deck. The praetorians were all shouting. Half the crew ran to the other side from instinct, bringing the boat level and then further.

Agrippina tugged feverishly at cloth that would drown her. The cloak came free but the folds tangled around her feet. Something snapped then in the couch, a dull and muffled sound. With no more warning, it folded around her, crushing her chest. She dropped into the sea, carried down and down.

Serenus heard the splash and made his way cautiously to the part of the deck that could be made to drop. He sank to his knees to look over that inner edge and saw the couch had vanished, taking the two women with it. It had been Nero's idea to use the boat from the arena sea battle. It had appealed to the emperor's sense of the dramatic to make the deep sea responsible. Even then, he had delayed the decision to the final moment.

Serenus grinned in the darkness. Nero's touch on the resin bracelet had been the signal he had expected. Agrippina had planned her own son's murder! There was no path back from that. Perhaps Nero had enjoyed the sense of making a decision, of telling his mother about Augustus and how he had condemned his grandson to death. The message had been clear enough, for those with ears to hear.

'Just one, but a lion . . .' Serenus murmured to himself.

Black water showed below, hidden even from the light of stars. He was not that familiar with the mechanism and unsure if wrenching the bar into place would restore the deck. The rowers might have to ease them back to shore with it all hanging open.

In the quiet of the night, he heard splashing. Serenus rose from where he had been peering and went to the boat's edge. He looked for white, for the splashes and froth of someone struggling to stay on the surface.

'I am Agrippina!' came a strangled voice. 'Save the emperor's mother!'

Serenus pointed to the spot, some dozen paces off to one side. He whistled to the helmsman then, his hand steady.

'Get me closer,' Serenus ordered.

The man took a quick look and running feet sounded as the orders were passed on. Below deck, one bank of oars rattled out and dipped, turning the prow slowly towards the thrashing figure. Serenus waited until he was sure they would intercept her and then dropped through the open hatch to the gloom below. He pushed through slaves at the oars then, taking up a seat and ripping the leather gasket from its place. He tossed it into the sea and looked out through the open side. Almost at the level of the water, he could see froth and hear the sound of someone drowning.

'Reach for this,' he called.

He gripped an oar and raised it on its pivot over the struggling woman. He saw pale hands strain for it, as if he held it out to save her. He smiled then.

Agrippina fought clear of the broken couch that gripped her like a lover. She had been dragged down until her ears hurt. When the couch gave way, she floated free, but the layers of her dress were so heavy she thought she might never make it back to the surface.

She could have given up then. The cold reached into her and she was sodden and slow. Yet there was still rage to keep her warm, a coal at her heart that all the black sea could not snuff out.

She wrenched at her dress as she rose up, kicking all the while. Her lungs ached and she was not sure she could hold her breath a moment longer. A memory returned of Caligula holding her under the water when she was very small. It had been a game, he said, but there had been something in his eyes even then.

She wanted to scream as the heavy stola drifted clear. It left her in just a slip of cloth, her arms bare. Agrippina thought she could see starlight above, as well as a great shadow blotting out the surface. She kicked away from that, though her thoughts had become ice, slower and slower. Her movements too were fading. She knew she was dying, just as her head broke the surface. She lay for a time then, breathing. The air bit like knives, but was still sweet.

She could see the boat, the prow turning slowly towards her. Agrippina was spent, her limbs leaden. She could only watch in growing horror as the dark shape loomed.

Somewhere close, a voice cried out. It was one she knew,

Conn Iggulden

though the words made no sense at all in her half-frozen state. Agrippina frowned in confusion as Polla shrieked, 'I am Agrippina! Save the emperor's mother!'

Agrippina's heart broke for the girl. Of course. Polla had not understood the danger she was in. She thought the men on board would move the earth to rescue Agrippina, leaving a maid to drown. In her terror, she had made a terrible mistake.

Agrippina dared not call to her. The cold was leaching in and she could only watch as one of the oars rose above the thrashing girl. Polla reached for it, desperate to be saved. For an instant, Agrippina thought those on board might relent, but then it came down hard, with a sound like bone breaking. Polla was knocked under the surface. When she rose again, her face leaned, dark with blood and shadow. The oar cracked down once more. Agrippina waited, but the thing that surfaced a third time no longer moved. The hissing froth eased and the sea was still.

Agrippina could see shadows shift on deck and heard orders carry across the night. She felt a pang in her side and touched it, feeling a deep gash she had not noticed before. No doubt some part of the couch had torn her as she went in with it. It was all numb, but her arm felt weaker on that side. She had the sudden thought of blood spilling in long threads, drawing monsters to her.

She stayed there, caught between the stars and a surface that reflected them as a blurred glitter. She could not hail the boat. Poor Polla had showed what they would do if she did. Nor could she remain afloat for much longer. As well as her wound, she was already exhausted – from all the hours of fear and strain that had gone before. She bared her teeth then, hearing them click and chatter. Her son had not chosen mercy. He was no lion, but a jackal, as she had always feared.

The boat had continued to drift as she trod water, fighting the urge to just give up, to sink, down and down into the blackness. Agrippina saw the shadow of the hull had shifted to one side, though whether it had moved or she had was beyond her. She narrowed her eyes then as something shone. Baiae was further around the curve of the bay, she remembered. It could not be that town. Yet a single light burned, clear and steady. It had to be the shore, or at least the direction of the shore. She was suddenly certain and half-lifted herself out of the water, fixing on that point. It vanished as she rose and fell with waves – then appeared once more.

The dock at Misenum. It was so far away, it made her want to weep, but she clamped her jaw and began to kick. Her left arm could barely make a stroke and she knew the wound was more than just a scratch. Yet she turned on her side and pulled at the sea, sweeping her good hand back, kicking for land.

She struck out as far and wide as she could from Serenus and his crew. Even then, Agrippina thought she could feel his foul gaze searching, but no cry went up. She became a numb and frozen thing, just pulling and kicking at the black water. When she heard oars rattle out once more, the boat passed east of her, leaving her behind – and alone.

A figure leaned over the prow, sweeping a lamp back and forth in a slow rhythm. They searched for her and she was afraid of them. She thought it was Serenus, but she could not be sure.

*

Nero was drunk, Burrus could see that much. After he had sent his mother to be escorted home, the emperor had begun to pour wine down his throat as if he wanted to make himself ill. The tasting slave had been dismissed after sampling half a dozen jugs without ill effect. Burrus too would have excused himself, but there was a sort of manic energy in Nero and he refused.

'Keep me company,' he insisted. 'Are we not friends, Burrus? I do not want to be alone tonight. Let us watch the sun rise together, shall we?'

That had been after enough wine to make his eyes glassy, his speech slurred. Burrus had acquiesced, of course, before Nero could make it an order. He understood the young man was still distressed at his mother's betrayal. Burrus could not imagine how it felt. It was one thing to have enemies, or be betrayed by friends even. To learn of Agrippina's plot was a bitter draught, a deeper wound. Burrus thought he could forgive Nero a few jugs of wine after that.

'Where is your cup, Burrus?' Nero demanded irritably, breaking into his thoughts. His lip stuck out like a truculent child.

Burrus hid his sigh. He had known three kinds of drunk in the legions. The cheerful singers were the best and good enough company. The fighters were the ones who caused the most trouble, who broke taverns and friendships in equal numbers. His least favourite were the ones who wept and dripped from the nose. Nero could be more than one sort, of course. On a bad night, he might even be all three.

Burrus raised the cup he had been given, knocking it back though his stomach churned. He had not eaten earlier and he could feel the fumes already spreading in his blood. He tried to sip as Nero gulped and refilled, driven by something Burrus could not begin to understand.

'*Drink*, Burrus! *Match* me! Like this!' Nero said.

He bustled forward to refill the praetorian's cup, already clumsy so that he staggered. Burrus dared not lay a hand on the young emperor in this mood. He stood like a statue until Nero had righted himself, peering at him and breathing sourness.

'You are a loyal man,' Nero mumbled, peering up at him. 'There is no one in the world I trust as I trust you to . . . this night. Tonight. No one. Another cup, Burrus! Falernian, sweet as love, pale as a woman's thighs. Do you know Otho's wife, Burrus? Poppaea Sabina?'

He pressed his fingers over his lips and shushed himself. Or perhaps Burrus, it was hard to say.

'She is the most extraordinary scarlet . . . down there,' Nero said, pointing at himself.

Burrus blushed as he suddenly understood. He did not want to hear anything the emperor might regret the next morning. His embarrassment was such he dared almost to interrupt him.

'I don't, er, know, Majesty. I am no longer young . . .'

Nero looked at him in confusion.

'A deep red, like ripe plums. What has age got to do with anything? Drink, man! Or are you pretending? Would you have me drink alone? A man should never drink on his own, Burrus. Didn't Seneca say that? *He* understood.' He leaned closer then. His eyes held a sort of cunning. 'I will tell you a secret, Burrus.'

'It isn't necessary, Majesty, I swear. I hear nothing, see nothing.'

'Shh, Burrus. It sat in me like a gold coin, shining, all the

Conn Iggulden

time I was speaking to my mother. My mother, Burrus! Did you hear the way she asked about the wombs? Did you hear the spite still in her? Well, did you?'

Burrus clenched his fists behind his back. He was loyal, he had proved that beyond any doubt. Yet to have a young man spraying him with flecks of spittle and white wine was trying his patience. He wished he could excuse himself.

'I didn't hear any spite, Majesty. Your mother was chastened, I would say.'

The young man gave a bark of laughter.

'Then you would be wrong. I didn't tell her, Burrus. I *could* have done! I could have sent her away with the knowledge that her line went on, but why should I give her that pleasure? She did not earn it. I'd rather she went to a watery grave thinking she had failed in all things, that I might never sire a child. Is that hatred, Burrus? Well, if it is, she has brought it about in me. Everything I am – is something she has made.'

He began to weep and Burrus looked at him in shock as he understood. Nero caught his stare and blinked at him. His expression cleared for a moment and he waved a hand.

'Not Octavia, Burrus. That dried-up little thing won't quicken, not for me. No, it is Poppaea whose monthly blood has stopped. She is the one with a boy of mine inside her!'

Burrus knew he was gaping.

'But Otho . . . I don't understand,' he said, though he just didn't want to.

The young emperor shook his head, gripping his praetorian by both shoulders.

'Otho has been safely away in Lusitania for a full year,

Burrus. I made sure of it. No, the child is mine, at last. I could have told my mother that. I could have spent that last coin with her, but she gets nothing from me. I kept it back.'

He slumped, his head drooping. He had poured wine into himself as fast as Burrus had ever seen. He would certainly vomit, probably many times. Burrus wondered if he should stay to make sure Nero didn't choke. He had lost a soldier like that once, when a celebration . . . He froze, thinking back over the ramblings.

'Majesty, is your mother safe? You said . . . I thought you said you would spare her.'

'Serenus knows,' Nero muttered, his lips barely moving. 'He has the boat . . . with the deck . . .'

He turned his head and wine poured out of him, mixed with shreds of liver and onions he had consumed from small plates. It began to pool on the stone floor, spattering his bare legs. He made a terrible sound and Burrus felt his eyes grow large as he understood.

'What order did you give?' Burrus said.

He was not sure Nero heard him. The young man mumbled words between the gushing wine.

'A son cannot order . . . the sea might take . . .'

'I must see to my men, Majesty,' Burrus said. 'It is the end of watch.'

Nero waved a hand and if it was not a formal dismissal, the praetorian took it as one. He passed through the outer doors and crossed the hall with the golden dome at a run.

Outside, he stopped at the docks. The boat was gone, of course it was. Serenus and Nero had plotted an ending between them. They had both lied to him, used his own praetorians for the purpose! Burrus looked south. Misenum was just a few miles around the coast. He could run it.

He did not know if he could save her, or whether he would be too late. Anger, wine and guilt mingled as he ran. Sweat began to pour and Burrus forced himself onward, racing through the night as the stars turned overhead.

27

Serenus jumped the gap between boat and dock, even as it closed. His crew were all hand-picked but he had not been able to include the praetorians in the plan. Six of them stepped ashore, visibly hostile as they surrounded him. Their optio was a hardbitten man with an ear like a scarred fist and twenty years of service under his belt. As soon as that man felt dry land under him, he stepped in close to Serenus, his voice a growl.

'You've overreached, you cocksure whelp,' the praetorian said. 'It'll be my pleasure to nail you to a tree for it. The emperor's own mother? I'll ask for your punishment detail as a special duty, I swear it.'

Serenus raised his hand very slowly, all too aware that this was a man who chose violence first – and usually second as well. There was a torch burning on that dock and it made what he held shine. The optio narrowed his eyes in suspicion. He dropped a hand to his sword hilt, but that was just habit rather than any sense of threat.

'What's that then?' he growled, peering at it. 'Some

Conn Iggulden

vigiles badge, is it? Seems to me your authority doesn't stretch much past the city walls. I don't see any fires on these docks. I don't hear anyone crying thief! No, son, you're *done*. Turn around and put your hands together. I've got a bit of twine that will do to hold you.'

Serenus didn't move. He just moved the medallion closer until the praetorian was forced to look at it properly.

'This is the emperor's personal seal,' Serenus said.

He made sure to keep any sign of triumph from his voice, not that he felt any. The plan had been neat and simple. One couch jamming the deck and it had all turned into chaos.

'Do you understand?' Serenus went on. 'It means you put yourself at my orders. It means for tonight at least, I am the emperor's word, his command walking. It means I have his approval and that I cannot be taken up or arrested. I could order your men to kill you right now – and if they refused, it would cost them all their lives. Or I could tell you to take your own life . . .'

'I understand,' the optio began, but Serenus went on.

'Or I could send your mates to whatever hovel you call a home and visit fire and violence on whoever they find there – and it would all be legal and right. That's what you face tonight, optio. So think hard before you say another word. All I want to hear from you is "I am at your orders." Can you say that?'

The man's eyes bulged, but there was something terrible in the calm way Serenus had explained. Nor had the optio missed the threat to his family. His desire to see the younger man arrested and held on charges of treason melted like morning mist. He nodded slowly.

'I am at your orders,' he said.

'Excellent,' Serenus said. He did not smile. He had beaten a young woman to death that night as she plunged and fought. There was no lightness in him.

'Then you will take your men and search the coast – east and west of this spot. I have a couple of dozen rowers in the hold, as well as a few crewmen. Make groups of them and set them to search. They are to look for bodies.' He leaned in, copying the aggression the man had shown before. 'If the emperor's mother somehow makes it to shore, she will not do so alive. Do you understand, optio? Just nod, you fool. I cannot waste another moment.'

'I . . .' The praetorian chose to use a term of honour to cover his confusion. 'I don't understand, dominus. I heard a woman cry out that she was Agrippina, the emperor's mother. I heard her, before . . .' He could not bring himself to describe the way Serenus had smashed her head in with an oar, not with the man staring at him.

'It wasn't her,' Serenus said, his anger at himself showing. 'I recognised her when I brought the lamp. It was her maid, optio. Perhaps the girl thought we would leave her in the water . . .' He waved a hand. 'Or perhaps she sought to distract us while her mistress escaped. The emperor's mother went into the water. I hope she drowned there. Pray she did. There will be no second chance – for any of us, not if she lives. Understand me. The emperor himself has decreed this. She is *already* dead, even if she makes it to shore.'

The optio saluted. He was used to the routines and disciplines of praetorians and legion life. All this, from killing women to the emperor's personal seal, was beyond him.

'I understand, dominus,' he said.

Serenus turned away, his gaze searching the distance. Dawn was coming, the eastern horizon lighting grey. The day would be cold and every moment revealed more and more of the shore.

Agrippina saw the day come as she flopped and choked on seawater. To drown within reach of land was an exquisite agony. Yet her strength had deserted her. Her limbs had grown numb and she could not seem to close the gap any further. Somehow, light still spread, revealing the hills around Misenum. She looked up at the great house on the cliffs, the place she had called home for a while. It was so close and yet . . . A wave entered her lungs and she thought she would just slip under.

Her foot touched something. She'd thought she was completely numb, uncertain if her limbs even moved. Yet she had felt that. Dull fear sprang to life, but then she felt it again. No great fish, but the touch of honest sand and stones underfoot. She plunged beneath the surface as she tried to heave forward, but the waves were pushing her on.

She collapsed onto dark sand, in the shadow of the cliffs. For a while, she rested there, panting and mindless. The sun had appeared in the east and the light was gold on her right hand. Slowly, she rose.

She had been lost, but found herself. She had died, somewhere in the blackness and the deep waters. Yet she stood there.

She looked up and up, at the bluffs. The house would have servants and clothes – and warm fires and drinks. She half-turned to Polla and then remembered. Serenus, though he was not responsible. She knew who was. Even as she shook with a sort of violence, she knew the one who had given the order.

'And that is it,' she said aloud.

Her voice strengthened with every word, a croak that became a growling rasp.

'I *am* Medea,' she said. 'And I will kill my son.'

She heard steps, the scrape of sandals slipping on loose stones. Agrippina whirled round to see two men. Praetorians. One of them wore an optio's crest, she saw. She watched them approach, her eyes dark, skin pale as dead flesh. There was something about the way they met her eyes that told her. She shook her head, looking for anyone else. There were other soldiers on that shore, she realised, searching the driftwood and shingle for her.

When she turned back, the optio plunged his dagger under her ribs.

'I'm sorry,' he said, already sickened.

She slid clear as her legs failed, falling to the sand. Both praetorians turned then as a voice shouted in agony. Agrippina watched as Burrus appeared. There was not too much pain, she thought. Not too much.

Burrus shone in the dawn light, his skin bright with sweat. He had discarded his uniform and wore a tunic of brown cloth, dark patches showing at his armpits. He had retained his sword.

The optio raised his hand, recognising the prefect of his own legion.

'Hold. I have orders, Burrus. Under the emperor's own seal. Speak to . . .'

He fell back then as Burrus drew his sword and hacked at him. The optio was so surprised, he took a gash on his arm and swore. He and his companion drew their own blades, though the optio still held up his free hand, as if he could hold Burrus back.

Conn Iggulden

'Put that away, sir, please! I told you. The emperor gave the order.'

Burrus looked past him to where Agrippina lay. She still breathed. He nodded grimly then.

'Get out of my way,' he said.

The optio looked back at the woman he had stabbed. Burrus attacked.

The prefect of the praetorians was not young, but he had no thought for his own life. Instead of blocking, he let the optio's sword part the skin of his side. It opened a terrible cut – but brought him close enough to slice the man's throat. He had known that optio for decades, but he killed him like a dog.

The other praetorian dropped his sword and backed away, wanting no part of whatever was happening. Burrus darted at him, making him run. He watched him long enough to be sure he would not return.

Burrus went back then to Agrippina, pushing his fingers into the damp sand to raise her head. Blood and stones and salt twined through her hair. He was still breathing hard and sweat poured in fat drops.

'I'm sorry,' he said.

She smiled at him, her hand rising to touch his cheek. In turn, he smoothed away a curl of her hair. A moment passed, and she was gone.

Burrus looked up into the morning, blind. Nero had done this. For all his drunken talk of the sea, it was by his hand. The boy he and Seneca had trained had turned on them, like a wolf raised in a home. Burrus did not know if there was a way back from what he had done. For any of them. Some sins were just too great.

Historical Note

Praetor Lucius Junius Silanus Torquatus did indeed take his own life on the wedding day of Agrippina to Emperor Claudius. He had previously been engaged to marry the emperor's daughter and Agrippina preferred her son Nero to set foot on that path to the throne. Children from that union would always have had a superb claim, not least because Agrippina and her son managed to remove every other descendant of the Augustan line. In a sense, the campaign began on her wedding day, as Junius Silanus was the grandson of the granddaughter of Augustus.

The history of this period comes from three main sources. Tacitus wrote around fifty years later and is probably the best surviving account of Nero's reign. Suetonius wrote his *Twelve Caesars* a decade or two after that, with access to original court documents. Dio Cassius wrote his account a full century further on – and the only surviving versions are rewrites from the middle ages. The Jewish historian Josephus also provides some useful detail. He was born in the same year as Nero, met him in Rome and though he knew three emperors personally, survived to old age. Some of the record also comes from Seneca, who wrote speeches, letters, plays – even an essay worrying about Serenus' state of mind.

There is no way of telling whether the nastier comments on Nero's character have any basis in truth. As with the character destruction of King Richard III of

England, when history is written to please a man's successors, it becomes important to look for inconsistencies. For example, it is true that Nero slept with Otho's wife – and married her. That much is beyond dispute, but can we then trust any account that might have been influenced by Otho?

The Romans understood the eye of history. Claudius himself was warned by an earlier wife to stop rewriting histories, as they had too many hands on them already. In one grim tale, we hear of a male eunuch 'married' to Nero, who is then said to have donned a bridal veil and shrieked like a virgin on her wedding night. Given that the slave was castrated, this story presents some obvious practical problems.

One common Roman insult was to suggest a man took a female role in the bedchamber. Another was to accuse a man of incest – in Nero's case with his mother. Such things were considered distasteful enough to damage a man's standing, which is why they work as insults.

The inconsistency is not Nero's marriage to Octavia, which was clearly more for political power than love, but the long-term relationship with the free Greek, Acte. Nero had his friend Serenus pretend Acte was with him and used Otho as a go-between, all to keep a private relationship from the public eye – which presumably included his mother. He gained nothing from it politically.

For what it's worth, I suspect there is a great deal of spite in the historical record around Nero. Those who hated him spread constant rumours of cruelty and violence, with the recent reigns of Caligula and Tiberius as inspiration – yet Nero was well loved by the people of Rome and is recorded as having forbidden gladiators from fighting to the death. He was the last of his line and his place in history has to be sifted through to see the man.

That said, it would be extraordinary if Nero hadn't been damaged in some way. His mother certainly was, as was his uncle Caligula. Nero lost his father at an early age, then his first stepfather to poison. He may not have remembered assassins coming to his crib, but he wore the snakeskin bracelet for most of his adult life. He grew up in a time of constant threatened violence, and though Emperor Claudius was nowhere near as chaotic or savage as his maniac predecessor, the axe still fell hardest on the noble class. Claudius had at least thirty senators killed in the last few years of his reign.

Note on Roman technology: Glass did exist in the first century AD. There were two main Roman sources – 'Alexandrian' and 'Judaean' glass, both territories of the empire at this time. Alexandrian clear glass was considered the best. It was extremely expensive and would have been used for drinking vessels at imperial feasts, to make decorative vases, or as small, clear panes set in bronze frames. Emperors like Claudius would have known glass windows, even a hand mirror. A frame of bronze with glass fragments was found in Pompeii. It is assumed that the large windows of bath-houses in Rome had to be sealed in a similar way, to allow light, but keep all the heat and steam in. (It is one of the strange aspects of the ancient world that for all but the richest, self-image had to rely on water or polished bronze, poor mirrors both. Make-up and hair could presumably be checked by others, but what subtle effect would it have on identity to see oneself so rarely?)

*

Seneca was indeed brought back from exile on Cyrnus – Corsica – to take a wild boy in hand and oversee all aspects of his education. It was a success, at least at first, with Seneca and Burrus becoming the main role models for young Nero. They appear to have been responsible for the impressive first years of his reign, where he showed restraint. Power, of course, does corrupt.

Seneca mentions breathing problems in his writings. It appears to have been asthma and becoming short of breath frightened him badly all his life. It is also true that Burrus had a maimed hand. Both men had endured suffering, which is perhaps part of why they became good friends, united in raising Nero. It is true that Nero was granted his toga virilis – the robe and status of a man – earlier than the usual fourteen or fifteen. The suggestion that this might have been to make him responsible under law is my own conclusion. However, Claudius did leave him in charge of Rome. Nero was meant to sit in judgement on minor law cases, but of course the noble families of Rome saw either a chance to get an easy verdict, or just an opportunity to please the emperor. They lined up the most serious cases of the day for a boy with no experience.

Note: It is also true that Agrippina had an awning put up in the senate house, where she could listen to debates. It is difficult to imagine a more subtle display of power. At any moment, they had to assume she was there. It meant she oversaw every senate debate, whether actually present or not. Nor could they have it taken down.

Her face can be seen just behind that of Claudius in coins from this period. It is interesting to see the way that face becomes more prominent over time. Her relationship with the mints is unknown, however. It is true that she had three members of the Silanus family killed – the younger son betrothed to Octavia, then the head of the family and years later, another son. The motive for the first is clear enough. The other two were apparently to head off their revenge.

Note on measurements: A Roman *mille passus* – thousand paces – from which the word 'mile' comes, was shorter than a modern mile. The exact figure is difficult to pin down, but from road mile markers left behind, it seems to have been around 0.9 of a modern mile, or 1,400 metres.

One huge question remains from this period. How on earth did Claudius not see the danger he was in? With that family history? Married to the sister of Caligula? Yet he allowed Nero to take his toga a year early. He allowed the betrothal and marriage to his daughter Octavia. He agreed to make Nero the official heir to the empire. With the benefit of hindsight, that looks like complete madness. I had to engineer a motive as a way of protecting Britannicus, but it says more about the extraordinary charisma of Agrippina. Such people do exist.

Mentioning no names, I knew a man who was engaged to a young woman from a very wealthy family. The young man was something of a fantasist and over time his fiancée began to suspect something was wrong. He was just too smooth, too plausible, too charming and funny. She caught him in a couple of lies and began to wonder. Yet her father adored him and was openly looking forward to having him as a son-in-law. In the end, this young woman broke off the engagement. Her father was so furious about it that he told the young man he could still keep coming to the family estate house – and *forbade his daughter from doing so*. In short, he chose a charming rogue over his own daughter and his own daughter's judgement.

When I heard that, I was reminded of the incredible power some individuals have to spin confusion, to weave lies and truths together into a cloud of helplessness. I suspect Agrippina had some of that quality. Nothing else explains why Claudius disinherited his own son at her request, not really. Nero was older, it's true. Adoption was both lawful and utterly ordinary in Rome of this period. Claudius had *physically heard* the murder of Caligula by his own guards, but never saw the danger he was in from his wife.

Agrippina favoured a number of astrologers, mystics and fortune-tellers. One of them actually was a Gaulish woman, the rather wonderfully named 'Locusta'. In later years, Nero too valued Locusta's services, granting her property and great wealth. Locusta became a woman of some influence during his reign, surviving both poison and politics.

Note on the naumachia: Emperor Claudius actually used a mountain lake some fifty miles east of Rome – the Fucine. That ancient site was famously malarial. Over time, it had to be part-drained – first by Claudius, who had a tunnel dug, then finally and permanently in the nineteenth century. It is rich farmland today. Nero staged his own naumachia when he was emperor. I needed the reader to 'see' the rigged drop deck, so switched locations. That allowed me to describe the action in more detail than would be possible on a distant lake battle with 19,000 men.

Nero's naumachia was three years after that of Claudius, in a wooden arena in Rome. It would have had to be water-proofed in overlapping wood and pitch, or possibly mortar. It is true Roman mortar would set even underwater, so must have made a good waterproof layer. The Colosseum wasn't yet built. Many details are lost, but the description of the ship with the drop deck is well attested – and in some ways, the least surprising part of these extraordinary public spectacles. Given the part it played in Agrippina's death, I wanted to introduce it earlier.

Note: Though Nero was renowned for his love of sport, and chariot racing in particular, there is no record of him allowing Britannicus to try a racing team, nor of his younger brother being knocked out. That scene is my own invention, aimed at increasing the tension between Agrippina and Claudius.

Caractacus of the Catuvellauni fought the Romans in Britain on a number of occasions. His brother Togodumnus did not survive the first invasion. Caractacus was handed over to them by the queen of the Brigantes in the north, then taken to Rome as a prisoner. I don't believe he was one of those made to fight for his freedom on the flooded arena. That part is my invention.

The line 'All this and they still wanted our huts?' is actually attributed to Caractacus, in awe at the city of Rome. He spoke very well to Claudius and was freed as a result. We do not know if he made it home.

Note: As hard as it is to separate truth from misinformation about Nero, the idea that he might have been involved in theft from shopkeepers and a stabbing actually rings true. I saw a few things like that when I was in my teens. Though we should avoid too much analysis on too little evidence, Nero was a young man who had lost three fathers – two to poison. Running wild in Rome is not too surprising after that. He did make his friend Serenus head of the vigiles, a position of some power and wealth-making ability. It is also true that Nero sent his mother away to Misenum, a house on the cliffs, with Capri in the distance.

At this point in his life, Nero had Seneca and Burrus around him, men he wanted to impress. He was involved with the vast responsibility of being emperor, from massive building projects to the administration of grain, the collection of taxes, the actions of twenty-eight legions and as many governors and vassal kings.

Note: Otho's wife Poppaea Sabina had already been divorced once and was some seven years older than her young husband. She seems to have wished to get close to Nero and made a play for him from the beginning. He was not unmoved by her interest, despite his continuing relationship with Acte and his own marriage – still without children.

As with the biblical story of David and Bathsheba, Nero sent her new husband very far away, to Lusitania – modern-day Portugal – as governor. Otho's story is an interesting one, with an extraordinary second act.

Note on sandals: In writing about Rome, I usually think of footwear as sturdy things on the feet of legionaries, with studs in the soles and wool stuffed in against the cold. Yet there were sandals of gold found in the tomb of Tut-ankhamun, made to a design recognisable on any beach today. That simple flat sole, with a Y-shaped strap between the toes, is apparently an ancient design – and of course Nero was pharaoh of Egypt at this time.

The death of Agrippina is, by necessity, a confusing moment of Nero's history. It is difficult to think of a worse crime than a son killing his mother, so it is no surprise to find aspects that are denied or concealed. Accounts conflict in the works of Suetonius, Tacitus and Dio Cassius, though the drop-deck boat appears more than once. The technology certainly existed in arena sea battles. Yet the motives and exact events will always be contested. We will never know, for example, why the maid Acerronia Polla called out, 'I am Agrippina! Save the emperor's mother.' She *may* have misunderstood the reason for being in the water and so made a terrible tactical error – or she could have been trying to distract them and give Agrippina a chance to get to shore. Hero or fool? It's a shame not to know for sure.

It is certain that Agrippina made it ashore. All the sources agree on that, which suggests the action was not very far off the coast of Misenum. After that, the fog of history descends and we do not know exactly where she was cut down, only that she was killed by legionaries. She was just forty-three years old: sister to one emperor, wife to another, mother to a third. She is one of the most extraordinary characters I have encountered.

In the end, she played the wrong card. Prefect Burrus of the praetorians was her appointment. It was Agrippina who made Burrus mentor to her son, along with Seneca.

Yet it was that close connection that meant in the end he chose Nero over her – and sealed her fate.

For the last book of this trilogy, the curtain will open on a young emperor. His will be a reign of hope, gold – and fire.

—Conn Iggulden,
London

**THE GRIPPING FINAL INSTALLMENT
IN CONN IGGULDEN'S NERO TRILOGY**

**First it was JULIUS CAESAR in EMPEROR.
Then GHENGIS KHAN in CONQUEROR.**

**Now 'master storyteller' (*Daily Express*)
Conn Iggulden turns to THE TYRANT OF ROME**

READ ON FOR AN EXCLUSIVE FIRST CHAPTER

I

The sea was cold under him, black as ink. On the surface, reflected stars smeared and broke apart. Nero felt suddenly afraid, too far from land. He knew it was a risk to swim at night and he struck out for shore.

He felt something touch his feet. Whatever it was moved against him in a great rough length. Almost gently, he was drawn beneath the surface. A silver shield twisted above his fingertips, just out of reach. His legs were held; he dared not look to see. His mother trod water, hair unbound, dress floating. Agrippina sneered at his fear, close enough to kiss.

He would *not* drown, not with her judging him! Nero kicked against whatever gripped his legs with all the wild strength of youth. In that instant, he cared nothing for pain or injury. His will, his rage, overrode all. He wrenched his flesh to escape, to surface for one more breath.

It slid around his thighs. He knew it was a snake, some frilled thing that dripped poison in milky strands. It had him. All his youth, all his strength, was as nothing to it.

His mother smiled, satisfied. His word had condemned her. Nero had given the order that pitched her into the sea with her maid. This sea. He felt his strength failing, numbness creeping in. The coils tightened on his chest, but he was already done. He looked into the face of Agrippina and wanted to say how sorry he was – and how glad. Emperor Caligula's sister, Emperor Claudius' wife . . . mother to Nero. While she had lived, she had remained a threat. No one was as broken, or as dangerous.

She came closer in the water, silver-eyed. He tried to scream rather than feel the touch of that flesh on his own. His last breath roared out of him and he knew seawater would enter in.

He woke with dawn's light showing, twisting against the ropes of his sheets. His gaze came to rest on the bangle he wore, one that his mother had given him. It shone gold with a strip of snakeskin embedded in resin, like insects in amber. He blinked at it. Somewhere close, all the palaces and temples of the city were waking. The beating heart of the world was splashing water on its face. Hundreds of thousands of men and women were kissing one another goodbye in that moment, separated by work and the need to eat.

The young emperor could hear the steps of soldiers and the scurry of slaves as they began the day. It felt like he had not slept at all, and for a time Nero just stared. The nightmares were not getting better. They stole his rest, leaving him exhausted through the day. He remembered his mother's face had been part of it, speaking in the green water, accusing. He swung his legs over the side of the bed. It was already fading and he was grateful for that. He vowed to tell Seneca about it. The old man knew a little bit of everything, so he said. It had sounded like a joke when Nero was a child, but it actually seemed to be true.

Perhaps Seneca would be able to make the dreams stop. Burrus had said it took time, but it had already been months.

Conn Iggulden

Wine didn't help, and the juice of the poppy made them worse.

He wiped his face with a hand. His waking had been noticed, of course. A troupe of imperial house slaves entered the room in silent column. Two of them opened shutters to the dawn, while another pair set up a barber's chair they had brought with them.

Nero clapped his hands twice, as much to wake himself up as to startle them into faster movement. He accepted a tray of square-cut cloths and walked on his own to a private toilet room. There were four seats, though he was the only occupant. By the time he had relieved himself and used the cloths, he was ready to be bathed. No soldier's sponge on a stick for the emperor! No toilet stones either, to leave a man raw. He hardly noticed the slaves who entered the little room as he left, ready to clean and polish until it was perfect once more. Nero left his loincloth on the floor for them as he strolled back to the main room, naked as a child.

The slaves' labour was the Palatine waking bell. Before first light, they brought ladders into every room, brushing cobwebs, dusting, cleaning silver. Others lit the fires in the kitchens, preparing food for the day ahead. Such work began in every house, rich and poor alike up at first light. Only drunks slept away the sun, Seneca said. The glory of the day was precious to consul and beggar.

Nero considered heading into another part of the complex, where plunge pools and heated baths steamed. He glanced at the sun and saw a line of gold showing. No, there was no time to sink and relax in warmth, not with the senate expecting him. Instead, he nodded to his personal slaves. They carried buckets of hot and cold water and they sluiced and brushed him like a prize bull as he stood there with arms apart. He was heavily muscled, a fine figure of a man. When he had spat scented water into a golden bowl, when his skin gleamed with fresh oil, he sat for his barber, Thalamus. Two more slaves surrounded him as he leaned back, working with quick skill. Nero's ears were cleaned and singed, his nose examined. Fresh oil was applied to his hair, arranging it in small curls. It was vanity, perhaps, but it was a lion's mane and Nero was proud of those locks. Half the senate had shiny brown pates rising like islands from the sea. He felt like the future of Rome when he sat amidst all those old men. He chuckled at the thought, while Thalamus stropped a blade of Hispanian steel, breathing through his nose.

Nero nodded to the fellow, giving permission. Thalamus took a cloth from a steaming bucket with a flourish, draping it over the emperor's features. The heat stung, but Nero endured. When he was revealed, Thalamus rubbed a little olive oil into his cheeks and set to work with his razor. No one who ruled in Rome had worn a beard, not since Julius Caesar. The fashion may even have begun with that old wolf, or at least become popular. Nero rather admired modern Greek styles, but Seneca had been so horrified at the thought of the first man in Rome going unshaven that Nero had ended up promising he would not consider it. It had become a compromise between them – Nero could keep his charioteer's curls, as long as he was shaved every morning.

The emperor clenched his jaw as Thalamus worked. Some barbers were so terrified of cutting their noble clients that they took an age. Thalamus may have been old but his hand was still quick. It took a moment of sheer surprise for Nero to realise the sting he felt was a rare cut. His gaze slid to Thalamus, suddenly still with wide eyes.

'How bad?' Nero asked.

The old man stammered as he replied.

Conn Iggulden

'A small n-nick, dominus, under the jaw. There is just a little blood.'

Thalamus was already reaching for his kit, where lengths of spiderweb had been prepared in oil and vinegar. Nero said nothing as a tiny strip of the stuff was pressed on. He was quietly proud of himself for not reacting badly. He had been thinking about the senate and distracted just long enough for the surge of anger to pass. Seneca would be pleased with him.

When the work was done, the barber stood with head bowed, still trembling. Nero ran a hand over his jaw and nodded. Thalamus knelt in relief then, stammering another apology until Nero held up a palm. Nothing would spoil his mood on such a day.

The chair was removed and four matronly women dressed Nero in a new loincloth, then a long tunic. Over that went the huge length that was a toga of blinding white. It was a weight he didn't love, but there was no help for that. Nero never wore the same one twice and felt his mind grow calm with the touch of new cloth, crisp against his skin. He had trained his slaves to the point where every morning was as close to perfect as he could make it. He touched the line on his jaw where he had been cut. That had broken the rhythm. Perhaps it was time to send Thalamus to retirement and find a younger man. Nero frowned at the thought. Choosing one who could be trusted to stand near an emperor's throat with a razor was no small thing.

In a chair by the door, Nero sat to have his sandals tied, then sprang up, making the slaves jump back in a tableau, raising their hands to their faces. He grinned at them. It was a game each morning. They played their parts well. In that moment, he was Odysseus, he was Achilles . . . He thought of Seneca's sour face and strained to find a Roman hero rather than Greek ones. He was Caesar at Pharsalus. He was Horatius at the bridge, ready to give his life for Rome.

Nero walked towards two huge bronze doors. Before they were opened, he paused, checking himself for one final moment of privacy before he showed his face to the world. A slave rushed up with a glass of pure water in that beat of time, kneeling and presenting it in the same instant. Nero waited for his taster to drink, then accepted the rest before it grew warm. It was a hobby he had taken up, to find the purest of mountain waters. The clear liquid in this glass had been brought from peaks above Gaul. The water had been sieved and boiled, then plunged into shavings of ice. It was cold enough to make his throat ache and he gasped, allowing them a small smile as reward for all their labours.

The doors opened. Nero did not look back as he went out to the world. Behind him, thirty slaves slumped and breathed, before they began to clear the private rooms.

Nero nodded to the advisers he favoured, already arranged in strict order of status and the importance of their business. He knew they jostled and argued for places outside his private doors. He approved. Competition kept them sharp and saved time. The most serious issues would reach his ears first.

As he strode along a cloister, he and his council passed a garden with a scent of jasmine and the sound of running water. Nero breathed it in, noting the Greek he employed as a finance minister was not in the front row. Good. Phaon may have been brilliant, but the problems of currency and loans were never his first choice to begin the day.

Nero eyed the prefect of the praetorians, standing on his right shoulder. Burrus was a fixture in his service and rarely gave way to any of the others, unless the need was very great. His presence was reassuring, as it was intended to be. At his left elbow, Nero glanced at the prosecutor Eprius Marcellus. That man was bald and ugly as a dog, his face seamed and deep brown from all the years under a Roman sun. Eprius carried rolls of papyrus, wrapped in ribbons of imperial purple. The man waited patiently for the emperor to acknowledge him.

Nero sighed and increased the pace. He almost looked back in apology at Seneca then. His childhood teacher was not a young man, but then his ailment had been with him all his life. Seneca would be wheezing and red-faced, fighting to breathe by the time they reached the forum at the bottom of the hill. Nero firmed his jaw. The business of the senate could not wait. He was expected to grant them his presence on the same day each week, to give his complete attention. Seneca would just have to suffer, or fall behind. They all endured in some way or other. Burrus had lost two fingers in military service. Seneca's throat closed with exercise, so that he lived with death on his shoulder. Nero . . . He thought of his mother's silver eyes and shuddered.

A final set of gates swung open and he brought his group out onto the stones of the street. A dozen praetorian guards joined in perfect formation, keeping the emperor safe. The view caught his breath, as it did every morning. He took a moment just to enjoy the sheer beauty and wonder of it.

All of Rome spread before him, a city of a million souls, slaves and free and freedmen and women, potters and paint- ers and masters of war. From the height of the Palatine hill, he could see the great Circus Maximus, the temples on the forum, the aqueducts that brought water to the city – and the hills themselves that teemed with people, all selling and making and buying food, though the sun had barely cleared the horizon. Nero felt light and loose as he nodded to the prosecutor.

'Eprius,' he said.

The man spoke immediately, a veteran of the morning charge down the hill.

'Dominus, the senate is convening to hear arguments around the murder of Senator Lucius Pedanius. As the case involves the killing of a senator, Your Majesty will be called upon for the judgement.'

'Give me the main points,' Nero said. He could hear Seneca's breathing worsen, even over the noise of sandals and praetorian boots.

'Ah . . . murdered by one of his slaves. The woman has been caught and held for punishment. There is no dispute as to the crime.'

'What judgement can I make, then?'

'Senator Pedanius had just over four hundred slaves, dominus. Law and custom would have them all put to death after such a murder.'

Nero cursed under his breath. He could almost feel Seneca's gaze on his shoulder blades.

'Men, women, children?' he asked.

Eprius dipped his head, tapping the scrolls he held, though he had memorised it all.

'Ninety women, dominus, from fourteen to sixty in age. Forty-eight children. Some of those will be the senator's by-blows, though without Pedanius alive to confirm the paternity . . .'

'I see. Very well. I will hear the arguments.'

Eprius bowed his head and moved back, allowing Nero's favourite architects to take the precious position. Nero eyed the pair. It was said Severus and Celer worked and lived together, sharing every intimacy. There were moments,

Conn Iggulden

usually when his wife or his mistress were angry with him, when he wondered ... A life lived solely with men might have *some* compensations. Of course, the price would be quite high. Nero smiled at that thought.

The young emperor had led the group most of the way down the hill by that point. He was not certain if he wished to broach a new subject, but then relented.

'Severus.'

'The theatre across the Tiber is almost finished, dominus,' Severus said immediately. He too had noted the forum coming closer. 'I just need to have your mark on the final bills. The gold leaf was harder to find in good quality than we ...'

'See Phaon,' Nero interrupted. 'Phaon? Agree those bills.'

He glanced at Burrus, seeing a familiar stony expression on the praetorian's face. Nero clenched his jaw and turned back to the architects.

'Pay yourself a bonus for the work, both of you. A fifth of the building cost. I will stage something on the first of next month – a private event, Burrus, there is no need to frown at me. Friends and family only.'

The praetorian bowed his head and both architects fell back. Nero saw the younger one grip the neck of his companion, shaking him in pleasure. If only all his tasks were as simple.

The group had reached the forum with unusual speed that morning. Not all those who wished to speak had been heard. Nero halted before the door to the senate house. They were no longer alone: citizens of Rome had already gathered around the door of the Curia building, straining to listen to the debates within. In the presence of the emperor, those men and women stood in awe.

Nero faced his group of advisers, aware once again of Seneca's struggle to breathe.

'Old friend, I have pushed you too far this morning,' Nero said softly.

Seneca shook his head.

'I will recover. My duty . . . is at your side.'

It was not quite an expression of adoration and Nero knew he was being rebuked. Seneca was a subtle man, but Nero wanted his approval. Perhaps Seneca was a father to him, in some ways. Boys needed a father and his own . . . well, he hardly remembered the men his mother had married. Emperor Claudius was the only one he recalled beyond a few moments of peace and some memory of gluing a chariot. He scowled at the thought. The Fates had taken his fathers, so that he'd had to find other men to teach him. He had done so with Seneca, with Burrus – with those he trusted.

'I must go in,' he said. 'Burrus? You may prepare the way. Find a spot for Seneca on the observers' benches.'

The prefect bowed and went inside. His entry would alert the senate to Nero's presence, if they hadn't heard already. He would be received then with proper dignity and respect. Not for himself, as Seneca had lectured a thousand times, but for the dignity of the role. Nero was princeps, first in Rome. He was the emperor, and all power rested in him.

Conn Iggulden